Cindi Myers is the author of more than fifty novels. When she's not crafting new romance plots, she enjoys skiing, gardening, cooking, crafting and daydreaming. A lover of small-town life, she lives with her husband and two spoiled dogs in the Colorado mountains.

Lena Diaz was born in Kentucky and has also lived in California, Louisiana and Florida, where she now resides with her husband and two children. Before becoming a romantic suspense author, she was a computer programmer. A Romance Writers of America Golden Heart® Award finalist, she has also won the prestigious Daphne du Maurier Award for Excellence in Mystery/ Suspense. To get the latest news about Lena, please visit her website, lenadiaz.com.

Also by Cindi Myers

Saved by the Sheriff
Avalanche of Trouble
Deputy Defender
Danger on Dakota Ridge
Murder in Black Canyon
Undercover Husband
Manhunt on Mystic Mesa
Soldier's Promise
Missing in Blue Mesa
Stranded with the Suspect

Also by Lena Diaz

Mountain Witness
Secret Stalker
Stranded with the Detective
SWAT Standoff
Missing in the Glades
Arresting Developments
Deep Cover Detective
Hostage Negotiation
The Marshal's Witness
Explosive Attraction

Discover more at millsandboon.co.uk

ICE COLD KILLER

CINDI MYERS

SMOKY MOUNTAINS RANGER

LENA DIAZ

This book is produced from independently certified FSC™
paper to ensure responsible forest management.

For more information visit: www.harpercollins.co.uk/green

Printed and bound in Spain
by CPI, Barcelona

MILLS & BOON

First Published in Great Britain 2019
by Mills & Boon, an imprint of HarperCollins*Publishers*
1 London Bridge Street, London, SE1 9GF

Ice Cold Killer © 2019 Cynthia Myers
Smoky Mountains Ranger © 2019 Lena Diaz

ISBN: 978-0-263-27411-0

0419

MIX
Paper from
responsible sources

FSC

ICE COLD KILLER

CINDI MYERS

Chapter One

Snow hid a lot of things, Colorado State Patrol Trooper Ryder Stewart mused as he watched the wrecker back up to the white, box-shaped clump near the top of Dixon Pass. Christy O'Brien, a sturdy blonde with chin-length hair beneath a bright red knit beanie, stopped the wrecker a few inches from the snow clump, climbed out and brushed at the flakes with a gloved hand, revealing the bumper of a brown delivery truck. She knelt and hooked chains underneath the truck, then gave Ryder a thumbs-up. "Ready to go."

Ryder glanced behind him at the barrier he'd set up over the highway, and the Road Closed sign just beyond it. Ahead of Ryder, a cascade of snow flowed over the pavement, part of the avalanche that had trapped the truck. "You're clear," he said.

Slowly, Christy eased the wrecker forward. With a sound like two pieces of foam rubbing together, the delivery truck emerged from its icy cocoon. When the truck was fully on the pavement, the wrecker stopped. The door to the delivery truck slid open, clumps of snow hitting the pavement with a muffled *floof*. "Took you long enough!" Alton Reed grinned as he said the words and brushed snow from the shoulders of his brown jacket.

"How many times is this, Alton?" Ryder asked, looking the driver up and down.

"First one this year—fourth overall." Alton surveyed the truck. "Got buried pretty deep this time. I'm thinking it's going to be a bad year for avalanches."

"The weather guessers say it's going to be a bad snow year." Ryder studied the pewter sky, heavy clouds like dirty cotton sitting low on the horizon. "This is the second time this week we've had to close the highway. Might not open again for a few days if the weather keeps up."

"You people ought to be used to it," Alton said. "It happens often enough. Though I can't say I'd care for being cut off from the rest of the world that way."

"Only four days last winter," Ryder said.

"And what—three weeks the year before that?"

"Three years ago, but yeah." Ryder shrugged. "The price we pay for living in paradise." That was how most people who lived there thought of Eagle Mountain, anyway—a small town in a gorgeous setting that outsiders flocked to every summer and fall. The fact that there was only one way in and out of the town, and that way was sometimes blocked by avalanches in the winter, only added to the appeal for some.

"Guess I'll have to find a place in town to stay until the weather clears," Alton said, eyeing the cascade of snow that spilled across the highway in front of them.

"You ever think of asking for a different route?" Ryder asked. "One that isn't so avalanche prone?"

"Nah." Alton climbed back into his van. "After the first scare, it's kind of an adrenaline rush, once you realize you're going to be okay. And this route includes hazard pay—a nice bonus."

Ryder waved goodbye as Alton turned his truck and steered around the barriers, headed toward town. He and the other commuting workers, delivery drivers and tourists trapped by the storm would find refuge at the local motel and B&Bs. Ryder shifted his attention to Christy, who was fiddling with the chains on her wrecker. "Thanks, Christy," he said. "Maybe I won't have to call you out anymore today."

"Don't you want me to pull out the other vehicle?" she asked.

The words gave him a jolt. "Other vehicle?" He turned to stare at the snowbank, and was stunned to see a glint of red, like the shine of a taillight. The vehicle it belonged to must have been right up against the rock face. Alton hadn't mentioned it, so he must not have known it was there, either. "Yeah, you'd better pull it out, too," he said. "Do you need any help?"

"No, I've got it."

He shoved his hands in the pockets of his fleece-lined, leather patrolman's jacket and blew out a cloud of breath as he waited for Christy to secure the vehicle. When she'd brushed away some of the snow, he could make out a small sedan with Colorado plates.

Wedged farther back under the packed snow, the car took longer to extricate, but it was lighter than the delivery van, and Christy's wrecker had tire chains and a powerful engine. She dragged the vehicle, the top dented in from the weight of the snow, onto the pavement.

Snow fell away from the car, revealing a slumped form inside. Ryder raced to the vehicle and tried the door. It opened when he pulled hard, and he leaned in to take a look, then groped for the radio on his shoulder. "I need an ambulance up at the top of Dixon Pass," he said. "And call the medical examiner."

Even before he reached out to feel for the woman's pulse, he knew she wouldn't be needing that ambulance.

The young, brown-haired woman was as cold as the snow that surrounded them, her hands and feet bound with silver duct tape, her throat slit all the way across.

He leaned back out of the car and tilted his head up into the cold, welcoming the feel of icy flakes on his cheeks. Yeah, the snow hid a lot of things, not all of them good.

DARCY MARSH RAN her fingers through the silky fur of the squirming Labrador puppy, and grinned as a soft pink tongue swiped at her cheek. For all the frustrations that were part of being a veterinarian, visits like this were one of the perks. "I'd say Admiral is a fine, healthy pup," she told the beaming couple in front of her. High school teacher Maya Renfro and Sheriff's Deputy Gage Walker returned the smile. "We'll keep an eye on that little umbilical hernia, but I don't expect it will cause any problems."

"Can Casey hold him now?" Maya asked, smiling at her young niece, Casey, who was deaf. The little girl's busily signing fingers conveyed her eagerness to cuddle her puppy.

"Yes, I think he's ready to come down." Darcy handed over the pup, and Casey cradled him carefully.

"You'll need to bring him back in a month for his second set of puppy vaccinations," Darcy said as she washed her hands at the exam room sink. "If you have any concerns before then, don't hesitate to give us a call."

"Thanks, Doc," Gage said. The family followed Darcy to the front of the office. "Are you all by yourself today?"

"It's Dr. Farrow's day off," Darcy said. "And I let Stacy go early, since you're my last client for today."

"Not quite the last," Maya said. She nodded toward the open waiting room door. An auburn-haired man in the blue shirt and tan slacks of a Colorado State Patrol-man stood at their approach.

"Ryder, what are you doing here?" Gage asked, step-ping forward to shake hands with the trooper.

"I just needed to talk to the vet for a minute," the of-ficer, Ryder, said. He looked past Gage. "Hello, Maya, Casey. That's a good-looking pup you have there."

"His name is Admiral," Maya said as Casey walked forward with the now squirming dog.

Ryder knelt and patted the puppy. "I'll bet you two have a lot of fun together," he said, speaking slowly so that Casey could read his lips.

Darcy moved to the office computer and printed out an invoice for Maya, who paid while Gage and Ryder made small talk about dogs, the weather and the upcom-ing wedding of Gage's brother, Sheriff Travis Walker. "We're thinking of throwing some kind of bachelor party thing in a couple of weeks," Gage said. "I'll let you know when I have all the details. We may have to stay in town, if the weather keeps up like this."

"That should be an exciting party—not," Maya said as she returned her wallet to her purse. "All the local law enforcement gathered at Moe's pub, with the entire town keeping tabs on your behavior."

"This is my brother we're talking about," Gage said. "Travis isn't exactly known for cutting loose."

Laughing, they said goodbye to Ryder and left.

"What can I do for you?" Darcy leaned back against her front counter and studied the trooper. He was young, fit and good-looking, with closely cropped dark auburn hair and intense blue eyes. She had only been in Eagle Mountain four months, but how had she missed running into him? She certainly wouldn't have forgotten a guy this good-looking.

"Are you Dr. Darcy Marsh?" he asked.

"Yes."

"Is Kelly Farrow your business partner?"

"Yes." The room suddenly felt at least ten degrees colder. Darcy gripped the edges of the front counter. "Is something wrong?" she asked. "Has Kelly been in an accident?" Her partner had a bit of a reckless streak. She always drove too fast, and with this weather…

"I'm sorry to have to tell you that Ms. Farrow—Dr. Farrow—is dead," Ryder said.

Darcy stared at him, the words refusing to sink in. Kelly…dead?

"Why don't you sit down?" Ryder took her by the arm and gently led her to a chair in the waiting room, then walked over and flipped the sign on the door to Closed. He filled a paper cup with water from the cooler by the door and brought it to her. At any other time, she might have objected to him taking charge that way, but she didn't see the point at the moment.

She sipped water and tried to pull herself together. "Kelly's really dead?" she asked.

"I'm afraid so." He pulled a second chair over and sat facing her. "I need to ask you some questions about her."

"What happened?" Darcy asked. "Was she in an accident? I always warned her about driving so fast. She—"

"It wasn't an accident," he said.

She made herself look at him then, into eyes that were both sympathetic and determined. Not unkind eyes, but his expression held a hint of steel. Trooper Stewart wasn't a man to be messed with. She swallowed hard, and somehow found her voice. "If it wasn't an accident, how did she die?" Did Kelly have some kind of undiagnosed heart condition or something?

"She was murdered."

Darcy gasped, and her vision went a little fuzzy around the edges. This must be a nightmare—one of those super-vivid dreams that felt like real life, but wasn't. This couldn't possibly be real.

Then she was aware of cold water soaking into her slacks, and Ryder gently taking the paper cup from her hand. "I need to ask you some questions that may help me find her murderer," he said.

"How?" she asked. "I mean, how was she…killed?" The word was hard to say.

"We don't have all the details yet," he said. "She was found in her car, buried in an avalanche on top of Dixon Pass. Do you know why she might have been up there?"

Why wasn't her brain working better? Nothing he said made sense to her. She brushed at the damp spot on her pants and tried to put her thoughts into some coherent order. "She told me she was going shopping and to lunch in Junction," she said. Leaving Eagle Mountain meant driving over Dixon Pass. There was no other way in or out.

"When was the last time you spoke to her?" Ryder asked.

"Yesterday afternoon, when we both left work. Today was her day off."

"Was that unusual, for her to take off during the week?"

"No. We each take one day off during the week so we can both work Saturdays. My day off is Wednesday. Hers is Tuesday."

"How long have you known her?"

Darcy frowned, trying to concentrate. "Five years? We met in college, then were roommates in vet school. We really hit it off. When she was looking for a partner to start a vet business here in Eagle Mountain, I jumped at the chance."

"Are you still roommates?" he asked.

"No. She lives in a duplex in town and I have a place just outside town—on the Lusk Ranch, out on County Road Three."

"Do you know of anyone who would want to hurt her?" he asked. "Does she have a history of a stalker, or someone from her past she's had a rocky relationship with?"

"No! Kelly got along with everyone." Darcy swallowed past the lump in her throat and pinched her hand, hard, trying to snap out of the fog his news had put her in. She couldn't break down now. Not yet. "If you had ever met her, you'd understand. She was this outgoing, sunny, super-friendly person. I was the more serious, quiet one. She used to say we were good business partners because we each brought different strengths to the practice." She buried her face in her hands. "What am I going to do without her?"

"Can you think of anyone at all she might have argued with recently—an unhappy client, perhaps?"

Darcy shook her head. "No. We've only been open a few months—less than four. So far all our interactions with clients have been good ones. I know, realistically, that won't last. You can't please everyone. But it's been a good experience so far. Well, except for Dr. Nichols." She made a face.

"Ed Nichols, the other vet in town?"

"Yes." She sighed. "He wasn't happy about our coming here. He said there wasn't enough business in a town this small for one vet, much less three. He accused us of undercutting his prices, and then I heard from some patients that he's been bad-mouthing us around town. But he never threatened us or anything like that. I mean,

I can't believe he would want to kill one of us." She wrapped her arms around herself, suddenly cold.

"Where were you this morning, from nine to one?" Ryder asked.

"Is that when she died? I was here, seeing patients. We open at eight o'clock."

"Did you go out for lunch?"

"No. We had an emergency call—a dog that had tangled with a porcupine. I had to sedate the poor guy to get the quills out. I ended up eating a granola bar at my desk about one o'clock."

"So you usually spend all day at the office here?"

She shook her head. "Not always. One of us is usually here, but we also treat large animals—horses and cows, mostly, but we see the occasional llama or donkey. Sometimes it's easier to go out to the animal than to have them brought here. That was something else Dr. Nichols didn't like—that we would do house calls like that. He said it set a bad precedent."

"Was Kelly dating anyone?" Ryder asked.

"She dated a lot of people, but no one seriously. She was pretty and outgoing and popular."

"Did she ever mention a man she didn't get along with? A relationship that didn't end well—either here or where you were before?"

"We were in Fort Collins. And no. Kelly got along with everyone." She made dating look easy, and had sometimes teased Darcy—though gently—about her reluctance to get involved.

"What about you? Are you seeing anyone?"

"No." What did that have to do with Kelly? But before she could ask, Ryder stood. He towered over her—maybe six feet four inches tall, with broad shoulders and muscular thighs. She shrank back from his presence, an involuntary action she hated, but couldn't seem to control.

"Can I call someone for you?" he asked. "A friend or relative?"

"No." She grabbed a tissue and pressed it to her eyes. "I need to call Kelly's parents. They'll be devastated."

"Give me their contact information and I'll do that," he said. "It's part of my job. You can call and talk to them later."

"All right." She went to the office, grateful for something to do, and pulled up Kelly's information on the computer. "I'll go over to her house and get her cats," she said. "Is it okay if I do that? I have a key." Kelly had a key to Darcy's place, too. The two looked after each other's pets and were always in and out of each other's homes.

"Yes. I already stopped by her place with an evidence team from the sheriff's department. That's how we found your contact information."

She handed him a piece of paper on which she'd written the names and numbers for Kelly's parents. He took it and gave her a business card. "I wrote my cell number on there," he said. "Call me if you think of anything that might help us. Even something small could be the key to finding out what happened to her."

She stared at the card, her vision blurring, then tucked it in the front pocket of her slacks. "Thank you."

"Are you sure you're going to be okay?" he asked.

No. How could she be okay again, with her best friend dead? And not just dead—murdered. She shook her head but said, "I'll be all right. I'm used to looking after myself."

The intensity in his gaze unnerved her. He seemed genuinely concerned, but she wasn't always good at reading people. "I'll be fine," she said. "And I'll call you if I think of anything."

He left and she went through the motions of closing up. The two cats and a dog in hospital cages were doing well. The dog—the porcupine victim—would be able to go home in the morning, and one of the cats, as well. The other cat, who had had surgery to remove a tumor, was also looking better and should be home by the weekend. She shut down the computer and set the alarm, then locked up behind her.

Outside it was growing dark, snow swirling over the asphalt of the parking lot, the pine trees across the street dusted with snow. The scene might have been one from a Christmas card, but Darcy felt none of the peace she would have before Ryder's visit. Who would want to hurt Kelly? Eagle Mountain had seemed such an idyllic town—a place where a single woman could walk down the street after dark and never feel threatened, where most people didn't bother to lock their doors, where children walked to school without fear. After only four months she knew more people here than she had in six years in Fort Collins. Kelly had made friends with almost everyone.

Was her killer one of those friends? Or a random stranger she had been unfortunate enough to cross paths with? That sort of thing was supposed to happen in cities, not way out here in the middle of nowhere. Maybe Eagle Mountain was just another ugly place in a pretty package, and the peace she had thought she had found was just a lie.

Chapter Two

A half mile from the veterinary clinic, Ryder almost turned around and went back. Leaving Darcy Marsh alone hadn't felt right, despite all her insisting that he go. But what was he going to do for her in her grief? He'd be better off using his time to interview Ed Nichols. Maybe he would call Darcy later and check that she was okay. She was so quiet. So self-contained. He was like that himself, but there was something else going on with her. She hadn't been afraid of him, but he had sensed her discomfort with him. Something more than her grief was bothering her. Was it because he was law enforcement? Because he was a man? Something else?

He didn't like unanswered questions. It was one of the things that made him a good investigator. He liked figuring people out—why they acted the way they did. If he hadn't been a law enforcement officer, he might have gone into psychology, except that sitting in an office all day would have driven him batty. He needed to be active and *doing*.

Ed Nichols lived in a small, ranch-style home with dark green cedar siding and brick-red trim. Giant blue spruce trees at the corners dwarfed the dwelling, and must have cast it in perpetual shadow. In the winter twilight, lights glowed from every window as if determined to dispel the gloom. Ryder parked his Chevy Tahoe at the curb and strode up the walk. Somewhere inside the house, a dog barked. Before he could ring the bell, the door opened and a man in his midfifties, thick blond hair fading to white, answered the door. "Is something wrong?" he asked.

"Dr. Nichols?" Ryder asked.

"Yes?" The man frowned.

"I need to speak with you a moment."

Toenails clicking on the hardwood floors announced the arrival of not one dog, but two—a small white poodle and a large, curly-haired mutt. The mutt stared at Ryder, then let out a loud *woof.*

"Hush, Murphy," Dr. Nichols said. He caught the dog by the collar and held him back, the poodle cowering behind, and pushed open the storm door. "You'd better come in."

A woman emerged from the back of the house—a trim brunette in black yoga pants and a purple sweater. She paled when she saw Ryder. "Is something wrong? Our son?"

"I'm not here about your son," Ryder said quickly. He turned to Nichols. "I wanted to ask you some questions about Kelly Farrow."

"Kelly?" Surprise, then suspicion, clouded Nichols's expression. He lowered himself into the recliner and began stroking the big dog's head while the little one settled in his lap. "What about her?"

"You might as well sit down," Mrs. Nichols said. She perched on the edge of an adjacent love seat while Ryder took a seat on the sofa. "When was the last time you saw Kelly Farrow?" he asked.

Nichols frowned. "I don't know. Maybe—last week? I

think I passed her on the street. Why? What is this about? Is she saying I've done something?"

"What would she say you've done?"

"Nothing! I don't have anything to do with those two."

"Those two?"

"Kelly and that other girl, Darcy."

"I understand you weren't too happy about them opening a new practice in Eagle Mountain."

"Who told you that?"

"Is it true?"

Nichols focused on the big dog, running his palm from the top of its head to the tip of its tail, over and over. "A town this small only needs one vet. But they're free to do as they please."

"Has your own business suffered since they opened their practice?" Ryder asked.

"What does that have to do with anything?" Mrs. Nichols spoke, leaning toward Ryder. "Are you accusing my husband of something?"

"You can't come into my home and start asking all these questions without telling us why," Nichols said.

"Kelly Farrow is dead. I'm trying to find out who killed her."

Nichols stared, his mouth slightly open. "Dead?"

"Ed certainly didn't kill her," Mrs. Nichols protested. "Just because he might have criticized the woman doesn't mean he's a murderer."

"Sharon, you're not helping," Nichols said.

"Where were you between nine and one today?" Ryder asked.

"I was at my office." He nodded to his wife. "Sharon can confirm that. She's my office manager."

"He saw patients all morning and attended the Rotary Club meeting at lunch," Sharon said.

"Listen, Kelly wasn't my favorite person in the world, but I wouldn't do something like that," Nichols said. "I couldn't."

Ryder wanted to believe the man, who seemed genuinely shaken, but it was too early in the case to make judgments of guilt or innocence. His job now was to gather as many facts as possible. He stood. "I may need to see your appointment book and talk to some of your clients to verify your whereabouts," he said.

"This is appalling." Sharon also rose, her cheeks flushed, hands clenched into fists. "How dare you accuse my husband this way."

"I'm not accusing him of anything," Ryder said. "It's standard procedure to check everyone's alibis." He nodded to Nichols. "Someone from my office will be in touch."

Ryder left the Nicholses' and headed back toward Main. He passed a familiar red-and-white wrecker, and Christy O'Brien tooted her horn and waved. Weather like this always meant plenty of work for Christy and her dad, pulling people out of ditches and jump-starting cars whose batteries had died in the cold.

Ryder pulled into the grocery store lot and parked. He could see a few people moving around inside the lit store—employees who had to be there, he guessed. People who didn't have to be out in this weather stayed home. The automatic doors at the store entrance opened and a trio of teenage boys emerged, bare-headed and laughing, their letter jackets identifying them as students at the local high school. Apparently, youth was immune to the weather. They sauntered across the lot to a dark gray SUV and piled in.

Ryder contacted his office in Grand Junction to update them on his progress with the case. Since state patrol personnel couldn't reach him because of the closed road, he had called on the sheriff's department to process the crime scene. After the medical examiner had arrived at the scene and the ambulance had transported the body to the funeral home that would serve as a temporary morgue, he had had Kelly's car towed to the sheriff's department impound lot. But none of the forensic evidence—blood and hair samples, fingerprints and DNA— could be processed until the roads opened again. Eagle Mountain didn't have the facilities to handle such evidence.

"The highway department is saying the road won't open until day after tomorrow at the earliest," the duty officer told Ryder. "It could be longer, depending on the weather."

"Meanwhile, the trail gets colder," Ryder said. "And if the killer is on the other side of the pass, he has plenty of time to get away while I sit here waiting for the weather to clear."

"Do what you can. We'll run a background check on this Ed Nichols and let you know what we find. We're also doing a search for similar crimes."

"I'm going to talk to the sheriff, see if he has any suspects I haven't uncovered."

He ended the call and sat, staring out across the snowy lot and contemplating his next move. He could call it a night and go home, but he doubted he would get any rest. In a murder investigation it was important to move quickly, while the evidence was still fresh. But the weather had him stymied. Still, there must be more he could do.

A late-model Toyota 4Runner cruised slowly through the parking lot, a young man behind the wheel. He passed Ryder's Tahoe, his face a blur behind snow-flecked glass, then turned back out of the lot. Was he a tourist, lost and using the lot to turn around? Or a bored local, out cruising the town? Ryder hadn't recognized the vehicle, and after two years in Eagle Mountain, he knew most people. But new folks moved in all the time, many of them second homeowners who weren't around enough to get to know. And even this time of year there were tourists, drawn to backcountry skiing and ice climbing.

Any one of them might be a murderer. Was Kelly Farrow the killer's only victim, or merely the first? The thought would keep Ryder awake until he had answers.

DARCY PARKED IN front of Kelly's half of the duplex off Fifth Street. Kelly had liked the place because it was within walking distance of the clinic, with easy access to the hiking trails along the river. Darcy let herself in with her key and when she flicked on the light, an orange tabby stared at her from the hall table, tail flicking. *Meow!*

"Hello, Pumpkin." Darcy scratched behind the cat's ears, and Pumpkin pressed his head into her palm.

Mroww! This more insistent cry came from a sleek, cream-colored feline, seal-point ears attesting to a Siamese heritage.

"Hello, Spice." Darcy knelt, one hand extended. Spice deigned to let her pet her.

Darcy stood and looked around at the evidence that someone else—Ryder, she guessed—had been here. Mail was spread out in a messy array on the hall table, and powdery residue—fingerprint powder?—covered the door frame and other surfaces. Darcy moved farther into the house, noting the afghan crumpled at the bottom of the sofa, a paperback romance novel splayed, spine up, on the table beside it. A rectangle outlined by dust on the desk in the corner of the room indicated where Kelly's laptop had sat. Ryder had probably taken it. From television crime dramas she had watched, she guessed he would look at her emails and other correspondence, searching for threats or any indication that someone had wanted to harm Kelly.

But Kelly would have said something to Darcy if anyone had threatened her. Unlike Darcy, Kelly never held back her feelings. Darcy blinked back stinging tears and hurried to the kitchen, to the cat carriers stacked in the corner. Both cats watched from the doorway, tails twitching, suspicious.

She set the open carriers in the middle of the kitchen floor, then filled two dishes with the gourmet salmon Pumpkin and Spice favored, and slid the dishes into the carrier. Pumpkin took the bait immediately, scarcely looking up from devouring the food when Darcy fastened the door of the carrier. Spice was more wary, tail twitching furiously as she prowled around the open carrier. But hunger won over caution and soon she, too, darted inside, and Darcy fastened the door.

She was loading the second crate into the back of her Subaru when the door to the other half of the duplex opened. A man's figure filled the doorway. "Darcy, is that you?"

"Hello, Ken." She tried to relax some of the stiffness from her face as she turned to greet Kelly's neighbor. Ken Rutledge was a trim, athletic man who taught math and coached boys' track and Junior Varsity basketball at Eagle Mountain High School.

He came toward her and she forced herself not to pull away when he took her arm. "What's going on?" he asked. "When I got home from practice two cop cars were pulling away from Kelly's half of the house." He looked past her to the back of her Forester. "And you're taking Kelly's cats? Has something happened to her?"

"Kelly's dead. Someone killed her." Her voice broke, and she let him pull her into his arms.

"Kelly's dead?" he asked, smoothing his hand down her back as she sobbed. "How? Who?"

She hated that she had to fight so hard to pull herself together. She tried to shove out of his arms, but he held her tight. She reminded herself that this was just Ken— Kelly's neighbor, and a man Darcy herself had dated a few times. He thought he was being helpful, holding her this way. She forced herself to relax and wait for her tears to subside. When his hold on her loosened, she eased back. "I don't know any details," she said. "A state patrolman told me they found her up on Dixon Pass— murdered."

"That's horrible." Ken's eyes were bright with the shock of the news—and fascination. "Who would want to hurt Kelly?"

"The cops didn't stop to talk to you?" she asked.

"When I saw the sheriff's department vehicles I didn't pull in," he said. "I drove past and waited until they were gone before I came back."

"Why would you do that?" She stared at him.

He shrugged. "I have a couple of traffic tickets I haven't paid. I didn't want any hassle if they looked me up and saw them."

She took a step back. "Ken, they're going to want to talk to you," she said. "You may know something. You might have seen someone hanging around here, watching Kelly."

"I haven't seen anything like that." He shoved his hands in his pockets. "And I'll talk to them. I just didn't feel like dealing with them tonight. I mean, I didn't know Kelly was dead."

She closed the hatch of the car. "I have to go," she said.

He put a hand on her shoulder. "You shouldn't be alone at a time like this," he said. "You're welcome to stay with me."

"No. Thank you." She took out her keys and clutched them, automatically lacing them through her fingers to use as a weapon, the way the self-defense instructor in Fort Collins had shown her.

His expression clouded. "If it was someone else, you'd accept help, wouldn't you?" he said. "Because it's me, you're refusing. Just because we have a romantic history, doesn't mean we can't be friends."

She closed her eyes, then opened them to find him glaring at her. Were they ever going to stop having this conversation? They had only gone out together three times. To her, that didn't constitute a *romantic history*, though he insisted on seeing things differently. "Ken, I don't want to talk about this now," she said. "I'm tired and I'm upset and I just want to go home."

"I'm here for you, Darcy," he said.

"I know." She got into the driver's seat, forcing herself not to hurry, and drove away. When she glanced in the rearview mirror, Ken was still standing in the drive, frowning after her, hands clenched into fists at his sides.

Dating him had been a bad idea—Darcy had known it from the first date—but Kelly had pressured her to give him a chance. "He's a nice man," she had said. "And the two of you have a lot in common."

They did have a lot in common—a shared love of books and animals and hiking. But Ken pushed too hard. He wanted too much. After only two dates, he had asked her to move in with him. He had talked about them taking a vacation together next summer, and had wanted her to come home to Wisconsin to meet his parents for Christmas. She had broken off with him then, telling him she wasn't ready to get serious with anyone. He had pretended not to understand, telling her coming home to meet his family was just friendly, not serious. But she couldn't see things that way.

He had been upset at first—angry even. He called her some horrible names and told her she would regret losing a guy like him. But after he had returned from visiting his folks last week, he had been more cordial. They had exchanged greetings when she stopped by to see Kelly, and the three of them spent a couple of hours one afternoon shoveling the driveway together. Darcy had been willing to be friends with him, as long as he didn't want more.

She turned onto the gravel county road that led to the horse ranch that belonged to one of their first clients. Robbie Lusk had built the tiny house on wheels parked by the creek as an experiment, he said, and was happy to rent it out to Darcy. His hope was to add more tiny homes and form a little community, and he had a second home under construction.

Darcy slowed to pull into her drive, her cozy home visible beneath the golden glow of the security light one hundred yards ahead. But she was startled to see a dark SUV moving down the drive toward her. Heart in her throat, she braked hard, eliciting complaints from the cats in their carriers behind her. The SUV barreled out past her, a rooster tail of wet snow in its wake. It turned sharply, scarcely inches from her front bumper, and she tried to see the driver, but could make out nothing in the darkness and swirling snow.

She stared at the taillights of the SUV in her rearview mirror as it raced back toward town. Then, hands shaking, she pulled out her phone and found the card Ryder had given her. She punched in his number and waited for it to ring. "Ryder Stewart," he answered.

"This is Darcy Marsh. Can you come out to my house? A strange car was here and just left. I didn't recognize it and I… I'm afraid." Her knuckles ached from gripping the phone so hard, and her throat hurt from admitting her fear.

"Stay in your car. I'll be right there," Ryder said, his voice strong and commanding, and very reassuring.

Chapter Three

Ryder met no other cars on the trip to Darcy's house. Following the directions she had given him, he turned into a gravel drive and spotted her Subaru Forester parked in front of a redwood-sided dwelling about the size of a train caboose. She got out of the car when he parked his Tahoe beside her, a slight figure in black boots and a knee-length, black puffy coat, her dark hair uncovered. "I haven't looked around to see if anything was messed with," she said. "I thought I should wait for you."

"Good idea." He took his flashlight from his belt and played it over the ground around the house. It didn't look disturbed, but it was snowing hard enough the flakes might have covered any tracks. "Let me know if you spot anything out of place," he said.

She nodded and, keys in hand, moved to the front door. "I know most people around here don't lock their doors," she said. "But I'm enough of a city girl, I guess, that it's a habit I can't break." She turned the key in the lock and pushed open the door, reaching in to flick on the lights, inside and out.

Ryder followed her inside, in time to see two cats descending the circular stairs from the loft, the smaller, black one bounding down, the larger silver tabby moving at a more leisurely pace. "Hello, guys." Darcy shrugged off her shoulder bag and bent to greet the cats. "The black one is Marianne. Her older sister is Elinor." She glanced up at him through surprisingly long lashes. "The Dashwood sisters. From *Sense and Sensibility.*"

He nodded. "I take it you're a fan of Jane Austen?"

"Yes. Have you read the book?"

"No." He couldn't help feeling he had failed some kind of test as she moved away from him, though she couldn't go far. He could see the entire dwelling, except for the loft and the part of the bathroom not visible through the open door at the end, from this spot by the door—a small sitting area, galley kitchen and table for two. The space was organized, compact and a little claustrophobic. It was a dwelling designed for one person—and two cats.

Make that four cats. "I stopped by Kelly's place and picked up her two cats," she said. "Will you help me bring them in?"

He followed her back to her car and accepted one of the cat carriers. The cat inside, a large gold tabby, eyed him balefully and began to yowl. "Oh, Pumpkin, don't be such a crybaby," Darcy chided as she led the way back up the walk. Inside they set the carriers side by side on the sofa that butted up against the table on one side of the little house. "I'll open the carrier doors and they'll come out when they're ready," she said. "They've stayed here before."

"I'll go outside and take a look around," he said, leaving her to deal with the cats.

A closer inspection showed tire tracks in the soft snow to one side of the gravel drive, and fast-filling-in shoe prints leading around one end of the house to a large back window. He shone the light around the frame, over fresh tool marks, as if someone had tried to jimmy it open.

Holding the light in one hand, he took several photos with his phone, then went back inside.

"I put on water for tea," Darcy said, indicating the teakettle on the three-burner stove. "I always feel better with a cup of tea." She rubbed her hands up and down her shoulders. She was still wearing her black puffy coat.

Ryder took out his notebook. "What can you remember about the vehicle you saw?" he asked.

"It was a dark color—dark gray or black, and an SUV, or maybe a small truck with a camper cover? A Toyota, I think." She shook her head. "I'm not a person who pays much attention to cars. It was probably someone who was lost, turning around. I shouldn't have called you."

Ryder thought of the 4Runner that had cruised past him in the grocery store parking lot. "There are fresh footprints leading around the side of the house, and marks on your back window, where someone might have tried to get in."

All color left her face, and she pressed her lips together until they, too, were bleached white. "Show me," she said.

She followed him back out into the snow. He took her arm to steer her around the fading shoe prints, and shone the light on the gouges in the wooden window frame. "I'm sure those weren't here before," she said. "The place was brand-new when I moved in four months ago."

"I'll turn in a report to the sheriff's office," he said. "Have you seen the vehicle you described before?"

"No. But like I said, I don't pay attention to cars. Maybe I should."

"Have you seen any strangers out here? Noticed anyone following you? Has Kelly mentioned anything about anyone following her?"

"No." She turned and walked back into the house. When he stepped in after her, the teakettle was screaming. She moved quickly to shut off the burner and filled two mugs with steaming water. Fear seemed to rise off her like the vapor off the water, though she was trying hard to control it.

"I know this is unsettling," he said. "But the fact that the person didn't stay when you arrived here by yourself tells me he was more likely a burglar who didn't want to be caught, than someone who wanted to attack you."

"I was supposed to be safe here," she said.

"Safe from what?"

She carried both mugs to the table and sat. He took the seat across from her. "Safe from what?" he asked again. "I'm not asking merely to be nosy. If you have someone you're hiding from—someone who might want to hurt you—it's possible this person confused you and Kelly. It wouldn't be the first time something like that happened."

"No, it's not like that." She tucked her shoulder-length brown hair behind her ear, then brought the mug to her lips, holding it in both hands. When she set it down again, her eyes met his, a new determination in their brown depths. "I was raped in college—in Fort Collins. I moved in with Kelly after that and she really helped me move past that. My mother and I aren't close and my father has been out of the picture for years."

He thought of what she had said before—that she was used to looking after herself. "Women who have been through something like that often have a heightened awareness of danger," he said. "It's good to pay attention to that. Have you seen anyone suspicious, here or at Kelly's or at your office? Have you felt threatened or uneasy?"

"No." She shook her head. "That's why I thought Eagle Mountain was different. I always felt safe here. Until now."

He sipped the tea—something with cinnamon and apples. Not bad. It would be even better with a shot of whiskey, but since he was technically still on duty, he wouldn't bring it up. He wondered if she even had hard liquor in the house. "I stopped by and talked to Ed Nichols and his wife after I left the clinic," he said.

Fine lines between her eyes deepened. "You don't really think he killed Kelly, do you?"

"I haven't made up my mind about anything at this point. He said he was at the clinic all morning, and then at the Rotary Club luncheon."

"How did she die?" Darcy asked. "You told me you found her up on Dixon Pass, but how?"

"Do you really want to know?"

"I have a very good imagination. If you don't tell me, I'll fill in too many horrid details of my own." She took another sip of tea. "Besides, the papers will be full of the story soon."

"She was in her car, over to the side, up against the rock face at the top of the pass. Her hands and feet were bound with duct tape and her throat had been cut."

Darcy let out a ragged breath. "Had she been raped?"

"I don't know. But her clothes weren't torn or disarrayed. We'll know more tomorrow."

"So someone just killed her and left her up there? Why there?"

"I don't know. Maybe he—or she—hoped what did happen would happen—an avalanche buried the car. We might not have found it for weeks if a delivery truck wasn't buried in the same place. When we pulled out the delivery driver, we found Kelly's car, too."

"Did you talk to her parents?"

"Yes. They wanted to fly down right away. I told them they should wait until the road opens."

"When will that be?"

"We don't know. A storm system has settled in. They're predicting up to four feet of new snow. Until it stops, no one is getting in or out of Eagle Mountain."

"The sheriff and Lacy Milligan are supposed to get married in a few weeks," she said.

"The road should be open by then," he said. He hoped so. He wasn't going to get far with this case without the information he could get outside town.

"When I moved here and people told me about the road being closed sometimes in winter, I thought it sounded exciting," she said. "Kind of romantic, even—everyone relying on each other in true pioneer spirit. Then I think about our weekly order of supplies not getting through, and people who don't live here being stuck in motels or doubling up with family—then it doesn't sound like much fun." She looked up at him. "What about you? Do you live here?"

"I do. I'm in a converted carriage house over on Elm."

"No pets? Or are you a client of Dr. Nichols's?"

Her teasing tone lifted his spirits. "No pets," he said. "I like dogs, but my hours would mean leaving it alone too long."

"Cats do better on their own." She turned to watch Pumpkin facing off with Marianne. The two cats sniffed each other from nose to tail then, satisfied, moved toward the stairs and up into the loft.

"I should let you go," she said. "Thank you for stopping by."

"Is there someone you could stay with tonight?" he asked. "Or you could get a motel room, somewhere not so isolated."

"No, I'll be fine." She looked around. "I don't want to

leave the cats. I have a gun and I know how to use it. Kelly and I took a class together. It helped me feel stronger."

He was tempted to say he would stay here tonight, but he suspected she wouldn't welcome the offer. He'd have to sleep sitting up on her little sofa, or freeze in his Tahoe. "Keep your phone with you and call 911 if you feel at all uneasy," he said.

"I will. I guess I should have called them in the first place."

"I wasn't saying I minded coming out here. I didn't. I don't. If you feel better calling me, don't hesitate."

She nodded. "I guess I called you because I knew you. I'm not always comfortable with strangers."

"I'm glad you trusted me enough to call me. And I meant it—don't think twice about calling me again."

"All right. And I'll be fine." Her smile was forced, but he admired the effort.

He glanced in the rearview mirror as he drove away, at the little house in the snowy clearing, golden light illuminating the windows, like a doll's house in a fairy-tale illustration. Darcy Marsh wasn't an enchanted princess but she had a rare self-possession that drew him.

He parked his Tahoe on the side of the road to enter his report about the vehicle she'd seen and the possible attempted break-in at her home. He was uploading the photos he'd taken when his phone rang with a call from the sheriff's department.

Sheriff Travis Walker's voice carried the strain of a long day. "Ryder, you probably want to get over here," he said. "We've found another body."

Chapter Four

Christy O'Brien lay across the front seat of her wrecker, the front of her white parka stained crimson with blood, her hands and feet wrapped with silver duct tape. The wrecker itself was nose-down in a ditch at the far end of a gravel road on the outskirts of town, snow sifting down over it like icing drizzled on a macabre cake.

Ryder turned away, pushing aside the sickness and guilt that clawed at the back of his throat. Such emotions wouldn't do anyone any good now. "I just saw her," he said. "Less than an hour ago."

"Where?" Sheriff Travis Walker, snow collecting on the brim of his Stetson and the shoulders of his black parka, scanned the empty roadside. Travis was one of the reasons Ryder had ended up in Eagle Mountain. He had visited his friend at the Walker ranch one summer and fallen in love with the place. When an opening in this division had opened up, he had put in for it.

"I was in the grocery store parking lot," Ryder said. "She passed me. I figured she was on a call, headed to pull someone out of a ditch."

"This probably happened not too long after that." Travis played the beam of his flashlight over the wrecker. "Maybe the killer called her, pretended his car wouldn't start—maybe a dead battery. When she gets out of the wrecker to take a look, he overpowers her, tapes her up, slits her throat."

"Then shoves her into the wrecker and drives it into the ditch?"

"He may not have even had to drive it," Travis said. "Just put it into gear and give it a good push in the right direction. Then he gets in his own car and drives away."

"Who called it in?" Ryder asked.

"Nobody," Travis said. "I was coming back from a call—an attempted break-in not far from here. I turned down this road, thinking the burglar might have ducked down here. When I saw the wrecker in the ditch, I knew something wasn't right."

"An attempted break-in?" Ryder asked. "Where? When?"

"Up on Pine." Travis indicated a street to the north that crossed this one. "Maybe twenty minutes ago? A guy came home from work and surprised someone trying to jimmy his lock. He thought it was a teenager. He thought he saw an Eagle Mountain High School letter jacket."

"I saw three boys in letter jackets at the grocery store just after Christy's wrecker passed me," Ryder said. "And someone tried to break into Darcy Marsh's place this evening—I was leaving there when you called me."

Travis frowned. "I don't like to think teenagers would do something like this, but we'll check it out." He turned back toward the wrecker. "I'll talk to the people in the houses at the other end of the road, and those in this area. Maybe someone heard or saw something."

"There would be a lot of blood," Ryder said.

"More than is in the cab of the wrecker, I'm thinking. It was the same with Kelly, did you notice? She wasn't killed in that car—and it was her car."

"I did notice," Ryder said. "There was hardly any blood in the car or even on her."

"I think she was killed somewhere else and driven up there," Travis said.

"So the killer had an accomplice?" Ryder asked. "Someone who could have followed him up to the pass in another car, then taken him away?"

"Maybe," Travis said. "Or he could have walked back into town. It's only about three miles. We'll try to find out if anyone saw anything." He walked to the back of his cruiser and took out a shovel. "I don't think Christy was killed very far from here. There wasn't time. I want to see if I can find any evidence of that." He followed the fast-filling tracks of the wrecker back to the road and began to scrape lightly at the snow.

Ryder fetched his own shovel from his vehicle and tried the shoulder on the other side of the road. The work was slow and tedious as he scraped, then shone his light on the space he had uncovered. After ten minutes or so, the work paid off. "Over here," he called to Travis.

The blood glowed bright as paint against the frozen ground—great splashes of it that scarcely looked real. Travis crouched to look. "We'll get a sample, but I'm betting it's Christy's blood," he said.

"Whoever did this would have blood on his clothes, maybe in his vehicle," Ryder said.

Travis nodded. "He could have gone straight home, or to wherever he's staying, and discarded the clothes—maybe burned them in a woodstove or fireplace, if he has one. There's no one out tonight to see him, though we'll ask around." He stood. "You said you were at Darcy's place?"

"Right. When she got home tonight, there was a strange vehicle leaving. I found signs that someone tried to break in."

"What time was this?" Travis asked.

Ryder checked his notes. "Seven forty."

"The person or persons who tried to break in to Fred Starling's place might have come from Darcy's, but I don't see how they would have had time to drive from Darcy's, kill Christy, then break in to Fred's," Travis said. "We'll see what the ME gives us for time of death." He glanced down the road. "He should be here soon."

"I didn't like leaving Darcy alone out there," Ryder said. "It's kind of remote."

"I've already called in one of our reserve officers," Travis said. "I'll have him drive by Darcy's place and check on her. Why did she call you?"

"I gave her my card when we spoke earlier and told her to call if she needed anything." Ryder shifted his weight, thinking maybe it was time to change the subject. Not that he thought Travis was a stickler over jurisdiction, but he didn't think Darcy would welcome any further attention from the sheriff. "What are you doing, pulling the night shift?" he asked. "Doesn't the sheriff get any perks?"

"The new officer who's supposed to be working tonight has the flu," Travis said. He shrugged. "I figured I'd make a quick patrol, then spend the rest of the night at my desk. I have a lot of loose ends to tie up before the wedding and honeymoon."

"I hope the weather cooperates with your plans," Ryder said. "The highway department says the pass could be closed for the next two or three days—longer if this snow keeps up."

"Most of the wedding party is already here, and the ones who aren't will be coming in soon," Travis said. "My sister, Emily, pulled in this afternoon, about half an hour ahead of the closure."

He turned to gaze down the street, distracted by the headlights approaching—the medical examiner, Butch Collins, followed by the ambulance. Butch, a portly man made even larger by the ankle-length duster and long knitted scarf he wore, climbed out of his truck, old-fashioned medical bag in hand. "Two dead women in one day is a little much, don't you think, Sheriff?" He nodded to Ryder. "Is there a connection between the two?"

Ryder checked for any lurking reporters, but saw none. He nodded to the ambulance driver, who had pulled to the side of the road, steam pouring in clouds from the tailpipe of the idling vehicle. "Both women had their hands and feet bound with duct tape, and their throats slit," he said. "It looks like they weren't killed in the vehicle, but their bodies were put into the vehicles after death."

Collins nodded. "All right. I'll take a look."

Ryder and Travis moved to Travis's cruiser. "Darcy said Kelly was going shopping today," Ryder said. "She couldn't think of anyone who would want to hurt Kelly. No one had been threatening her or making her feel uneasy. You're a little more tied in with the town than I am. Do you know of anyone who might have had a disagreement with her—boyfriend, client or a competitor?"

"I didn't know her well. My parents had Kelly or Darcy out to the ranch a few times to take care of horses. I remember my mom said she liked them. I knew them well enough to wave to. I don't think she was dating anyone, though I'll ask Lacy. She keeps up with that kind of gossip more than I do." Travis's fiancée was a local woman, near Kelly's age. "I never heard anything about unhappy clients. As for competitors, there's really only Ed Nichols."

"What do you know about him?" Ryder asked. "Darcy

said he wasn't too happy about them opening up a competing practice."

"Ed's all right," Travis said. "He might have grumbled a little when the two women first arrived, but it's understandable he would feel threatened—two attractive, personable young women. I imagine it cut into his business."

"I talked to him and his wife this afternoon," Ryder said. "He seemed genuinely shaken by the news that Kelly was dead."

"It's hard to picture Ed doing something like this," Travis said. "But we'll check his alibi for the time of Christy's death."

"What about a connection between Kelly and Christy?" Ryder asked. "Were they specific targets, or random?"

"Maybe Kelly was the target and the killer went after Christy because she was the one who pulled the car with Kelly's body in it out from its hiding place?" Travis shook his head. "It's too early to make any kind of hypothesis, really."

"I've got a bad feeling about this."

"I don't like to use the words serial killer," Travis said. "But that could be what we're looking at."

"After I found Kelly's body, I was worried her murderer had gotten away before the road closed," Ryder said. "If he did, we might never find him."

"Looks like he didn't get out," Travis said. "Which could be a much bigger problem."

"I hear you," Ryder said. As long as the road stayed blocked, the killer couldn't leave—but none of his potential victims could get very far away, either.

DARCY CONSIDERED CLOSING the clinic the next day, out of respect for Kelly. But what would she do, then, other than sit around and be sad? Work would at least provide a distraction. And the clinic had been her and Kelly's shared passion. Keeping it open seemed a better way to honor her than closing the doors.

The morning proved busy. Most of the people who had come in had heard about Kelly and were eager to share their memories of her. Darcy passed out tissues and shed a few tears of her own, but the release of admitting her grief felt good. Knowing she wasn't alone in her pain made it a tiny bit more bearable.

The office manager, Stacy, left for lunch, but Darcy stayed behind, claiming she had too much work to do. If she was being honest with herself, however, she could admit she didn't want to go out in public to face all the questions and speculation surrounding Kelly's murder, especially since one of her last patients of the day had told her the newest edition of the *Eagle Mountain Examiner* had just hit the stands, with a story about the two murders filling the front page. The editor must have stayed up late to get the breaking news in before the paper went to the printer.

Murder. The word sent a shiver through her. It still seemed so unreal. Who would want to harm Kelly? Or Christy? Darcy hardly knew the other woman, but she had seemed nice enough. Not that nice people didn't get killed, but not in places like Eagle Mountain. Maybe she was wrong to think that, but she couldn't shake her belief that this small, beautiful town was somehow immune to that kind of violence.

She was forcing herself to eat a cup of yogurt from the office refrigerator when the phone rang. She should have let it go straight to the answering service, but what if it was Ryder, with news about Kelly? Or Kelly's parents, wanting to talk?

She picked up the receiver. "Hello?"

A thin, quavering voice came over the line. "Is this the vet?" The woman—Darcy thought it was a woman—asked.

"Yes. This is Dr. Marsh. Who is this?"

"Oh, my name is Marge. Marge Latham. You don't know me. I'm in town visiting my cousin and I got trapped here by the weather. Me and my dog, Rufus. Rufus is why I'm calling."

"What's the problem with Rufus?" Darcy called up the scheduling program on the office computer as she spoke.

"He's hurt his leg," the woman said. "I don't know what's wrong with it, but he can't put any weight on it and he's in a lot of pain. It's so upsetting." Her voice broke. "He's all I have, you see, and if something happens to him, I don't know what I'd do."

"If you can bring Rufus in at three today I can see him," Darcy said. The patient before that was routine vaccinations, so that shouldn't take too long. The patient after might have to wait a little, but most people understood about emergencies.

"I was hoping you could come here," Marge said. "He's such a big dog—he weighs over a hundred pounds. I can't possibly lift him to get him into the car."

"What kind of dog is Rufus?" Darcy asked.

"He's a mastiff. Such a sweet boy, but moving him is a problem for me. I was told you do house calls."

"Only for large animals," Darcy said. "Horses and cows." And llamas and goats and one time, a pig. But they had to draw the line somewhere. Most dogs were used to riding in the car and would climb in willingly—even mastiffs.

"Well, Rufus is as big as a small horse," Marge said.

"Is there anyone who can help you get him to the office?" Darcy asked. "Maybe your sister or a nephew—"

"No, dear, that isn't possible. Won't you please come? The other vet already said no and I don't know what I'll do. He's all I have." She choked back a sob and Darcy's stomach clenched. She couldn't let an animal suffer— or risk this old woman hurting herself trying to handle the dog by herself.

"I could stop by after work tonight," she said. "But we don't close until six today, so it would be after that."

"That would be wonderful. Thank you so much."

The address the woman rattled off didn't sound familiar to Darcy, but that wasn't unusual. Four months was hardly enough time to learn the maze of gravel roads and private streets that crisscrossed the county. "Let me have your number, in case I'm running late," Darcy said.

"Oh, that would be my sister's number. Let me see. What is that?" The sounds of shuffling, then Marge slowly read off a ten-digit number. "Thank you again, dear. And Rufus thanks you, too."

Darcy hung up the phone and wrote the woman's information at the bottom of the schedule, and stuffed the notes she had taken into her purse.

Five and a half hours later, Darcy drove slowly down Silverthorne Road, leaning forward and straining her eyes in the fading light, searching for the address Marge had given her. But the numbers weren't adding up. She spotted 2212 and 2264 and 2263, but no 2237. Had Marge gotten it wrong?

Darcy slowed at each driveway to peer up the dark path, but usually she couldn't even make out a house, as the drive invariably turned into a thick tunnel of trees. Growing exasperated, she pulled to the side of the road and took out her phone and punched in the number Marge had given her. A harsh tone made her pull the phone from her ear, and a mechanical voice informed her that the number she had dialed was no longer in service or had been changed.

Darcy double-checked the number, but she had it right. And she was sure she hadn't written it down wrong. So was Marge completely confused, or was something else going on? "I should have asked her sister's name," Darcy muttered. "Then maybe I could have looked up her address."

Or maybe there wasn't a sister. A cold that had nothing to do with the winter weather began to creep over her. No. She pushed the thought away. There was no reason to turn this into something sinister. It was simply a matter of a confused old woman, a stranger in town, getting mixed up about the address. Darcy would go into town and stop by the sheriff's department. The officers there knew the county front to back. They might have an idea where to find a visitor with an injured mastiff and her sister.

With shaking hands, Darcy put the car in gear and eased on to the road once more, tires crunching on the packed snow, even as more of the white stuff sifted down. As soon as she found a place to turn around, she would. But houses were far apart out here, and the narrow driveways difficult to see in the darkness. She missed the first drive, but was able to pull into the next, and carefully backed out again and prepared to return to town.

She had just shifted the Subaru into Drive when lights blinded her. A car or truck, its headlights on bright, was speeding toward her. She put up one hand to shield her eyes, and used the other hand to flash her high beams. Whoever was in that vehicle was driving much too fast, and didn't he realize he was blinding her?

She eased over closer to the side of the road, annoyance building, but irritation gave way to fear as she realized the other car wasn't slowing, and it wasn't moving over. She slammed her hand into the horn, the strident blare almost blocking the sound of the racing engine, but still, the oncoming vehicle didn't slow or veer away.

Panic climbed her throat and she scarcely had time to brace herself before the other car hit her, driving her car into the ditch and engulfing her in darkness.

Chapter Five

Travis had offered one of the sheriff's department conference rooms as a temporary situation room for the investigation into the murders of Kelly Farrow and Christy O'Brien. Until the roads opened and Colorado State Patrol investigators could take over, Ryder would work with Travis and his officers.

On Wednesday evening, he met with Travis and deputies Dwight Prentice and Gage Walker, to review what they knew so far. Travis yielded the whiteboard to Ryder and took a seat at the conference table with his officers.

"Our interviews with neighbors and our calls for information from anyone who might have seen anything in the vicinity of both crime scenes have turned up nothing useful," Ryder began. He had spent part of the day talking to people in houses and businesses near where the crimes had taken place. "That's not terribly surprising, considering both murders took place in isolated areas, during bad weather."

"That could mean the murderer is familiar with this area," Dwight said. "He knows the places he's least likely to be seen."

Ryder wrote this point on the whiteboard.

"It's a rural area, so isolated places aren't hard to find," Gage said.

"Point taken," Ryder said, and made a note. He moved on to the next item on his list. "We didn't find any fingerprints on either of the vehicles involved."

"Right. But everyone wears gloves in winter," Dwight said.

"And even dumb criminals have seen enough movies or television to know to wear gloves," Gage said.

"What about the tire impressions?" Ryder asked. "There was a lot of fresh snow at both scenes."

"We don't have a tire impression expert in the department," Travis said. "But we know how to take castings and photographs and we've compared them to databases online."

Dwight flipped pages in a file and pulled out a single sheet. "Best match is a standard winter tire that runs on half the vehicles in the county," he said. "We've even got them on one of the sheriff's department cruisers."

"And the snow was so fresh and dry that the impressions we got weren't good enough to reveal any unusual characteristics," Travis said.

Ryder glanced down at the legal pad in his hand for the next item on his list. "We have blood samples, but no way to send them for matching until the roads open up," he said.

"Could be tomorrow, could be next week," Gage said. "One weather station says the weather is going to clear and the other says another storm system is on the way."

Impatient as the news made him, Ryder knew there was no point getting stressed about something he couldn't control. "What about the duct tape?" He looked at the three at the table.

"Maybe a fancy state lab would come up with something more," Gage said. "But as far as we could tell, it's the standard stuff pretty much everybody has a roll of."

Ryder nodded. He hadn't expected anything there, but he liked to check everything off his list. "Have we found any links between Kelly and Christy?" he asked.

"Christy had a cat," Gage said. "Kelly saw it one time, for a checkup."

"When was that?" Ryder asked.

"Three months ago," Gage said.

"Anything else?" Ryder asked. "Did they socialize together? Belong to the same groups or organizations?"

The other three men shook their heads. "I questioned Christy's mom and dad about who she dated," Gage said. "I thought I might be able to match her list to a list of who Kelly went out with. I mean, it's a small town. There are only so many match-ups. But I struck out there."

"How so?" Ryder asked.

"Christy is engaged to a welder over in Delta," Gage said. "They've been seeing each other for three years. I talked to him on the phone. He's pretty torn up about this—and he couldn't have gotten here last night, anyway, since the road was still blocked."

"What about Kelly's dating history?" Ryder asked. "Anything raise any questions there?"

Gage shook his head. "That was harder to pull together, but Darcy gave me some names. One of them moved away two months ago. The other two have alibis that check out."

Ryder had to stop himself from asking how Darcy was doing. She obviously hadn't had any more trouble from whoever had tried to break into her place. He might find an excuse to stop by there later, just to make sure.

"Ed Nichols was home with his wife, watching TV last night when Christy was killed," Travis said.

"I'm guessing he wasn't too happy to see you," Ryder

said, recalling his own less-than-warm reception in the Nicholses' home.

"Ed was okay, but his wife is furious," Travis said. "But I think they were telling the truth. There was six inches of snow in the driveway when I pulled in last night, and no sign that Ed's truck or her car had moved in the last few hours."

Ryder consulted his notes again, but he had reached the end of his list. "What else do we have?" he asked.

"I questioned some of the high school kids this afternoon," Gage said. "And I talked to the teachers. No one knew anything about any guys in letter jackets who might have been out last night, trying to break into homes. I got the impression some of the students might not have been telling me everything they knew, but it's hard to see a connection between attempted break-ins and these murders."

"If students were in that area last night, they might have seen the killer, or his vehicle," Travis said. "I want to find and talk to them."

"Anything else?" Ryder asked.

"The ME says both women had their throats cut with a smooth-bladed, sharp knife," Travis said. "No defensive wounds, although Christy had some bruising, indicating she might have thrashed around quite a bit after the killer taped her hands and feet."

"So the murderer was able to surprise the women and bind them before they fought much," Dwight said.

"Might have been two men," Gage said. "No woman is going to lie still while you tape her up like that."

"One really strong man might be able to subdue a frightened woman," Travis said.

"Or maybe they were drugged," Dwight said. "A quick

jab with a hypodermic needle, or chloroform on a rag or something."

Ryder frowned. "I don't think there are any facilities here to test that," he said. "And even if we collect DNA from the bodies, we don't have any way of testing or matching it here."

"Right," Travis said. "We'll have to hold the bodies at the funeral home until the roads open."

Meanwhile, whoever did this was running free to kill again. "I spoke with the friends and family of both women," Ryder said. "None of them were aware of anyone who had made threats or otherwise bothered Kelly or Christy."

"There was no sexual assault," Travis said. "Whoever did this was quick. He killed them and got out of there. No lingering."

"We can't say they weren't targeted killings, but right now it feels random," Ryder said.

"Thrill killings," Gage said. "He did it because he could get away with it."

"If that's the case, he's likely to kill again," Travis said.

The others nodded, expressions sober. Ryder's stomach churned. He felt he ought to be out doing something to stop the murderer, but what?

Travis's phone buzzed and he answered it. "Sheriff Walker." He stilled, listening. "When? Where? Tell the officer we'll be right there."

He ended the call and looked to the others. "A 911 call just came in from Darcy Marsh. Someone attacked her tonight—ran her car off the road."

"DARCY! DARCY! Wake up, honey." Darcy struggled out of a confused daze, wincing at the light blinding her. She moaned, and the light shifted away. "Darcy, look at me."

She forced herself to look into the calm face of a middle-age man who spoke with authority. "What happened?" Darcy managed, forcing the words out, the effort of speaking exhausting her.

"You were in a wreck. I'm Emmett Baxter with Eagle Mountain EMS. Can you tell me what hurts?"

"Everything," Darcy said, and closed her eyes again. She had a vague recollection of dialing 911 earlier, but her memories since then were a jumbled mess.

"Don't go to sleep now," Emmett said. "Open your eyes. Can you move your feet for me?"

Darcy tried to ignore him, then the sharp odor of ammonia stung her nose and her eyes popped open. "That's better." Emmett smiled. "Now, tell me your name."

"Darcy Marsh."

He asked a few more questions she recognized as an attempt to assess her mental awareness — her address, birthdate, telephone number and the date.

"Now try to move your feet for me," he said.

Darcy moved her feet, then her hands. The fog that had filled her head had cleared. She took stock of her surroundings. She was in her car, white powder coating most of the interior, the deflated airbag spilling out of the steering wheel like a grotesque tongue. "My face hurts," she said.

"You're going to have a couple of black eyes and some bruises," Emmett said. He shone a light into each eye. "Does anything else hurt? Any back or neck pain, or difficulty breathing?"

She shook her head. "No."

He released the catch of Darcy's seat belt. "I'm going to fit you with a cervical collar just in case." He stripped the plastic wrapping from the padded collar and fit it to her neck, the Velcro loud in her ears. "How do you feel about getting out of the car and walking over to the ambulance?" he asked. "I'll help."

"Okay." Carefully, she swung her legs over to the side of the car, Emmett's arm securely around her. They both froze as the bright beams of oncoming headlights blinded them.

"I'm not sure why the state patrol is here," Emmett said.

Ryder, a powerful figure in his sharp khaki and blue, emerged from the cruiser and strode toward the car. His gaze swept over the damaged vehicle and came to rest on Darcy's face. The tenderness in that gaze made her insides feel wobbly, and tears threatened. "Darcy, are you okay?" he asked.

She clamped her lips together to hold back a sob and managed, almost grateful for the pain the movement caused. At least it distracted her from this terrible need to throw her arms around him and weep.

"We're just going to get her over to the ambulance where we can get a better look at her," Emmett said.

"Let me help." Not waiting for a response, Ryder leaned down and all but lifted her out of the car. He propped her up beside him and walked her to the back of the ambulance, then stepped aside while Emmett and a female EMT looked her over.

"You're going to be pretty sore tomorrow," Emmett pronounced when they were done. "But there's no swelling or indication that anything is broken and I can't find any sign of internal damage. How do you feel? Any nausea or pain?"

"I'm a little achy and still shaken up," Darcy said. "But I don't think I'm seriously injured."

"With the highway still closed, we can't transport you to the hospital, but I'd recommend a visit to the clinic in town. They can do X-rays and maybe keep you overnight for observation."

"No, I really don't think that's necessary," she said. "I think I just had the wind knocked out of me. If I start to feel worse, I promise I'll see a doctor."

Emmett nodded. "Don't hesitate to call us if that changes or you have any questions." He glanced over his shoulder at Ryder, who stood, arms folded across his chest, gaze fixed on Darcy. "Your turn."

For the first time Darcy realized there were other people at the scene—Travis and another man in a sheriff's department uniform, and several people in jeans and parkas who might have been neighbors. Ryder sat beside her on the back bumper of the ambulance while Travis came to stand beside them. "What happened?" he asked.

She took a deep breath, buying time to organize her thoughts. "I got a call at lunchtime today," she said. "When I was alone in the office. A woman who said her name was Marge asked me if I could make a house call to look at her mastiff who had hurt his leg. She said she was staying with her sister and had been trapped by the weather. She gave me an address on this street, but I couldn't find the number. I tried to call her, but the phone number she had given me wasn't a working number. I turned around and started to head back toward town when this vehicle blinded me with its headlights and ran into me." She put a hand to her head, wincing. "I must have blacked out for a minute, then I guess I came to and called for help, then passed out again. I didn't come to completely until the ambulance was here."

"A man backing out of his driveway saw the accident and called 911, too," Travis said. "He didn't get a good look at the vehicle that hit you, though he thinks it was a truck. He said it drove off after it put your car in the ditch."

Darcy looked toward her car, which was canted to one side in a snowbank. "He hit me almost head-on," she said. "My car's probably ruined."

"Had you ever heard from this Marge person before?" Ryder asked.

"No. She said her name was Marge Latham. I didn't think to ask for her sister's name."

"What was the address she gave you?" Travis asked.

"Two two three seven Silverthorne Road," Darcy said. "She said her dog's name was Rufus. She sounded really old, and said he was a mastiff, and too big for her to lift."

"You say you were alone in the office when the call came in?" Ryder asked.

"Yes. I had just sent Stacy to lunch. I stayed in to catch up on some work."

"So anyone watching the office would have known you were alone," Ryder said.

She stared at him. "Why do you think someone was watching the office? Why would they do that?"

His grim expression sent a shiver of fear through her. "I think someone made that call to get you out here, so they could run you off the road," he said. "The neighbor backing out of his driveway probably scared him off."

She hugged her arms across her stomach, fighting nausea. "Do you think it's the same person who killed Kelly and Christy?"

Ryder and Travis exchanged a look. "Is there anyone you can stay with for a while?" Ryder asked.

"No," she said. If Kelly was still alive, Darcy might have stayed with her, but that wasn't possible now. And the thought of leaving her little home was wrenching. "I don't want to leave the cats. I'll be fine."

A young uniformed officer approached. "The wrecker is here," he said. "Where do you want the car towed?"

All three men looked at Darcy. "Oh. Is there a mechanic in town?"

"There's O'Brien's," the officer said. "That's where the wrecker's from."

"Then I guess tow it there," she said.

"I'll drive you home," Ryder said.

There was no point in refusing—she didn't have any other way to get home, and she could see he wasn't going to take no for an answer. He helped her to his Tahoe and she climbed in. They rode in silence; she was still numb from everything that had happened. At the house he took the keys from her and opened the door, then checked through the house—which took all of a minute—the cats observing him from their perches on the stairs to the loft.

Darcy unbuttoned her coat and Ryder returned to her side to help her out of it. He draped it on the hook by the door, then hung his leather patrolman's jacket beside it. "Sit, and I'll make you some tea," he said.

She started to protest that he didn't have to wait on her. He didn't have to stay and look after her. She wanted to be alone. Instead, she surrendered to her wobbly knees and shakier emotions and slid onto the bench seat at the little table and watched while Ryder familiarized himself with her galley kitchen. Within minutes he had a kettle heating on the stove and was opening a can of soup.

"You don't have to stay," she said.

"No." He took two bowls from a cabinet and set them on the counter. "You've had a fright. I figured you could use some company." His eyes met hers. "And I'd rather stay here than go home to my empty place and worry about you out here alone."

"I'll be fine," she said. "I can see anyone coming, the locks are good and I have my gun and my phone."

"Use the phone first."

"Of course." She shivered. She had only ever fired the gun at the range. Could she really use it on a person? Maybe. If her life depended on it. "But I think I'm safe here." If she kept repeating the words, she might make them true.

"You should install an alarm system," he said.

"That's a great idea. But the nearest alarm company is in Junction—on the other side of Dixon Pass." Not accessible until the road reopened.

He stirred the soup, the rhythmic sound calming. Elinor the cat settled onto the bench next to Darcy, purring. She stroked the cat and tried to soak in all this soothing comfort. "Why is this happening?" she asked.

"Have you thought of anything at all that's happened the past few weeks that's been out of the ordinary?" he asked. "A client who was difficult, a man who leered at you in the grocery store—anything at all?"

"No."

"And no one who might have a grudge against you, or resentment—other than the other vet."

She hesitated. There was Ken, but he didn't really hate her. He had only had his feelings hurt because she had refused to continue dating him. But she had never felt threatened by him. Ryder turned toward her. "Who are you thinking of?"

She sighed. "There was a guy I went out with a few times—Ken Rutledge. He lives next door to Kelly, in the other half of the duplex. I thought he was getting too serious too quickly, so I broke things off. He wasn't happy about it, but I can't believe he would *kill* anyone. I mean, he's just not the violent type." She would have said the same about the man who raped her, too, though.

"I'll have a talk with him," Ryder said. He poured soup into the two bowls and brought them to the table. "I won't tell him you said anything. If he was Kelly's neighbor, I need to talk to him, anyway."

"Thank you." She leaned over the bowl of soup and the smell hit her, making her mouth water. Suddenly, she was ravenous. She tried not to look like a pig, but she inhaled the soup and drained the cup of tea, then sat back. "I feel much better now," she said.

Ryder smiled. His eyes crinkled at the corners when he did so. A shadow of beard darkened his chin and cheeks, giving him a rakish look. "You're not as pale," he said. "Though I bet you're going to be pretty sore tomorrow."

"But I'll heal," she said. "I'm not so sure about my car. And how am I going to get to work?" Her predicament had just sunk in. "It's not as if Eagle Mountain has a car rental agency."

"I'm pretty sure Bud O'Brien keeps a couple of loaner vehicles for customers," Ryder said.

"I hate to bother him," Darcy said. "The man just lost his daughter." Her stomach clenched, thinking of the woman who had been murdered.

"The people who work for him will be there," Ryder said. "Too many people would be left stranded in this weather if they closed their doors. Call them in the morning and someone will work something out for you. If not, give me a call and I'll put out some feelers."

"Thanks."

Ryder insisted on staying to help clean up and do the dishes. They worked side by side in her tiny kitchen. He seemed too large for the compact space, and yet comfortable in it, as well. Finally, when the last dish was returned to its place in her cabinets, he slipped on his jacket.

"You're sure you'll be comfortable here by yourself?" he asked.

He was standing very close to her so that she was very aware of his size and strength. She wasn't exactly uncomfortable, but her heart beat a little too fast, and she had trouble controlling her breathing.

"Darcy?"

He was looking at her, waiting on an answer. She cleared her throat. "I'll keep my phone with me and I'll call 911 if I see or hear anything suspicious."

"Call me, too," he said. "I'm going to have the phone company try to track the number the call came from, but if you hear from Marge again, you'll let me know."

It wasn't a request—more of an order. "I will," she said. "Part of me still hopes it was a mistake—a confused woman who wasn't familiar with the area gave me the wrong address and phone number."

"It would be nice if that were the case," he said. "But I think it's better to act as if it was a genuine threat and be prepared for it to happen again."

His words sent a shudder through her, but she braced herself against it and met his gaze. "I'll be careful," she said.

He rested his hand lightly on her shoulder. "I'm not trying to frighten you," he said.

She wanted to lean into him, to rest her cheek against his hand like a cat. Instead, she made herself stand still and smile, though the expression felt weak. "I know. I'm already frightened, but I won't let the fear defeat me."

"That's the attitude." He bent and kissed her cheek, the brush of his lips sending a jolt of awareness through her. She reached up to pull him to her, but he had already turned away. She leaned in the open doorway.

He strode to his car, his boots crunching in the snow. He lifted his hand in a wave as he climbed into the Tahoe, then he was gone. And still she stood, with the door wide open. But she didn't feel the cold, still warmed by that brief kiss.

Chapter Six

Ryder's first impression of Ken Rutledge was an overgrown boy. On a day when the temperatures hovered in the twenties, Rutledge wore baggy cargo shorts and a striped sweater, and the sullen expression of a teen who had been forced to interact with dull relatives. "You're that cop who's investigating Kelly's murder," he said by way of greeting when he opened the door to Ryder.

"Ryder Stewart." Ryder didn't offer his hand—he had the impression Rutledge wouldn't have taken it. "I need to ask you some questions."

"You'd better come in." Rutledge moved out of the doorway and into a cluttered living room. A guitar and two pairs of skis leaned against one wall, while a large-screen TV and a video gaming console occupied most of another. Rutledge clearly liked his toys.

Rutledge leaned against the door frame of the entrance to the kitchen, arms folded across his chest. "What do you want to know?" he asked.

"How well did you know Kelly Farrow?" Ryder asked.

"Pretty well. I mean, we lived right next to each other. We were friends."

"Did you ever date her?"

Rutledge grinned. "She flirted with me. I think she

would have gone out with me if I'd asked, but she wasn't my type."

Ryder wondered if this meant he'd asked her out, but Kelly had turned him down. "What is your type?"

"I like a woman who's a little quieter. Petite. Kelly had too much of a mouth on her."

Quiet and petite—like Darcy. Ryder took out his notebook and pen—more to have something to do with his hands than to make notes. He wasn't likely to forget anything this guy said. "You dated Darcy Marsh," he said.

Rutledge shifted, uncrossing his arms and tucking his thumbs in the front pockets of the cargo shorts. "We went out a few times."

"She says you weren't too happy when she broke it off."

"Yeah, well, she would say that, wouldn't she?"

"What do you mean?"

"Women always try to make themselves look like the victim."

"So what did happen between you two?" Ryder asked.

"I was really busy—I teach school and coach basketball. Darcy was a little too needy. I didn't give her the attention she wanted." He shrugged. "I let her down easy but I guess I hurt her feelings, anyway."

Ryder pretended to consult his notebook. "Where were you last night about six thirty?" he asked.

"Why? Did they find another body?"

"Answer the question, please."

"Yeah, sure. Let's see—there was a game at the high school. The varsity team—I coach JV—but I was there to watch."

Ryder made a note of this. It ought to be easy enough to check. "What about Tuesday night?" he asked.

"I was home, playing an online game with a couple of friends."

"I'll need their names and contact information."

"Sure. I can give that to you." He moved to a laptop that was open on a table by the sofa and manipulated a mouse. While he made notes on a sheet of paper torn from a spiral notebook, Ryder looked around the room. There were no photographs, and the only artwork on the wall was a framed poster from a music festival in a nearby town.

"Here you go." Rutledge handed Ryder the piece of paper. "And since I know you're going to ask anyway, the day Kelly was killed, I was teaching school. That'll be easy for you to check."

Ryder folded the paper and tucked it into the back of his notebook. "Do you have any idea who might have wanted to kill Kelly Farrow?" he asked. "Did she ever mention anyone who had threatened her, or did you ever see anyone suspicious near the house?"

Ken shook his head. "It could have been anybody, really," he said.

Most people said things like "everybody liked Kelly" or "she never made an enemy." "Why do you say that?" Ryder asked.

"Like I said, she had a mouth on her. And she dated lots of men—though none for very long. Maybe she said the wrong thing to one of them."

"And you think that would justify killing her?"

Ken took a step back. "No, man. I'm just saying, if the wrong guy had a hair trigger—it might be enough to make him snap. There are a lot of sick people in this world."

Ryder put away the notebook and took out one of his cards. "Call me if you think of anything," he said. Though

Rutledge's alibis sounded solid enough, he couldn't shake the feeling the man was hiding something. Ryder would be keeping an eye on him.

AT SEVEN THIRTY Thursday morning a mechanic from O'Brien's Garage delivered a battered pickup truck in several shades of green and gray to Darcy's door. "She looks like crap, but she runs good," the young man said as he handed over the keys. He rode off with the friend who had followed him to her place, and Darcy hoisted herself up into the vehicle, wishing for a step stool, it was so high off the ground. She felt tiny in the front seat—even the steering wheel felt too big for her hands. But as promised, the truck ran smoothly and carried her safely into town.

She had discarded the cervical collar that morning. While much of her was sore, none of the aches and pains felt serious. Her patients might all have fur or feathers, but she considered herself competent to assess her own injuries.

She stopped by Eagle Mountain Grocery, hoping the store would be mostly empty this time of morning. All she needed was a deli sandwich, since she planned to eat lunch at her desk again. She had layered on makeup in an attempt to hide the worst of the bruising, but she was sure she faced a day full of explaining what had happened to her.

As hoped, the store was mostly empty when she arrived. She hurried to the deli and ordered a turkey sandwich on cranberry bread, and debated adding a cookie while the clerk filled her order. A few more minutes and she'd be safely out of here.

"Darcy Marsh, you've got a lot of nerve!"

The strident voice rang through the store like a crack

of thunder. Darcy turned to see Sharon Nichols steering her grocery cart toward her. For a tense moment Darcy thought Sharon intended to run her over. She had a flash of herself, pinned to the glass-fronted deli case by the cart.

But Sharon stopped a few inches short of hitting Darcy. "Haven't you done enough to hurt us?" she demanded, lines etched deeper in her face than Darcy remembered.

"I don't know what you're talking about." Darcy spoke softly, hoping Sharon would lower her voice, as well. As it was, the two workers in the deli had both turned to stare.

"You complained about my husband to that cop and now he won't leave us alone." Sharon leaned closer, but didn't lower her voice. "He had the nerve to suggest Ed murdered those girls. Ed—who wouldn't hurt a fly! Why do you hate us so much?"

Darcy took a step back, desperately wanting to get away from Sharon and the angry words, which battered her like a club. "I don't hate you," she said. "And I never suggested Ed killed anyone. I don't believe that."

"You should go back to wherever you're from and leave us alone. Ed has lived here all his life. He had a good business, taking care of the animals in this county, then you and your friend had to move in and try to take over."

"We didn't try to take over. There's room enough in Eagle Mountain for all of us."

"That's a lie and you know it!" Sharon inched closer until the end of her cart pressed against Darcy's hips. "You came in with your fancy new office and pretty faces, undercutting us, trying to put us out of business."

"That's not true." If anything, the fees she and Kelly charged were higher than Ed's, but there was no use pointing that out to Sharon. Darcy glanced around. Two women peered from the end of one aisle, and one of the checkout people and a stocker had gathered to watch, as well. "I think you should go," she said softly.

"You won't run us out of town," Sharon said, tears streaming down her face. "You won't. We'll force you to leave first."

She turned and, seeing her chance, Darcy fled. She fumbled the keys into the ignition of the truck and drove out of the lot, scarcely seeing her surroundings, her mind too full of the image of Sharon Nichols's furious face.

Her final words, about making Darcy leave town, left a sick feeling in the pit of Darcy's stomach. She had never seen anyone so angry. Was Ed that angry, too? Were the Nicholses angry enough to kill?

RYDER STEPPED INTO the clinic and was greeted by furious barking from a small white terrier, who strained on the end of its leash. "I'm sorry about that." A middle-age woman with red curly hair scooped up the barking dog. "He thinks he has to protect me from everyone."

"Hello, Officer." The receptionist, a blue-eyed blonde with long, silver-painted fingernails, greeted him from behind the front counter. "What can I do for you?"

"I'd like a word with Darcy, if she's free."

"Wait just a few minutes."

He took a seat. The terrier glared at him from the redhead's lap. The office smelled of disinfectant. A brochure rack on the wall offered information on various ailments from arthritis to kennel cough, and a locked cabinet displayed a variety of cat and dog food and treats.

The door to the back office opened and a gray-haired couple emerged, the man toting a cat carrier. Darcy followed them out. "Bring her back on Tuesday and we'll remove the bandage," Darcy said. "And don't let her near any more mousetraps." She looked over Ryder's shoulder and sent him a questioning look.

He stood and as the couple moved to the front desk to pay, he slipped through the door and followed her into a small exam room where she sprayed the exam table with disinfectant and began to wipe it down. "Stacy said you wanted to talk to me," she said.

He shut the door to the room behind him. "Just to tell you that I talked to Ken Rutledge and his alibis for last night, and the times of the murders check out." Several people remembered seeing Ken at the basketball game, his online buddies had vouched for the times he had been involved in their game and he had had a full load of classes the day Kelly was murdered, including lunchroom and bus duty.

"I'm glad to hear it." She all but sagged with relief. "I hated to think I'd misjudged him so badly—that he was capable of something like that."

"He had a different story about your relationship, though," Ryder said.

"Oh?" She went back to wiping down the table and counters.

"He says he broke it off because you were too clingy."

She let out a bark of laughter. "That's not what happened, but if it makes him feel better to say so, it doesn't make any difference to me."

"He also said Kelly flirted with him, but she wasn't his type."

"Oh, please. Kelly was gorgeous. She was nice to everyone, which I guess some men take as flirting, but she wasn't interested in Ken." She tucked the bottle of disinfectant back in a cabinet over the sink and dropped a handful of used paper towels in the trash can by the door.

"To tell you the truth, I think she introduced him to me as a way to get him off her back."

"So he may be a jerk, but I don't think he's the person who's harassing you." He leaned against the end of the counter. "Have you heard any more from Marge?"

"No. And I doubt I will."

"I checked with Ed Nichols. He says he never got a call from a woman about a large dog that needed a house call."

A shadow passed over her face as if she was in pain. "What is it?" Ryder asked. "What's wrong?"

She glanced over his shoulder as if making sure the door was still closed. "I ran into Sharon Nichols at the grocery store this morning," she said. "She cornered me and demanded to know why I was trying to ruin her husband's life. She was so furious, she was almost… unhinged."

Ryder tensed. "Did she threaten you?"

"Not exactly."

"What did she say—exactly?"

"She said I wouldn't run them out of town—that they would make me leave first."

"She didn't elaborate?"

"No. And I really think she was just talking. She was so upset."

"I'll have a word with her."

"No." She grabbed his arm. "Please. You'll only make things worse."

His first inclination was to deny this. If the Nicholses had any intention of harming Darcy, he wanted to make it clear he would see they were punished, swiftly and harshly.

But the pleading look in Darcy's eyes forced him to

calm down. "I won't say anything to them," he said. "But I will keep an eye on them."

She took her hand from his arm. He wanted to pull it back—to pull her close and comfort her. Last night he had kissed her cheek on impulse, but he had wanted to kiss her lips. Would she have pushed him away if he tried?

"I need to get back to work," she said, glancing toward the door again.

"Just one more question," he said. "Though you may not like it."

"Oh?"

"What happened with the man who raped you?"

She hadn't expected that, he could tell. "If he's not in prison, I think it would be worth tracking him down," he said. "Just to make sure he isn't in Rayford County."

She nodded. "He was caught. I testified at the trial. I think he's still in prison."

"What was his name?"

"Jay Leverett. You don't think he's come after me again—not here?" Her skin had turned a shade paler.

"I'm just going to check."

She nodded. "This whole thing scares me. But I can't let that stop me from living my life."

"I don't like you out there at that little house by yourself." He'd meant to keep his fears to himself, but suddenly couldn't.

"It's my home. And my cats' home." She frowned. "Ken asked me to move in with him. I told him no way."

If Ryder asked her to move in with him, would she lump him in the same category as Ken? "You could move into Kelly's place," he said. "It's right in town, with more people around."

"No. I can't make you understand, but it's important to me to be strong enough to stay put. One thing I learned after I was raped was that fear was my worst enemy. Let me put it this way—if you were the one being threatened, would you move out of your home?"

"Probably not." He wanted to argue that he was a trained professional—but that wasn't what she wanted to hear. "I'll be keeping an eye on you," he said. "And keep your phone charged and with you at all times, with my number on speed dial. Call 911 first, then call me."

"I will. And thank you." She reached past him for the doorknob. "Now I have to get back to my patients."

The terrier growled at him as he passed. He ignored the dog and went back outside. Snow swirled around him in big white flakes. The sun that had shone earlier had disappeared and there was already an inch of snow on his Tahoe. The city's one snowplow trundled past him as he waited to turn onto Main Street. From the looks of things, the highway wouldn't be opening back up today. Was the killer getting antsy, looking for his next victim? If he was the person who went after Darcy last night, he had failed. How long would he wait before trying again?

Chapter Seven

Friday afternoon Darcy watched the young woman lead the horse the length of the barn and back and nodded. "I think she's more comfortable with the leg wrapped, don't you?" she said.

"Yes, I do." Emily Walker, younger sister to Travis and Gage Walker, brushed back a sweep of long, dark hair and smiled at Darcy. "Thanks so much for coming out here to look at her." She rubbed the horse's nose. "I've only ridden her once since I got here and she was fine then. I couldn't believe it this morning when I came out and found she'd gone lame."

"Keep the wrapping on, let her rest and give her the anti-inflammatories I prescribed," Darcy said. "If she's not better in a couple of days, call me and we can do some more extensive testing, but I think she'll be okay."

"I hope so." Emily gave the horse another pat, then both women exited the stall. "Thanks again for driving out here. I wasn't really looking forward to pulling a horse trailer on these snowy roads."

"I take it you're here for the wedding?" Darcy asked.

"It's my winter break, so I'd probably be here, anyway, but of course I'm staying over for the wedding." Emily grinned. "It's going to be so beautiful. I adore Lacy and though my big brother likes to play it all serious and unemotional, I can tell he's over the moon in love. I'm so happy for them both."

"You're from Denver?" Darcy asked.

"Fort Collins. I'm in grad school at Colorado State University."

"That's where I went to school," Darcy said.

"I love it there," Emily said. She stretched her arms over her head. "But I can't tell you how great it is not to have to think about classes and data analysis and lab reports and all of that for a few weeks. I'm determined to make the most of my time at home, snow or no snow." She put a hand on Darcy's arm. "What are you doing tomorrow?"

"I have office hours until noon." With Kelly gone, she was working six days a week—six long days, since she was handling all the office visits as well as house calls. She had rearranged her schedule this afternoon in order to make this call, but she had a full slate of patients for the rest of the afternoon. She hadn't had time to think much about how she was going to manage to keep up with such a schedule.

"Come here for the afternoon," Emily said. "I'm hosting a snowshoe scavenger hunt for the wedding party and any other young people I can get up here. We might all be trapped by the snow, but that doesn't mean we can't enjoy it."

Kelly would have jumped at that kind of invitation—she adored parties and meeting new people. Darcy, on the other hand, had been looking forward to an afternoon curled up on the sofa with the cats around her and a good book. "Oh, thanks so much," she said. "But I don't think I'll be able to make it. Since my partner died I'm pretty much buried under work." Not a lie.

Emily looked as disappointed as a child who had been

told she couldn't have a puppy. "I was so sorry to hear about Kelly." She squeezed Darcy's arm. "If you change your mind, come anyway. The more the merrier."

They emerged from the barn and Darcy was startled to see Ryder striding toward them. Dressed in his uniform with the black leather coat, he somehow didn't look all that out of place in the corral. "Hello, Emily, Darcy." He nodded to them. "Is everything all right?"

"It is now," Emily said. "Darcy has taken very good care of my favorite mare." She touched Darcy's arm. "Darcy, do you know Ryder Stewart? He's one of Travis's groomsmen."

"We know each other," Ryder said. A little current of heat ran through Darcy as his eyes met hers.

"If you're looking for Travis, he went somewhere with Dad," Emily said. "But they should be back pretty soon for supper. Our cook, Rainey, doesn't like it if people are late for meals, and Dad doesn't like to cross her."

"I'll catch him later," Ryder said. "It's not that important."

"Well, I'm glad you stopped by, anyway," Emily said. "You've saved me a phone call. I'm having a get-together for the wedding party and friends tomorrow afternoon— a snowshoe scavenger hunt." She turned to Darcy. "I'm trying to talk Darcy into coming, too."

"You should come," Ryder said. "It'll be good to be around other people."

She heard the unspoken message beneath his words: no one is going to bother you with half a dozen law enforcement officers around. And maybe socializing would be a good way to distract herself from worries about everything from the business to her own safety. "All right. I guess I could come."

"Wonderful," Emily said. She looked past Ryder, toward the ranch house. "My mom is waving to me—she probably needs my help with something for the wedding. With most of the wedding party staying here, you wouldn't believe how much there is to do." She waved goodbye to both of them and hurried away.

Ryder fell into step beside Darcy as they headed for the parking area near the stables where she had left the borrowed truck. Ryder laughed when he saw the green and yellow monster. "I saw this outside your office," he said. "But I had no idea it was yours."

"It's the official loaner vehicle for O'Brien's Garage," she said. "A little horrifying, but it runs well. I was glad to get anything at all, since my car will need some pretty major repairs."

"I think anyone will have a hard time running you off the road in that," Ryder said.

"Good point." The idea cheered her. She took out the keys and prepared to hoist herself into the cab, then paused. "Is everything all right?" she asked. "You aren't here to see Travis about a development in the case?"

He shook his head. "He asked me to help find extra chairs for the wedding guests and I wanted to get a look at the space where the ceremony will be. I have a couple of places that have agreed to loan some chairs, and I wanted to see what would work best."

"That's nice of you," she said.

"I'm the backup plan, really," he said. "They have a wedding planner out of Junction who's supposed to supply all that stuff, but this is in case the roads don't open in time."

"But the wedding is still over three weeks away," Darcy said. "Surely, the road will be open by then."

"Probably," he said. "But it's probably not a bad idea to plan, just in case."

"I need to go through our medical supplies and make sure we have enough of everything," she said. "I can see it will be a good idea to keep extra stock on hand in the winter." She climbed into the truck.

Ryder shut the door behind her. "Have a good evening," he said. "See you tomorrow."

"Yeah. See you tomorrow." While part of her still longed for that quiet afternoon at home, curled up with a book, she could see the sense in spending her free time around other people. That one of those people would be Ryder made the prospect all the more pleasing.

RYDER HAD JUST turned onto Main Street when his phone rang with a call from Travis. "I was just up at your place, looking at the wedding venue," Ryder said.

"I ended up getting detoured to the office," Travis said. "When you get a chance, swing by here. I've got something to show you."

"I'll be right over."

Adelaide Kinkaid, the seventy-something woman whose title Ryder didn't know, but who kept the sheriff's department running smoothly, greeted Ryder as he stepped into the station lobby. "Trooper Stewart," she said. "We're seeing so much of you lately we should make you an honorary deputy."

"Do I get to draw double pay?" Ryder asked.

Adelaide narrowed her blue eyes behind her violet-rimmed glasses. "I said *honorary*. To what do we owe the pleasure of your company today?"

"I need to speak with the sheriff."

"Of course you do. You and half the county. Don't you people know he has a wedding to prepare for?"

"I thought the bride did most of the work of weddings," Ryder said.

Adelaide sniffed. "We live in a new age, haven't you heard? Men have to pull their weight, too."

"I'm more concerned about this case than the wedding right now." Travis stood in the hallway leading to the offices. "Come on back, Ryder."

Instead of stopping at his office, Travis led the way down the hall to a conference room. He unlocked the door and ushered Ryder inside. Items, some of which Ryder recognized as being from the crime scenes, were arrayed on two long folding tables. He followed Travis around the tables. "When we originally towed Kelly's car, our intention was to secure it and leave it to the state's forensic team to process," Travis said. "After Christy's murder, with the road still closed, we felt we no longer had that luxury, so I put my team on it."

He picked up a clear plastic envelope. "They found this in Kelly's car, in the pocket on the driver's side door."

Ryder took the envelope and studied the small rectangle of white inside. A business card, with black letters: Ice Cold. "What does that mean?" he asked. "Is it supposed to be the name of a business?"

"We don't know. We didn't turn up anything in our online searches. It's not a business that we can find."

Ryder turned the packet with the card over. The back was blank, but on closer inspection, he could see that the edges of the card were slightly uneven, as if from perforations. "It looks like those blanks you can buy at office supply stores," he said. "To print your own cards at home."

"That's what we think, too," Travis said. "We think it was printed on a laser printer. The card stock is pretty common, available at a lot of places, including the office supply store here in town, though the owner doesn't show having sold any in the past month. But it could have been purchased before then."

Ryder laid the envelope back on the table. "We don't know how old it is, either," he said. "Kelly could have dropped it months ago."

"Except we found another card just like this in Christy's wrecker." Travis moved a few feet down the table and picked up a second envelope.

The card inside was identical to the one in the first envelope. A brief tremor raced up Ryder's spine. "We found it wedged between the cushions of the driver's seat," Travis said.

"Whoever left it there had to know we'd find it," Ryder said.

"I don't think he's going to stop with two murders," Travis said. "He's going to want to keep playing the game."

Ryder thought of Darcy, her car run off the road, and felt a chill. "Darcy could have been the third."

"Maybe," Travis said. "But Christy's murder, at least, feels more like a crime of opportunity. She was one of the few people out that night. The killer saw her and decided to make her his next victim."

"How do we stop him?" Ryder asked.

"I'm putting every man I can on the streets, and I'm asking the newspaper to run a story, warning everyone to be careful about stopping for strangers, suggesting they travel in pairs, things like that. I don't want to alarm people, but I don't want another victim."

"That may not be enough," Ryder said. "Some people think they're invincible—that a place like Eagle Mountain has to be safe."

"I'm trying to make it safe," Travis said. "We'll do everything we can, but we're at a disadvantage. The killer knows us and that we're looking for him." He picked up the business card again. "We'll keep trying to track down the meaning of Ice Cold."

"I'll get folks at state patrol working on it, too. We can transmit the images electronically. At least we've still got that. Did you find anything else in the vehicles that we can use?"

"Nothing. No fingerprints, no hair. Of course, with the weather, he was probably bundled up—cap, gloves, maybe even a face mask."

"Which makes it even more certain the business card was left deliberately." Anger tightened Ryder's throat. "He's treating this like some kind of game—taunting us."

"It's a game I don't intend to lose," Travis said.

Ryder nodded. But the cold knot in his stomach didn't loosen. If whoever did this killed again, someone would lose. Someone—probably a woman—would lose her life. And the awful reality was that he and Travis and the other officers might not be able to stop it from happening.

A LATE CANCELLATION allowed Darcy to keep her pledge to take an inventory of veterinary supplies at her office Friday afternoon. To her relief, she was well stocked on most items, though her stockpile of some bandages and Elizabethan collars were running low. Fortunately, Kelly kept overflow supplies in her garage and Darcy was sure she could find what she needed there.

After closing up that evening, she drove to Kelly's duplex. She parked the truck in the driveway, then let herself in with her key and switched on the living room light. Already, the house looked vacant and neglected. Kelly's furniture and belongings were still there, of course, but dust had settled on the furniture, and the air smelled stale. She swallowed back a knot of tears and forced herself to walk straight through to the connecting door to the garage. She would get what she needed and get out, avoiding the temptation to linger and mourn her missing friend.

Darcy flipped the switch for the garage light, but only one bulb lit, providing barely enough illumination to make out the boxes stacked along the far wall. Without Kelly's car parked inside, the space looked a lot bigger. Darcy wondered what would happen to the duplex now. The rent was presumably paid up through the end of the month. Once the road opened, she assumed Kelly's parents would clean the place out.

The boxes of supplies on the back wall contained everything from paper towels and toilet paper for the veterinary office restrooms to surgical drapes and puppy pads. The friends had found a supplier who offered big discounts for buying in bulk, and had stocked up on anything nonperishable.

The bandages and plastic cones she needed were in two separate boxes on the bottom of the pile, the contents of each box noted on the outside in Kelly's neat handwriting. Darcy set her purse on the floor and started moving the top layer of boxes out of the way. At least all this activity would warm her up a little. The temperature had hovered just above freezing all day, plunging quickly as the sun set. The concrete floor of the garage might as well have been a slab of ice, radiating cold up through Darcy's feet and throughout her body.

She shifted a heavy carton labeled surgical supplies and set it on the floor with a rattling thud. The noise echoed around her and she hurried to pull out the box of bandages. She'd carry the whole thing out to the truck, then come back for the collars. She only needed a few of them, in small and medium sizes.

She picked up the bandage carton—who knew all that

elastic and cloth could be so heavy?—and headed back toward the door to the kitchen. She had her foot on the bottom step when the door to the kitchen opened and the shadowy figure of a man loomed large. "What do you think you're doing?" he demanded. A flashlight blinded her, then someone knocked the box from her hand and she was falling backward, a scream caught in her throat.

Chapter Eight

Darcy tried to fight back, but the man's arms squeezed her so tightly she could scarcely breathe. She kicked out and clawed at his face, screaming and cursing. Then, as suddenly as he had grabbed her, the man let go. "Darcy! Darcy, are you okay? I had no idea it was you."

Eyes clouded with angry tears, she stared at Ken, who stood at the bottom of the steps leading into the house, a flashlight in one hand, the other held up, palm open. Darcy swiped at her eyes and straightened her clothes. "What are *you* doing here?" she asked. "And why did you attack me?"

"I didn't know it was you." He looked truly flustered. "I saw the truck in the driveway and didn't recognize it. Then I heard a noise in the garage—I thought someone was trying to rob the place."

She gathered up the scattered contents of the carton of bandages, trying to gather up a little of her dignity, as well. "Let me help you with that," Ken said, bounding down the stairs to join her. "Why are you driving that old truck?"

"My car is in the shop," she said. "Someone ran me off the road the other night."

"Oh, Darcy." He put a hand on her shoulder and looked

into her eyes. "You need to be careful. Do you think it was the serial killer?"

"Serial killer?" The word struck fear into her. Could he be a serial killer if he'd only killed two people? Or had Ryder and the sheriff discovered others?

"That's what the paper is saying," Ken said. "They even printed a statement from the sheriff, telling everyone to be careful around people they don't know, and suggesting people not go out alone."

She clutched the box to her chest, pushing down the flutters of panic in her stomach. "I'm being careful," she said. So careful she was beginning to feel paranoid, scrutinizing the driver in every car she passed, looking on every new male client with suspicion.

"You shouldn't be out at your place alone," Ken said. "The offer is still open to stay with me."

"I'm fine by myself," she said. "And I couldn't leave the cats."

She pushed past him and he let her pass, but followed her into the living room. "I talked to that cop," he said. "That state trooper."

She set the box down and pulled on her gloves. "Oh?"

"He thinks I had something to do with Kelly and Christy's deaths—that I killed them, even."

She looked up, startled. "Did Ryder say that? Did he accuse you of killing them?" He had told her that Ken's alibis for the times of the murders checked out, but maybe he had only been shielding her. Or maybe he even thought she might share information with Ken.

"He didn't have to. He grilled me—asking where was I and what was I doing when the women were killed. And he wanted to know all about my relationship with Kelly."

"He just asked you the same questions he asked everyone who knew Kelly," she said. "He wasn't accusing you of anything. And you haven't done anything wrong, so why be upset?"

"Cops can frame people for crimes, you know," he said. "Especially people they don't like, or who they want to get out of the way."

"Don't be ridiculous." She regretted the words as anger flashed in his eyes. "I mean, why would he do that?" she hastened to add. "Ryder doesn't even know you."

"He wanted to know about my relationship with you, too," Ken said. "I think he's jealous that we're friends. That we used to date."

Darcy didn't think three dates amounted to a relationship, but she wasn't going to argue the point now. "I think he's just doing his job," she said.

"I think that cop is interested in you," Ken said. "You should be careful. What if he's the serial killer?"

"Ryder?" She almost laughed, but the look on Ken's face stole away any idea that he was joking.

"It's not so far-fetched," he said. "Crooked cops do all kinds of things. And he was the one who found Kelly's body."

"Ryder was with me when Christy was killed," she said.

Ken's eyes narrowed to slits. "What was he doing with you?" He took a step closer and she forced herself not to move away, though her heart pounded so hard it hurt.

"Someone tried to break into my house," she said. "He came to investigate."

Ken's big hand wrapped around her upper arm. "I told you it's not safe for you out there," he said, squeezing hard.

She cried out and wrenched away. She searched for her car keys and realized she had left her purse in the garage. She could do without the collars if she had to, but she couldn't go anywhere without her keys. "You can go home now," she said. "I'll let myself out."

Not waiting for an answer, she pushed past him and all but ran to the garage where she retrieved her purse, threaded half a dozen plastic, cone-shaped collars over one arm and returned to the living room. Ken had picked up the box of bandages. "I'll carry these for you," he said.

At the truck, he slid the box onto the passenger seat. She dropped the collars onto the floorboard and slammed the door, then hurried around to the driver's side. "You look ridiculous in this big old wreck," he said, coming around to the driver's side as she hoisted herself up into the seat.

"I've got more important things to worry about." She turned the key and the engine roared to life.

"Be careful," he said. "And be careful of that cop. I don't trust him."

"I do," she said, and slammed the door, maybe a little harder than necessary. She drove away, but when she looked in the rearview mirror, Ken was still standing there, watching her. She didn't think he was a killer, but she was glad she had decided not to date him anymore. She had never been completely comfortable with him. And while she trusted Ryder to have her best interests at heart, she couldn't say the same about Ken.

ON SATURDAY AFTERNOON the parking area around the ranch house at the Walker Ranch was so packed with vehicles that a person could have been forgiven for thinking the wedding day had been moved up, Darcy thought as she maneuvered the truck into a parking spot. A steady stream of young people made their way to the bonfire in front of the house where Darcy found Emily Walker greeting everyone.

Ryder caught her eye from the other side of the bonfire and joined her. "Are all these people in the wedding party?" Darcy asked. She recognized Tammy Patterson, who worked for the *Eagle Mountain Examiner*, and Fiona Winslow, who waited tables at Kate's Kitchen. Dwight and Gage from the sheriff's department were there, and Dwight's new wife, Brenda Stinson. A few other people looked familiar, though she couldn't name them.

"Some of them. Others are people from town, and some visitors." He indicated a dark-haired man in a sheepskin jacket and cowboy hat. "That's Cody Rankin, a US Marshal who's one of the groomsmen. To his left is Nate Hall. He's a fish and wildlife officer—another groomsman."

"We ought to be safe here with all these law enforcement officers," she said.

"When you're in the profession, you end up hanging out with others in the profession a lot," Ryder said. "But there are plenty of civilians here, too." He nodded toward a pair of men in puffy parkas, knit caps pulled down low over their ears. "Those two are students Emily knows from Colorado State University. They came to Eagle Mountain on their winter break to ice climb and got trapped by the snow."

As she was scanning the crowd, Ken arrived. He saw her standing with Ryder and frowned, but didn't approach. Darcy was glad. After their uncomfortable encounter last night, she intended to avoid him as much as possible.

Emily climbed up on a section of tree trunk near the fire and clapped her hands. She wore a white puffy coat, and a bright pink hat, skinny jeans tucked into tall, fur-topped boots. Her long, dark hair whipped in the wind and her face was flushed from excitement or the fire, or both. "All right, everybody. I think everyone's here," she said. "I think you all know each other, but I wanted to introduce Jamie Douglas. She's been in town for a while, but she's the newest deputy with the Rayford County Sheriff's Department."

A rosy-cheeked brunette, who wore her hair in twin braids, waved to them.

"And last, but not least, we have Alex Woodruff and Tim Dawson." Emily indicated the two men Ryder had pointed out. "They live in Fort Collins and go to school at CSU."

Everyone waved or said hello to Alex and Tim, who returned the greetings. "All right," Emily said. "Let's get this party started." She pulled a handful of cards from her coat pocket. "I want everyone to form teams of two to three people each. Here are the lists of items you need to find. The first team to find all the items on the list wins a prize. Gage, please show everyone the prize."

Gage stepped forward and held up a liquor bottle. "What if you don't like Irish cream?" someone in the crowd asked over the oohs and ahhs of other guests.

"Then you give it to me, because it's my favorite," Emily said. She held up her phone. "It's two o'clock now. Everybody meet back here at four and we'll see who has the most items. We have plenty of food and drinks to enjoy around the bonfire, too. Now, come get your lists."

Ryder took Darcy's arm. "Let's team up together," he said.

"All right."

He went forward and got one of the cards, then rejoined her and they leaned in close to read it together. "A bird's nest, animal tracks, red berries, spruce cones, old horseshoe, mistletoe," Ryder read. "How are we supposed to collect animal tracks?"

"We can take a picture," Darcy said. "Where are we going to find a rock shaped like a heart with all this snow?"

"Maybe down by the creek." He handed her the list. "Did you bring snowshoes?"

They retrieved their snowshoes and put them on, then set out in the wake of other partygoers, everyone laughing and chattering. For once it wasn't snowing. Instead, the pristine drifts around them sparkled in the sun, the dark evergreens of the forest standing out against an intensely turquoise sky. "Emily must live a charmed life to get weather like this for her party," Darcy said as she tramped across the snow alongside Ryder.

"I'm hoping this break in the weather lasts," Ryder said. "The highway department is blasting the avalanche chutes today, and they've got heavy equipment in to clear the roads. With luck they can get everything open again by Monday morning."

"Will that help you with your case?" she asked. "Having the roads open?"

He glanced at her. "It will. But I don't want to talk about that today." He pointed a ski pole toward an opening in the woods. "Let's head to the creek, see if we can find that rock. And maybe the bird's nest, too."

"Are birds more likely to nest along creeks?" she asked.

"I have no idea. You're the animal expert here."

She laughed. "I can tell you about dogs and cats, some livestock, and a little about ferrets and guinea pigs. I don't know much about wild birds except they're pretty."

"Did you always want to be a veterinarian?" he asked.

"I wanted to be a ballerina, but short, awkward girls don't have much a chance at that," she said. "Then I wanted to be a chef, an astronaut or the person who ran the roller coaster at Elitch Gardens. That was just in third grade. I didn't settle on vet school until I was a sophomore in college, after I got a part-time job working at an animal hospital. I thought I would hate it, but I loved it."

"It's good to find work you love."

"What about you?" she asked. "Do you love your job?"

He glanced down at her, his expression serious. "I do. I like doing different things every day and solving problems and helping people."

"Is it something you've always wanted to do?" she asked.

"I went to college to study engineering, but attended a job fair my freshman year where the Colorado State Patrol had a booth. I'd never even thought about a law enforcement career before, but after I talked to them, I couldn't let go of the idea. I talked to some officers, did a couple of ride-alongs—and the rest is history." He stopped and bent to peer into the underbrush. "There's red berries on that list, right?"

"Yes."

He leaned forward and reached into the brush, and came out with a half dozen bright red berries clustered on a stem. "That's one down," he said. He handed the berries to her. "Stash those in my pack."

She had to stand on tiptoe—not an easy feat in snowshoes—in order to unzip the pack and put the berries inside. He crouched a little to make it easier. "Ready to keep going?" he asked.

She nodded and fell into step behind him this time as the woods closed in and the path narrowed. "How did you meet the sheriff?" she asked.

"We met in the state police academy," he said. "We just really hit it off. We kept in touch, after he signed on with the sheriff's department in Eagle Mountain and

I went to work for CSP. I visited him here on a vacation trip and fell in love with the place. When a job opening came up, I jumped on it." He looked over his shoulder at her. "How did you end up in Eagle Mountain?"

"Kelly visited here and came back and told me it was the perfect place to open a practice," she said. "There were a lot of people moving in, a lot of area ranches, and only one solo vet, so she thought we'd have plenty of business. I was ready to get out of the city so I thought, why not give it a try?"

"Will you stay, now that she's gone?"

She stopped. "Why wouldn't I stay?" Leaving hadn't crossed her mind.

He turned back toward her. "I hope you will stay," he said. "I just didn't know if it was something you'd want to do—or be able to afford to do."

She nodded. "Yeah, the money thing might be a problem. But I'm going to try to find a way to make it work. This is home now."

"An awfully tiny home," he said.

She laughed. "It's cozy and it's cheap," she said. "Maybe it wouldn't be practical for a family, but it's perfect for me right now."

The clamor of shouts ahead of them distracted her. Something crashed through the underbrush toward them, and Tim Dawson emerged onto the trail just ahead of them. "It's mine!" he shouted, waving what at first appeared to be a ball of sticks over his head. As he neared them, Darcy realized it was a bird's nest. Laughing and whooping, he ran past her, followed by his friend, Alex Woodruff.

She and Ryder started forward again, only to have to move off the trail again to allow Ken and Fiona to pass. "That jerk stole our bird's nest," Fiona said as she passed them.

"It was a jerk move, but there are probably other nests," Ryder said.

Fiona stopped, panting. "That's what I told Ken, but he's too furious to listen to reason." She bent forward, catching her breath. "Fortunately, those two are too fast, so I don't think he'll catch them."

"Do you want to hunt with us, instead?" Darcy asked. Not that she wasn't enjoying spending this time alone with Ryder, but she knew enough about Ken in a bad temper that she didn't want Fiona's afternoon ruined.

"Good idea to switch teams," Fiona said. She straightened. "It's sweet of you to offer, but I saw Tammy and Jamie up the creek a ways. I think I'll join them." She waved and headed back the way she had come.

Ryder and Darcy set out again and in another few minutes they reached the creek. The area near the trail was deserted, but tracks in the snow veered to the left along the bank. Ryder turned right. A few minutes later he stopped, putting an arm out to stop Darcy. "Animal tracks," he said, pointing to a row of tiny paw prints in the snow.

While he pulled out his camera and took several photographs, Darcy crouched to examine the tracks more closely. "I think they might be a weasel or something."

"I thought you didn't know about wild animals," he said.

"No. But they look a lot like a ferret. And ferrets are related to weasels."

Ryder pocketed his phone. "We have berries and animal tracks. What else is on the list?"

"The bird's nest and the rock shaped like a heart. A horseshoe—I don't think we're going to find that here."

"We can save the horseshoe for last. I know where the Walkers put all their old ones."

"Then we also need a spruce cone and mistletoe."

He scanned the trees around them, then took a few steps forward and plucked an oval brown cone from a tree. "One spruce cone," he said and handed it over.

She closed her hand around the cone and turned toward his backpack, but froze as her gaze landed on a familiar clump of leaves in the tree over their heads. "Isn't that mistletoe?" she asked.

Ryder looked up, and a grin spread across his face. "It is."

"How are we going to get it down?" It had to be ten feet up the tree.

He looked down again, into her eyes, and her heart fluttered as if she'd swallowed butterflies as she realized they were standing very close—so close she could see the rise and fall of his chest as he breathed, and make out the individual lashes framing his blue eyes. He put a hand on her shoulder and she leaned in, arching toward him, and then he was kissing her—a slow, savoring caress of his lips, which were warm and firm, and awakening nerve endings she hadn't even known she had.

She moaned softly and darted her tongue out to taste him, and the gentle pressure of the kiss increased until she was dizzy with sensation, intoxicated by a single kiss. She opened her eyes and found he was watching her, and his mouth curved into a smile against his. She pulled back a little, laughing. "That's some really powerful mistletoe," she said.

"I'm thinking we have to get some to keep now." He looked up at the green clump of leaves, which grew at the end of a spindly branch of fir.

"You can't climb up there," Darcy said. "The tree

would never support your weight. And there aren't any branches down low to hold on to."

"Maybe I can throw something and knock some down."

"Throw what?"

"I don't know. A big rock?"

She looked toward the creek. Though snow obscured the banks and ice glinted along the edges, the water in the center of the channel was still flowing, and lined with rocks. "I'm not going to stick my hand in that freezing water," she said.

He stripped off his gloves and handed them to her. "I will."

"A picture is probably good enough," she said as he kicked out of his snowshoes.

"I told you, I like to solve problems." He took a step forward and immediately sank to his knees in the soft snow.

She put a hand over her mouth, trying to suppress a giggle. "Ryder, I really don't think—"

A scream cut off her words—an anguished keening that shredded the afternoon's peace and tore away the warmth Darcy had wrapped herself in after Ryder's kiss. "Who is that?" she asked.

Ryder fought his way out of the drift and shoved his boots back into the snowshoes. "It came from downstream," he said and headed out, leaving Darcy to keep up as best she could.

Chapter Nine

The screams had died down by the time Ryder reached the crowd of people on the stream bank. Gage turned at Ryder's approach, his expression grim. Next to him, his sister Emily stood with her face in her hands, drawing in ragged breaths, clearly trying not to cry. Tammy and Jamie both knelt in the snow, Tammy sobbing loudly.

"What's going on?" Ryder asked Gage. But then he saw the woman half-submerged in the shallow creek, hands and feet bound with silver duct tape, blood from the gash at her throat staining the water pink.

Behind him, Darcy made a choking noise. He turned to look at her, but Emily had already put her arm around her and was leading her away. "Travis is on his way," Gage said. "And Dwight. And probably Cody and Nate, too."

Ryder made himself look at the body in the water again. Fiona's knit cap had come off and her shoulder-length brown hair was spread out around her head, moving in the current of the stream as if blown by a gentle wind. "This must have just happened," he said, keeping his voice low. "Darcy and I saw her maybe half an hour ago. She and Ken Rutledge were chasing those two college guys—Tim and Alex—down the trail. She said Tim had stolen a bird's nest they had found. Ken was going after them. She decided to turn around and try to find Tammy and Jamie." He nodded to the two women kneeling in the snow. Emily and Darcy were beside them now, urging them up and away from the creek.

Tammy's sobs had quieted, and Jamie helped her to stand, then joined Gage and Ryder on the bank. "We didn't touch anything," she said. "I looked and I didn't see anyone else around here, or any obvious tracks."

Thrashing sounds in the brush heralded the arrival of Travis. "I sent Dwight to round up the rest of the guests and get them to the house," Travis said. He scowled at the scene beside the creek. "We need to get everybody out of here," he said.

"I'll take the others up to the ranch house," Emily said. Pale, but composed, she took Darcy's hand. "Darcy will help me."

The lawmen stood beside a large cottonwood, the bare branches forming a skeletal canopy over their heads while Emily and Darcy persuaded Tammy to come with them. When the others were out of sight up the trail back to the house, they began to work.

Gage and Jamie cordoned off the scene while Ryder took photographs. All the blood had washed away by now, leaving Fiona looking more like a mannequin than a human, her skin impossibly pale. Or maybe it only helped to think of her that way. She looked cold, sprawled in the icy water, though he knew she couldn't feel the chill anymore. She would never feel anything again, and the fact that she had been killed minutes after he saw her, when he was located less than a quarter mile away, gnawed at him.

Travis returned from a walk down the creek bank and the lawmen gathered under the tree once more. "The snow is churned up on this side of the creek for a good five hundred yards," he said. "There are some indistinct snowshoe tracks—probably from the guests on the scavenger hunt. No tracks on the opposite bank that I could find. My guess is the murderer walked in the water when he had to, and on trampled ground the rest of the time."

"So we're looking for a person or persons with blood on his clothes and wet feet," Gage said.

"He might not have any blood on him," Jamie said. "If he had her in the creek, facing away from him, he could reach in front of her, cut her throat and all the spray would go out in front and into the water."

"You say she was with Ken when you and Darcy met her on the trail?" Travis asked Ryder.

"He passed us first," Ryder said. "Well, Tim and Alex ran past us, and a few seconds later Ken ran past. Fiona was a few seconds behind him. She stopped to talk to us for a few more seconds, then turned and went back the way she came. She said she was going to catch up with Tammy and Jamie and hunt with them."

"She never found us," Jamie said. "We didn't hear or see anything of her until we came across her body."

Ryder was silent, recreating the scene in his head. "When Darcy and I got to the creek, where the trail stops at the creek bank, all the other tracks had turned left," he said. "We turned right and didn't see any other tracks."

"Could she have turned off the trail before she reached the creek?" Travis asked.

"I don't think so," Ryder said. "The brush is pretty thick on either side of the trail in there. She was wearing snowshoes, like us, so it would have been tough to maneuver through the underbrush."

"Emily and I were searching along the creek and we saw Jamie and Tammy ahead of us," Gage said. "We stopped to talk to them, and then started all searching together. We didn't see Fiona until we stumbled over her body."

"Did you see anyone else?" Travis asked.

Gage shook his head. "No."

"I told Dwight not to let anyone leave until we've questioned them," Travis said. "I want to know where everyone was and what they were doing when she was killed."

"The murderer isn't necessarily one of your guests," Ryder said. "It wouldn't have been that hard to find out this party was going on up here this afternoon. The killer might have taken it as a personal challenge to kill under a bunch of cops' noses, so to speak."

"Or maybe it's a copycat," Jamie said. "Someone with a grudge decides to get rid of Fiona and make it look like a serial killing."

"We'll look into Fiona's background," Travis said. "But I never heard anything about her having trouble with anyone."

"Why doesn't anyone around here get killed in a nice warm building?" Medical Examiner Butch Collins trudged into view, his booming voice the only clue to his identity, the rest of him concealed by a calf-length leather duster, a yards-long red wool scarf wrapped several times around his throat, the ends trailing down his back, a black Stetson shoved low over his ears, oversize dark glasses shading his eyes. He stopped in front of them and whipped off the glasses. "And while I'm ordering up the perfect murder, it needs to happen on a weekday, when coming to see you people is a good excuse for getting out of the office, instead of away from a nice warm fire in my own home."

"When we catch the killer, we'll be sure to pass along your request," Gage said.

Butch surveyed the body in the creek. "I hope you

catch him soon," he said. "I'm tired of looking at lovely young women whose lives have been cut short." He shrugged out of his backpack and set it in the snow. "I'll be done here as soon as I can, so we can all get warm."

"Ryder, I want you and Gage to go up to the house and start questioning people," Travis said. He didn't say *before one of them tries to leave* but Ryder knew that was what he meant.

The two men didn't say anything on their trek to the ranch house. Ryder's mind was too full of this new development. How had the killer been so close, and he hadn't had any inkling? Was one of the people waiting for him at the ranch house responsible for this and the other murders?

Emily must have been watching for them. She met them at the front door. "Everyone is in the living room," she said. "I had Rainey make hot chocolate for everyone—with whiskey or schnapps if they wanted—and plenty of snacks."

Conversation rose from behind them. "They don't sound too upset," Gage said.

"They were, at first," Emily said. "Then I had everyone show their scavenger hunt finds and got them to talking. It's not that everyone isn't horrified, but I didn't see any point in dwelling on the tragedy—and I didn't think you'd want them talking about it amongst themselves. Not before you'd had a chance to question them."

"Good thinking." Gage patted her shoulder. "Is everyone here?"

"Everyone," she confirmed.

A woman appeared in the doorway behind Emily. Nearly six feet tall, her blond hair pulled back in a tight ponytail, blue eyes lasering in on them from a weathered face. "These are for you," she said, pushing two mugs of hot chocolate toward them. "Get those coats and boots off and warm up by the fire before you go to work."

"Ryder, this is our cook, Rainey Whittington," Gage said. "In case you haven't noticed, she's bossy."

"Hmmph." She turned and left the room.

Ryder sipped the chocolate—it was rich and creamy. His stomach growled—he'd have to snag some of the hors d'ouevres he'd spotted on trays around the room to go with the chocolate.

He and Gage left their boots and coats in the foyer and moved into the next room—a large space with windows on two sides, a massive stone fireplace, soaring ceilings and oversize cushioned sofas and chairs. Almost every seat was filled with men and women, who looked up when Gage and Ryder entered.

Some of the women looked as if they had been crying. Most of the men showed tension around their eyes. "What's going on out there?" Ken Rutledge demanded.

"The medical examiner is at the scene," Gage said. He sipped his chocolate, watching the others over the rim of his cup. The two college guys, Alex and Tim, fidgeted. Tammy looked as if she was going to cry again. Ken prodded the fire with the poker.

Darcy cradled a mug with both hands and met Ryder's gaze. She looked calm, or maybe a better word was resigned.

"We're going to need to question each of you," Gage said. "To find out where you were and what you were doing shortly before Fiona's body was found."

"You don't think one of us killed her, do you?" Alex asked.

"You might have seen or heard something that could lead us to the killer," Gage said.

Rainey appeared in the doorway with a fresh tray

of hors d'ouevres, a thin, freckled young man behind her with a second tray. She began passing the food. The young man walked up to Ryder with his tray. "I'm Rainey's son, Doug," he said.

Ryder took a couple of the sausage balls from the tray. "Thanks."

Gage shook his head and Doug moved on. "Ken, why don't you come in the library with me and Ryder," he said.

Ken jumped up and followed them down a short hallway to a small room just past the area where everyone had gathered. "You think because I was teamed up with Fiona that I had something to do with her death," he said. "But I don't know what happened to her. She didn't even tell me she wanted to split up—she just left."

"Why don't you sit down?" Gage motioned to an armchair. He and Ryder arranged the desk chair and another armchair to face him. Ken looked flushed and agitated, his face pale. His jeans, Ryder noted, were wet from the knees down.

"When I saw you on the trail, you were chasing Alex and Tim," Ryder said. "What was that about?"

"They stole the bird's nest Fiona and I found by the creek," Ken said. "I wasn't going to let them get away with that, so I chased them."

"Did you catch them?" Gage asked.

Ken looked sullen. "No. They must have veered off the trail into the woods."

"How far did you chase them?" Gage asked.

"I don't know. Not that far, I guess. It's too hard to run in snowshoes."

"What did you do after you stopped chasing them?" Ryder asked.

"I went looking for Fiona. I figured she'd be waiting for me, back on the trail, but she'd disappeared."

"Did that upset you?" Gage asked. "When you couldn't find her?"

"I was a little annoyed, sure. But I didn't kill her."

"You were annoyed because she ditched you," Ryder said.

"I thought maybe she got lost or something. Most women aren't good with directions."

Gage and Ryder both stared at him. "What?" Ken asked. "It's true."

"Okay, so you were by yourself, for how long?" Gage asked.

"I don't know. Twenty minutes? I was trying to find the others."

The desk chair squeaked as Gage shifted his weight. "Did you find them?" he asked.

"No," Ken said. "I finally gave up and came back here. That's when I heard what happened to Fiona. I feel sick about it."

"How did your pants get so wet?" Ryder asked.

Ken flushed. "I fell in the creek getting the bird's nest out of the tree. That's when those jerks came along and got it, while I was in the water. Fiona was screaming at them to stop and they just laughed."

"How did you and Fiona come to team up?" Ryder asked.

"I asked her to come with me. She wasn't here with anybody, so I figured, why not?"

"Had the two of you ever dated?" Ryder asked.

"Nah. We'd flirted some, when I had dinner at Kate's Kitchen. I was thinking about asking her out. I figured this would be a good way to get to know each other better."

"While you were looking for Fiona, did you see anyone else?" Gage asked. "Talk to anyone?"

He shook his head. "No. Not until I got back to the house. Travis was here, and his fiancée. Maybe some other people." He shrugged. "I just wanted to get inside and get warm. Then they told me about Fiona and I couldn't believe it. I mean, I thought this guy killed women in their cars. What's he doing out in the woods?"

Good question, Ryder thought. They sent Ken on his way. "What do you think?" Gage asked when he and Ryder were alone again.

"I don't know," Ryder said. "Maybe he's telling the truth. Or maybe he caught up with Fiona and slit her throat."

"But first he bound her wrists and ankles with duct tape and no one else saw or heard a thing?" Gage grimaced. "I'm thinking it had to be a job for two people."

"Let's talk to Tim and Alex," Ryder said.

Tim Dawson and Alex Woodruff had the easy-going, slightly cocky attitudes of young men for whom everything in life came easy. They dressed casually, in jeans and fleece pullovers and hiking boots, but the clothes were from expensive designers. They had straight teeth and stylish haircuts, and Alex wore a heavy copper and gold bracelet that wouldn't have looked out of place in an art gallery. He and Tim shook hands with Ryder and Gage, and met their gazes with steady looks of their own. "You've certainly got your hands full, investigating something like this," Alex said. "I don't imagine a sheriff's department in a place like Eagle Mountain is used to dealing with serial murderers."

"You might be surprised," Gage said, which had the two younger men exchanging questioning looks.

"How did you two end up in Eagle Mountain?" Gage asked when they were all seated in the library.

"We heard the ice climbing here was good," Tim said.

"Tim heard the ice climbing was good and wanted to come," Alex said. "I sort of invited myself along."

"Why is that?" Gage asked.

Alex shrugged. "I didn't have anything better to do. Getting away for a few days sounded like a good idea."

"We didn't plan on getting stuck here," Tim said.

"But we're making the best of it," Alex said.

"What are you studying at the university?" Ryder asked.

"Business," Tim said.

"Psychology." Alex's smile flashed on and off so quickly Ryder might have imagined it. "So this whole case interests me—as an observer."

"How did you come to be invited here today?" Gage asked.

"We know Emily from school," Alex said.

"Alex knows her," Tim said. "He introduced me when we ran into her in town a few days ago and she invited us to come." He shrugged. "It was fun until that girl was killed."

"Did you know the woman who died?" Gage asked.

They both shook their heads.

"Take us through the afternoon," Gage said. "What you did and when."

The two exchanged glances. Alex spoke first. "We got the list and decided to head to the creek. I guess a lot of people did that, but we ran to get ahead of them."

"Why the creek?" Ryder asked.

"It seemed to me that a lot of the items on the list could be found there," Alex said. "And I was right. We found the heart-shaped rock and the red berries right away. And then we got the bird's nest."

Tim made a noise that was almost like a snicker. "Where did you find the bird's nest?" Ryder asked.

"That big blond guy—Ken—was standing on the creek bank in the snow, trying to get to this nest up high. He had hold of a branch and was trying to bend the tree down toward him."

"Except he slipped and fell into the water," Alex said. "When he let go of the branch, the tree sprang back upright, and the nest flew out of it and landed practically at Tim's feet."

"So I picked it up and ran," Tim said. "The guy was screaming bloody murder, and so was the woman, too, but hey, I figure 'finders keepers.'"

"Losers weepers," Alex added.

"What happened next?" Ryder asked.

"You know," Tim said. "You saw. We took off, with the blond coming after us. He couldn't run that fast in snowshoes, and he gave up pretty quick."

"What did you do next?" Gage asked.

"We kept on finding the stuff on the list," Tim said. "We had everything but the horseshoe when the cops herded everyone back to the house."

"We figure we must have more items than anyone else," Alex said. "We're bound to win the prize."

"Did you see Fiona or Ken again after you ran off with the bird's nest?" Ryder asked.

"No," Alex said. "We didn't see anyone until that cop told us to go back to the house." He stretched his arms over his head. "Are you going to keep us here much longer?"

"Do you have somewhere else you need to be?" Gage asked.

"Not really." Alex grinned. "But it's Saturday night.

We thought we'd go out, have a few beers, maybe meet some women."

"Where are you staying?" Gage asked.

"My aunt has a little cabin on the edge of town," Tim said. "It's a summer place, really, but it's okay. At least we're not paying rent."

Gage took down the address and both men's cell phone numbers. "That's all the questions I have." He looked at Ryder.

"That's all I have for now," Ryder said.

Tim and Alex stood. "You know where to find us if you need more," Alex said.

They ambled out of the room, shutting the door softly behind them. Gage let out a sigh. "Both of them working together could have done it," he said.

"They could have," Ryder said. "Or they could just be a couple of cocky college guys who didn't do anything but swipe a bird's nest that really didn't belong to anyone, anyway. They're not wet from being in the creek and they don't have blood on them."

"They might have a change of clothes in their vehicle or their pack," Gage said. "And Jamie was right about the blood—if they were careful, they wouldn't get much, if any, on them."

"We'll check their backgrounds, maybe talk to the aunt and their neighbors at that cabin," Ryder said.

A knock on the library door interrupted him. "Come in," Gage called.

Travis stepped inside and closed the door behind him. "How's it going?" he asked.

"Not much to go on yet," Gage said. "We've talked to Ken and Tim and Alex. That's all the non-law enforcement men. Except for Doug, the cook's son. I guess we'd better talk to him."

"I sent Jamie back early and she and Dwight interviewed the women," Travis said. "None of them saw or heard anything."

"Anything turn up at your end?" Ryder asked.

"We'll go over the body more closely tomorrow, but we found this." He took an evidence envelope from the inside pocket of his jacket and passed it over. Ryder stared at the single square of water-soaked pasteboard. A business card, the words Ice Cold barely legible on the front.

"It's the same killer," Ryder said. "Not a copycat. The same man or men who killed Kelly and Christy."

"It's the same one," Travis said. "He's challenging us right under our noses now."

Chapter Ten

Darcy arrived home to a chorus of complaining cats and the beginnings of more snow. She dealt with the cats by serving up fresh seafood delight all around, and dispensed with the snow by turning her back on it, drawing the shades and standing under the strong stream of a hot shower until the icy chill that had settled over her hours ago had receded and the tension in her shoulders and neck began to relax.

She and Ryder had exchanged a brief goodbye as she filed out of the ranch house with the rest of the non-law-enforcement guests. Earlier she had given her version of their encounter on the trail with Ken and Fiona to the female deputy, Jamie. "I'll call you when I can," Ryder said, and squeezed her hand.

She checked the locks on her doors and windows again, turned on the outside lights and settled on the sofa with a fresh cup of tea and a peanut butter sandwich—her idea of comfort food. She had just picked up a favorite Regency romance novel and turned to the first chapter when strains of Vivaldi sounded from her cell phone.

Spirits lifting, she snatched up the phone, but her mood dropped again when she saw that the call wasn't from Ryder as she had hoped, but from Kelly's mother. "Darcy, I hope I haven't caught you at a bad time." Cassidy Farrow spoke with a tremor as if she was very old, though she was probably only in her early fifties.

"Not at all." Darcy tucked her feet up beside her and pulled a knitted blanket up to her knees. "What can I do for you?"

"I don't know, really. I just… I just wondered if you've heard anything about…about Kelly's case. If they're any closer to finding out who did this awful thing." Her voice caught, and Darcy pictured her struggling to regain her composure.

"I know the officers are working very hard to find out who killed Kelly," Darcy said. Should she mention the other women who had died? No. That would only be more upsetting, surely.

"I hate to keep calling the Colorado State Patrol," Mrs. Farrow said. "They're always very nice, of course. And they tell me they'll contact me when they know something, but then I don't hear anything, and we can't even get there to see our girl, or to take her…her body for the funeral. It's just so awful."

"It is," Darcy said. "It's the most awful thing I can imagine." She grieved terribly for her friend—how much worse the pain must be for Kelly's mother.

"It doesn't even seem real to me." Mrs. Farrow's voice was stronger now. "I don't think it will be until I see her. I keep dreaming that there's been some mistake, and that she's still alive."

"I catch myself thinking that, too," Darcy said. "I wish she were still here. I miss her all the time."

"The officer I spoke to said they were sure the woman they found was Kelly."

"Yes," Darcy said, speaking softly, as gently as she could. "It really was Kelly."

The sobs on the other end of the line brought tears to

her own eyes. As if sensing her distress, Elinor crawled into her lap, and the other cats arranged themselves around her, a furry first-aid team, offering comfort and protection.

"I'm sorry," Mrs. Farrow said. "I didn't mean to call and cry like this. I just wanted to talk to someone who knew her, who understood how wonderful she was."

"Call anytime," Darcy said. "It helps to talk about her. It helps me, too."

"Thank you. I'll say goodbye now, but we'll be in touch."

"Goodbye."

She ended the call and laid the phone back on the table beside her. She turned back to her book but had read only the first page when headlights swept across the windows, and the crunch of tires on her gravel drive made her clamp her hand around the phone again. She glanced toward the loft where the gun lay in the drawer of the table beside her bed. Then she shook her head and punched 911 on her phone. She wouldn't hit the send button yet, but she'd be ready.

The car stopped and the door creaked open. Darcy wanted to look out the window, but she didn't want to let whoever was out there know her location in the house. Footsteps—heavy ones—crossed to the house and mounted the steps to her little front porch, then heavy pounding shook the building. "Darcy, it's me, Ken. Please let me in. I need to talk to someone."

Her shoulders sagged, and annoyance edged out some of her fear. "Ken, I really don't want to have company right now," she said.

"Just let me in for a few minutes," he said. "Today has been so awful—for us both. I just need to talk."

She wanted to tell him no—that she just wasn't up to

seeing him right now. But he sounded so pitiful. Fiona had been his partner in the scavenger hunt—to have her killed must have been a shock to him. Sighing, she unlocked the door and let him in. "You can only stay a few minutes," she said. "I really am exhausted."

He had changed clothes since leaving the ranch and wore baggy gray sweatpants and a University of Wisconsin sweatshirt. His hair was wet as if he had just gotten out of the shower. "Thanks," he said. "I was going crazy, sitting at the house with no one to talk to."

"Do you want me to make you some tea?" Darcy asked.

"No. That's okay." He began to pace—four steps in one direction, four in another. "I can't believe this is happening," he said.

"I can't believe it, either." Darcy settled on the sofa and hugged a pillow to her chest. Three women dead—it was hard to accept.

"That cop as good as accused me of murdering that woman."

Of course. Ken wasn't upset because Fiona had died. He was agitated because he had been questioned. "He's just doing his job," she said. "The cops questioned everyone."

Ken stopped and faced her. "Why are you defending him? Is there something going on between you two?"

"No!" But her cheeks warmed at the memory of the kiss they had shared under the mistletoe. Maybe *something* was happening with her and Ryder—but she wasn't clear what that something might be. Or what it might turn into.

Ken began to pace again, running his fingers through his hair over and over, so that it stood straight up on his head, like a rooster's comb. "You shouldn't be here by yourself," he said. "You should come and stay at my place. No one will bother you with me around."

"No one is going to bother me here."

"You can't know that."

She wasn't going to waste her breath arguing with him. She picked up her now-cold tea and sipped, waiting for him to calm down so she could ask him to leave.

More headlights filled her window. "Who's that?" Ken demanded.

"I don't know." She stood and went to the door. A few moments later a light knock sounded. "Darcy? It's me, Ryder."

Relief filled her and she pulled open the door. She wanted to throw her arms around him, but thought better of it, feeling Ken's stare burning into her back. "What are you doing here?" Ken asked, his tone belligerent.

"I wanted to make sure Darcy was all right after the upsetting events of this afternoon," Ryder said. He moved into the room and shut the door, but kept close to Darcy. "Why are you here?"

"Darcy and I are friends. I wanted to make sure she was all right, too."

"Thank you for checking on me, Ken," Darcy said, hoping to defuse the situation by being gracious. "I'll be fine. You can go now."

"Is he staying?" Ken asked.

"That really isn't your concern," she said. She patted his arm. "Go home. Try to get some rest."

He hesitated as if he intended to argue, then appeared to think better of it and moved past Ryder and out the door. As he pulled out of the drive, Ryder gathered Darcy close. "Your heart is pounding," he said into her hair. "Did he frighten you?"

"No. Just annoyed me." She looked up at him. "I think he has a habit of rubbing people the wrong way."

"What did he want?"

"He was upset. He seemed to think you believe he killed those women."

"We haven't identified anyone as our main suspect."

"Ken is annoying, but I can't believe he's a killer," she said. "And you said his alibis checked out."

"Alibis can be faked," he said. "And right now it's my job to be suspicious of pretty much everyone."

She started to protest again that Ken couldn't be the murderer—but how much of that was a true belief in his innocence, and how much was her desperate desire not to be wrong again about a man she had trusted? She probably would have defended the man who raped her, too—until he turned on her. Was she making the same mistake with Ken?

She put her hand on his shoulder, the leather of his jacket cold beneath her palm. "You're freezing," she said. "And you must be exhausted."

"I'm all right," he said.

"At least let me fix you some tea or soup."

"I wish I could stay, but I need to get over to the sheriff's department. I just wanted to make sure you were okay."

"You're going back to work?" she asked. "Does this mean you have a suspect?"

He shook his head. "I couldn't tell you if I did, but no. No suspects yet. We need to look at the evidence we gathered today and see if we find something we've missed before."

"You don't really think one of the party guests is the killer?" she asked. Everyone had seemed so nice—people she either already thought of as friends, or whom she looked forward to getting to know better.

"We just don't know." He kissed her cheek. "All you can do is be extra careful."

He started to pull away, but she wrapped her arms around his neck and tugged his lips down to hers. She hadn't intended to kiss him so fiercely, had only wanted to prolong the contact between them, but as soon as their lips met the last bit of reserve in her burned away in the resulting heat. She lost herself in the pleasure of that kiss, in the taste of him, in the power of his body pressed to hers, and in her own body's response.

He seemed to feel the same, his arms tightening around her, fitting her more securely against him, his lips pressed more firmly to hers, his tongue caressing. She felt warmed through, safer and happier than she had felt in a long time. They broke apart at last, both breathing hard, eyes glazed. He stroked his finger down her cheek. "I wish I didn't have to go," he said.

"I wish you didn't have to go, either."

He stepped back, and she reluctantly let him. "Lock the door behind me," he said.

"I will."

"If Ken comes back here, don't let him in," he said.

"All right," she said.

She didn't want to let anyone in—into her home, or her life, or her heart. That had been her policy for years. But Ryder had breached those barriers and the knowledge both frightened and thrilled her. He wasn't a killer. Ryder would never hurt her. She knew that, but that didn't mean he didn't have the power to hurt her. Maybe not physically, but if you gave your heart to someone, you risked having it broken. She had been so wrong about a man before—would she ever really be able to trust her judgment again?

RYDER WAS THE last to arrive in the situation room at the sheriff's department. He filled a mug from the coffeepot at the back of the room, then settled at the table next to Gage. Like Ryder, most of the others still wore the clothes they had had on that afternoon. Only the sheriff and Dwight were in uniform—Ryder assumed because they were on duty.

"Let's get started," Travis said from the front of the room. "I've asked Cody and Nate to sit in, since they were at the ranch this afternoon."

US Marshal Cody Rankin and Department of Wildlife officer Nate Hall nodded to the others.

Travis moved to the whiteboard. "Let's start by summarizing the information we learned this afternoon," he said. "Jamie, you helped interview the women. Anything there?"

"Ryder and Darcy appear to be the only people who saw Fiona after she and Ken set out on the scavenger hunt," Jamie said. "No one thought it was odd for her to be with him. Several said they were laughing together when they split up from the rest of the group to start the hunt. No one saw any strangers or anything they thought was odd or out of place."

Travis nodded. "About what we got from the men, too."

"I don't think any of the women had the physical strength to overcome Fiona," Jamie said. "Even two women working together would have had a hard time, and she would have fought and screamed. Someone would have heard."

"There were no signs of struggle in the stream or on the bank," Dwight said.

"There were a lot of footprints in the soft snow," Ryder said. "Too many to tell who they belonged to."

Travis picked up a sheet of paper from a stack on the end of the conference table. "The medical examiner says Fiona was struck on the back of the head," he said. "It wasn't enough to kill her, but it probably would have knocked her out, at least long enough to restrain her."

"So whoever killed her comes up behind her, hits her in the head with a big rock before she can say anything," Gage said. "She falls, he wraps her up in duct tape, slits her throat and leaves."

"That's different from the way he handled Kelly and Christy," Ryder said.

"Probably because he was in a hurry," Gage said. "He was out in the open, with lots of people around. He needed to get her down quickly."

"So we're pretty sure it's a man," Travis said. "I think it's safe to rule out the law enforcement personnel who were at the party."

"That leaves Ken, Alex and Tim," Ryder said.

Travis wrote the names on the whiteboard. "Ken was the last person seen with Fiona," he said. "He's big and strong enough to take her down without too much trouble, and he was alone with her. Alex and Tim could have worked together. They're new to the area, and we don't know much about them."

"Ken has strong alibis for the other two murders," Ryder said. "And we're assuming all three women were murdered by the same person because of the business card."

"Do we have any idea what the significance of Ice Cold might be?" Jamie asked.

"I've been working on that." Dwight, who had been rocked back in his chair, straightened. "Online searches haven't turned up anything—no businesses by that name. Maybe the killer is bragging about how 'cool' he is."

"Or how fearless and unfeeling?" Jamie suggested. "Nothing can touch him because he's ice cold."

"We know this guy likes to show off," Ryder said. "Leaving the cards at the scene of each killing is a way of bragging. And killing Fiona when he was pretty much surrounded by cops is pretty arrogant."

"Tim and Alex struck me as arrogant," Gage said.

"Let's check their alibis for the other two killings," Travis said. He glanced at his note. "And there's one other man on the scene we need to check."

"Doug Whittington," Gage said.

"Right," Travis said.

"The cook's son," Ryder said, remembering.

"It would have been fairly easy for him to slip away from the house and follow Fiona and Ken into the woods," Travis said.

"What do you know about him?" Ryder asked. "Has he worked for your family long?"

"Rainey has been with us for at least ten years," Gage said. "Doug only showed up a couple of months ago."

"My parents agreed he could stay to help Rainey with the extra workload of so many wedding guests," Travis said. "She promised to keep him in line."

"What do you mean, *keep him in line*?" Ryder asked.

"He has a record," Travis said. "In fact, he just finished a fifteen-month sentence in Buena Vista for assault and battery."

"He beat up his girlfriend," Gage said. "Broke her jaw and her arm."

Jamie made a face. "So a history of violence against women. That definitely moves him up my list."

"Let's check him out," Ryder said. "But be careful. Make it seem routine. Not like we suspect him."

"We'll keep a close eye on all our possible suspects," Travis said. "Whoever did this may think he can kill right under our noses, but he'll find out he's wrong." He laid aside the marker he'd been using to make notes on the whiteboard. "Dwight, I want you and Ryder to interview Doug tomorrow. Since his mother is so closely associated with our family, Gage and I should keep our distance for now."

"I want to talk to Alex and Tim tomorrow, too," Ryder said. "Double-check their alibis for the other murders."

"If the roads open up tomorrow, we'll have someone rush the forensic evidence we've collected to the lab," Travis said.

"I wouldn't hold your breath on that," Gage said. "The snow is really coming down out there."

"We'll do what we can," Travis said. "For now the rest of you go home and think about what we know so far. Maybe you'll come up with an angle we haven't examined yet."

Ryder said good-night to the others and climbed into his Tahoe. But instead of driving to the guest house he rented on the edge of town, he turned toward the address for the cabin Alex and Tim said belonged to their aunt. He wouldn't stop there tonight; he just wanted to check it out and see what those two might be up to. And if they weren't home, he might take a little closer look at the place.

He had just turned onto the snow-covered forest service road that led to the cabin when he spotted a dark gray SUV pulled over on the side of the road. The vehicle was empty, as far as he could tell, but there were no houses or driveways nearby. Had someone broken down and left the car here? An Eagle Mountain Warriors bumper sticker peeked out from the slush that spattered the vehicle's bumper. Where had he seen this vehicle before?

He parked his Tahoe in front of the SUV and debated calling in the plate, which was almost obscured by slush. He climbed out of his vehicle and walked back toward the SUV to get a better look. He had just pulled out his flashlight when shouting to his right made him freeze. A cry for help, followed by cursing and what might have been jeers. He played the light over the side of the road and spotted an opening in the brush. It appeared to be a trail. As the shouting continued, he sprinted down the narrow path into the woods.

Chapter Eleven

The trail ended in a clearing at the base of ice-covered cliffs. Ryder shut off his light and stopped, watching and listening. Moonlight illuminated two young men in Eagle Mountain High School letter jackets standing at the base of a frozen waterfall, while a third young man dangled precariously from the ice. "Help!" the man stranded on the ice called.

"Chicken!" one of his companions jeered.

"You don't get credit unless you make it all the way up," the third man said.

"This ice is rotten," the first man said. "This was a stupid idea."

"You took the dare," the second man said. "That's the rules. To get credit, you have to complete it."

Ryder switched on the light, the powerful beam freezing the three teens. They stared at Ryder, expressions ranging from defiance to fear. Ryder moved toward them. "I heard the shouting," he said. "What's going on?"

"Just doing some climbing." The first young man—blond, with acne scars on his cheeks—spoke. He slouched, hands in pockets, not meeting Ryder's eyes.

Ryder played the beam of light over the young man on the ice. He balanced on a narrow ledge on one foot, hands dug into the ice in front of his chest. "You okay up there?" he called.

"I'm fine." The man spoke through clenched teeth.

"Odd time of night to be climbing," Ryder said. "And shouldn't you have ropes and a helmet?"

"He said he's fine." The second young man spoke. "Why don't you leave us alone?"

"He doesn't look fine." Ryder pulled out his phone. "I'm going to call for help."

"No!" The man on the ice sounded frantic. "I'll be okay. I just need to find the next footho—" But the word ended in a scream as the ledge holding him broke and he slid down the ice.

Ryder sprinted forward, though the young man's companions remained frozen in place. He was able to break the kid's fall, staggering back under the sudden weight, then dropping hard to his knees on the snowy ground, the young man collapsed against him. They stayed that way for a long moment, catching their breath.

The sound of an engine roaring to life made Ryder jerk his head around. The climber's companions were gone. "Looks like your friends ditched you," he said.

The young man grunted and tried to stand, but his left leg buckled when he tried to put weight on it.

Ryder knelt beside him. "You're hurt," he said. "Lie still. I'll call for help."

"I don't need help." The young man tried to stand and succeeded this time, though he favored his left leg. "It's just a sprain." He glared at Ryder. "I would have been fine if you hadn't interfered."

"I'd better take you home," Ryder said.

Sullen, the young man limped ahead of him down the trail. Ryder waited until he was buckled into the passenger seat of the Tahoe before he spoke. "What's your name?" he asked.

"Greg Eicklebaum," he said. "You can drop me off at the school. I'll walk home from there."

"You can't walk home with a bad ankle." Ryder started the Tahoe. "What's your address?"

Greg reluctantly rattled off an address in one of Eagle Mountain's more exclusive neighborhoods. "My parents are going to freak when a cop shows up at the door," he said.

"What did your friends back there mean about the climb not counting if you didn't finish?" Ryder asked.

"It was nothing. Just stupid talk."

"I gathered you made the climb on a dare."

Greg said nothing.

"What other dares have the three of you tried?" Ryder asked.

Greg stared out the window. "I don't know what you're talking about."

"Did you decide to break into some houses on a dare? Maybe the tiny house out at Lusk Ranch where the veterinarian lives? Or the Starling place on Pine Drive? Fred Starling said he thought the guy he surprised was wearing a letter jacket like the one you've got on."

Greg slumped down farther in his seat. "I don't have to talk to you," he said. "I'm a minor and you can't question me without my parents around."

"You're right. Let's wait and talk to your parents. I'm sure they'll be interested in hearing about this dare business."

Greg sat up straighter. "We're not doing anything wrong," he said. "It's just, you know, a way to pass the time. So we dare each other to do stuff, like climbing without ropes. Stupid, maybe, but it's not against the law."

"Attempting to break in to someone's home is against the law."

"I don't know anything about that."

"What other kinds of dares have you done?" Ryder asked.

"Gus ate a live cricket." Greg grinned. "It was disgusting."

"So there's you and Gus. Who's the third kid?"

Greg's expression grew closed off again. "I don't have to say."

"That's okay. I'll run the plate on his vehicle and find out."

Greg glared at him, then slumped down in his seat.

"The night of those break-ins, a woman was murdered," Ryder said.

"Are you trying to pin that one on us, too?" Greg asked.

"The murder wasn't far from the Starling house. The weather was bad and there weren't many people out. The person or persons who attempted the break-in might have seen the murderer, or his car."

"Can't help you."

"Think about it," Ryder said. "The sheriff might be willing to overlook an attempted burglary charge in exchange for evidence that helps us track down a killer."

"Right."

When Ryder pulled into the driveway at the Eicklebaum house, no lights showed in the windows. Greg unsnapped his seat belt and was opening the door before Ryder came to a complete stop. "Looks like nobody's home," he said. "Thanks for the ride." Then he was out of the Tahoe and sprinting up the drive.

Ryder waited until the young man was in the house, the door shut behind him. He could have waited for the parents to return, or he could come back later to talk to them, but he doubted they would be able to shed any light on the situation. He'd run the plates on the SUV, and let Travis and his men know about the three young men and their series of dares. He couldn't prove they were the ones behind the break-in at Darcy's house, but it felt right. And if he could find the right pressure to put on them, they might have some evidence that could help break this case.

"GOOD MORNING, Trooper Stewart."

Ryder was startled to be greeted by Adelaide Kinkaid when he entered the sheriff's office Sunday morning. "What are you doing working on a Sunday?" he asked.

"No rest for the wicked," she said.

"She doesn't think we can manage without her," Gage said as he joined Ryder in the lobby.

"You can't," she said. "And as long as there's a killer terrorizing my town, I don't see any sense sitting at home twiddling my thumbs. It's not as if at my age I'm going to take up knitting or something."

"I have a job for you," Ryder said. He handed her a piece of paper on which he'd written the license plate information from the SUV Greg's friends had driven. "Find out who this vehicle is registered to."

Adelaide studied him over the top of her lavender bi-focals. "Does this have something to do with the killer?"

"Probably not. But I still need to know."

"All right. But next time call it in to the highway patrol."

"Yes, ma'am." Ryder grinned, then followed Gage into his office where Dwight was already slouched in the visitor's chair.

Dwight straightened and stifled a yawn. "I guess

you're here to go with me to interview Doug Whitting-ton," he said.

"That's the plan." Ryder leaned against the doorjamb. "No rush. I'd like to get the information on that license plate from Adelaide first."

"What's up with the plate?" Gage asked.

Ryder told them about his encounter the night before with Greg Eicklebaum. "The plate belongs to the SUV they were in. His friends drove off without him, so I didn't get their names, though I take it one of them has the first name of Gus."

"Gus Elcott." Adelaide spoke from the doorway. "The SUV is registered to his father, Dallas, but Gus is the one who drives it."

"What do you know about Gus?" Ryder asked her. Adelaide was known for having her finger on the pulse of the town.

"He's the star forward on the high school basketball team. An only child of well-off parents, which means he's spoiled, but aren't they all these days?" Her eyes behind the bifocals narrowed. "Why? What's he done?"

"Nothing that I know of," Ryder said. "I caught him and some friends ice climbing in the dark without safety equipment. One of them fell and sprained his ankle and I took him home."

"Oh. Well, I suppose if that's the worst trouble they get into, we should be thankful." She left them.

Gage moved over to the door and shut it. "Now, tell us what's really going on," he said.

"I'm not sure," Ryder said. "Greg said something about a series of dares they were doing, and apparently there's some kind of point system. I take it whoever racks up the most points wins. Wins what, I don't know, and Greg wouldn't elaborate. But I think Greg and Gus and one other kid, whose name I don't know yet, were behind the attempted break-ins at Darcy's house and at Fred Starling's the night Christy O'Brien was killed."

"Fred said he thought the burglar wore a high school letter jacket," Gage said.

"Yeah," Ryder said. "And Darcy said the car that pulled out of her driveway that night was a dark SUV. And I saw three high school boys at the grocery store not long before the break-ins."

"It doesn't sound like we have enough evidence to charge them with anything," Dwight said.

"No," Ryder agreed. "But there's a chance those boys saw something that night that could help us track down the murderer—a vehicle, or maybe the murderer himself. We just have to find a way to make them talk."

"Maybe we gather more evidence about the burglaries and use that to put pressure on them," Gage said. "Offer to make a deal."

"It's worth a try," Ryder said. "Right now we don't have much else."

Dwight stood. "Maybe after today we'll have more," he said. "You ready to go interview Doug?"

"Be warned that Rainey isn't going to welcome you with open arms," Gage said. "She's very protective of her son."

"Any particular reason why?" Ryder asked.

"Apparently, his dad was out of the picture early on, and she raised him by herself. It really broke her heart when he went to jail. She's determined to keep him from going back." He pulled a folder from a stack on the corner of his desk. "Take a look at this before you go out there. Dwight's already seen it."

Ryder read through the file. Doug Whittington had been convicted two years previously of beating up his

girlfriend during a drunken argument. He broke her jaw
and her arm and cracked several ribs. She had ended up
in the hospital, and he had ended up in jail. After he had
served fifteen months of a two-year sentence, he was eli-
gible for parole. He looked up at Gage. "Did he come to
the ranch right after he was paroled?"

Gage nodded. "Rainey begged my parents to let him
stay with her on the ranch until he could get on his feet
again. He had completed both anger management and alcohol rehab while behind bars, and wasn't going to mess
up in a household with two lawmen as part of the family."

"If he is the killer, he's taking a big risk, murdering
women while two lawmen are in and out of the house
practically every day," Dwight said.

"This particular killer seems to enjoy taking risks and
taunting lawmen," Ryder said. "So he would fit that pat-
tern."

Gage took the folder Ryder handed him. "I hope he
has nothing to do with this. It's going to be messy for my
folks if he does, but we have to check it out. Still, Rainey
isn't going to be happy."

Twenty minutes later Ryder parked in front of the
ranch house and he and Dwight made their way up a recently shoveled walkway. Emily answered their knock,
dressed in ripped jeans and a button-down shirt, her hair
piled in a loose knot on her head and her feet bare. "Mom
and Dad are away, but Travis told me you were coming," she said, ushering them inside. "He asked me not
to say anything to Doug. He and Rainey are both in the
kitchen."

She showed them into the kitchen, a modern, light-
filled space with expanses of cherry cabinets and black
granite countertops. The cook, Rainey, was rolling dough
on the kitchen island while Doug chopped carrots by the

sink. Rainey looked up as they entered, her gaze sweeping over them. "Hello, officers," she said, her tone wary.

"You remember Sergeant Stewart and Deputy Prentice from my party yesterday, don't you?" Emily asked.

"We need to ask Doug a few questions," Ryder said.

At the sink, Doug stopped chopping and raised his head, but he didn't turn around.

"Doug can't tell you anything," Rainey said.

"You don't know what we need to ask him," Ryder said.

"It doesn't matter." Rainey went back to rolling dough. "He doesn't socialize with folks in town. He stays here at the ranch with me and keeps his nose clean. He's had culinary training, you know. He plans to open his own restaurant one day, or maybe do catering. He's been a big help to me, preparing for this wedding."

"If he hasn't done anything wrong, then he doesn't have anything to worry about," Dwight said.

Rainey sniffed. "Go ahead and ask, then. He doesn't have anything to hide, do you, Doug?"

Doug wiped his hands on a dish towel and turned to face them. He had a square, freckled face under closely cropped hair, his nose off-kilter as if it had been broken and not set properly. "What do you want to know?" he asked.

"I'll leave you all to it," Emily said and slipped out the door.

Ryder turned to Rainey. "If you could excuse us a moment," he said. "This won't take long."

"It's my kitchen and I'm not leaving." She assaulted the dough on the counter with vigorous strokes from her rolling pin. "And he's my son. Anything you want to ask him, you can ask in front of me."

Ryder and Dwight exchanged looks. They could always insist on taking Doug down to the sheriff's department to interview, but that would no doubt cause trouble for the sheriff and his family. And it might be interesting to see how Rainey reacted to their questions. There was still the possibility that the killer had had an accomplice. "All right," he said and took out his notebook. "During the party yesterday, what were you doing?"

"I worked with Mom, in the kitchen here," he said. "We made snacks for the party."

"Did you take a break from the work anytime?" Ryder asked. "Maybe step outside for a cigarette?"

Doug looked at his mother, who had given up all pretense of rolling out dough and stood with her arms crossed, watching them. "Mom doesn't like me to smoke," he said.

"But did you smoke?" Ryder pressed. "Maybe stepped outside to grab a quick cigarette?"

Doug nodded slowly.

"When?" Ryder asked.

"I dunno. A couple of times. But I didn't go far." He nodded toward the back door. "Just behind the woodpile out there."

Ryder walked to the door and looked out the glass at the top. A wall of neatly stacked wood extended from the corner of the house, forming a little alcove between the back door and the side of the house. "Did you see anyone while you were out there?" he asked. "One of the party guests, or maybe someone who wasn't supposed to be there? Did you speak to anyone?"

"No. I try to stay back, so no one sees me."

"How long were you out there?" Dwight asked.

"A few minutes. Maybe ten. As long as it takes to smoke a cigarette."

"What about last Tuesday?" Ryder asked. "What were you doing that day?"

He looked again to his mother, his gaze questioning. "I dunno," he said. "I guess I was here."

"That's the day they found those women," Rainey said. "And yes, he was here. With me. What are you implying?"

Ryder ignored the question. "You were here all day?"

"Are you calling me a liar?" Rainey moved around the counter toward him. She was almost as tall as Ryder, and though she had left the rolling pin on the counter, he was aware that it was still within reach, as were half a dozen knives in a block on the edge of the counter.

"If you can't remain quiet, Mrs. Whittington," Ryder said, "I'll have to ask you to leave."

She said nothing, but didn't advance any farther toward him.

Trusting Dwight to keep an eye on her, Ryder turned his attention to Doug. "Did you know Kelly Farrow or Christy O'Brien or Fiona Winslow?" he asked.

"No," Doug said.

"You'd never seen any of them around town, or spoken to them?" Ryder asked.

"I saw Fiona at the restaurant where she worked," he said. "She waited on my table once."

"Did you speak to her?" Ryder asked.

"I maybe said hello." He shifted his weight and shoved his hands in the pockets of his jeans. "There's no law against that."

"She was a very pretty woman," Ryder said.

"They were all pretty," Doug said.

An innocent statement, maybe, but it gave Ryder a chill. "I thought you said you didn't know Kelly or Christy."

"I saw their pictures in the paper."

"Did you ask Fiona to go out with you?" Ryder asked.

"What makes you think that?" Doug asked.

"Just a guess. Maybe you asked her out and she turned you down. When you saw her at the party, it reminded you of that and made you angry. Maybe you followed her into the woods and confronted her."

"No!" Doug and Rainey spoke at the same time.

"How dare you make up lies like that about my son," Rainey said. "Just because he made a mistake once, people like you want him to keep paying for the rest of his life. Instead of going out and finding the real killer, you can just pin these murders on him and your job is done."

"I haven't accused your son of anything," Ryder said.

"Does the sheriff know you're here?" she asked. "I can't imagine he'd put up with you bullying someone who is practically a member of his own family."

"Can Mr. or Mrs. Walker, or someone else, confirm that you didn't leave the ranch on Tuesday?" Ryder asked Doug.

"I don't know," he said. "I guess you'd have to ask them."

"Please don't ask them." Rainey's tone had turned from strident to pleading. "You'll only embarrass all of us. Doug was here because he was with me. I make it a point to keep him busy. He doesn't need to go to town for anything."

"He obviously went to town at some point and met Fiona at the restaurant," Dwight said.

"He was with me that day," Rainey said. "I keep him with me."

Dwight returned his notebook to his pocket. "That's all for now," he said. "I may have more questions later."

They left the kitchen. The living room was empty, so they let themselves out of the house. Ryder stopped on the way back to the Tahoe and looked around. Four cars were parked in front of the house, with another couple of trucks over by the horse barn. "A lot of vehicles," he said.

"The Walkers and Emily live here, along with Rainey and Doug, a ranch foreman and a couple of cowboys," Dwight said. "Cody Rankin is staying here until the wedding, and there are probably people in and out all day—delivery people, the veterinarian and farrier, other service people."

"So it would be easy for Doug to have slipped away while his mother was busy," Ryder said.

"Maybe," Dwight said. "But what's his motive?"

"He thought the women who were killed were pretty. If they turned down his advances, he might have taken it personally."

"He served time for assaulting a woman," Dwight said. "Not a stranger, but a woman he knew. And the crime was more violent and spontaneous. These crimes feel more planned out to me."

Ryder nodded. "His mother is worried about something," he said and resumed the walk to his vehicle. "Something to do with Doug."

"I got that feeling, too," Dwight said. "He might not be guilty of murdering Fiona and the others, but she thinks he's guilty of something."

"Or maybe she's lying about Doug having been with her every day, all day," Ryder said. "Her guilt over the lie is what I'm picking up on."

"She said she keeps him on the ranch with her, and pretty much doesn't let him out of her sight," Ryder said. "But it might be possible he could slip out without her knowing."

"Anything is possible," Dwight said. "We could get a

warrant to search his room. Maybe we'd get lucky and find a stack of Ice Cold calling cards."

"I don't think we have enough evidence to get a warrant," Ryder said. "Right now he has an alibi we can't disprove for all the killings. We don't have a motive, and the crime he was convicted of isn't similar enough to these murders to justify a search—at least not from a judge's point of view."

"I wonder if he has access to a computer and printer?" Dwight asked.

"I'll bet there's one somewhere in that house." Ryder glanced over at the big ranch house. "But without a warrant, we can't legally find out what's on it."

"We don't have much of anything, really," Dwight said. "That's the problem with this case—lots of guys who might be a killer, but no proof that any of them are."

"Yeah." Ryder's hands tightened on the steering wheel. "It feels like we're in a race, hurrying to catch this guy before he strikes again." A race that, right now at least, they were losing.

Chapter Twelve

By Monday Darcy was feeling much calmer. Fiona's murder had been very upsetting, but Darcy had managed to bring her feelings under control and focus on her work. "You've got a new patient in room two," Darcy's receptionist, Stacy, said when Darcy emerged from the kennels that afternoon where she'd been checking on a corgi who had had a bad tooth removed that morning. Churchill the corgi, more familiarly known as Pudge, was sleeping peacefully in a kennel, cuddled up on his favorite blanket, supplied by his indulgent owner.

"Oh?" Darcy accepted the brand-new patient chart, labeled Alvin. The information sheet inside listed a three-month-old Labrador puppy, Spike.

"The pup is adorable," Stacy said. "I should prepare you for the owner, though."

Darcy checked the sheet again. The puppy's owner was listed as Jerry Alvin. "What about him?" Had he given Stacy trouble already?

"He seems very nice," Stacy said. "But he's recovering from some kind of accident—his face is all bandaged and one arm is in a sling. I thought I should prepare you since it's a little shocking when you first see him."

"Oh, okay. Thanks." She closed the folder, then opened the door to exam room two.

Jerry Alvin's appearance was indeed a little shocking. Most of his head—with the exception of his eyes, ears and chin, was wrapped in bandages, and his left arm was enclosed in a black sling. He wore a black knit hat pulled down to his ears, tufts of blond hair sticking out from beneath it. "Hello, Dr. Marsh," he said, rising to greet her, and offering his hand.

"Hello, Mr. Alvin." She turned to greet the dog. "And hello, Spike."

Spike, a dark brown ball of fur, seemed thrilled to see her, jumping up and wagging his whole body. Darcy rubbed behind his ears and addressed his owner once more. "What's brought you in to see me today?"

"I was in a car accident." Alvin indicated the bandages. "Got pretty banged up. Spike was thrown from the car. He acts okay, but I just wanted to make sure he isn't hurt."

"When did this accident happen?" Darcy asked.

"Yesterday. I hit an icy spot on the highway and ran off the road, hit a tree. My head went through the windshield. I guess I'm lucky to be alive."

Darcy knelt and began examining Spike. The pup calmed and let her run her hands over him. "You say he's acting fine," she said. "No limping or crying out?"

"No. He landed in a snowbank, so I guess that cushioned his fall."

Spike certainly looked healthy and unharmed. Darcy picked him up and put him on the exam table. "He has a little umbilical hernia," she said. "That's not uncommon with some puppies. Chances are he'll outgrow it, but we should keep an eye on him."

"I'll do that. Thanks."

The hernia made her think of another puppy she had seen recently, with an almost identical umbilical hernia. Gage Walker's lab puppy was a twin to this dog—same age and size. He even had the same cloverleaf-shaped white spot on his chest. A chill swept over Darcy as she continued to examine the dog. If this wasn't the same puppy Gage had brought to her, then it was an identical twin. She glanced at Alvin. "Is something wrong?" he asked, leaning toward her.

"Nothing." She picked up the puppy and cradled it to her chest. "I'm going to check something in the back right quick. It won't take a minute." Before he could stop her, she exited the room and hurried to the back. She found her microchip reader in the drawer of the lab table and switched it on. With shaking hands, she ran it over the pup's shoulder. A number appeared on the screen. Darcy made note of the number, then carried the puppy to an empty kennel and slid it inside. The pup whined at her. "You'll only be in here a minute," she said and shut the door and slid the catch in place.

Then she hurried to the front office. "What's going on?" Stacy asked. "Did something happen back there?"

"What do you mean?" Darcy pulled Gage Walker's folder from the filing cabinet and spread it open on the desk.

"Mr. Alvin just ran out of here—without his dog."

Darcy looked up. "What?"

"He couldn't get out of here fast enough," Stacy said.

Darcy went to the window and peered out at the parking lot. Only her and Stacy's cars were visible. "Did you see what he was driving?" she asked.

"No." Stacy folded her arms. "Are you going to tell me what's going on or not?"

"Just a second." Darcy returned to the folder and compared the code the microchip scanner had displayed with the code registered to the microchip she had implanted in Gage's puppy, Admiral. They matched.

Stacy peered over her shoulder. "What are you doing with Gage's folder?"

"The puppy back there—the one Jerry Alvin called Spike—is Gage Walker's new dog."

"You mean that guy stole it?" Stacy's eyes widened. "So all those bandages must have been a disguise. But why bring it here?"

"I don't know." Darcy picked up the phone and punched in Gage's cell number. He answered on the third ring.

"Darcy," he said. "What can I do for you?"

"Gage, I have your puppy, Admiral, here at the office," she said.

"What? What happened? Where's Maya?"

"A man who said his name was Jerry Alvin brought him in to see me," Darcy said. "He was calling the dog Spike. As soon as I went into the back to check the dog's microchip, he ran out the front door."

"I'll be right over," Gage said.

Darcy went to the back and retrieved the puppy from the kennel. She wasn't comfortable letting it out of her sight until its real owner arrived. Ten minutes later Gage walked into the office, along with Maya and Casey. The little girl squealed and ran to envelop the puppy in a hug.

"We got in from school just a few minutes ago," Maya said. "We were frantic when we couldn't find Admiral. Gage called while we were looking for him."

"He's perfectly fine," Darcy reassured them. "Whoever took him didn't hurt him."

Gage took a small notebook from the pocket of his uniform shirt. "Tell me about this Alvin," he said. "What did he look like?"

"That's the thing," Darcy said. "I can't really tell you." She explained about the bandages and sling.

"It looked like a Halloween costume," Stacy said. "He said he'd been in a car wreck."

"He told me he ran off the road and hit a tree," Darcy said. "Even when he said that, I was thinking it didn't sound right. He said his face went through the windshield, but wouldn't the airbag have protected him from that? And even if he wasn't wearing a seat belt, it seemed he would have been hurt worse. And do they really bandage people up like that—like mummies?"

"How tall was he?" Gage asked. "What kind of build?"

Darcy and Stacy exchanged glances. "Just—average," Darcy said.

"Maybe five-ten," Stacy said. "Not too big, not too little."

"Hair color?" Gage asked. "Eye color?"

"He had a knit cap pulled over his hair, but there were some blond strands sticking out," Darcy said. "And I was so distracted by the bandages, I didn't notice his eyes."

"How was he dressed?" Gage asked.

"Jeans, a dark blue or black parka and the hat," Darcy said. "I didn't notice his shoes."

"The bandages and sling really drew all your attention, you know," Stacy said. "I guess that was the idea."

"Did you get a look at his car?" Gage asked.

Both women shook their heads.

Gage pocketed the notebook. "I'll ask the neighbors if they saw anyone around the house this afternoon."

"I'm so glad you thought to check the microchip,"

Maya said. She held the puppy now, stroking the soft brown fur. "I don't know what we'd have done if we lost him."

The front door opened and Ryder entered. "Darcy, are you all right?" he asked.

"I'm fine," she said. "Why wouldn't I be?"

"I stopped by the sheriff's department and Adelaide told me a guy showed up at your office who had stolen Gage's dog."

"He did, but he ran away when I took the dog into the back room to check the microchip," she said.

"I don't understand," Stacy said. "Why bring the dog here in the first place? It wasn't sick or hurt, and he had to have realized that in a town this small, the odds were good we had already seen the puppy." She tapped her chin. "You know, the more I think about it, the more I think this guy was trying to seem older than he was. Like—I don't know—a kid playing dress-up."

"You think this was a kid?" Darcy stared at her.

Stacy scrunched up her nose. "Not a little kid, but maybe a teenager?"

"I have an idea," Ryder said. "Maya, do you have a high school yearbook at your house?"

"Sure," Maya said. "I have a copy of last year's."

"Could you bring it to us? Now?"

"Oh. Okay." She took Casey's hand. "Come on, honey. Let's take Admiral home and get a book Trooper Stewart wants to look at."

"Why do you want to look at the school yearbook?" Darcy asked.

"Just a hunch I have about who might have done this. You take care of your next patient and I'll call you when Maya gets back with the book."

Darcy vaccinated a dachshund, and Maya and Gage returned together with the Eagle Mountain High School yearbook. "You think those daredevil high school students were behind this?" Gage asked as he handed over the yearbook.

"I think it's a possibility." Ryder opened the book. "What year is Greg Eicklebaum?" he asked.

"He's a junior," Maya said.

Ryder flipped to the pages for the junior class and found Greg's picture and showed it to Stacy and Darcy. They both peered at it, then shook their heads. "I was paying attention to the dog, not its owner," Darcy said.

"That's not the guy," Stacy said. "The hair was a lot lighter, and I'm pretty sure at least some of it was real."

"Try Gus Elcott," Gage said.

Ryder found Gus's picture, but it got a no also. "Try Pi Calendri," Maya said.

"Who names their kid Pie?" Ryder asked as he turned pages.

"It's short for Giuseppe," Maya said. "Apparently, a lot of Italians settled in this area at the turn of the last century to work in the mines. The Calendris have been here for generations. The story I heard is that Giuseppe is Italian for Joe. Someone started calling him Joe Pi, then it got shortened to Pi." She shrugged. "He hangs out with Dallas and Greg."

Ryder studied the photograph of a mature-looking blond. He turned the page toward Stacy. "What about him?"

"Bingo." She nodded. "That's him."

Darcy leaned over to take a look. "I think it could be him," she said. "Something about the chin…"

Ryder closed the book. "Why would Pi Calendri

steal our dog?" Maya asked. "He's not even in any of my classes."

"Why don't we go talk to him and find out," Gage said.

Chapter Thirteen

The Calendri home was in the same neighborhood as the Eicklebaums', though the house was larger, with more spectacular views. An attractive blonde answered the door, and her carefully groomed brows rose at the sight of two law enforcement officers on her doorstep. "Is something wrong?" she asked.

"Mrs. Calendri?" Ryder asked.

She nodded. "We'd like to speak to Pi," Ryder said. "Um, that is, Giuseppe."

"What is this about?"

"We have a few questions for him," Gage said. "We'd like you and your husband, if he's home, to be present while we talk to him, of course."

"My husband isn't here," she said. "Should I call our lawyer?"

"It's just a few questions," Ryder said. "May we come in?"

She stepped back and allowed them to pass, then shut the door behind them. "Excuse me," she said and hurried up the stairs to their left. A few moments later not-so-muffled tones of argument sounded overhead, though the words were too garbled for Ryder to make them out. A few seconds later mother and son descended the stairs.

"Hello, officers." A handsome young man, neatly dressed in jeans and a button-down shirt, stepped forward and offered his hand. "My mother said you wanted to speak to me. Is this about that fender bender in the school parking lot yesterday afternoon? I'm afraid I wasn't there. I had practice."

"Pi is rehearsing for the school's production of *Guys and Dolls*," Mrs. Calendri said. "He has the male lead."

"So you're in drama," Gage said. He and Ryder exchanged looks. A drama student would know how to change his appearance and assume a different identity.

"Yes, sir. You're Ms. Renfro's husband, aren't you?" Pi asked.

"Yes."

"Come into the living room and have a seat and tell us what this is all about." Mrs. Calendri led them into a room that looked straight out of a top-end designer's showroom—all leather and hammered copper and carved cedar. A fire crackled in a massive gas fireplace. A large white dog rose from a bed in front of the fire and padded over to greet them, tail slowly fanning back and forth.

"Beautiful dog," Ryder said, scratching the animal's ears.

"That's Ghost," Pi said. He sat on the end of the sofa. Ryder and Gage took chairs facing him. The dog sat beside the young man, who idly patted its back.

"You like dogs, I see," Ryder said.

"Sure," Pi said. "Who doesn't?"

"What is this about?" Mrs. Calendri asked.

"I have a dog," Gage said. "A chocolate Lab puppy, Admiral."

"Labs are great dogs," Pi said. "Do you plan to train him to hunt?"

"I hope to." Gage scratched his chin. "Funny thing, though. Someone took Admiral out of my yard this afternoon."

"That's terrible." Pi looked suitably shocked, though Ryder thought he wasn't ready for his professional acting debut just yet. "Do you know who did it?"

"We have a very good idea," Ryder said. "And we think you do, too."

"Are you accusing Pi of taking your dog?" Mrs. Calendri poised on the edge of her seat as if prepared to leap up and do battle on behalf of her child.

"Funny thing about cops," Gage said. "We're very security conscious. And when you have a family, you can't be too careful. Lots of us install security cameras in our homes." Ryder noticed that Gage hadn't said that he personally had a security camera, though he wanted Pi to think so.

"Not to mention, the receptionist at the vet clinic where you tried to pass off Admiral as your own made you for a teenager right away," Ryder said.

Pi tried to hold his expression of surprise, but Ryder's words broke his resolve. He slumped, head in his hands. "It was just supposed to be a joke," he said. "I would never have hurt your dog, I promise. I would have returned him to your house before you even knew he was gone."

"Giuseppe! What are you saying?" Mrs. Calendri glared at her son. "You stole this officer's dog? Why?"

"You did it on a dare, didn't you?" Ryder asked.

Pi nodded. "At first, the dare was just to snatch the dog. But there's nothing really difficult or dangerous about taking a dog out of someone's yard." He sent Gage an apologetic look. "We didn't know about the security camera. So then we decided it would be worth more points if I tried to pass the dog off as my own. So we thought I should take it to the vet. If I could have fooled her, I'd be way ahead of the other guys on points."

"How many points would breaking into someone's house be worth?" Ryder asked.

Pi flushed. "I don't know anything about that."

"Pi, what are you talking about?" Mrs. Calendri asked. "What other guys?"

"Greg Eicklebaum and Gus Elcott," Ryder said. "They've been egging each other on in a series of dares, to see who can get away with various stunts without getting caught." He turned back to Pi. "Who's ahead?"

"Right now Gus is," Pi said. "After he put the bear statue from the city park on the high school gym roof the week after Christmas. He was sure nobody could beat that. That's why I had to do something really outrageous to top him." He buried his head in his hands. "Am I in big trouble for taking your dog? I promise I wouldn't have hurt him."

"You could be," Gage said. "That depends on whether or not you're willing to help us in another matter."

"Of course he'll help you," Mrs. Calendri said.

Pi sighed. "What do you want?"

"The night Christy O'Brien was killed—Tuesday, the fifth," Gage said. "You and Greg and Gus were out that night, in the snowstorm."

"I saw you in the parking lot of the grocery store," Ryder said. "You stood out because almost no one else was out in that weather."

"So? There's no law against being out at night," Pi said.

"Who else did you see that night? You may have seen the murderer, or his car."

"We didn't see anybody," Pi said. "That's the point, you know? Not to see anyone and not to let them see you."

"Except the veterinarian, Darcy Marsh, came home and surprised you trying to break in to her house, and a little while later Fred Starling did the same," Ryder said.

"I don't know what you're talking about," Pi said.

"We don't care about that right now," Gage said. "We want to know if you saw anyone else out that night. Any other car on the road, especially near Fred Starling's place."

"We weren't near Fred Starling's place," Pi said. "I can't help you."

"How do you know where Fred Starling lives?" Ryder asked. "We didn't mention an address."

Pi scowled. "This town is like, three blocks wide. I grew up here. I know where everyone lives. Mr. Starling was my Cub Scout leader when I was in second grade."

"He said he doesn't know anything that can help you." Mrs. Calendri stood. "If you want to talk to him anymore, you'll have to wait and do it when his father and our lawyer are present."

Ryder and Gage rose also and followed Mrs. Calendri to the door. In the hallway Gage turned back to Pi. "If you think of anything that might be helpful, call anytime," he said. "Oh, and if anything else happens to my dog, I'll come looking for you, and I won't just ask questions."

"I would never hurt a dog," Pi said. "I promise you."

Gage nodded, and both officers left.

When they were in Ryder's Tahoe again, he leaned back against the driver's seat and let out a long breath. "Those boys were responsible for both those attempted break-ins," he said.

"We'll never prove it," Gage said. "But at least we know it wasn't the murderer targeting Darcy."

"The boys didn't pretend to be an old woman with a dog, and I don't think one of them ran her off the road," Ryder said. "All three of them were playing on the varsity basketball team that night. I saw the roster when I checked Ken Rutledge's alibi."

"Right," Gage said. "I'm still holding out hope they saw something that night that can help us. We'll try questioning all three of them, but we'll have to be careful—probably bring them in to the station with their parents and their attorneys. I'll talk to Travis and see what he thinks."

"Good idea." Ryder started the Tahoe. "Want me to drop you at the station or your house?"

"My vehicle is at my house. And I need to check in with Maya and Casey. Casey isn't going to want to let Admiral out of her sight for the next month."

"I'm glad your dog is okay," Ryder said.

"Me, too. I believe Pi when he said he wouldn't hurt him, but we need to stop these stunts before somebody does get hurt." He was silent a moment, then chuckled.

"What's so funny?" Ryder asked.

"I can't believe a high school kid got that bear statue up on the roof of the gym. The statue is made of bronze. It must weigh a ton. I took the call and the look on the principal's face was priceless. It was all I could do to keep a straight face."

"Maybe we can declare Gus the winner of the contest and put an end to the dares," Ryder said.

"Yeah," Gage agreed. "We've got better things to do than deal with high school delinquents." They had a murderer to stop, and Ryder hated that it didn't feel like they were any closer to him than they had ever been. It was only a matter of time before he struck again, and every woman in town was vulnerable—even, or especially, Darcy.

DARCY WASN'T SURPRISED to see Ryder waiting for her as she ushered her last patient of the day back into the lobby. She busied herself removing her lab coat and smoothing her hair while the woman paid her bill. As soon as the door shut behind the woman, Stacy demanded, "Well? Did you find out who took Gage's pup?"

"It was a high school kid," Ryder said.

"I knew it!" Stacy pumped her fist.

"What did he want with Gage's dog?" Darcy asked.

"He did it on a dare." Ryder came around the counter to join them in the little office space. "We think he and his friends were behind the attempted break-in at your house, and at another house, the night Christy O'Brien was killed."

Darcy sagged against the counter. "That's a relief," she said. "I mean, to know it was just a bunch of kids." And not the killer—though she couldn't bring herself to say the words out loud.

"Yes and no," Ryder said. "The kids aren't dangerous, but this does show how vulnerable you are to someone who could mean harm. Especially while we've got a killer running loose, you should be wary of new clients."

"I'm not going to turn away paying customers—or hurt animals," Darcy said.

He opened his mouth to protest and she rushed to cut him off. She wasn't going to debate her business practices. "I've already made a policy of not going on any more house calls for new patients," she said. "And I won't see anyone if I'm here alone."

"I'll start asking every new patient for a copy of their driver's license," Stacy said. "They do it at my doctor's office—I don't see why I can't do it here."

"That's not a bad idea," Darcy said. "We'll be careful, I promise."

Ryder studied her, clearly displeased, but not saying anything. Stacy slung her purse over her shoulder. "I think I'll head home now." She looked from Ryder to Darcy. "You two don't need me here."

When she was gone Darcy steeled herself to argue with Ryder. "I can't shut down my business or put my life on hold because of the killer," she said. "Of course I'll be careful, but teenagers playing pranks don't have anything to do with that. They're a nuisance, but they're not dangerous."

"They aren't the ones who ran you off the road when you went on that bogus call," Ryder said. "We still don't know who was responsible for that. They might try again."

Her stomach hurt, the old fear squeezing at her. But she couldn't let fear run her life. If Ryder had his way, he'd want her to shut down the practice and move into a spare cell at the sheriff's department. As pleasant as it was to know he was concerned for her, she couldn't live like that. "I'll be careful," she said, softening her voice. "It's all any of us can do."

He nodded. "That doesn't mean I won't worry."

"And I think your worrying is sweet." She reached for her coat and he took it and held it while she slipped her arms into the sleeves. It was a little gesture, but it touched her. She turned and put her hands on his chest. "It means a lot to me," she said. "Knowing you care. But it unsettles me a little, too. I'm not used to that."

He covered her hands with his own. "I hope you could get used to it."

"Maybe I can. But I need time. And I need space, too. Okay?"

He looked into her eyes. Searching for what? she wondered. He stepped back. "Okay," he said. "I'll walk you to your car, then I have to get back to work. I won't rest easy until we've found this guy."

"I think all of us can say that," she said. And she wouldn't deny that it was comforting to have him walk her to her car—to have him watching over her.

RYDER REMINDED HIMSELF that Darcy was a smart, careful woman who would be on her guard against anyone who might harm her. She was perfectly capable of looking out for herself, and he really ought to be concentrating on the case. He'd always made it a point to seek out easy, uncomplicated relationships—that worked out best for everyone involved. But there was nothing easy or uncomplicated about Darcy. Yet, the thought of distancing himself from her set up a physical ache in his chest.

He tried to push the thought aside as he headed back to the sheriff's department—his home away from home these days, since his regular office on the other side of Dixon Pass was off-limits due to the still-closed roads. Gage saluted him with a slice of pizza. "There's more in the break room, if you hurry," he said.

Ryder helped himself to the pizza. "I thought you'd be home with your dog," he said when he rejoined Gage in his office.

"I'm on duty this evening," Gage said. "And the dog is fine—being showered with treats by Maya and Casey, who have vowed not to let him out of their sight."

Ryder sank into the chair across from Gage's desk. "I don't even know why I'm here," he said. "Except I keep hoping for a break in the case."

"You can help sort through the calls we've had from the public." Gage picked up the top sheet from a stack of printouts on his desk. "'My neighbor has a lot of guns and looks at me funny whenever I go out to my car. Maybe he's your killer.'" He tossed that sheet aside and selected another. "'I overheard a man at the café the other morning tell his wife that Fiona Winslow probably got in trouble because she was such a big flirt. I didn't get a good look at him, but if you find him, maybe he knows something.'"

"Are they all like that?" Ryder asked.

"So far. But we have to look at them all. Someone might come up with something. Oh, and I almost forgot." He pulled another sheet of paper from a different stack. "This came into the office for you this morning."

Ryder set aside the half-eaten slice of pizza and took the paper—a printout from the Colorado Department of Corrections. "Who is Jay Leverett and why do you want to know if he's been released from prison or not?" Gage asked.

"It's a man Darcy dated in Fort Collins," Ryder said. "The relationship didn't end well."

"And you thought he might have tracked her down here?"

"It's always possible." He glanced up. "You saw what he served time for?"

Gage nodded. "Sexual assault. And he was released two months ago."

"And the DOC has no idea where he is now." Ryder tossed the paper back onto the desk. "Do you know of anyone in town who fits his description?"

"Not offhand," Gage said. "But we have a lot of strangers stranded here by the storms. He could be one of them."

"And he could be our killer," Ryder said. "Or not. But it's one more lead to follow."

Adelaide appeared in the doorway. "If you men are finished stuffing your faces, there's someone here who wants to speak with an officer," she said. "Actually, two someones. Tourists."

"I'll take this," Gage said.

Ryder and Dwight followed Gage and Adelaide to the lobby, where Tim and Alex stood, studying the photographs displayed on the walls. "Hey, long time no see," Alex said.

"Adelaide said you wanted to talk to an officer?" Gage asked.

"Yeah," Tim said. "We want to report a crime."

"What sort of crime?" Gage asked.

"Someone tried to kill us," Alex said. "You've got a lunatic running around in your little town."

Chapter Fourteen

"You say someone tried to kill you?" Ryder studied the two men before him. Tim looked visibly shaken, but Alex was red-faced with anger. "What happened?"

"Come take a look at this." Alex motioned them toward the door.

Ryder, Dwight and Gage followed Alex and Tim out into the small front parking lot. Alex led the way to a gray Toyota 4Runner. "Some maniac tried to run us off the road," Tim said. "Look what he did to my ride." He walked around the car and indicated the bashed-in driver's side front quarter-panel.

"Was it a traffic accident, or was it deliberate?" Gage asked.

"Oh, it was deliberate," Alex said. "He aimed right at us."

"Come inside and tell us what happened," Gage said. He led the way to an empty conference room. He sat on one side of the table, with Alex and Tim on the other. Dwight sat next to him, while Ryder stood by the door. This wasn't his case—the two men had come to the sheriff's department to report a crime. But his interest in the men as suspects in his case made it reasonable for him to be present for the interview, though he planned to keep quiet and let Gage take the lead.

Gage leaned over and switched on a digital recorder that sat in the middle of the table. "I'm going to make a record of this," he said. "We'll transcribe your statements later and have you sign them. All right?"

Both men nodded. "Okay," Gage said. "Tell us what happened—where were you, when and all the details you can remember."

"We were out near Tim's aunt's cabin," Alex said. "On County Road Five. We were headed into town for dinner when this guy in a dark pickup truck turned out of a side road and headed toward us. He was driving really fast."

"Yeah, like maybe eighty miles an hour," Tim said. "Crazy, because the road has a lot of snow on it—packed down and drivable, but not that fast."

"Tim laid on the horn and moved over as far as he could, but the guy just kept coming," Alex said.

"It was like he was playing chicken or something," Tim said. "He headed straight for us and at the last minute sideswiped us."

"If he was going that fast and hit you, why didn't he lose control and go crashing into the trees?" Dwight asked.

Tim glanced at Alex. "He was lucky, and a good driver," Alex said.

"It would have been better if you had remained at the scene and called us," Gage said. "We'll send someone out to take a look. We may be able to determine his speed by skid marks."

"Good luck with that," Alex said. "It's all snow out there."

"You can see where we went into the ditch," Tim said. "And there's, like, glass and stuff from my busted headlight."

"All right," Gage said. "We'll check. In the meantime, can you tell us where you were Tuesday?"

Tim laughed. "I can't even remember what I had for breakfast yesterday."

"That was the day after that first big snowstorm, right?" Alex said. "The day those two women were killed."

"Yes," Gage said. "What were you doing that day?"

"We were hanging out at Tim's aunt's place, moaning about being stuck here for who knows how long," Alex said.

"Did you go out to a restaurant or bar or maybe to the store to buy groceries?" Gage asked. "Did you see or talk to anyone else?"

"Nah. We stayed in and got drunk," Tim said.

"No offense, but the idea of being stuck here with nothing to do when we could be back in the city, hanging out with friends, really bummed us out," Alex said.

"I thought you came here to ice climb," Gage said.

"Sure. But you can't even do that when it's snowing so hard you can't see in front of your face," Alex said.

"Yeah," Tim agreed. "We've pretty much climbed all the good local routes, so doing them again would be kind of lame."

"How have you been occupying your time while you're stranded here?" Dwight asked.

"Watching a lot of TV, playing video games," Tim said.

"That's why it was so nice of Emily Walker to invite us to her party," Alex said. "It was a lot of fun until that poor woman was killed."

"Did you get a good look at the driver of the truck that hit you?" Gage asked. "Did you get a license plate number?"

"I'm pretty sure the vehicle didn't have a front license plate," Alex said. "And the windows were tinted. I had the impression of a big person—probably a man, with broad shoulders. He was wearing some kind of hat, like a ball cap."

Gage looked at Tim, who shrugged. "Like he said, the windows were tinted. And I was too terrified to notice much of anything. I really thought we were going to be killed."

"Were either of you hurt by the impact?" Gage asked.

"My neck is pretty sore." Alex rubbed the back of his neck. "I think I might have whiplash."

"I'm just generally banged up," Tim said. "No permanent damage, I don't think."

"Your airbag didn't deploy," Dwight said.

Again, the two friends exchanged a look. "No," Tim said. "I wondered about that. Maybe it's defective."

"We were both wearing seat belts," Alex said. "I'm sure that saved us from more serious harm."

"We'll get someone out to the site and check it out," Gage said. "We don't have a lot to go on, but we'll do what we can, though I think you realize we're a small department, and we have more pressing concerns at the moment."

"I wanted to ask you about that," Alex said. He smiled, a tight grimace that made Ryder think he didn't use the expression often. "I think I told you I'm studying psychology at the university. I have a special interest in serial killers. I'm actually thinking of pursuing a career as a profiler, helping law enforcement."

"I really can't talk about the case," Gage said.

"Oh, I get that," Alex said. "I wouldn't ask you to reveal anything confidential. But I read in the paper that the killer has been leaving cards with the bodies of his victims—cards that say Ice Cold. I wonder what you think the significance of that might be. Is he trying to send a particular message? And to whom? Does he kill women because he sees them as emotionally cold? Does he think this about all women or do his victims symbolize a particular woman?"

"I don't have any answers for you," Gage said. He stood. "If you could stop by the station again tomorrow, we'll have your statements ready for you to sign, and we may have some photographs from the scene for you to look at and verify. Thanks for stopping by."

He and Dwight escorted the two out to the truck and watched them leave. When they returned to the lobby, Ryder asked, "What do you make of that?"

"They're lying about something," Gage said.

Dwight nodded. "I got that, too," he said.

"The truck was damaged," Ryder said.

"It was," Gage said. "I'm just not sure the damage happened the way they said."

"What about those questions he asked?" Ryder asked. "About the killer?"

"Lots of people are fascinated by serial killers," Dwight said. "I imagine most psychology students find the topic interesting."

"How did the information about those cards get in the paper?" Ryder asked.

"Tammy Patterson was at the party at the ranch Saturday," Gage said. "She's a reporter for the paper. She probably heard about the cards there."

"I wish she hadn't publicized it," Ryder said.

"Nothing we can do about it now." Gage shoved his hands in his pockets. "Alex raised some interesting points," he said. "Ones we should look at."

"They don't have an alibi for the day Kelly and Christy were killed," Ryder said.

"No," Gage said. "But the weather was bad that day.

Most people were probably staying at home, watching TV, playing video games and drinking. It doesn't prove they were guilty of anything."

"We aren't getting anywhere with this case," Ryder said.

"When we find out what those two are lying about, maybe we'll have something to work with," Gage said.

"I AM NOT going to let you eat lunch cooped up here in the office again." Stacy, purse in hand, handed Darcy her coat after she had sent her last patient of the morning on her way Tuesday.

"I don't mind staying in." Darcy slipped out of her lab coat and hung it on a peg by the door. "It's a good time to catch up on paperwork." Since Kelly's death, she had fallen into the habit of bringing food from home or from the grocery store deli, and eating at her desk.

"Lunch is supposed to be a break from work," Stacy said. "So you come back in the afternoon refreshed. Besides, if you go to lunch with me, neither one of us is alone. It just seems safer to me for women to travel in groups around here, at least until that Ice Cold Killer is caught."

"Ice Cold Killer?" The name gave her a jolt. "Where did you get that?"

"That's what the paper is calling him. Apparently, he leaves a business card with those words on it with each of the bodies of the women he's killed." She shuddered. "Creepy. I wouldn't stay anywhere by myself for ten seconds, much less a whole lunch hour."

"I'm sure I'm perfectly safe here," Darcy said, though even as she uttered the words, a shiver of fear ran through her. "I keep the door locked."

"You keep thinking that way if it helps you sleep at night," Stacy said. "As for me, I'm scared half to death, and I'd appreciate the company."

Though Stacy's tone was joking, Darcy sensed some truth behind her words. She hadn't read the latest issue of the paper, but news of a serial killer snowed in with the rest of the town had everyone on edge. And she had noticed an uptick of men accompanying the women who brought their pets in to see her. Maybe she and Stacy keeping each other company wasn't such a bad idea. She collected her purse from the bottom drawer of the filing cabinet. "All right. I'll go to lunch with you."

They headed for Kate's Kitchen, always a favorite. But the black ribbons adorning the door reminded them that Fiona Winslow had worked here, which momentarily quieted their conversation. Stacy waited until they had placed their orders before she spoke. She stripped the paper off a straw and plopped it into her glass of diet soda. "It's just so weird that a serial killer would end up here, in little Eagle Mountain. What's the attraction?"

"I guess killers take vacations and go to visit relatives, like anyone else," Darcy said. "He got caught by the snow like a lot of other people."

"And while he's here he decides he should kill a few people?" She grimaced. "It's beyond creepy."

"I know the sheriff's department and every other law enforcement officer in the area is working really hard to track him down," Darcy said. "They're bound to catch him soon. There aren't that many people in this town, and he can't leave."

"Yeah. You have to hope the killer really is a stranger who got stuck here—and not someone we've all known for years. That would freak me out. I mean, how could someone hide that side of himself?"

"It happens all the time," Darcy said. The man who had raped her had seemed like another good-looking, charming fellow student—until he had refused to let her leave his apartment one night, and had turned what had started as a pleasant date into a nightmare.

"I guess it does," Stacy said. "I mean, the news reports always have some neighbor talking about 'He was such a nice, quiet man. He kept to himself and didn't hurt anybody.'"

The waitress—an older woman whose name tag identified her as Ella—delivered the soup and sandwiches they had both ordered. Darcy picked up her spoon.

"Speaking of law enforcement officers," Stacy said. "What's the story with you and Ryder?"

Darcy blinked. "Story?"

"He's not hanging around the office so much because of the case," Stacy said. "Or at least, that's not the only reason." She picked up half a sandwich. "And didn't the two of you team up at Emily Walker's party last Saturday? How was that?"

"It was fun." Darcy sipped her own drink. "Until it wasn't."

"Yeah, not the most romantic of circumstances," Stacy said. She leaned across the table, her voice lowered. "Still, you have to admit he is one gorgeous man. And I can tell he's really into you."

How can you tell? Darcy wanted to ask, but she didn't. Because it didn't really matter what someone else thought was going on. The only gauge that counted was what she and Ryder felt. She could assess her own feelings, but the emotions of the other party in a relationship were impossible to plumb. Probably even people who had been together for years had a tough time of it.

So what about her feelings for him? Ryder was gorgeous. And his kisses certainly hadn't been casual pecks on the lips. But they had been thrown together under such odd circumstances. How much of her attraction to him was fueled by fear? If anyone could protect her from this Ice Cold Killer, surely it was a lawman who wore a gun pretty much all the time. And what if she was mistaking his sense of duty to protect her for something more? "I like him," she said. "But it's not as if we've even had a real date." The party had been a good start, but they had been interrupted before they had spent all that much time together.

"You can fix that," Stacy said.

"Fix what?"

"Not having had a date. Ask him out."

"Oh. Well, he's really busy right now."

"He can't work all the time," Stacy said. "He has to eat, right? Take him to dinner. Or better yet, offer to cook at your place."

Yes, she and Ryder had shared tea and conversation and even soup at her place, but it wasn't a real date. A real date, where she dressed up and cleaned the house and put some effort into a meal, felt like too much just yet. Too intimate and confining.

Maybe a little too reminiscent of her date-turned-nightmare with the man who had raped her.

"Okay, you're not digging that idea," Stacy said. "I can see it on your face. So what about an activity? Maybe something outdoors? Go ice-skating at City Park."

"I don't know how to skate." A broken bone didn't sound very romantic.

"Then something else. You're smart. You can think of something."

"What if he says no?"

"He won't." Stacy pointed her soup spoon at Darcy. "Don't be a coward. And hey, think of it this way—when you're out with a cop, Mr. Ice Cold isn't going to come anywhere near you."

Chapter Fifteen

As the highway closure stretched to its second week, what had been a fun, short-term adventure began to wear on everyone's nerves. Tempers were shorter, complaints were louder and signs on the doors of stores and restaurants warned of limited menus and items no longer available. All the fresh milk and bread in town were gone, though a couple of women were making a killing selling their home-baked loaves, and the local coffee shop had converted more than a few people to almond milk and soy milk lattes. One of the town's two gas stations was out of gas. The city had made the decision to not plow the streets, and people made the best of the situation by breaking out cross-country skis for their commutes.

Darcy figured she had enough fuel to take her through another week. Weather prognosticators were predicting a break in the storms any day now—but they had been saying that for a while.

Four days had passed since Fiona's murder, and though tensions in town were still high, Darcy had stopped flinching every time the door to the clinic opened, and she had stopped looking over her shoulder every few seconds as she drove home in the evening.

"Ryder is here." Stacy made the announcement Wednesday afternoon in a singsong voice reminiscent of a schoolgirl on the playground teasing another girl about her crush.

Darcy finished vaccinating Sage Ryan's tortoise-shell cat and frowned at Stacy. They'd have to have a discussion about interrupting Darcy while she was with a client.

"Do you mean that hunky highway patrolman?" Sage asked as she gathered the cat—Cosmo—into her arms once more. "He's easy enough on the eyes that I might not even mind getting a ticket from him."

"Cosmo should be good for another three years on his rabies vaccine," Darcy said. "He's a nice, healthy cat, though it wouldn't hurt for him to lose a few pounds. I'll ask Stacy to give you our handout on helping cats lose weight."

"Oh, he's just a little pudgy, aren't you, honey?" Sage nuzzled the cat, who looked as if he was only tolerating the attention in hopes it would pay off with a treat. "He's so cute, I can't help but spoil him."

"Try spoiling him with toys and pats instead of treats," Darcy said. "He'll be much better for it in the long run."

"I'll try." She caught Darcy's eye, her cheeks reddening slightly. "And I'm sorry if I said anything out of line about your boyfriend. I promise I didn't mean anything by it."

Darcy opened her mouth to protest that Ryder was not her boyfriend, but the eager look in Sage's eyes changed her mind. No sense providing more fuel for the town gossips.

She followed Sage out to the front. "Now's your chance," Stacy whispered as Darcy passed.

In the waiting room, Ryder rose from the chair he had taken by the door. Dressed in his sharp blue and buff uniform, tall leather boots accenting his strong legs and the leather jacket with the black shearling collar adding to the breadth of his shoulders, he definitely was *easy on the eyes*, as Sage had said. "I didn't mean to interrupt," he said.

"I can give you a few minutes," she said and led the way past Stacy, who didn't even pretend not to stare, into the exam room she'd just exited. "What can I do for you?" she asked, picking up the bottle of spray disinfectant.

"I just wanted to see you, make sure you haven't had any more suspicious customers or disturbances at your home," he said.

"No." She sprayed down the metal exam table. "I promise I'll let you know if anything happens."

"I know." He leaned against the wall, relaxed. "I guess I just wanted to see you. I've been so busy we haven't seen much of each other the past couple of days."

The knowledge that he missed her made her feel a little melted inside. "It's really good to see you, too." She set aside the spray bottle. Her palms were sweating, but it was now or never. "I've been meaning to call you," she said.

"Oh?"

"I wondered if you wanted to go skiing this weekend. I mean, if you're free. I know you're putting in a lot of overtime on the case, but I thought—"

He touched her arm. "I'd love to," he said. "Unless something urgent comes up, I can take a day off. When?"

"Sunday? The office is never open then, and the forecast is for clearing weather."

"Sounds great. I'll pick you up. Is ten o'clock good?"

"Sure." She couldn't seem to stop grinning. "I hope nothing happens to keep you from it. Things have been pretty quiet lately, right?"

"Yeah. But it feels like we're waiting for the other

shoe to drop. We know the killer hasn't gone anywhere, because he can't."

"Maybe he's decided to stop killing people."

"That's not usually the way it works with serial killers. I think he's waiting for something."

"Waiting for what?"

"I don't know." He patted her shoulder, then kissed her cheek. "Don't let down your guard," he said. "And I'll see you Sunday morning."

She opened the door of the exam room just wide enough to watch him saunter down the short hallway to the door to the lobby. Now she would be the one waiting, anticipating time alone with Ryder and where that might lead.

THE SNOW THAT had been falling when Ryder awoke Sunday morning had all but stopped by the time he reached Darcy's house, and patches of blue were starting to show through the gray clouds. But Darcy, dressed in a bright yellow and blue parka and snow pants, would have brightened even the dreariest day. Ryder's heart gave a lurch as she walked out to meet him, her smile lighting her face. Oh yeah, he was definitely falling for this woman, though it was harder to read what she felt for him.

At least she looked happy enough to see him today, though maybe it was just the break in the snow that had her smiling. "I'm so relieved to see a change in the weather," she said.

"This was a great idea," he said, opening up the back of the Tahoe and taking the skis she handed to him. "Nothing like getting out in the fresh air to clear away the cobwebs."

"I've been looking forward to a little time off from work," she said, handing him her ski poles.

"I guess it hasn't been easy, handling the practice by yourself," he said. On top of grieving the loss of her friend, she was having to do the work of two people.

"In some ways it's been a blessing." She stepped back and tucked a stray lock of hair beneath her blue stocking cap. "I haven't had too much time to brood. But I haven't had much time off, either. One day soon I need to sit down and draw up a new schedule. I can't keep the office open ten hours a day, six days a week by myself."

"You could bring in another partner," he said.

She wrinkled her nose. "That would be hard to do. The partnership with Kelly worked because we had been such good friends for years. I don't know if I could bring in a stranger. If it were the other way around—if Kelly was the one having to look to replace me—it wouldn't be so hard. She loved meeting new people and she got along with everyone. It takes me a lot longer to warm up to people."

Her eyes met his and he wondered if she was warning him off—or letting him know how privileged he was to be invited closer to her.

She looked away and moved past him to deposit her backpack next to the skis. "I imagine you could use a break, too," she said. "With the roads closed, you're the only state patrol officer in town."

"Yes, though most of my patrol area is closed due to the snow," he said. "Which isn't so bad. It's left me more time to concentrate on the case."

Worry shadowed her face. "You're probably tired of people asking you if you have any suspects."

"I only wish I had a better answer to give than no." He shut the back of the Tahoe. "Maybe a day in the woods will give me a new perspective on the case."

They climbed into the truck and he turned back onto

the road. "Where should we go skiing?" she asked. "I know the trails up on Dixon Pass are popular."

Ryder shook his head. "The avalanche danger is too high up there right now. I thought we'd head down valley, to Silver Pick Recreation Area. There are some nice trails through the woods there, sheltered from the wind."

"Kelly and I hiked there this fall," she said. "Right after we moved here. The color in the trees was gorgeous." She settled back in her seat and gazed out the side window. "One of the things I love about living here is there are so many places to go hiking or skiing or just to sit and enjoy nature. The city has plenty of parks, but it's not the same." She glanced at him. "And before Kelly died, I always felt safe out here, even when I was alone. I guess I couldn't imagine any harm could come to me in such a peaceful place."

He tightened his grip on the steering wheel. "I hate that this killer has taken that peace away from you—and from a lot of other people."

"I guess we're naive to think small towns are immune from bad things and bad people," she said. "Or maybe, because crime is so rare in a place like this, it has a bigger impact."

"You would think that a killer hiding in a small population like this would be easier to find," he said. "But that isn't proving to be the case."

She leaned over and squeezed his arm, a gentle, reassuring gesture. "Today let's try not to think about any of that," she said. "Let's just enjoy the day and each other's company."

He covered her hand with his own. "It's a deal."

There were several cars and trucks parked at the recreation area, including a couple of trailers for hauling snow machines. "Snowmobilers have to use the trails on the other side of the road," Ryder said. "We'll probably hear them, but the trails on this side are only for skiers and snowshoers."

They unloaded their skis and packs and set out up an easy groomed trail. After a few strides they fell into a rhythm. The snow had stopped altogether now, only the occasional cascade of white powder sifting down from the trees that lined the trail. The air was sharp with cold, but the sun made it feel less biting and more invigorating.

They had traversed about a half mile up the trail when a loud boom shook the air. Darcy started. "What was that?"

Ryder looked in the direction the explosion had come from. "Sounds like avalanche mitigation up on the pass," he said. "That's good news. The weather forecast must call for clear weather and they're working to get the roads open."

"Oh." Darcy put a hand to her chest. "I guess I knew they used explosives—I just didn't expect for them to sound so loud."

"Sound carries a long way here. And those howitzers they use can be pretty loud."

"Howitzers?" she asked. "As in military weapons?"

"Yeah. They're actually on loan from the army. A lot of the avalanche control crews are ex-military. Their experience with explosives comes in handy. They'll try to bring down as much snow as possible, then get heavy equipment in to haul it off."

"So the highway could be open soon?"

"Maybe as early as tomorrow."

She grinned. "Everyone will be glad to hear it. You wouldn't think a whole town could feel claustrophobic, but it can. And it'll be good to restock all the stores."

"Hopefully the roads will stay clear for all the wedding guests who'll be arriving at the Walker ranch over the next few weeks," Ryder said. "Since some of the party live far away, the family has asked them to stay for an extended visit. They're making kind of a reunion of it, I guess."

"That sounds nice," she said. "It should be a beautiful wedding."

"Would you like to come to the ceremony and reception?" he asked. "I'm allowed to bring a date."

"Oh. Well…"

He cringed inwardly as her voice trailed off. Had he asked too much too soon?

"Yes. I'd love to come with you," she said.

"Good." He faced forward and set out again, though it felt as if his skis scarcely touched the snow.

They paused several times to rest and to take pictures. She snapped a shot of him posed near a snowman someone had built alongside the trail, then they took a selfie in front of a snow-draped blue spruce.

Their destination was a warming hut at the highest point of the trail. They reached it just after noon and raced to kick off their skis and rush inside. The rough-hewn log hut contained a wooden table, several benches and an old black iron woodstove that someone had stoked earlier in the day, so that the warmth wrapped around them like a blanket when they entered.

They peeled off their jackets and Ryder added wood to the stove from the pile just outside the door, while Darcy unpacked a thermos of hot cocoa, two turkey and cheese sandwiches, clementines and peanut butter cookies.

"What a feast," Ryder said as he straddled the bench across from her. He sipped the cocoa, then bit into the sandwich. "Nothing like outdoor exercise to make such a simple meal taste fantastic."

She nodded her agreement, her mouth full of sandwich, laughter in her eyes. A few moments later, when they had both devoured about half the food, she said, "Kelly and I didn't hike this far in the fall. I didn't even know this was up here."

"At the solstice a bunch of people ski or hike up here and have a bonfire," he said. "You should come."

"Maybe I will."

Maybe she would come with him. It felt a little dangerous to think that far ahead, but satisfying, too. Maybe the two of them would have what it took to make it as a couple. This early in their acquaintance, when they were just feeling their way, getting to know each other, anything felt possible.

"Did you make these?" he asked, after taking a bite of a soft, chewy cookie.

She nodded. "I like to bake."

"They're delicious."

They sat side by side on a bench in front of the hut's one window, a view of the river valley spread out before them. "Road closure or not," he said, "I can't think of anywhere I'd rather be right now than here." He turned to her. "With you."

"Yes," she said. "I feel the same."

There wasn't anything more that needed saying after that. They sat in companionable silence until the cocoa and cookies were gone. "Ready to ski back down?" he asked.

"Yes. I want to stop near the river and take some more pictures of the snow in the trees."

They traveled faster going downhill, racing each other to the flat section of the trail along the river where they stopped and she took more pictures. By the time they started out again, the light was already beginning to fade, the air turning colder and the wind picking up.

When Ryder first heard the snowmobile, he mistook the noise for the wind in the trees. But Darcy, skiing ahead of him, stopped abruptly. "Is that a snowmobile?" she asked. "It sounds like it's heading this way."

"The snow and the trees can distort sound," he said. "All snowmobile traffic is on the other side of the road."

They skied on, but the roar of the machine increased as they emerged into an open area just past the river. "It's probably someone headed to the parking lot," Darcy called over her shoulder.

Ryder started to agree, then saw a flash of light over Darcy's shoulder. The snowmobile emerged from the trees ahead, a single headlight focused on them, a great rooster tail of snow arcing up behind the vehicle.

"What is he doing?" Darcy shouted as the machine bore down on them. She sidestepped off the main trail, but there was nowhere they could go that the snowmobile wouldn't be able to reach. The driver, face obscured by a helmet, leaned over the machine and gunned the engine. He was headed straight for them and showed no sign of veering away or slowing down.

Chapter Sixteen

Darcy stared at the snowmobile charging toward them. The roar of the engine shuddered through her, and the stench of burning diesel stung her nose. *Move!* a voice inside her shouted, but her limbs refused to obey, even as the machine closed the gap between them with alarming speed.

And then she was falling as Ryder slammed into her. They rolled together, a tangle of skis and packs and poles. The snowmobile roared past, a wave of snow washing over them in its wake.

"We've got to get out of these skis!" Ryder shouted. He reached back and slammed his hand onto the release of her skis, then untangled his own legs and pulled her to her feet. The snow off the trail was deep and soft, and she immediately sank to her knees, but Ryder held on to her, keeping her upright. "We have to get into the trees!" he shouted.

She followed his gaze behind them and her stomach turned over as the snowmobile driver made a wide turn and headed back toward them.

"Come on." Ryder tugged on her arm. In his other hand, he held a gun. Was he really going to shoot the driver? If he did, would that even stop their attacker in time?

The snowmobile bucked forward, and she lurched

ahead, as well, Ryder still gripping her arm tightly. They fought their way through heavy snow, every step like walking in a dream, her legs heavy, trapped in the snow. They were in an open field, the line of trees fifty yards or more away, the roar of the snowmobile ever louder as it raced toward them again.

"He's crazy!" she shouted. "How can he hit us without wrecking?"

Ryder shook his head but didn't answer, all his energy divided between breaking a path for them through the drifts and keeping an eye on the snowmobile.

We aren't going to make it, Darcy thought, when she dared to look back and saw the snowmobile only a few dozen yards from them.

The report of Ryder's gun was deafening, and she screamed in spite of herself. The snowmobile veered, then righted. Ryder fired again, and the bullet hit the windscreen, shattering it.

The snowmobile wobbled, then righted itself once more, then the driver turned and headed back the way he had come, away from them.

"I have to go after him," Ryder said. He tucked the pistol into the pocket of his parka. "Can you make it back to the parking lot okay on your own? I'll meet you there."

She nodded, too numb to speak.

He half jogged through the snow, back to the trail and his skis, then took off, kicking hard, making long strides, and was soon out of sight.

She moved much more slowly, her legs leaden. By the time she reached the trail she had begun to shake so hard it took her half a dozen tries to put on both skis. Then she started slowly back toward the parking lot, her movements more shuffle than glide, tears streaming down her face, her mind replaying over and over the sight of that snowmobile bearing down on them.

Ryder met her near the end of the trail. He took her pack from her and skied beside her all the way to the Tahoe, saying nothing. Then he helped her out of her skis and into the truck. "He was gone by the time I got here," he said. "I followed his tracks across the road, but he disappeared into the woods."

"Do you think you hit him when you fired?" she asked, struggling to keep her voice steady.

"No. I hit the machine, but not him."

Neither of them spoke on the drive back to her house. Ryder turned the heat up and Darcy huddled in her seat, unable to get warm. At the house he took her keys and unlocked the door, then she followed him inside.

He closed the door behind them, then pulled her close. They stood with their arms wrapped around each other for a long moment.

"I thought we were going to die," she said, unable to keep her voice from shaking.

He cupped her face in his hands and stared into her eyes. "We didn't die," he said. "We're going to be okay."

She slid her hands around to the back of his head and pulled his mouth down to hers. She kissed him as if this might be the last chance she ever had of a kiss. Need surged through her—the need to be with him, to feel whole again with him.

She had wasted so much time being cautious, waiting to be sure. Sure of what? What was more sure than how much she wanted him right this minute? What could be more sure than the regret she would have if she didn't seize hold of this moment to live fully?

Ryder returned the kiss with the same ferocity, sliding

his hands down to caress her ribs, then bringing them up to cup her breasts. She leaned into him and moved her own hands underneath his sweater, tugging at the knit shirt he wore underneath the wool.

His stomach muscles contracted at her touch, and heat flooded through her. She spread her fingers across his stomach, then slid up to his chest, the soft brush of his chest hair awaking every nerve ending.

He nipped at her jaw, then pulled her fleece top over her head and tossed it aside, followed by her silk long underwear top. Then he began kissing the top of her breasts where they swelled over her bra, and her vision lost focus and she sagged in his arms.

He paused and looked up at her. "How far do you want this to go?" he asked. "Because if you want me to leave, I should probably stop now."

She hugged him more tightly. "Don't leave." Smiling, she reached back and unhooked her bra, then sent it sailing across the room. Out of the corner of her eye, she watched as one of the cats—Pumpkin, she thought—pounced on the lacy toy, which only made her grin more broadly.

The look in Ryder's eyes was worth every bit of the cold chill that made her nipples pucker. He started to reach for her, but she intercepted his hands. "Come on," she said, and led the way to the stairs to the loft.

The stairs were steep and narrow, but they negotiated them in record speed. In the loft Ryder had to duck to avoid hitting his head on the ceiling, but once sprawled on the queen-size bed, his height didn't matter so much. They wasted no time divesting each other of their clothes, then, naked, they slid under the covers.

"This is nice and cozy," he said, pulling her close. "I like the flannel sheets."

"Not as sexy as silk, maybe, but a lot warmer," she agreed.

"Trust me, with you in them, flannel is incredibly sexy." He kissed her, long and deep, while his hands explored her body, learning the shape and feel of her while she did the same with him.

Their leisurely movements gradually became more intense and insistent. Ryder leaned back to study her face. "I probably should have asked this before," he said. "But do you have any protection?"

Smiling, she rolled away from him and opened the drawer in the bedside table. She handed him the box of condoms.

"This has never been opened," he said. "Did you buy them just for me?"

"That's right," she said. "I've been planning to seduce you for weeks now." Then she grew more serious. "Actually, Kelly gave them to me in a whole box of things when I moved into this place. She said coming here was my chance to get out of my shell and improve my social life. I told her she was being overly optimistic, but maybe I was wrong."

"She was a good friend," Ryder said. "I wish I'd known her better."

"Ha! If you had known her, you never would have looked twice at me," she said. "Men took one look at her blond hair and knockout figure and they couldn't see anything else."

"I prefer brunettes." He took a condom from the box. "And your figure definitely knocks me out."

She sat up and watched him put on the condom, almost

dizzy with desire, and then he started to push her back down on the mattress. She stiffened in spite of herself, then tried to force herself to relax. This was Ryder. He wasn't going to hurt her. Everything was going to be fine.

Ryder stilled, then took his hands from her and sat back. "What's wrong?" he asked.

"Nothing's wrong."

"Something's wrong. I felt it. Tell me what I did so I won't do it again."

She looked away, ashamed, and then angry at the shame. "I just… I don't like someone looming over me. A man. I… I can't relax."

Understanding transformed his face. "I should have realized," he said. "I'm sorry."

"No, it's okay." She sat up, arms hugged across her stomach, fighting back tears. Things had been going so well, and she had to ruin it.

"Hey." He touched her shoulder lightly. "It's okay." He lay down and patted the sheet beside him. "We don't have to rush. We'll take our time and do what feels good for both of us."

Hesitantly, not trusting herself, she lay down beside him again. He stroked her arm, gently, then moved her hand to rest on his chest. "Feel that?" he asked.

She waited, then felt the faint beat of his heart beneath her palm. She looked into his eyes. "Your heartbeat," she said.

He lifted her palm and kissed it, the brush of his tongue sending a jolt of sensation through her. "That's the sound of me, wanting you," he said.

She closed her eyes and he kissed her eyelids, then she was kissing his forehead, his cheek, his ear. They began to move together, desire rebuilding, but somehow deeper, more intense, this time. Facing him, she draped her thigh over his and, eyes open, watching him, she guided him into her. She didn't feel afraid or overwhelmed or anything but aware of her own body and of his—of the tension in his muscles and the heat of her own skin and the wonderful sensation of being filled and fulfilled.

She kept her eyes open as they moved together, and when her climax overtook her, he kissed her, swallowing her cries, and then she saw his face transform with his own moment of release. They held each other, rocking together and murmuring words that weren't really words yet that conveyed a message they both understood.

When at last he eased away from her to dispose of the condom, she let him go reluctantly. When he returned, he pulled her close again, her head cradled on his shoulder, his arm securely around him. The steady beat of his heart lulled her to sleep, the message it sent more powerful than any words.

Chapter Seventeen

Ryder breathed in the perfume of Darcy's hair, and reveled in her softness against him. The comfortable bed in this cozy loft seemed a world apart from the snowy landscape outside where a murderer might lurk. But he could only hide from that world so long, before duty and his conscience drove him to sit up and reach for his clothes.

"You're not leaving, are you?" Darcy shoved up onto one elbow, one bare shoulder exposed, tousled hair falling across her forehead. She looked so alluring, he wondered if he really had the strength to resist the temptation to dive back under the covers with her.

"I'm not leaving," he said, standing and tugging on his jeans. "But I have to call in a report about that snowmobiler." Later he'd have to file a report for his commander, explaining why he had discharged his weapon. "I should have called it in earlier."

"We were both a little distracted," she said, and the heated look that accompanied these words had him aroused and ready all over again.

"I'll, uh, be right back," he said, grabbing a shirt and heading for the stairs.

Three of the four cats met him at the bottom of the steps, studying him with golden eyes, tails twitching.

"It's okay," Ryder said, stepping past them. "I'm not the enemy."

He punched in Travis's number and while he waited for the sheriff to answer, he studied the view out the window. The sun was setting, slanting light through the trees and bathing the snow in a rosy glow. It was the kind of scene depicted in paintings and photographs, or on posters with sayings about peace and serenity—not the kind of setting where one expected to encounter danger.

"Ryder? What's up?" Travis's voice betrayed no emotion, only brisk efficiency.

"Darcy and I were skiing over at Silver Pick rec area and a snowmobiler tried to run us down," Ryder said. "I fired off a couple of shots and he fled. I followed, but I lost him on the snowmobile trails on the other side of the road."

"When was this?" Travis asked.

Ryder looked around and spotted the clock on the microwave, which read four thirty. "Around three o'clock," he said.

"And you're just now calling it in?"

"Yes."

Travis paused as if waiting for further explanation, but Ryder didn't intend to offer any. "All right," the sheriff said. "Can you give me a description of the guy, or his snowmobile?"

"It was a Polaris, and one of my shots hit the windscreen and shattered it. The driver was wearing black insulated coveralls and a full helmet, black. That's all I've got."

"Let me make sure I'm clear on this," Travis said. "You and Darcy were on the ski trails, on the east side of the highway, closest to the river, right?"

"Right. We were headed back to the parking lot and

were in that open flat, maybe a quarter mile from the parking area. He came straight toward us. We bailed off the trail and tried to make it through the woods, but the snow there is thigh-deep and soft. He missed us his first pass, then turned and came back toward us. That's when I fired on him."

"How many shots?" Travis asked.

"Three. One hit the windscreen and two went wide."

"Hard to hit a moving target like that with a pistol," Travis said. "This doesn't sound like our serial killer. For one thing, running over someone with a snowmobile is a pretty inefficient way to kill someone."

"If he had hit us, chances are he'd have been injured himself," Ryder said. "He probably would have wrecked his machine and could have been thrown off it, too."

"So maybe he wasn't trying to hit you," Travis said. "Maybe he was playing a pretty aggressive game of chicken."

"Maybe," Ryder said. "But he sure looked serious to me."

"Ed Nichols has a Polaris snowmobile," Travis said. "Gage saw it when he interviewed him about his alibi for Kelly's murder."

Nichols. Ryder hadn't focused much attention on the veterinarian after all his alibis had checked out. Clearly, that had been a mistake. "We need to find out what he was doing this afternoon," Ryder said. "And check the windscreen of his snowmobile. Maybe he was the one who ran Darcy off the road that night, too."

"He has an alibi for that evening," Travis said. "He was cooking for a church spaghetti supper."

"It doesn't seem likely we'd be dealing with two different attackers," Ryder said. What could Darcy have done to make herself such a target?

"Question Darcy again," Travis said. "See if she can come up with anyone who might want to get back at her for something. Maybe she failed to save someone's sick dog, or someone disagreed with her bill—it doesn't take much to set some people off."

"I'll do that," Ryder said. "Let me know if you spot any snowmobiles with the windscreens shot out."

He ended the call and turned to find Darcy, wrapped in a pink fleece robe, standing at the bottom of the steps, watching him. "Do you have to go?" she asked.

"No." He pocketed the phone. "I can stay if you want."

"I'd like that." She moved to him and put her arms around him. He kissed the top of her head, wondering how she'd react if he suggested they go back to bed.

"I'd like to take a shower," she said, pulling away from him. "Unfortunately, my shower isn't big enough for two people."

"You go ahead," he said. "I'll clean up when you're done."

She nodded and headed for the bathroom. Once the water was running, Ryder called into his office. His supervisor was out, but he made his report to the duty officer and promised to follow up with the appropriate paperwork. When Darcy emerged from the shower, pink-cheeked, damp hair curling around her throat, he was studying a photo of her standing with an older couple. "Are these your parents?" he asked.

"My mom and her boyfriend." Darcy came to stand beside him. "That was taken the day I graduated from veterinary school."

"Where does she live?" Ryder asked.

"Denver. Though she isn't home that much. She travels a lot. Right now she's in China, I think. Or India?" She frowned. "It's hard to keep up. We're not close."

"I'm sorry," he said and meant it. Though he didn't see them often, he had always felt embraced by his own family.

"It's okay," she said.

"Where is your father?" he asked.

"I have no idea. He and my mother divorced when I was six months old. I never knew him."

His instinct was to tell her how sad this was, but clearly, she didn't want any sympathy. "What about your family?" she asked.

"My mom and dad are in Cheyenne," he said. "I have a brother in Seattle and a sister in Denver. We're all pretty close."

"That's nice." She patted his arm. "The shower is all yours."

When he emerged from the shower—which, in keeping with everything else in the house, was tiny—she handed him a glass of wine. "I don't have anything stronger in the house," she said. "I figured we could both use it."

She sat on the sofa, legs curled up beneath her robe, and he moved aside a couple of throw pillows and sat beside her, his arm around her shoulders. She snuggled close. "What a day, huh?" she said.

He stroked her shoulder. "Are you okay?"

"Better." She sipped the wine, then set the glass on the low table in front of them. "I can't promise I won't have nightmares about that snowmobile headed straight for us. I mean, it was scary when that guy ran me off the road, but this was worse. I felt so vulnerable, out there in the open. And he seemed closer, without a vehicle around him. The attack seemed so much more personal." She shuddered, and he set aside his glass to wrap his other arm around her.

They were both silent for a long moment. Ryder wondered if she was crying, but when she looked up at him, her eyes were dry. "Why is someone trying to kill me?" she asked.

"Kill you—or frighten you badly," Ryder said. He leaned forward and handed her her wineglass and picked up his own. "I know I've asked you this before, but can you think of anyone who might want to hurt you? A client or someone who wanted to rent this place and you beat them to it? Anything like that?"

She shook her head. "I've thought and thought and there isn't anyone."

"We checked on Jay Leverett," he said, not missing how she stiffened at the mention of the name.

"Oh?" she asked.

"He was released from prison two months ago. We're still trying to find out where he went after that."

"I'm sure I would recognize him if he was here in Eagle Mountain," she said. She set her now-empty wineglass aside and half turned to face Ryder. "Why would he come after me now—after all this time? It's been six years since he raped me, and I wasn't the first woman he had hurt—or the only one. Mine wasn't even the crime he was sentenced for—he was caught when he broke into a girls' dorm and attacked one of the women there. Why would he come after me?"

"What he did to you before didn't make sense, either," Ryder said. "And this may have nothing to do with him. We just need to be sure."

"Did whoever is after me kill Kelly and Christy and Fiona, too?" she asked.

"We don't know," Ryder said. "Your attacker could be someone different. As far as we know, Kelly and the others were never pursued prior to their deaths."

"How did I get to be so lucky?" She tried to smile but failed, and her voice shook.

He took both her hands in his—they were ice cold. "We can find you a safe place to stay until we've tracked this guy down," he said. "Travis's family probably has room at their ranch—or you could stay with me. My place isn't much, but you'd be safe there."

She nodded. "Maybe it's time for something like that," she said. "I mean, I don't want to be stupid about this—I just hate being chased out of my own home."

"I understand." He admired her independence, but was relieved she was smart enough to accept help. "My place isn't set up for cats, but if you tell me what you need…"

"I think I'll leave them here," she said. "I can come by and check on them every day."

"Do you want me to call Travis and have him ask his parents if you can stay with them, or are you comfortable moving in with me?"

"I'll stay with you." She leaned toward him once more, her hands on his shoulders. "I think I can trust you."

He knew how much those words meant, coming from her. He pulled her close. "We don't have to be in any hurry," he said. "What would you think if I spent the night here tonight?"

A slow smile spread across her lips. "I think that's a very good idea," she whispered and kissed him, a soft, deep kiss that hinted at much more to come.

HALF OF DARCY's clients canceled their appointments the next day. The highway had opened at last, and everyone was anxious to drive over the pass to do shopping and run errands. A steady stream of delivery trucks flowed into town. The prospect of new supplies, along with the abundant sunshine, had everyone in a jubilant mood.

"If I call the patients who still have appointments today and convince them to come in early, do you think we could close up ahead of schedule?" Stacy asked after yet another client called to move their appointment to another day. "I'd really like to get over to Junction and do some shopping."

"That sounds like a good idea," Darcy said.

"You could come with me, if you like."

"Thanks, but I've got plenty to keep me busy here." She and Ryder had agreed that she would head back to her place after work, pack up whatever she thought she needed for the next few days, make sure the cats were settled, then drive over to his house.

It's only temporary, she reminded herself. *It's not as if we're really moving in together.* After all, they had known each other only a few days, even though it felt as if he already knew her better than anyone ever had. He had learned to read her moods and anticipate her thoughts, attuned to her in a way that was both touching and awe-inspiring.

When they reopened the office after lunch, Darcy was surprised to find Ken waiting outside the clinic. "What can we do for you?" Stacy asked as she waited for Darcy to unlock the door. "Are you overdue for your rabies shot?"

"Very funny." He followed them into the clinic. "I just stopped by to see how you're doing," he said to Darcy.

"I'm fine." Had word somehow gotten out about her encounter with the homicidal snowmobiler the day before?

"Why wouldn't she be fine?" Stacy asked.

Ken glared at her. "Don't you have work to do?"

"It's much more fun to annoy you."

Ken turned his back on her. "The sheriff's department and that highway patrolman haven't done anything to stop this Ice Cold Killer. Everyone is wondering who he's going to kill next."

"The local law enforcement officers are working very hard to try to stop the killer," Darcy said.

"But they aren't getting anywhere, are they? They don't have any suspects, do they?" He stared at her as if expecting an answer.

"I wouldn't know," she said.

"I thought you might, since you and that highway patrolman are so cozy."

He looked as if he expected her to confirm or deny this. She did neither. She certainly wasn't going to tell Ken she was moving in with Ryder. She had decided not to share their plans with anyone. Not because she was ashamed, but because she and Ryder had agreed the fewer people who knew where she was, the safer she would be.

She took her white coat from its peg and put it on. "Thanks for stopping by," she said. "I have to get ready to see my afternoon patients."

"I know the female teachers at my school are terrified," he continued. "The male teachers have agreed to walk them to their cars, kind of like bodyguards."

"That's very thoughtful of you," Darcy said.

"You should do something like that here," he said.

"I'm being careful."

"Now that the highway is open, maybe the killer will take the opportunity to get out of here," Stacy said. "Maybe he's already gone."

"I guess that would be good," Ken said.

"I'd rather see him caught and stopped," Darcy said. "I hate to think of him moving on to somewhere else to kill more women."

"Now that the road is open, maybe they'll get some experts in who can track him down," Ken said.

Darcy resisted the impulse to defend Ryder. She sensed Ken was only trying to bait her, and she wasn't going to waste energy sparring with him.

He shifted his weight to his other hip, apparently prepared to stay until she ordered him away. "I guess now that the road is open, Kelly's parents will be coming to clear her things out of the duplex," he said.

"I guess so." She frowned, thinking of all the clinic supplies in the garage. "I'll need to clear out the garage," she said. "And find some place to store all that stuff here."

"Why don't you just move in, instead?" Ken asked. "My landlord would be happy to find a renter so easily. You'd be closer to work and town and you could still use the garage for storage."

"I like the place where I am now," she said.

"Sure. But it's not safe for you out there. You're way too vulnerable without other people around. If you lived in town, I'd be right next door, and there are other neighbors nearby."

She couldn't tell him that having him right on the other side of her living room wall wasn't something she looked forward to. "I'll be fine. And now I really do need to get ready for my patients." Not waiting for an answer, she turned and walked into the back room, closing the door from the waiting room firmly behind her.

A few moments later Stacy joined her in the section of the big back room they used as their in-house laboratory, where Darcy was unpacking a new supply of blood collection tubes. "Poor Ken," Stacy said. "He's still crazy about you. He can't get over losing you."

"He never had me to lose," Darcy said. "We only went out three times." And she had only agreed to the third date so that she could tell him to his face that she didn't have romantic feelings for him and didn't believe she ever would. She had tried to let him down gently, but she had also been clear that she didn't want to date him again.

"Still, I feel sorry for him," Stacy said. "He's one of these guys who tries too hard."

"Then you date him."

"I'm married, remember?" She leaned back against the lab table. "I didn't say I thought you ought to go out with him. Ryder is a much better guy for you." She grinned. "How did your date go yesterday?"

"It went…well."

"Uh-oh. I distinctly heard a 'but' in there. What happened?"

Darcy pushed aside the half-empty box of tubes. "You can't tell anyone, okay?"

"Cross my heart." She made an X across her chest with her forefinger.

"We had a great time," Darcy said. "It was a beautiful day and we skied up to the warming hut at the top of the hill and had lunch."

Stacy looked disappointed. "That's not a 'but.'"

"I'm getting to the bad part." She took a deep breath. Better to just come out with it. "On the way back down, a guy on a snowmobile tried to run us over."

"I thought snowmobiles weren't allowed on the ski trails," Stacy said.

"They're not. But he deliberately tried to kill us. When he missed the first time, he turned around and headed for us again."

"Sheesh, woman! What is with you and guys trying to run you down?" She touched Darcy's arm. "Sorry. I wasn't trying to be insensitive. Are you okay?"

Darcy nodded. "I was terrified at the time. But Ryder

pulled his gun and shot at the guy and he raced off. Ryder tried to follow, but he got away."

"Do you have any idea who it was?"

"No. He was wearing a full helmet with a visor. There was no way to know."

The bells on the front door announced the arrival of their first afternoon patient. A dog's insistent bark confirmed this. "That will be Judy Ericson and Tippy," Stacy said. She squeezed Darcy's arm. "I'm so glad you're okay. And I hope they find out who it was."

"One of Ryder's bullets hit the windshield of the snowmobile," Darcy said. "He's hoping that will help him find the guy."

"Ryder should talk to Bud O'Brien—he rents snowmobiles out of his garage," Stacy said. "If this maniac was a tourist who's stuck here, he might not have his own snowmobile. He'd have to rent one."

"That's a great idea. I'll pass it on."

Stacy headed to the door, but stopped before she opened it and turned to face Darcy again. "I think I agree with Ken on this one—you shouldn't be out at your place by yourself. You're welcome to stay with me and Bill."

"I'll be fine," Darcy said. "I promise."

Stacy nodded. "At least you have one thing going for you," she said.

"What's that?"

"You've got Ryder on your side. That's worth a lot."

Chapter Eighteen

"Now that the highway is open, the Colorado Bureau of Investigation is sending in its own team to investigate the murders," Ryder told Travis when they met at the sheriff's department Monday morning.

"So I hear," Travis said. "Good luck to them. So far we don't have a lot to go on."

"When I spoke with my boss this morning, he told me to deliver the physical evidence to the state lab in Junction as soon as possible," Ryder said. "I had to tell him we didn't have any physical evidence—no blood, no hair or fibers, no prints."

"I checked with Ed Nichols about his whereabouts yesterday afternoon," Travis said. "He says he was home with his wife, watching television."

"That's a hard alibi to disprove if his wife backs him up," Ryder said. "What about the snowmobile?"

"It wasn't there," Travis said. "He said it's at O'Brien's Garage, waiting on a part."

"A new windscreen?"

"I don't know. O'Brien's was closed when I went by there, and the phone goes to an answering machine. Bud didn't answer his home phone, either."

"I'll go by his house," Ryder said. "He'll want as much as anyone to get to the bottom of this. But first, I want to interview Tim and Alex again. I want to see what they were up to yesterday afternoon."

"There was only one man on that snowmobile," Travis said.

"Maybe it was one of them—maybe it wasn't," Ryder said.

"The problem I have is with motive," Travis said. "Why go after Darcy?"

Gage joined them. "I heard about what happened yesterday," Gage said. "Is Darcy okay?"

"She's holding up," Ryder said. He turned to Travis once more. "She tried again to think of someone who might have a grudge against her and came up with nothing." He hesitated. He wanted to honor the trust Darcy had placed in him by revealing her past, but he couldn't keep information pertaining to the case from Travis. "She does have an ex-boyfriend who went to jail after kidnapping and raping her," he said. "It happened six years ago, and he was released from prison two months ago, after serving time for another crime. I received a report about him yesterday—no current address. But Darcy is sure she hasn't seen him here in town."

"He could have avoided her," Travis said. "He wouldn't want her to know he was behind the attacks."

"Right. His name is Jay Leverett," Ryder said. "I gave his description to the other officers, and it's on your desk."

"We'll be on the lookout for him," Travis said. He turned to Gage. "I need you to contact Bud O'Brien," he said. "Find out why Ed Nichols's snowmobile is at his garage, how long it's been there and if it has a damaged windscreen."

"Will do," Gage said.

Travis turned back to Ryder. "I'll go with you to interview Tim and Alex."

"We should try to get Darcy into a safe house," Travis said when he and Ryder were in Travis's cruiser. "I can make some calls…"

"She'll never go for that," Ryder said. "And she has a business to run here in town."

"I can try to run extra patrols out her way, but I don't really have the personnel," Travis said.

"It's okay. I talked her into moving in with me."

Travis glanced at him, one eyebrow quirked, but all he said was, "All right, then."

No vehicles were parked in the driveway at the cabin where Alex and Tim were staying, and no one answered Travis's knock. "Maybe they left town already," Ryder said. He scanned the snow-covered yard. A black plastic trash can on rollers sat against the house, next to a half cord of firewood. No snowmobile.

Travis walked along the narrow front porch and peered into a window. "If they did, they left behind most of their stuff," he said.

Ryder cupped his hands against the windowpane and studied the clothing, shoes, beer cans, half-empty bags of chips and video game controllers scattered across the sofa and coffee table. "Yeah, it doesn't look like they went back to Denver yet," he agreed.

The two men returned to Travis's cruiser. "What now?" Ryder asked.

"I need to run up to my folks' ranch," Travis said. "I've got a couple of guests that are supposed to arrive now that the road is open. One of them is the caterer and I want to make sure she has everything she needs."

"Rainey and Doug Whittington aren't doing the food for the wedding?"

"They wanted to, but this woman is a friend of Lacy's. It was important to her to have her do the wedding and I wasn't going to argue. And Rainey is always complaining about how much work all the wedding guests are for her, so she should appreciate the help."

Rainey struck Ryder as the type who wouldn't want to share her kitchen with anyone, but he kept that opinion to himself. "Speaking of the Whittingtons, does Doug have a snowmobile?" he asked.

"He doesn't own one," Travis said. "But he certainly has access to several. I'll check on that while I'm up there."

Ryder glanced back toward the house. "I'll swing by here later and try to catch these two—try to find out what their plans are." He started to mention the lack of a snowmobile but was interrupted by the insistent beeping from his shoulder-mounted radio. "Report to Dixon Pass for one-vehicle accident. Vehicle is blocking the road."

"Guess that means the pass is closed again," Travis said. "It's going to be a long winter."

Ryder nodded. "It's already too long for me."

DARCY WAVED GOODBYE to Stacy and headed for the Green Monster. As long as she still had the truck, she might as well move the boxes from Kelly's garage to the office. She told herself she was being practical, tackling the job now, and tried to ignore the voice in the back of her head that said she was only delaying taking her things to Ryder's house.

Not that she wasn't looking forward to spending more time with him—she definitely was. And she knew she would be much safer with what amounted to her own personal bodyguard. But moving in with a man, even temporarily, was a big step. One she wasn't sure she was ready to take. She certainly wouldn't be doing this now when they had known each other so little time, if circumstances—or rather, a deranged man who was possibly a killer—hadn't forced her hand.

She pulled into the driveway of the duplex, relieved to see no sign of Ken or his truck. The house looked even more neglected when she stepped inside, the air stale, the furniture lightly covered with dust. She made her way to the garage and opened the automatic door from the inside, then set about transferring boxes to the back of the truck. Fortunately, none of the cartons was particularly heavy, though by the time she had filled the truck bed, she felt as if she had had a workout. She slammed the tailgate shut and surveyed the full bed. She had managed to get everything in.

Something cold kissed her cheek and she looked up into a flurry of gently falling white flakes. More snow felt like an insult at this point, but she reminded herself this was what winter in the mountains was all about. She needed to get used to it.

She went back inside to shut the garage door, but stopped just inside the doorway. This might be the last time she was ever in this house—a place that held so many memories. She and Kelly had spent countless evenings here, drinking wine and eating pizza, binge-watching television or planning the next steps for the veterinary practice. She could almost see her friend, seated in the corner of the sofa, a bowl of popcorn in her lap, her hair pulled up in a messy ponytail, head thrown back, laughing. The memory made her smile, even as unshed tears pinched at her throat.

From the living room she walked down a short hallway to the master bedroom, the bed unmade as it almost always was, clothes thrown over a chair, shoes discarded just inside the doorway. She bent and picked up a red high heel. Kelly loved shoes, and was always encouraging Darcy to go for prettier, sexier footwear. She understood Darcy had no desire to call attention to herself with provocative clothing, but she tried to do whatever she could to help her friend get over the fear behind those inhibitions.

The two had met only a few months after Darcy's rape. Kelly had come in late to a class and taken the vacant seat next to Darcy. In the next five minutes she had borrowed a pen, some notepaper, shared half a carrot cake muffin and invited Darcy to have lunch with her. Swept along in what she later thought of as Hurricane Kelly, Darcy had found herself befriended by this vibrant, fearless woman. Though their personalities were so different, they bonded quickly. When Kelly learned about Darcy's traumatic experience, she had become her biggest cheerleader and defender.

When she had first visited Darcy's apartment and seen the array of locks on the door—and learned that Darcy left the lights on all night, even though it made it hard to sleep—she had invited Darcy to move in with her. Gradually, Darcy had gained the confidence to sleep without the lights on. Kelly had found a therapist who specialized in helping rape victims, and had accompanied Darcy to the first appointment.

Though Kelly had been nurturing and protective, she had refused to let Darcy become dependent on her. At every turn, Kelly encouraged Darcy to try new things, take new risks and expand her boundaries. She could be overbearing, and the two friends had had their share of disagreements. But in the end Kelly had saved her. It grieved Darcy beyond words that she hadn't been able to save her friend.

She shook her head, set the shoe on the dresser and left the room. Time to get on with it. As she passed through the kitchen on her way to the garage, she decided to check Kelly's pantry for more cat food. No sense letting it go to waste. She found an unopened bag of dry food, and half a dozen cans, as well as a brand-new catnip mouse. The cats would appreciate a new toy, and it would help assuage her guilt at abandoning them while she stayed with Ryder.

She was searching for a bag to put the food in, humming to herself, when pain jolted her. The cat food cans tumbled from her arms and rolled across the kitchen floor as blackness overtook her.

Chapter Nineteen

The eighteen-wheeler had slid sideways across the highway near the top of Dixon Pass, until the back wheels of the trailer slipped off the edge, while the rest of the truck sprawled across both lanes. The driver had somehow managed to stop, and gravity and one large boulder had prevented the rig from sliding farther. The road was at its narrowest here, with almost no shoulders and no guardrails. The driver, who had bailed out of the cab, now stood in the shelter of a rock overhang, staring through a curtain of falling snow, hands shoved in the pockets of his leather coat, while they waited for a wrecker to come and winch the rig all the way back onto the road.

"The wrecker should be here in about ten minutes," Ryder told the driver, ending the call from his dispatcher. "What are you hauling?"

"Insulation." He wiped his hand across his face. "Yesterday I had a load of bottled water. All those heavy bottles probably would have shifted and taken me on over the side." His hand shook as he returned it to his pocket.

"You got off lucky," Ryder said.

"Yeah. I guess so."

Ryder moved away and, shoulders hunched against the falling snow, hit the button to call Darcy. He needed to let her know he was going to be late. She should let herself into the house with the key he had given her and make herself at home. Even though they had both agreed this stay would only be temporary, he wanted her to feel she could treat his place as her own. He let the call ring, then frowned as it went to voice mail. Maybe she was with a late patient and couldn't be interrupted. He left a message and stowed the phone again as a man in a puffy red coat and a fur hat strode toward him through the falling flakes.

"How much longer is the road going to be closed?" the man asked in the tone of someone who is much too busy to be stalled by petty annoyances.

"Another hour at least," Ryder said. "Maybe more. It depends on how long it takes to move the truck."

"You people need to do a better job of keeping the highway open," the man said. "Isn't that what we're paying you for?"

"I'm charged with keeping the public safe," Ryder said.

"They should keep these big rigs off the road when the weather is like this," the man said. "They're always causing trouble."

Ryder could have pointed out that passenger cars had more accidents than trucks, but decided not to waste his breath. "A wrecker is on the way to deal with this truck," he said. "If you don't want to wait, you can turn around."

"I can't turn around," he said. "I have business in Eagle Mountain."

"Then you'll need to go back to your vehicle and wait."

The man wanted to argue, Ryder could tell, but a stern look from Ryder suppressed the urge. He turned and stalked back toward his SUV. Ryder didn't even give in to the urge to laugh when he slipped on the icy pavement and almost fell.

Ryder's phone rang and he took the call from Travis.

"I checked at the ranch and none of our snow machines are damaged," Travis said. "And Rainey swears Doug was helping her in the kitchen all yesterday afternoon. I haven't heard yet from Gage about Ed's snowmobile."

"Thanks for checking," Ryder said. "Did your caterer make it?"

"She called Lacy a little while ago and told her she's stuck in traffic. Apparently, a wreck has the highway closed again."

"Yeah. We're going to get it cleared away in an hour or two." He looked up at the gently falling snow. "I'm hoping the highway department can keep it open. Looks like we've got more snow."

"I'll try to get by Alex and Tim's place tomorrow to talk to them," Travis said.

"I'll do it on my way home this afternoon," Ryder said. "It's on my way." He really wanted to talk to those two before they slipped out of town.

Two hours later the wrecker had winched the eighteen-wheeler to safety. The driver, and all the cars that had piled up behind him, were safely on their way, and a Colorado Department of Transportation plow trailed along behind them, pushing aside the six inches of snow that had accumulated on the roadway. As long as the plows kept running and no avalanche chutes filled and dumped their loads on the highway, things would flow smoothly.

Ryder turned traffic patrol over to a fellow officer and headed back into Eagle Mountain. He tried Darcy's phone again—still no answer. Maybe she'd forgotten to charge it, or was simply too busy to answer it, he told himself. He resisted the urge to drive straight to his house, hoping to find her there, and stuck with his plan of interviewing Tim and Alex.

But first, he had to stop for gas. He was fueling the

Tahoe when a red Jeep pulled in alongside him. "Hello, Ryder," Stacy said.

"Hi, Stacy," he said. "You're getting off work a little late, aren't you?"

"Oh, I've been off hours," she said, getting out of her car and walking around to the pump. "We closed up early and I went into Junction to do some shopping. I made it back just before the road closed again, but then I had more errands to run here in town." She indicated the back of the Jeep, which was piled high with bags and boxes. "It's been a while."

If she had closed the clinic early, then Darcy probably hadn't been with a patient when he called earlier. So why wasn't she answering her phone? "Do you know where Darcy headed after you closed?" he asked.

"She said she had things to do," Stacy said.

"Did she say what?"

"Easy there, officer. Is something wrong?"

He reined in his anxiety. "I've tried to call her a couple of times and she isn't answering."

Stacy frowned. "That isn't like her. She said something earlier about needing to get all the clinic supplies out of Kelly's duplex. I guess now that the highway is open again, Kelly's parents want to come and clean it out. Maybe she decided to take care of that."

Maybe so. Though that still didn't explain why she hadn't answered his calls.

He headed for Tim's aunt's cabin next, determined to get that interview out of the way. The gray Toyota with the dent in the front quarter-panel sat parked in the driveway of the cabin, a frosting of snow obscuring the windows. Ryder parked his Tahoe behind the Toyota and made his way up the unshoveled walk to the vehicle. A deep indentation ran the length of the driver's side front quarter-panel, the metal gouged as if by a sharp object.

Ryder straightened and made his way to the front door. Alex answered his knock, dressed in black long underwear pants and top. "Hey," he said. "What you need?"

"Can I come in?" Ryder asked. "I need to ask a few questions."

Alex shrugged. "I guess so." He held the door open.

Tim was sprawled across the sofa, wearing green-and black-check flannel pants and a Colorado State University sweatshirt, a video game controller in his hands. He sat up and frowned at Ryder. "What do you want?"

"The highway is open," Ryder said, stepping around a pile of climbing gear—ropes and packs and shoes. "I figured the two of you would be headed back to Denver."

"We took advantage of the great weather to go climbing." Alex sat on the end of the sofa and picked up a beer from the coffee table. "We don't have to be back in class until the end of the month, anyway."

"What do you care?" Tim asked, his attention on the television screen, which was displaying a video game that seemed to revolve around road racing.

"What did the two of you do Sunday?" Ryder asked.

"What did we do Sunday?" Tim asked Alex.

"We went climbing." Alex sipped the beer.

"Where did you go?" Ryder asked.

"Those cliffs over behind the park," Alex said. "And before you ask if anyone saw us, yeah, they did. Two women. We went out with them that night."

"I'll need their names and contact information," Ryder said.

"Why?" Tim asked. "Did another woman get iced?" He laughed, as if amused by his joke.

"Have you visited Silver Pick Recreation Area while you've been in town?" Ryder asked.

"We checked it out," Alex said. "We didn't see any good climbing."

"Good snowmobile trails," Ryder said.

"We talked about renting a couple of machines," Tim said. "Too expensive. Climbing's free."

"Since when are you concerned about us having a good time?" Alex asked.

"We're looking for a snowmobiler who threatened a couple of people out at Silver Pick Sunday afternoon. He tried to run them down with his snowmobile."

"It wasn't us," Alex said.

"Maybe it was the same idiot who smashed my truck," Tim said.

"Yeah," Alex said. "What are you doing about trying to find that guy?"

"I don't think there's a guy to find," Ryder said.

"What?" Tim sat up straight. "Are you calling us liars?"

"I took another look at that dent on your truck," Ryder said. "It's too low to the ground to have been made by another car. And too sharp."

"It is not," Tim said.

"The more I think about it, the more it looks like it was made by those big chunks of granite that edge the parking lot near the ice climbing area out on County Road Fourteen," Ryder said. "It's easy enough to do—don't pay attention to what you're doing and you can run into one of them, scrape the heck out of your car."

"You can't prove it," Tim said.

"I'll bet if I went out there, I'd find paint from your truck on one of the rocks," Ryder said.

Tim and Alex exchanged looks. "Why would we

bother making up a story and getting the police involved if it wasn't true?" Alex asked.

"If someone else caused the damage to your car, maybe you thought you could get your insurance to pay for it under your uninsured motorist coverage," Ryder said. "It works like that in other states—for instance, in Texas, where you said you were from. But it doesn't work that way in Colorado. In Colorado you have to have collision coverage in order for the insurance to pay."

"No way!" Tim looked at Alex. "You told me we could get the insurance company to pay. Now what am I going to do?"

Alex ignored his friend. He looked at Ryder. "If you think you can prove something, have at it. Otherwise, why don't you leave us alone?"

"I'll leave for now," Ryder said. "But you'll be hearing from me again." Tomorrow he would go to the parking lot and try to find the rock they had hit. Filing a false report to a peace officer was at best a misdemeanor, but the charge would be a hassle for the two young men, and having to deal with it might teach them a lesson.

From the cabin to the place Ryder rented was only a short drive. His heart sank when he saw that the driveway was empty. He hurried into the house, hoping to see some sign that Darcy had been there, but everything was just as he had left it. No suitcases or bags or any of Darcy's belongings. He pulled out his phone and dialed her number again. Still no answer. What was going on?

DARCY WOKE TO familiar surroundings, sure she was in her own bed, but with the terrible knowledge that something was very wrong. When she tried to sit up, she discovered that her hands were tied to the headboard, and her ankles were bound together. She began to shake with terror, almost overwhelmed with the memory of another time when she had been tied to a bed, unable to escape her tormentor.

"Don't struggle now. You don't want to hurt yourself." Ken leaned over her, his smile looking to her eyes like a horrible grimace.

"What are you doing?" she asked. The memory of being in Kelly's kitchen flooded back. She had been looking at cat food and the next thing she knew, she woke up here. "Did you hit me on the head?"

"It was for your own good," Ken said. "If you had listened to me when I offered to let you move in with me, it wouldn't have been necessary."

"Let me go!" She struggled against the ropes that held her. The bed shook and creaked with her efforts, but she remained trapped.

"No, I can't do that," Ken said. "If I do that, you'll only call the sheriff, or that state trooper, Ryder. Then I'd have to leave and you'd be here all alone and unprotected."

"I don't need protection," she said.

"But you do. There's a serial killer in town who's murdering young women just like you. You don't want to be his next victim, do you?"

She stared at him, searching for signs that he had lost his mind. He looked perfectly ordinary and sane. Except every word he uttered chilled her to the core.

He sat on the side of the bed, the mattress dipping toward her. "What are you doing?" she asked, trying to inch away from him.

He put his hand on her leg. "I'm going to protect you."

"Did you kill Kelly and those other women?" she asked. If he was the murderer, was confronting him this way a mistake? But she had to know.

His hand on her leg tightened. "Is that what you think

of me?" he asked. "That I'm a killer? A man who hates women?" He slid his hand up her leg. "I love women. I love you. I've loved you since the first time I saw you with Kelly. I kept waiting for you to see it, but you couldn't. Or you wouldn't." His fingers closed around her thigh, digging deep.

"Stop!" She tried to squirm out of his grasp. "You're hurting me."

"I decided I had to do something to wake you up," he said, continuing to massage her thigh painfully. "To make you see how much I love you."

"If you loved me, you wouldn't frighten me this way," she said. "You wouldn't hurt me."

"I won't hurt you." He leaned over her, his voice coaxing. "In fact, I'm going to show you how gentle I can be." He moved his hand to the waistband of her slacks.

She closed her eyes and swallowed down a scream. There was no one to hear her, and if she screamed, she might give in to the panic that clawed at her. Hysterics wouldn't help her. She had to hang on. She had survived before, and she would survive again.

How long before Ryder came looking for her? He would be expecting her at his house, but what if he had to work late? She had no idea what time it was, though the window at the end of the loft showed only blackness. If could be seven o'clock or it could be midnight—she couldn't tell.

But no matter the hour, she had to find a way out of this situation. So far Ken hadn't threatened her with a gun. As far as she knew, he didn't own one. He was counting on his size and strength to overpower her, and so far it was working for him, but she had to find some advantage and figure out a way to use it against him.

"You need to untie me," she said, surprised at how

calm she sounded. "I can't relax and…and I can't focus on you if I'm tied up."

"You don't like being tied up?" He looked genuinely puzzled. "I thought it would be fun." He grinned. "A little kinky."

She swallowed nausea. "I just… I want to put my arms around you," she said.

He sat back, searching her face. "You won't try to fight me?"

"Of course not," she lied.

"I'll untie your hands," he said and leaned forward to do so. "But I'll leave your feet the way they are. I don't want you running away."

She forced herself to remain still while he fumbled with the knots at her wrists. "Maybe you need a knife," she said.

"Good idea." He stood, then winked at her. "Don't go away. I'll be right back."

"I'll be waiting." Saying the words made her feel sick to her stomach. But she would be waiting when he returned with the knife—then she would do everything to get her hands on that blade. He thought she was passive, but he would learn she was a fighter.

Chapter Twenty

The parking lot of the veterinary clinic was empty, the only tracks in the smooth coating of snow the fresh ones made by Ryder's Tahoe. He tried the door, anyway, and peered through the glass. A single light behind the front desk illuminated the empty counter. The only sound was the crunch of his own boots on the snow.

He tried Darcy's phone again, and this time the call went straight to voice mail. He hung up without leaving a message, stomach churning. Where was she?

He headed for her house, but since Kelly's duplex was on the way, decided to swing by there first. Stacy had mentioned that Darcy had planned to pick up some supplies from there. Maybe she had gotten distracted, or the task took more time than he would have thought. But even as he thought these things, instinct told him something was wrong.

The driveway to the duplex was vacant, and no lights shone from either half. The snow was falling harder now, filling in Ryder's tracks on the walkway to the door within minutes of his passing. He knocked on Kelly's door, then tried the knob. It was locked. With a growing sense of urgency, he moved to Ken's door and pounded on it. "Ken, it's Ryder! I need to talk to you."

He turned and headed back across the porch and up

the walk toward his Tahoe. But a dark bulk along the side of the duplex caught his eye. He unclipped the flashlight from his utility belt and shone it over a tarped snowmobile. Heart pounding, he stepped through the deepening snow to the snowmobile and unhooked the bungie cord that held the tarp in place.

His flashlight illuminated first the Polaris emblem. Then he arced the beam upward to the spiderweb of cracks in the windscreen that spread out from the neat, round bullet hole.

KEN CUT THE plastic ties that had bound Darcy's wrists and laid the knife on the floor beside the bed. She stretched her arms out in front of her, wincing at the pain, and struggled to sit up. Ken pushed her back onto the bed with one hand, reaching for the fly of his jeans with the other.

"Wait," she cried, squirming into a sitting position. She forced a smile to her trembling lips. "Let's talk a little bit first. You know—get in the mood."

He frowned but moved his hand away from his fly. "What do you want to talk about?"

"Were you the one on the snowmobile on the ski trail at Silver Pick Sunday afternoon?"

"What about it?"

"I just wondered." She swallowed, trying to force some saliva from her dry mouth. "I figure you were trying to show me how dangerous it was," she said. "How much I need to depend on you to protect me."

His expression lightened. "That's it." He sat beside her and took her hand in his. "I didn't want to frighten you, but I had to make you see the danger you were in. I did it to protect you."

"And were you the one who ran me off Silverthorne

Road?" she asked. "You pretended to be that woman with the hurt mastiff?"

He laughed. "That was pretty clever, wasn't it?" He leaned closer. "If only you weren't so stubborn. You would have saved us all so much trouble if you had accepted my help from the first."

She pushed him gently away, trying hard to hide her revulsion and fear. "Did you try to break in to this place, the night Kelly was killed?"

He frowned. "No. I wouldn't do something like that."

Hitting her over the head and kidnapping her, not to mention threatening her with both a truck and a snowmobile, apparently weren't as bad as jimmying a lock? But she believed him when he said he hadn't tried to break in that night. But was he the killer?

Ken forced his lips onto hers and slid his hands under her sweater. Her stomach churned and she wondered if it was possible to vomit from fear. Would that be enough to scare him off?

"I'm ready now." He stood and, so quickly she hardly registered what was happening, shoved his jeans down. She reacted instinctively, drawing up her legs, ankles still bound together, and shoving hard against his chest. He stumbled back and she dove for the floor, grabbing for the knife.

He straddled her, hands around her throat, choking her, as she felt blindly for the knife, which had slid under the bed. Her fingers closed around the handle, as he shoved his knee into her back, forcing her flat onto the floor. And all the while his hands continued to squeeze until her vision fogged and she felt herself slipping away.

A mighty crash shook the whole house, and the pressure on her throat lessened. "What the—"

"Darcy!" Ryder's shout was followed by pounding footsteps as he vaulted up the stairs.

His weight still grinding her into the floor, Ken swiveled to face the entrance to the loft. Darcy tightened her grip on the knife.

"Darcy!" Ryder shouted again.

"I'm here," she said, her voice weak, but she thought he heard.

"Get off her!" he roared.

"You can't have her." Ken stood, bringing her with him, and clasping her in front of him like a shield. She held the knife by her side, half-hidden in the folds of her trousers, and prayed he was too focused on Ryder to notice.

Less than six feet away, Ryder stood at the top of the stairs, both hands steadying his pistol in his hands. His eyes met Darcy's, and there was no mistaking the fear that flashed through them. He lowered the gun. "Don't do anything stupid," he said.

"You're the one who's stupid." Ken moved sideways, away from the bed. "Thinking you could have her. She belongs with me."

"I don't want to be with you!" She squirmed, but he held her so tightly her ribs ached.

"Get out of the way," Ken told Ryder. "Let us pass. And if you try anything, I'll kill her."

Why did he think *he* got to determine who she wanted to be with and what happened to her? Rage at the idea overwhelmed her. In one swift movement, she brought the knife up and plunged it into his thigh. It sank to the hilt, blood gushing. Ken screamed and released her.

Ryder grabbed her hand and thrust her away from the other man. She slid to the floor as Ryder shoved Ken against the wall, the gun held to his head. "Don't move," Ryder growled. "Don't even breathe hard."

"I'm bleeding!" Ken cried. "Do something."

"Sit down," Ryder ordered, and Ken slid to the floor.

Ryder pulled cuffs from his belt and cuffed Ken's hands behind him, then grabbed a pillow from the bed and held it over the bleeding. He looked over at Darcy. "Are you okay?"

She nodded. She felt sick and shaky, but she was alive. She had fought back. She would be okay—eventually.

He slipped a multi-tool from his belt and slid it across the floor to her. "Can you cut the ties on your ankles?"

Though her hands were still unsteady, she managed to sever the ties and stand. "I should call 911," she said.

"Do that." He saw her hesitation and softened his voice. "I'll be okay," he said.

She went downstairs and found her phone and made the call, then collapsed on the sofa and began to sob. She didn't know why she was crying, exactly, except that it had all been so horrible, and she was so relieved it was over.

She didn't know how long it was before Ryder came to her. He wrapped her in a blanket, then drew her into his arms and held her tightly. She clung to him, sobbing. "I was s-so scared," she said through her tears.

"You were great," he said, gently kissing the side of her face. "It's over now. You're safe."

Some time after that the ambulance came, along with Travis and Gage Walker. A paramedic checked out Darcy and gave her a sedative, while two others carried a howling and complaining Ken down the narrow stairs and out to the ambulance. "What will happen to him?" Darcy asked, the medication having soothed the hard, metallic edge of fear.

"He's under arrest," Travis said. "For kidnapping and menacing and probably a half a dozen other charges we haven't sorted out yet. He'll be placed under a guard at the clinic here and when the road opens again we'll transport him to jail to await his trial."

"The road's closed again?" Ryder asked.

Travis nodded. "I'm afraid so."

"I found a snowmobile at Ken's duplex, with the windscreen shot out," Ryder said.

"He admitted he tried to run us down at Silver Pick," Darcy said. "And he was the one who pretended to be an old woman with a mastiff, who ran me off Silverthorne Road that night." She studied the faces of all three lawmen, trying to figure out what they were thinking. "I don't think he killed Kelly or the others," she said. "Maybe I'm wrong, but…"

"I don't think he killed them, either," Ryder said. "He was teaching a class full of students when Kelly was killed."

"He was supposedly at a basketball game when that truck ran Darcy off the road," Gage said.

"That one was easy enough to fake," Ryder said. "He went to the basketball game, made sure he saw and talked to a lot of people, then slipped out. People would remember he was there, but they wouldn't necessarily remember the exact time they saw him. The classroom is tougher to fake. Everyone we talked to said he was there the whole time."

"So the killer is still out there?" Darcy asked.

"Maybe," Travis said. "Or maybe he took advantage of the break in the weather and left town."

"I'm still hoping Pi and his friends saw something that will help us," Ryder said.

"So far they're still not talking," Travis said. "But I've

contacted all their parents and they all agreed this business of daring each other to do risky things has to stop. They've agreed that the boys should spend their spare time for the next few weeks doing community service."

"What kind of service?" Darcy asked.

"They can start by shoveling snow. We have a lot of it to move at the school and at the homes of elderly residents. That should keep them out of trouble."

"So what do you do about the killer?" Darcy asked.

Ryder's arm around her tightened. "We wait."

DARCY WAS SURPRISED to learn it was only a little after seven o'clock when Ryder had arrived at her house. By nine, the two of them had moved her belongings—including all four cats—into the house he rented on the other side of town. She had located the cats hidden in various places around the house—behind books on a shelf, under a sofa cushion, in a cubby in the kitchen. She dosed them all with an herbal sedative and Ryder helped her stow them in their carriers and gather their food, treats, toys and litter boxes. He didn't ask why she had changed her mind about leaving the cats at the house, merely helped her move them. She hoped it was because he understood she needed them with her. They were part of her home—and the tiny house would never feel like home again.

When they had unloaded the cats and her belongings at Ryder's place, he made macaroni and cheese and served it to her with hot tea spiked with rum. "This tastes better than anything I've ever eaten," she said, trying hard not to inhale the bowl full of orange noodles that had to be the ultimate comfort food.

"I'm not a gourmet cook, but you won't starve while you're here," he said.

She wouldn't have to be afraid while she was here, either, she thought.

After supper he persuaded her to leave the dishes until the next day, and he built a fire in the fireplace. Then they settled on the sofa and he wrapped a knitted throw around them both. "Do you want to talk about what happened?" he asked, his voice quiet.

"The sheriff said I'll need to give a statement to him tomorrow."

"You can wait until then if you like," he said. "We can try to find a victim's advocate for you to talk to, too. You don't have to tell me anything."

"I want to tell you." It was true. She laced her fingers through his. "Talking can help. I learned that before—after Jay kidnapped and raped me." It had taken her a long time—years, really—before she had been able to name the crimes done against her so boldly. But naming them was a form of taking control, she had learned.

Ryder settled her more firmly against him. "All right," he said. "I'm listening."

So she told him everything—from the moment in the kitchen through everything that had happened until his arrival at her house. Reciting the facts, along with admitting her terror in the moment, made her feel stronger. "As bad as it was, it could have been so much worse," she said. "That's one reason I don't think Ken is the one who killed Kelly and the others. He's a terrible man, but I don't think he's a murderer."

"No, I don't think so," Ryder agreed. "But I'm glad he's behind bars now—or will be, as soon as his doctors okay his release. And I'm not sure I can put into words how relieved I am that you're safe."

She turned into his arms and kissed him, a kiss that

banished the chill from the last cold places within her. "Ken was right about one thing," she said.

"What is that?"

"I was wrong to insist on continuing to stay out at that isolated house by myself. Not that I would have ever accepted his offer to stay with him, but I could have gone to Stacy's."

"I'm glad you're here right now," he said.

"I'm going to stay as long as you'll have me," she said.

"How about forever?"

She stared at him, her heart having climbed somewhere into her throat. "I love you," he said. "And I want to keep on loving you. But I don't want to pressure you or control you or ever have you think I'm like Ken or Jay or anyone else who would try to hurt you."

She put her fingers over his lips. "Shhh. I know the difference between you and those others." She moved her hand and kissed the place where her fingers had been. "I love you, too," she said. "And I want to be with you." She kissed him again.

"To forever," he said and kissed her, softly and surely.

"Forever," she echoed. Saying the word was like uttering a magical incantation that opened the last lock on her heart. She felt lighter and freer—and more safe and secure—than she ever had.

* * * * *

SMOKY
MOUNTAINS
RANGER

LENA DIAZ

This book is dedicated to my dear friends and fellow authors Jan Jackson and Connie Mann. Your constant cheerleading and friendship is priceless. Jan, thank you for helping me through my plot tangles on this one. I hope you approve of the final product.

Chapter One

Adam ducked behind a massive, uprooted tree, the tangle of dead roots and blackened branches his only cover on this wildfire-blighted section of the Great Smoky Mountains. Had the man holding the pistol seen him? He ticked off the seconds as he slid his left hand to the Glock 22 holstered at his waist. When half a minute passed without sounds of pursuit, he inched over to peer up the trail and moved his hand to the radio strapped to his belt. After switching to the emergency channel, he pressed the button on his shoulder mic.

"This is Ranger McKenzie on the Sugarland Mountain Trail." He kept his voice low, just above a whisper. "There's a yahoo with a gun up here, about a quarter mile northwest of the intersection with the Appalachian Trail. Requesting backup. Over."

Nothing but silence met his request. He tilted the radio to see the small screen. After verifying the frequency and noting the battery was fully charged, he pressed the mic again.

"Ranger McKenzie requesting backup. Over." Again he waited. Again, the radio was silent. Cell phone coverage in the Great Smoky Mountains National Park was hit-or-miss. It didn't matter if someone was coming up from the Tennessee side, like Adam, or hiking in from the North Carolina border. Cell phones up here were unreliable. Period.

Which was why he and the rest of the staff carried powerful two-way radios that worked everywhere in the park.

With one exception.

The Sugarland Mountain Trail, where the devastating Chimney Tops wildfire had destroyed a communication tower.

Budget cuts meant the rebuilding was slow and had to be prioritized. Rehabilitating habitats, the visitors' center and the more popular, heavily used trails near the park's entrance were high on that list. Putting up a new tower was close to the bottom. So, naturally, the first and only time that Adam had ever encountered someone with a gun in the park, it happened in the middle of the only dead zone.

There would be no backup.

If the guy was just a good old boy out for target practice, the situation wouldn't even warrant a call back to base. Adam could handle it on his own and be on his way. But the stakes were higher today—much higher—because of two things.

One, the faded blue ink tattoos on the gunman's bulging biceps that marked him as an ex-con, which likely meant he couldn't legally possess a firearm and wouldn't welcome a federal officer catching him with one.

Two, the alarmingly pale, obviously terrified young woman on the business end of Tattoo Guy's pistol.

Even from twenty yards away, peering through branches, Adam could tell the gunman had a tenuous grasp on an explosive temper. He gestured wildly with his free hand, his face bright red as he said something in response to whatever the petite redhead had just said.

Her hands were empty and down at her sides. Unless she'd shoved a pistol in the back waistband of her denim shorts, she didn't appear to have a weapon to defend herself. The formfitting white blouse she wore didn't have any pockets. Even if she'd hidden a small gun, like a derringer, in her bra, there was no way she could get it out faster than the gunman could pull the trigger.

Did they know each other? Was this a case of domestic violence? Since the two were arguing, it seemed likely that they *did* know each other. So what had brought them to the brink of violence? And what had brought them to *this* particular trail?

Neither of them was wearing a backpack. Unless they had supplies at a base camp somewhere, that ruled them out as NOBOs on the AT who'd gone seriously off course and gotten lost. Not that he'd expect any northbound through-hikers on the Appalachian Trail in the middle of summer anyway. Most NOBOs started out on the two-thousand-plus-mile hike around March or April so they could reach Mount Katahdin in Maine before blizzards made the AT impassable. But even if they were day hikers, they had no business being on the Sugarland Trail. It was closed, for good reason. The wildfire damage made this area exceedingly dangerous. Now it was dangerous for an entirely different reason.

An idiot with a pistol.

So much for the peaceful workday he'd expected when he'd started his trail inspection earlier this morning.

He switched the worthless radio off, not wanting to risk a sudden burst of static alerting the gunman to his presence. The element of surprise was on his side and he aimed to keep it that way as long as possible, or at least until he came up with a plan.

He belatedly wished he'd dusted off his Kevlar and put it on this morning. But even though he was the law enforcement variety of ranger, as opposed to an informational officer, the kind of dangers he ran into up here didn't typically warrant wearing a bullet-resistant vest. The heat and extra weight tended to outweigh the risks of not having a vest on since the possibility of getting into a gunfight while patrolling half a million acres of mostly uninhabited mountains and forests was close to zero.

Until today.

Still, it wasn't the bullets that concerned him the most. It was the steep drop-off behind the woman. One wrong step and she'd go flying off the mountain. The edge was loose and crumbling in many places, particularly in this section of the trail. The couple—if that's what they were—couldn't have picked a worse spot for their argument.

Sharp boulders and the charred remains of dozens of trees littered the ravine fifty feet below. Branches stuck up like sharp spikes ready to impale anything—or any*one*— unlucky enough to fall on them.

Twenty feet farther north or south on this section of the Sugarland path would provide a much better chance of survival if the worst happened. The slope wasn't as steep and was carpeted with thick wild grasses. Fledgling scrub brush dotting the mountainside might help break someone's fall if they lost their footing. They'd still be banged up, might twist an ankle or even crack a bone. But that was preferable to plunging into a rocky ravine with no chance of survival.

The gunman and the woman were still arguing. But Adam couldn't figure out what they were saying. Sometimes sounds carried for miles out here. Other times a person could barely hear someone a few yards away. It all depended on the wind and the configuration of mountains, rocks and trees nearby.

At the man's back, a vertical wall of sheer rock went straight up to a higher peak. In front of him was the woman and the sharp drop-off. Sneaking up on him just wasn't going to happen. Either by luck or by design, he'd chosen a spot that was impossible to approach without being seen.

As Adam watched, the man gestured with his pistol for the woman to head south, away from Adam. When she didn't move, he stepped forward. She backed up, moving perilously closer to the edge. Adam drew a sharp breath. If he didn't do something fast, this was going to end in tragedy. He'd have to approach openly, giving up his element of surprise, and hope that cooler heads prevailed.

He unsnapped the safety flap on his holster—just in case—and straightened. Keeping his gaze trained on the ground, he boldly stepped onto the path in plain sight and whistled a tune—AC/DC's "Highway to Hell." It seemed appropriate at the moment.

Continuing to look down and pretending not to notice the couple, his hope was to get as close to them as possible and appear nonthreatening—just a ranger in the mountains, doing his job. Most people didn't realize the difference between informational officers and federal law enforcement rangers anyway. They'd assume the pistol holstered on his belt was for protection against bears or other dangerous wildlife. Usually, it was.

In his peripheral vision, he saw the man shove his pistol into his pants pocket. Adam kept moving forward, head down, increasing the volume of his whistling and tapping his thigh to the beat.

"You gonna run into us or what?" the man's voice snapped.

Adam jerked his head up as if in surprise, stopping a few feet away from the couple. "Sorry, folks. Must have been daydreaming. Pretty morning for it, don't you think?" He smiled and waved toward the mountains around them. "Even with the blight from the wildfires, it's still beautiful up here."

The man watched him with open suspicion as if sizing him up and trying to decide whether Adam really hadn't seen the gun. The woman stared at him, her green eyes big and round behind matching green-framed glasses. But instead of seeming relieved to have help, she appeared to be even more terrified than before.

Adam struggled to maintain his smile. "I'm Ranger Adam McKenzie. You folks lost? Got to admit I'm a bit surprised to see you on this particular trail. Know why?"

Tattoo Guy seemed to come to some kind of decision and offered his own smile that didn't quite reach his dark eyes. "Afraid I don't. Why?"

"Because the trail is closed, for your safety. It's because of the fires last season. You heard about those? Burned over seventeen thousand acres, ten thousand of them right here in the park. Killed fourteen people, too." He didn't have to fake his wince. The fire had been horrible, tragic. Innocent civilians—including children—had perished in the flames. Families had been destroyed. The community was still struggling to recover as best they could. But nothing could replace the precious lives that were lost.

The man glanced at the woman, his eyes narrowed as if in warning. "Can't say that I've heard about that. I'm not from around here."

"What about you, miss?" Adam grinned again. "Sorry. Where are my manners? I didn't catch your name. I'm Adam McKenzie. And you are?" He held out his hand to shake hers, purposely leaving enough space between them so that she'd have to move away from the edge to take his hand.

She looked at the other man as if for permission, then leaned toward Adam, her hand out. As soon as she grasped his hand, he pumped it up and down in a vigorous shake, pulling her even farther away from the edge.

"Your name, ma'am?"

"I, um… Jody. My name's Jody Ingram." She shook his hand, eyes wide with fear.

"Pleased to meet you." Adam let her go and held his hand out toward the gunman. "And you are?"

The man's nearly black eyes dropped to Adam's outstretched hand while he clearly debated his response. A handshake required that he use his right hand, his dominant hand, the one that had held the pistol earlier. He'd be giving up precious seconds of reaction time if he decided that Adam was a threat and he needed to draw his gun. Which of course was exactly why Adam wanted to shake his hand.

Adam was left-handed.

And his pistol was holstered just a few inches from where his left hand currently hung down by his side.

Come on, come on. Shake the clueless cop's hand.

An awkward silence stretched out between them as no one moved. Adam pretended not to notice. He kept his hand out, waiting, a goofy grin on his face. From the corner of his eye, Adam saw the woman watching them closely, her gaze sweeping back and forth.

Finally, the man mumbled something beneath his breath that sounded suspiciously like "stupid hillbilly" before gripping Adam's hand.

Adam yanked hard, jerking the man off balance. The man stumbled as Adam grabbed the butt of his gun in the holster. But Tattoo Guy was lightning fast. Even as Adam began to draw his pistol, the other guy was already drawing his and swinging it toward him.

Chapter Two

"Drop your weapon. *Now.*" Adam had both hands wrapped around the butt of his Glock. The bore of his gun was aimed directly at the other man's head.

Tattoo Guy stood statue still, his weapon aimed slightly to Adam's left, frozen in midmotion. But one quick twist and a squeeze of the trigger would blast a hole through Adam's gut. The only question was whether Adam could blow the man's brains out before that happened. Not exactly a competition he wanted to wage, especially with a woman a few feet away who was dangerously close to the kill zone.

The seconds ticked by. They stood frozen. The only sounds were the woman's short gasping breaths as she watched the standoff, apparently too terrified to back away to a safer location—preferably behind a thick, solid tree.

Adam didn't dare say a word to her. He didn't even blink as he kept his gaze glued to his opponent and his finger on the frame of his gun, just millimeters from the trigger. He narrowed his eyes, letting the stranger know that he wasn't kidding, wasn't bluffing and wasn't the head-in-the-clouds idiot he'd pretended to be moments earlier.

Tattoo Guy must have read the truth and determination in Adam's eyes, in his stance. He tossed his gun to the ground.

Adam kept his finger right above the trigger, ready to

fire at the slightest provocation. Everything about the man screamed danger, and he wasn't taking any chances. "Turn around."

The man hesitated, his gaze darting past Adam.

The urge to check over his shoulder to see what Tattoo Guy was looking at was almost impossible to resist. Did the man have a partner in crime creeping up on Adam? Or was he trying to trick him, distract him? His shoulder blades itched, expecting a bullet to slam into them any second. But he didn't turn around. He focused on the known threat in front of him and waited.

The man finally did as Adam had ordered and turned to face the wall of rock.

Adam kicked the pistol out of reach. "Down on the ground. Put your hands behind your back."

Again Tattoo Guy hesitated. Adam pulled a pair of handcuffs from one of the leather cases attached to his utility belt. He desperately wanted to check on the woman, make sure she was safe, that no one was sneaking up behind *her*. But he didn't dare. Not until he had this guy secured.

When the man finally put his hands behind his back, Adam holstered his pistol in one smooth motion and dropped down on top of him, jamming his knee against the man's spine to hold him down. The man cursed and tried to buck him off. But Adam used every bit of his six-foot-three-inch bulk to keep the stranger pinned.

He slapped the cuffs on the man's wrists, then sat back, drawing deep breaths as adrenaline pumped through him. A bead of sweat ran down the side of his face in spite of the mild, springlike temps this high up in the mountains. From the moment he'd seen the gunman to the moment he'd cuffed him had probably only been five minutes. But it had felt like an eternity.

He stood and pulled his prisoner up with him. After

patting the man down to make sure he wasn't hiding more weapons, he grabbed the man's pistol and popped out the magazine. After ejecting the chambered round and verifying that the weapon was now empty, he pocketed the gun and the magazine. Then he slid the man's wallet out of his back jeans pocket, jumping back when the man jerked around, glowering at him.

"Give that back." The man's tone communicated a deadly, unmistakable threat.

"After I check your ID."

A smug look crossed the man's face, a look Adam understood when he opened the wallet. Tucked inside was a hefty amount of cash: twenties, tens, a few ones—a thousand dollars, easy. A heck of a lot of money for someone wandering through the mountains. But that was it. No driver's license, no credit cards, nothing that could shed any light on his identity.

He forced the man to face the rock wall again and returned the wallet with its cache of money to the man's pocket. "What's your name?"

Silence met his question.

"What were you doing up here on a closed trail with a pistol? Why were you pointing it at Miss Ingram?"

Tattoo Guy turned his head to the side, watching Adam over his shoulder. Still, he said nothing. He just studied Adam intently, his eyes dark and cold, like a serpent.

Adam glanced toward the woman, then stiffened. During the altercation between him and the gunman, instead of moving down the trail or ducking for cover behind a tree, she'd backed up close to the edge again.

"Miss Ingram." He kept his voice low and soothing so he wouldn't startle her. "Jody, right?"

She swallowed, then nodded.

"Jody, I'd feel a whole lot better if you'd step away from that sharp drop-off."

She glanced over her shoulder. A visible shudder ran through her as she hurried forward and to the side. She'd been mere inches from falling off the cliff and was exceedingly lucky the unstable edge hadn't given way.

"How about you move over there?" He directed her closer to the wall of rock, a little farther up the path and out of reach of his prisoner if the man decided to launch himself at either of them.

She did as he'd directed. But instead of looking relieved that she no longer had a pistol pointing at her, she seemed even more anxious than before. Her face was chalk white, making her green eyes and matching glasses stand out in stark contrast. Even her lips had lost their color, and her whole body was shaking.

Why?

"Everything's okay now," he reassured her. "You're safe. What's this guy's name?"

She exchanged an uneasy glance with the handcuffed man, then shook her head. "I… I don't know. We, ah, ran into each other on the trail."

Adam glanced back and forth between them, beginning to wonder whether he should put her in handcuffs, too. They were hiding something. What was going on here?

"You're strangers? You've never met before?"

She swallowed. "We've never met. I'd just rounded the curve and he was…there. I…ah…startled him, which is why he drew his gun." She gave a nervous laugh. "I guess he thought I was a bear." Again, she gave a nervous laugh that was anything but convincing.

A smile creased Tattoo Guy's lips as he watched the exchange over his shoulder.

"You don't know each other's names?" Adam asked, giving her another chance to answer him truthfully.

"No."

He shook his head, not even trying to hide his disbelief. "You have a habit of getting into heated arguments with strangers?"

Her face flushed guiltily. "He drew a gun on me. I wasn't happy about that. Things did get a bit…heated…with him demanding to know why I'd snuck up on him. Which, of course, I hadn't. But looking back, I can see how it appeared that way to him." She wouldn't meet his gaze. Subterfuge obviously didn't come naturally to her. So why was she covering for this guy? Or was she covering for both of them?

He tried again, working hard to inject patience into his tone. "You were arguing with each other over him putting the gun down?"

She cleared her throat. "Yes, pretty much." Another nervous laugh.

Her story had more holes in it than a white-tailed fawn had spots. Instead of rescuing her from a domestic dispute between a couple, had he interrupted a disagreement between a couple of criminals? Were they out here doing something illegal and they'd turned on each other? Or maybe whatever they'd planned was still to come, something far worse than trespassing on a closed trail or carrying a gun into a national park. Adam backed up the path several feet so he could keep Jody—if that was her real name—in his line of sight at a safer distance, just in case she and Tattoo Guy decided to join forces against him.

"Let me guess," he said. "You don't have ID on you, either?"

She cleared her throat again. "Actually, no. I don't. I left my purse in my car, at the trailhead. All I have with me are my keys and my phone."

"Empty your pockets."

Her brow furrowed, and she finally looked at him. "Excuse me?"

"Would you prefer that I pat you down like I did your friend?"

Twin spots of color darkened her cheeks, making her freckles stand out in stark contrast to her pale complexion. Her eyes flashed with anger. "I assure you, he's *not* my friend."

That statement, at least, appeared to be true. But he could tell she immediately regretted her outburst by the way her teeth tugged at her full lower lip.

His prisoner's eyes narrowed at her, as if in warning. Something was definitely rotten in the state of Denmark, or in this case, the Smoky Mountains. And Adam was determined to get to the bottom of it.

"Your pockets, ma'am?"

Without a word, she pulled her phone out of one pocket, a set of keys out of the other. Clutching them both in one hand, she turned out the lining of her pockets to show they were empty. "That's it. There's nothing else."

"Back pockets, too."

Her mouth tightened but she turned around and turned those pockets inside out.

"All right," Adam conceded. "You can turn around." To perform a complete search, he should pat down her bra. But his years of reading people told him that wasn't necessary. She wasn't carrying.

"Where do you live?"

Again, another look at the handcuffed man as she shoved her keys and phone back into her pockets. "Not far from here. I've got an apartment in town."

"Gatlinburg?"

Again, she hesitated. "Yes."

"Why were you two up here today?"

She chewed her bottom lip.

Tattoo Guy simply stared at him, eyes narrowed with the promise of retribution over Adam's interference in whatever was going on.

"Maybe my question wasn't clear," Adam said. "Why were you both on a closed trail?"

"Closed?" The man sounded shocked. "Really? Miss Ingram, did you see any signs saying the trail was closed?" Laughter was heavy in his voice as he watched her.

"N...no." Her voice was barely above a whisper. "I didn't. I guess I was...enjoying nature too much and wasn't paying attention."

Disgusted with both of them, Adam flipped the radio on again. "Ranger McKenzie to base. Come in. Over." He tried two more times, then gave up.

"I don't know what you two are hiding. But at a minimum you're guilty of criminal trespass. This trail is closed for a reason. The recent wildfires have burned away brush that used to hold the topsoil in place. What the high winds and fire didn't destroy, recent rains did. Entire sections of the trail have been washed away. Trees have been toppled, their roots ripping up most of what was left. The trail is more a memory than a reality anymore. The part we're standing on is one of the best sections left. But it's the exception rather than the rule. You already know that, of course. Because you had to climb over and around some of the damage on your way up. No way you missed it."

He waited for their response and wasn't surprised when neither of them said anything.

"It's also against the law for civilians to carry guns into the park. Care to explain why you had a loaded pistol up here, sir?"

"Protection, of course. I've heard there are all kinds of

dangers in these mountains." He kept his gaze fastened on Jody.

As if she felt his eyes on her, she shivered.

What the heck was going on? Had Tattoo Guy just given the woman a veiled threat? Was *he* one of the dangers he'd just mentioned? Even though Adam had zero doubt that Jody Ingram was covering something, his instincts were telling him that she was a victim here. But since neither of them would talk, he had no choice but to bring both of them in.

"Am I under arrest, *Ranger*?" The man drew out Adam's title into several extra syllables, then chuckled. He wasn't the first to make fun of the ranger title. But Adam wasn't inclined to care. He just wanted this guy off the mountain before he hurt someone.

"For now, you're just being detained, for everyone's safety. We'll sort it all out at headquarters. Those are prison tats on your arms, aren't they? I'm sure your fingerprints are on file. Won't take but a minute to find out who you are once I get you back to base. And if you're a felon with a gun, well, we'll just have to deal with that issue, won't we?"

If looks could kill, Adam would be six feet under right now.

He'd dealt with all types over the years, the worst of the worst back when he'd first started out in law enforcement as a beat cop in some of the rougher parts of Memphis. But because of Adam's own intimidating size, he could count on one hand the number of men who made him uncomfortable. This man was one of them. There was something sinister, jaded, so…empty about him. As if long ago he'd poured out his soul and filled the emptiness with pure evil.

He motioned for him to start down the trail, in the direction toward the Appalachian Trail intersection and Clingmans Dome—a famous lookout point high in the Smoky Mountains. "Take it slow and easy."

His prisoner calmly pushed away from the rock wall. As he started walking down the path, he whistled the same tune that Adam had whistled earlier, "Highway to Hell."

Jody watched him go, fear and trepidation playing a game of tug-of-war across her face. Adam wanted to reassure her. But she'd done nothing but lie to him. Trusting her would be a mistake. Instead, he gestured for her to fall in beside him and they started down the steep incline about ten feet behind his prisoner.

"He can't hear you now." Adam kept his voice low as they carefully stepped around boulders and climbed over downed trees. "What was really going on back there?"

She accepted his hand to help her over a pile of rocks and busted branches. There were pieces of splintered wood and rocks everywhere, making it slow going. The prisoner up ahead navigated the same obstacles with surprising ease for a man with his hands behind him. There was now twelve feet of space between them. Adam frowned and motioned for Jody to speed up.

"Well?" he prodded, watching Tattoo Guy's back.

"I already told you. I didn't see the closed-trail signs and I was walking through the park enjoying the scenery. I rounded a curve and scared that man. He drew his gun. I'm sure he would have put it away, but then you came up and things got…complicated."

"That's how you're going to play this?"

She stared straight ahead.

Frustration curled inside him. "You don't have to be afraid of him. I can protect you, help you find a way out of whatever trouble you're in. Just tell me the truth."

She made a choked sound, then cleared her throat. "I am telling you the truth."

He let out a deep sigh. This was going to be a very long day.

Up ahead, the rock wall made a sharp curve to the left.

"Hold it," Adam called out to Tattoo Guy. "The trail gets much steeper and more treacherous there. I'll have to help you."

The man took off running.

Adam grabbed his pistol out of the holster. "Stay here!" He sprinted after his prisoner.

Chapter Three

Stay here? Was he worried that she'd run after the bad guy? It took courage to chase a man who'd pointed a pistol at you and made threats. She wasn't courageous. If she was, she would have fought harder after the auditor absolved her adoptive father of any wrongdoing in regards to her trust. She would have taken back what she believed he'd stolen from her. But she hadn't. She wouldn't. Because she was a coward. Being courageous and fighting back had never done her any good. It had only made things worse. So somewhere along the line, just giving in had become a habit.

Still, not at least checking on the ranger seemed wrong. So she kept moving forward, toward where he'd disappeared, even though she had no idea what she'd do if he needed help. She certainly hadn't done anything to help her best friend, the friend who was the only reason she'd survived her awful foster, later turned adoptive, family.

Where are you, Tracy? That man had to be lying. You have to be hiding somewhere, safe, not some thug's prisoner.

The curve where the ranger and his prisoner had disappeared loomed up ahead. What was the officer's name? Adam something. McKenzie, maybe? Yes, that was it. Cool name for a hot guy. Of course, she hadn't been thinking about his good looks during that frightening standoff. She'd stared up into those deep blue eyes and all she could think was that her friend Tracy was about to die, because of Jody's own stupidity. Her only chance to save her friend had been to lie, or so she'd thought. But she hadn't lied convincingly. She'd been too dang scared to pull it off.

Hysterical laughter bubbled up in her chest. Pull what off? What had she thought she could do? Convince a police officer that someone pointing a gun at someone else was no more significant than changing lanes on a highway without signaling? That Adam McKenzie would give them a warning and let them go on their merry way?

Once again, she'd had a choice to make. Once again, she'd made the wrong one. What she should have done was be honest, tell the ranger exactly what was going on. The time for going it alone had evaporated the second a man with scary tattoos had pulled a gun on her. What was she supposed to do now? If she told McKenzie the truth, would that sign Tracy's death warrant? Probably. Maybe. All she knew for sure was that Tracy needed help. But when help had arrived, in the form of a handsome, dark-haired ranger, she'd squandered the opportunity. And put him in danger, too.

Why hadn't he come back yet?

She stopped and peered down the trail, or what was left of it. McKenzie hadn't exaggerated its hazardous condition. She'd leaped over rock slides and logs a dozen times as she'd run from the man with the gun. He'd caught her, of course. Had she really thought she'd get away? Just like one of those too-stupid-to-live women in a horror movie, she'd run up the stairs instead of out of the house. Or, in this case, up the trail instead of back to her car.

Idiot. Stupid, cowardly idiot.

Her hands fisted at her sides. To be fair, she couldn't have reached her car. He was standing in the way, and there really had been nowhere else to go. Self-recriminations weren't helping. She was in deep, deep trouble and had no clue how to fix it, or even whether it *could* be fixed. But she at least needed to try. Standing here, waiting, wasn't accomplishing anything. It certainly wasn't finding her missing friend or saving an officer who might be in trouble.

She took a hesitant step toward the curve, then another. Her hand itched for the security of her pistol. But, of course, the one time she actually needed her gun it was locked in the safe in her apartment. That decision, at least, she couldn't feel bad about. There was no way she could have predicted what would happen when she drove up here in response to Tracy's text. That she might be in danger had never entered her mind.

When she reached the curve, she squatted down by the wall of rock and peered around the edge. Her stomach sank, as if she'd plummeted down a steep roller-coaster drop. McKenzie no longer had his gun. Instead, he stood about twenty feet away from her, hands in the air. And directly in front of him was another man pointing a pistol directly at McKenzie's chest.

The man McKenzie had handcuffed was still cuffed. But he was leaning against a tree another ten feet beyond the ranger and the other gunman. His face bore an angry, impatient expression as he watched the standoff.

McKenzie shifted slightly, revealing some bloody cuts on the right side of his face. She drew a sharp breath. All three men jerked their heads toward her. She pressed a hand to her throat, belatedly realizing she must have made a sound.

"Nice of you to join us, Jody," the handcuffed man called out, his earlier cocky grin back in place. "Stay right where you are. Remember what I told you." He half turned, looking over his shoulder at the other gunman as he flexed his hands. "Owen, just get the dang keys already and get these things off me. Officer Mayberry can wait."

Jody swallowed, his earlier threats running through her mind. Somehow he'd gotten it into his head that she had something he wanted. And he was using Tracy as leverage. It stood to reason that she could do the opposite, couldn't she? Leverage whatever he thought she had in return for Tracy's safety? If she helped McKenzie, wouldn't the bad guy have to keep Tracy alive until he got what he wanted?

She curled her nails against her palms. Why was she even debating with herself? It wasn't like she could just run away. No matter what, she couldn't ignore the fact that Adam McKenzie was right here, unarmed and outnumbered, with a gun pointed at him. He needed help. She had to do something. But what could she do?

The man named Owen had keys in his left hand now, keys that he must have taken from McKenzie. His gaze stayed on the ranger as he trained the pistol on him and backed toward the tree.

McKenzie's gaze locked on Jody. He glanced to the right, toward the curve of rock wall and subtly jerked his head. Clearly, he wanted her to run up the path, to escape while she could.

She shook her head, even though she really, *really* wanted to give in to her cowardice and do exactly that—retreat, run, hide. But she'd just had this particular argument with herself. And lost.

His jaw clenched. He obviously wasn't happy with her response. He jerked his head again.

Ignoring his unspoken command, she studied the other two men. The one with the gun was fumbling with the set of keys. Their attention was temporarily diverted. McKenzie must have realized the same thing. He edged toward her. One foot. Two feet. When he was about ten feet away, he took off running toward her.

A shout sounded behind him. He grabbed Jody's arm and yanked her around the corner as more shouts and curses sounded.

"The cuffs, the cuffs! Hurry!" The handcuffed guy was apparently ordering Owen to remove the cuffs before they took off in pursuit.

"Go, go, go!" McKenzie's fingers tightened around her upper arm, pulling her up the trail. When a downed tree blocked their way, he lifted her up as if she weighed nothing and leaped over the tree. He set her on her feet and they took off again.

The *clomp-clomp* of boots pounding up the path sounded behind them. She looked over her shoulder. The first gunman didn't have his hands cuffed anymore. The short delay of removing them had given her and McKenzie a head start. But their lead was dwindling.

"Come on." McKenzie pulled her around rocks, over branches, at an impossibly fast pace.

"I'm trying," she gasped, struggling to match his long strides. She already knew she couldn't outrun the man behind them going uphill. She'd tried once and failed. Keeping up with the tall, long-legged McKenzie was impossible.

"Stop or we'll shoot!" the man named Owen yelled at them.

She started to look over her shoulder again. But McKenzie tugged her forward.

"Don't look back. It'll only slow you down." He yanked her around another curve in the trail.

A shot rang out. Jody instinctively ducked. But McKenzie was already pulling her under some thick branches from another downed tree. He came out the other side, hopped over more branches, then lifted her over.

A bullet whined past them. She let out a startled gasp and pressed a hand to her galloping heart. Good grief, that was close. McKenzie didn't react at all. Was the man used to getting shot at? He pulled her behind a huge boulder that was clustered with several others and pushed her down. He scanned the area around them, up the trail, out toward the open vista of mountains that alternated between blackened bald spots and new spring greenery poking up through the ashes.

The twin peaks of the Chimney Tops, two of the higher mountains in the park, stood out in stark relief from the destruction around them. She'd never even been in the park before, other than sitting in a car looking out the window as her adoptive father wheeled and dealed for yet another parcel of land. The only reason she recognized that particular landmark was because a new client had shown her pictures of them a few weeks ago and was considering hiring her to take new ones for a tourist brochure. What she didn't understand was why McKenzie was looking at the Chimney Tops. It wasn't like they had a helicopter and could magically fly to them and escape.

His gaze flicked back to her. "I need to know whether I can trust you."

The cuts on his face had guilt flooding through her. "I could have run when you told me to. But I didn't leave you behind. Isn't that proof enough?"

He seemed to consider that, then shrugged. "For now, *you're* going to have to trust *me*."

She gave a nervous laugh. "Well, I certainly don't trust the guys shooting at us. Where are they?" She tried to peek around the largest boulder. He stopped her with a hand on her shoulder.

"Don't. They've hunkered down behind the last tree we jumped over, about forty feet back. I imagine they're waiting to see if I'm going to pull a weapon from my backpack, since they made me toss my pistol into the ravine and took Tattoo Guy's pistol away from me."

Hope unfurled in her chest. "Do you? Have a backup gun?"

He shook his head. "I've got a hunting knife. But you know the saying about bringing a knife to a gunfight."

"I'm really good with a knife. I could throw it at them. All I'd need is some kind of diversion to get one of them to stand up and give me a clear target."

As soon as she said it, she realized she'd made a mistake. He was looking at her with open suspicion again.

"In college," she rushed to explain, "I hired a guy who ran a gun range to teach me to defend myself. He taught me to shoot. But he also taught me how to throw a knife."

"Ever thrown a knife at a real, live person?"

"No, of course not, but—"

Bam! Bam!

They both ducked at the shockingly loud sound of pistol fire.

She drew a shaky breath. "Well?" She held out her hand for the knife.

"I'm not giving up my only weapon just yet."

She dropped her hand. "You have a better suggestion?"

He looked toward the Chimney Tops again. "I'm considering a few possibilities."

"Is one of them to crouch down and use these boulders to block them from seeing us retreat up the path, back the way you came? We might be able to get pretty far up the trail before they realize we're gone."

"That's a good suggestion, except for one problem." He shrugged out of his backpack and unzipped the top. "The trail straightens out after that next curve, with no cover of any kind for about three hundred yards. It's also unstable.

There's a lot of debris but nothing sizable enough to hide us from view. The odds of us making it that far before those guys work up the courage to storm our little hideout are too low to make it worth the risk." He pulled out a length of white nylon rope and the knife he'd mentioned earlier.

She was about to argue with him, but the rope made her pause. "What's the rope for?"

"So we don't die."

It took several seconds for her to realize he wasn't going to expand on his cryptic answer. Instead, he shoved the knife into a leather holder and tucked it into his backpack. After slipping the pack onto his shoulders, he connected some extra straps on the pack that he hadn't bothered to fasten earlier. One went over his chest. Two more attached the pack to his belt loops with metal clips. She thought they might be called carabiners, like she'd used when Tracy had badgered her into going on a zip-lining trip in Pigeon Forge to celebrate Jody's new, second job at Campbell Investigations.

"What are you doing?" she tried again.

He picked up the length of rope that he'd cut. His fingers fairly flew as he tied knots and created loops.

She watched him with growing frustration. The gunmen could be creeping up on them this very minute. So why was he tying knots? She hated being kept in the dark. Her life was on the line just as much as his.

And Tracy's.

He pulled on one of the loops as if testing it, then let out a few more inches, making it larger.

"Are you going to tie them up or try to lasso them or what?" she snapped, unable to hide her frustration any longer.

For the first time since he'd appeared on the trail with a goofy, dumb-as-a-rock grin, he gave her a genuine smile.

It lit up his eyes and made him look years younger than the thirty-one or -two that she'd assumed him to be. Maybe he was only in his late twenties?

"Lasso them? Can't say that's ever been part of my law enforcement training. Might be a good skill to learn, though."

He continued to work the rope through the metal clips. "Hypothetical. We figure out a way to get Owen or Tattoo Guy to stand up and give us a clear target. You do a Wonder Woman move and take him out. That leaves the second thug with two pistols, and potentially other weapons we don't even know about. We're left without even a knife to defend ourselves. What would we do then?"

"Maybe I do another Wonder Woman move and lasso the second guy."

His lips twitched as if he was trying not to laugh. He looped the rope through one of the backpack's metal clips.

She curled her fingers against her thighs. It was either that or shake him. She closed her eyes for a moment and drew deep, calming breaths. Their lives were on the line and this man was pushing all her buttons. What she needed to do was calm down and think. There had to be something they could do instead of just waiting here playing with a rope. She opened her eyes again, then frowned. "What *are* you doing?"

He swept the ground between them clear of debris, scattering several broken pieces of branches and twigs, then motioned for her to move toward him. Exasperated, but curious enough to see if he actually had some kind of plan, she scooted toward him on her knees. He closed the distance and slid the rope through one of the belt loops on her shorts.

"McKenzie. What are—"

"Give me a minute."

She blew out an irritated breath and held her hands out

of the way as he threaded the rope through all the loops on her shorts. When he was done, he tied the end of the rope to another metal loop on his backpack, effectively anchoring them to each other, with just a few feet in between.

"McKenzie?"

He tilted her chin up so she was looking into his eyes. "Is your name really Jody?"

She swallowed, her whole body flushing with heat when she realized just how close her breasts were to his chest, her lips to his. "Y...yes. Jody Vanessa Ingram." She hated that her voice came out a breathy whisper.

"Pretty name."

"Vanessa was my biological mom's name." Why had she said that? It didn't matter one bit under the circumstances.

He smiled. "Well, Jody Vanessa. We're about to explore one of those possibilities I mentioned earlier. And I think it's time you called me Adam. Don't you?"

His deep voice and cool blue eyes seemed to cast a spell on her. She couldn't think with him this close, could barely even breathe.

"Come on out from behind that rock and we won't kill you," Owen shouted. "All we want to do is talk."

She blinked. The spell was broken. Thank goodness. "McKenzie... I mean, Adam. What's the plan here? Why did you—"

He tugged the rope, pulling them even closer together. "This is where that trust part comes into play."

She licked her suddenly dry lips. "I'm not sure what you—"

He grabbed one of the short, broken pieces of branch that he'd swept out of the way earlier and tossed it over the top of the boulder.

Boom! The stick exploded into sawdust.

Jody ducked down, even though she was already behind the boulder.

Adam winced but didn't duck. "They're better shots than I'd hoped. This is going to be close."

"Close? What are you—"

He grabbed her around the waist.

She read the truth in his eyes and suddenly realized what he was going to do. The rope. The fact that he'd tied the two of them together. Him staring out at the Chimney Tops and telling her she needed to trust him. Her stomach lurched, and she pushed against his chest, to no avail. He didn't budge and the rope wouldn't have let her move very far anyway. "No. No, no, no. *Please.* I can't do this. I'm too scared. I *can't*."

Sympathy filled his gaze. He brushed a featherlight caress down the side of her face. "Then I'll just have to do it for both of us." He grabbed two more sticks and threw them high into the air. Shots rang out. He yanked her forward, clasping her tightly against his chest as he raced in a crouch behind the boulders toward where the trail disappeared over the edge of the mountain.

"No!" she cried, desperately pushing against him. "Please!"

The gunmen shouted.

Adam yanked her forward. She screamed as they tumbled over the cliff.

Chapter Four

They hit the ground hard, a tangle of arms and legs flopping end over end. Jody's head snapped against Adam's chest. Blood filled her mouth. She was too busy trying to grab a tree, a root, anything to stop their out-of-control roll down the steep mountainside to even cry out in pain.

"Hold on," his voice rumbled next to her ear as his arms squeezed her against his chest.

She caught a glimpse of another steep drop, then sucked in a startled breath and closed her eyes. Shots rang out from somewhere above them as they plummeted into open space again.

We're going to die.

Strong arms clasped her so tightly she thought her body would break in two. Then she hit something hard—or he did, because she was on top of him. Their entwined bodies bounced several more times and slid a heart-stopping few more yards. Then, just as suddenly as their wild flight had begun, it was over. His chest rose and fell beneath hers, his ragged breaths fanning against the top of her head. But other than that, and her own gasping breaths, the world was blessedly still.

We didn't die.

Yet.

Her eyes flew open. Miraculously, her glasses had somehow survived the tumble down the mountain and were still on. Which gave her a startlingly clear view of a pair of brilliant blue eyes staring directly into hers from just inches away. It was only then that she realized just how intimately she was pressed against him. Her breasts were crushed to his chest, her cleavage straining the top of her lacy bra, her blouse having surrendered several buttons. Her right thigh was sandwiched between both of his legs, pressing against a very warm spot that left little to the imagination about just how well-proportioned he was to his taller-than-average height. Her cheeks flaming, she tried to scramble off him.

"Hold it, wait." His harsh whisper had her going still as his hands tightened on her arms. He tilted his head back and looked up the mountain they'd just tumbled down, apparently searching for the gunmen.

Her gaze followed his. She didn't see anyone. But what she did see had her shaking again. How they'd managed to fall so far through such rough terrain without being killed was a mystery. As she noticed the deep skid and slide marks down the grassy and rocky terrain, and the broken tree branches that marked their path, she realized that maybe it wasn't such a mystery after all. Her benefactor had rolled and tugged and pulled her to him the entire ride down. That was the only thing that explained how they hadn't crashed into boulders and trees and been killed. He'd done that. He'd protected both of them.

Or he'd protected *her*, at least.

Her eyes filled with tears as she realized just what his noble actions had cost him. Blood was drying on his face from his earlier cuts, likely from an altercation or ambush by the second gunman, the one named Owen. More blood streaked his arms and neck. A long gash marred his left biceps, blood trickling from a wound that was smeared with dirt. A black shadow was already darkening on his forehead where he'd obviously smacked it against something. And her? Other than a bitten tongue, dirty and torn clothes, and a few stinging minor cuts on her arms and legs, she was unharmed.

"You're hurt," she said. "I'm so sorry. Do you have a first-aid kit in your backpack? I can dress your wounds."

His gaze shot to hers. "Are you okay? You're crying."

The concern in his voice as he reached a hand toward her had shame and guilt flaring up inside. She jerked back to scramble off him but slammed down against his chest because of the rope that still connected them.

"Sorry, sorry. Dang it." She wiped the tears away and tried to tug the rope free.

"Here, let me." His deep voice was soft again, gentle, as he pressed the carabiners on each side of his pack. A few quick tugs on the knots and they seemed to magically unravel. Another yank and the slick nylon rope pulled free from her belt loops.

She pressed against the ground on either side of his chest and pushed herself up off him, then sat back on her heels and yanked the ends of her blouse back together to cover her bra.

"Are you okay?" he asked again, sitting up.

She nodded. "Thanks to you, I'm fine. But you're not." She waved toward the dozens of cuts on his arms, his face. "You took the brunt of the fall to protect me. Why would you do that?"

He frowned as if in confusion. "Why wouldn't I? It's my job."

She shook her head, unable to fathom such selfless thinking. "First-aid kit?"

"Later." He pushed to his knees and looked up again. "I don't see our two friends."

She followed his gaze to the cliff, which seemed impossibly far away. She still couldn't believe they'd rolled down the mountain and hadn't gotten killed, or shot, or both. But thankfully the gunmen weren't standing there, aiming a pistol at them.

"Why aren't they still up there, trying to shoot us?" she asked. "Maybe they didn't think we'd survive the drop?" She shivered and wrapped her hands around her waist. "Maybe they're worried someone heard the shots, so they took off?"

He shook his head. "Unless there are more trespassers ignoring the trail-closed signs, there's no one else to hear the gunshots. And I don't see our friends just moseying to their car and heading back where they came from after all the trouble they went to. They're after something. And they don't have it yet." His eyes stared deep into hers, once again darkening with suspicion. "How much motivation do they have, Jody? Enough to figure out a way down that mountain to come after us?"

A cold chill shot through her. She looked up again. But the only thing above them was a bright blue sky and a hawk gliding over the mountaintops.

"Jody? Who were those men? Why are they after you?" He climbed to his feet and helped her stand.

She stepped back so she could meet his gaze without getting a crick in her neck. "You're bleeding. I really think we should get the first aid kit." She took another step back.

He grabbed her waist and yanked her to the side. "Haven't you ever been in the mountains before? Never back up without looking first."

She glanced over her shoulder and sucked in a breath. The blood seemed to drain from her body, leaving her cold and shaking. Once again, she'd been close to the edge of another drop-off and had nearly plunged over the side.

Swallowing hard, she pressed a shaking hand to her

throat. "Thank you. You've saved me more times than I can count and we've known each other for less than an hour."

"We need to go." He put a hand to the small of her back and urged her toward the charred woods to their right.

"Go where? It looks like we're heading toward another cliff." She tried to stop, but his hand was firm, pushing her forward.

"We'll make our own path. We have to. Out here we're too much in the open." He held back a branch on a new sapling that had sprouted from the destruction.

They rounded a curve in the mountain, the going steep, treacherous, with loose rocks underfoot. A few yards farther and they were surrounded by trees, half of them scorched but miraculously still standing. Some of them supported canopies of new growth in spite of their blackened trunks. The underbrush had resurged here. Many of the bushes were taller than both of them.

Far below, water gurgled and rushed over boulders. She caught glimpses of it through breaks in the trees. Rocks in the middle of the stream created eddies and little rapids. The artist in her craved a few moments to stand there and gape at the beauty below, to frame it in her mind's eye like she'd frame a camera shot. But the reality of their situation, and the imposing ranger beside her, had her hurrying as fast as she could manage through the rough terrain.

He took the outside, near the steep drop, using the rise of the mountain as a barrier against her falling over the edge. His gaze was never still. He constantly scanned the woods around them, looking up at the mountain that rose above their heads. His constant vigilance should have made her feel secure. Instead, it only reminded her of the danger they were in.

She finally grabbed one of the saplings they were passing and used it as an anchor in the sea of fear that threatened to pull her under. "Wait."

He stopped beside her, brows raised in question.

"Your arms—some of the cuts are still bleeding. And they need to be cleaned so they don't get infected. Do you have medical supplies in your pack?"

"You're stalling, Jody. We need to get moving."

She waved a hand toward the trees surrounding them. "Unless those gunmen take a swan dive over a cliff or have billy goat ancestors, I don't see how they could follow us. It's too steep and rocky."

"They don't have to get too close. They just need one clear shot. Up on the trail, we were jumping over downed trees and weaving around curves. Plus, their adrenaline was probably pumping pretty good. Otherwise they wouldn't have missed. I don't want to hang around in one spot and give them a perfect target."

Her hand tightened around the sapling. "You're not helping."

He frowned again. "Helping with what?"

She huffed out an impatient breath. "I'm scared, okay? Right now I'm more afraid of plunging headfirst over a cliff again than some gunmen who may or may not be following us."

His expression softened. "I wish I didn't have to force you to keep going. But I don't see those guys giving up that easily."

She swallowed. "Why do you say that?"

"Because they thought nothing of trying to shoot a federal officer. Your average thug thinks twice in a situation like that. They don't want to risk bringing the wrath of the feds down on them. But our guys not only shot at us multiple times, they risked their own lives running up a dangerous trail to do it. My guess is they might lie low for a little while to see whether backup arrives. But not for long. Then they'll be looking for a way to hike down here and find us."

He motioned toward the radio hooked to his belt. "I've turned this thing on half a dozen times since our flight down the mountain. There's no signal, not even a burst of static. One of the radio towers was destroyed in the wildfires. What we have to do is get within range of another tower so we can radio for help. Until then, we keep going." He arched a brow. "Unless you can tell me why those men might decide to hightail it out of here without finishing us off. Just what are they after? Who are they?"

She hesitated.

His jaw tightened. "Jody—"

"I don't know their names, other than the one calling the other Owen in front of both of us."

"You're splitting hairs. Not knowing their full names and not knowing what they want are two very different things. You were arguing with the first man when I approached. He later warned you to remember what he'd told you. What were you arguing about? What did he want you to remember?"

Without waiting for her reply, he pried her hand from the tree and tugged her through the woods.

Her foot skidded on some loose rocks. She let out a yelp, but he grabbed her around the waist and steadied her before she could fall.

"I've got you," he said. "Try not to worry. My boots hold the trail a lot better than your sneakers. I'm not going to let anything happen to you, okay?"

His voice was gentle again. But there was an underlying thread of steel. He wanted answers. And he deserved them. Even if it meant she might go to jail, or at the least, have all her career aspirations ruined. All those years of college, the sacrifices she'd made, the two jobs she was holding down were for nothing. In one stupid week, she'd destroyed it all.

She jerked to a halt, pressing a hand to her throat. "I can't believe how selfish I'm being, thinking about my future career and prison when Tracy's missing." She moved her hand to her stomach. "That's just the kind of thing my adoptive father would do." She squeezed her eyes shut. "I think I'm going to be sick."

"Your career? Prison? Wait, who's Tracy?"

Chapter Five

Jody groaned and whirled around, gagging as she dropped to her knees and emptied the contents of her stomach.

Suddenly a strong arm was around her waist and a gentle hand swept her hair back from her face, holding it loosely behind her as Adam spoke soothing words in her ear. She was too sick and miserable to protest his help. The spasms wouldn't seem to stop and she started dry heaving.

"Deep breaths," he said. "Slow, deep breaths. You'll be okay. Slow and easy."

Somehow the sound of his voice calmed her. She dragged in a deep breath, then another. The knots in her stomach eased, and she could finally breathe normally without feeling like her stomach was trying to kill her.

Her world suddenly tilted as he scooped her up into his arms. Before she could even ask him what he was doing, he'd set her down several feet away beneath the branches of a thick stand of trees. The realization that he was giving them cover in case the bad guys were around had her stomach clenching with dread. She pressed a hand to her belly.

"This should help." A bottle of water and a wet cloth appeared as if by magic as he handed them to her from the backpack he'd been carrying.

She rinsed her mouth out and spit. After a long drink, she washed her face with the cloth.

"Better?" He was on his knees in front of her, his brow furrowed with concern.

"Better. Thank you." She swept her hair back from her shoulders. Heat flushed her skin at the realization of what had just happened. She groaned and covered her face. "I can't believe you witnessed that. And that you helped me. I'm so embarrassed."

He tugged her hands down. "Jody, what made you so upset? Who's Tracy? Is she in trouble?"

She nodded miserably. "I think so. She texted me. That's why I was on the trail. Well, partly, anyway. I mean, I was in the parking lot. But she wasn't there, so I checked the bathrooms, and when I came out, that guy was there… and he started toward me. I saw his gun sticking out of his pocket, so I ran. I just ran. Then he was there, on the trail, with the gun—"

"Take a breath." He took one of her hands in his. "Back up. Who is Tracy?"

A ragged breath shuddered out of her. "My sister." She waved her hand. "Not a real sister. She's my friend. My very best friend. I don't have any biological siblings, just adoptive sisters and brothers. Not that I'm knocking adoptive families in general. I think they can be wonderful, for other people. But it hasn't turned out so well for me. We don't exactly visit each other or exchange Christmas cards." She drew a deep breath. "Tracy is not part of my adoptive family. She's my friend, my best friend, more of a sister to me than my adoptive sisters ever were. And her family is more of a family to me than my adoptive one." She closed her eyes and fisted her hands against the tops of her thighs.

"Tattoo Guy, he did something to her? To Tracy?"

She nodded and looked at him. "He abducted her. At least, that's what he told me. I didn't know, or I swear I would have called the police. I would never do anything to risk her life." She pressed her hand to her throat. "I think I may have just killed her. By running, with you. I shouldn't have done that." She squeezed her eyes shut again.

"Jody, I need you to be strong. For your friend, okay? I know it's hard. But you have to hold it together so we can figure out what to do. All right?"

She nodded and opened her eyes. "Okay. I'm sorry."

"Nothing to apologize for. I'm going to ask you some questions and I need you to give me the answers. Short and to the point. And we need to keep moving while we talk." He pulled her to her feet. "Can you do that?"

"I'll try. Yes. I'm sorry." She grimaced. "I know. Quit saying that."

He smiled and pulled her with him through the trees. "What's Tracy's full name?"

"Larson. Her name is Tracy Larson."

"Is she your age?"

"Yes. Twenty-four. We went to school together, from grade school through high school. She didn't go to college. I went to TSU, Tennessee State University, I... Sorry. Short and to the point. I forgot. Sorry."

"It's okay. I went to TSU, too. When's the last time you saw her?"

She patted her pocket to check the time of Tracy's last text messages on her phone. But her pocket was empty. They all were. "My phone and keys are gone." She shook her head. "I know. Doesn't matter. I think the last I heard from her was at work yesterday. She's full-time. I'm part-time. I left at my usual two o'clock."

He steered her around a downed tree. "Friday at 2:00 p.m.? You're sure?"

"Pretty sure. I'm not counting the fake text this morning. The guy with the gun must have sent that. He tricked me."

"We'll get to that in a second. Are you sure you didn't talk to Tracy on the phone after 2:00 p.m.?"

"Talk?"

His mouth quirked up in a smile. "Forgive me. I'm a doddering thirty-year-old who actually uses phones for spoken conversations. Let me rephrase. Did you text each other? Share anything on social media?"

She surprised herself by laughing, which seemed obscene given the situation. She quickly sobered. "Sorry. But the idea of you being described as doddering is ridiculous. Trust me, most women my age would count themselves lucky to be with a guy as smokin' hot as you."

Her face flushed with heat as soon as the words left her mouth. She absolutely refused to look at him. "Text, yes, we texted a few times. Nothing seemed out of the norm. Then, this morning, I got a new text from her saying she needed to meet me, that it was urgent. She said she'd be waiting in the parking lot at the Sugarland Mountain trailhead. I went to the visitor center, and her car wasn't there. I texted her to ask where she was, and she said in the parking lot on the other end of the trail, not the visitor center. So I headed there. Only, when I got there, her car wasn't there, either."

Tears burned the backs of her eyes, but she refused to give in to the urge to cry again. She swallowed against her tight throat and continued. "There were a couple of cars besides mine on the other side of the lot. One of them was a minivan with a family and kids. I didn't see anyone in the other car, a black Charger. Not then. The family went to use the public facilities by the beginning of the trail. Tracy texted back that she'd be there in a few minutes and to wait. I ducked into the restroom, chatted with some of the people from the minivan. They left before me. When I came out, they were just pulling out of the parking lot. That's when he got out of the car."

"Who? The guy with the tattoos?"

"Yes. I started toward my car, then stopped. He was walking really fast, straight toward me. But there wasn't anyone else around. And the men's restrooms were on the other side of the lot. There was no reason for him to be hurrying toward me. I don't know how to explain it. But he gave me the creeps, and he was between me and my car. I didn't want to let him get too close. So I walked toward the trail. I looked over my shoulder, and that's when I saw the gun." She swallowed. "He had a pistol sticking out of his pants pocket. I ran. I hopped over the cattle gate blocking the trail and took off. And he took off after me."

"Did he fire the gun?"

She frowned. "No. No, he never did. Not until you and I were running up the trail later."

He nodded as if that made sense to him. "Go on. You ran. Then what happened?"

"I used to run track in high school. I was pretty fast. But I'm not used to running up mountains or having to hop over downed trees. I couldn't sprint and pull away like I would in a flat footrace. He caught up to me right where you saw us. And he...he pointed his gun at me. And he..." She drew a ragged breath.

"You're doing great, Jody. Slow, deep breaths. What did he do next? What did he say to you?"

As much as she wanted to be strong for her friend, she was having a hard time holding back her terror. What was happening to Tracy right now? What had that man done to her? Was she even alive or had he lied to her?

"Jody. What did the man do when he caught you on the trail?" He steered her around a particularly rocky section and past some thorny shrubs.

She murmured her thanks and straightened. She could do this. She had to. For Tracy's sake. "He told me I had something of his and he wanted it. He said if I didn't give it to him, he would…he would kill Tracy." In spite of her efforts to stay calm, tears tracked down her cheeks. "He had her phone, showed it to me. That's how I knew he was telling the truth. He must have texted me to meet him there, pretending he was her. No way could he have gotten her phone without taking it from her. That thing is practically attached at her hip."

He pulled her to a halt and grasped her shoulders. "What do you have that he wants?"

"I don't have anything. I swear. He insisted I have pictures, maybe a video, or knew where they were. He said my boss had seen something he shouldn't have and that there was a gap in the time stamps on the pictures."

"Your boss?"

"Sam Campbell. He's a private investigator. Tracy and I work for him." She looked away, panic swelling inside her again. She'd been so stupid. So very, very stupid.

"You know what he's after, don't you?" The thread of steel was back in his voice.

She glanced up at him and wiped at the tears on her cheeks. "Not specifically, no. I assume that Sam performed surveillance on him, that he's one of Sam's clients. But all of Sam's pictures and videos are locked up at the office. I told him that. He shook his head, said that he'd searched there already. That's when we heard you whistling. He told me to keep my mouth shut, that Tracy would die if I told you anything."

His eyes widened. "You lied to me up on the trail to get me to leave you two alone, knowing he had a gun? If I'd bought your story, you would have been all alone with him. He could have killed you."

"I know. Looking back, it was stupid. But I didn't know what else to do. Tracy—" Her voice broke.

"You thought he would kill her if you didn't do what he told you. You risked your life for her. Whatever happens, you can't blame yourself. You did what you could."

She shook her head. "No. I was stupid, too scared to think straight. You don't make deals with criminals. What I should have done was shove him or something when you came up and yelled a warning." Her hand shook as she raked her hair back from her face. "You could have been killed."

He frowned. "Is that why you came looking for me after I chased Tattoo Guy down the trail? You were trying to save me?"

She snorted. "Fat lot of good it did. I just slowed you down. And now you're all scratched up and out here with me, without a weapon, with a couple of thugs possibly coming after us. I'm such an idiot."

His warm, strong hand gently urged her chin up so she had to look at him.

She pushed his hand away. "Go ahead. Yell at me. My stupidity has probably gotten my friend killed and nearly got you killed. Every decision I made was wrong. You'd have thought I would have learned better at college."

"What do you mean?"

"I studied criminal justice, graduated with honors. Not that it means I have any sense. Might as well tear up that piece of paper."

He frowned. "Aren't you being a bit hard on yourself? You drove up here because a friend said she needed you. A man chased you with a gun, threatened to kill your friend if you didn't do what he said. And as soon as you had a chance to escape, instead, you went *toward* trouble, to help a law enforcement officer you thought was in need. From where I stand, that's pretty darn amazing."

She blinked. "What?"

"You have the education, but not the training or the experience. And you're a civilian, unarmed. You did the best you could. I can't find fault with any of your decisions."

"Th...thank you?"

He smiled. "Come on. There are a lot of gaps in your story, like why someone with a criminal justice degree is working part-time as a private investigator." He tugged her hand, then stopped and looked over his shoulder at her when she pulled back. "Jody?"

"I'm not a private investigator," she confessed. "And when I tell you the rest, you aren't going to think I did the best I could or made good decisions. I didn't."

He turned to face her. "Go on."

"Tracy pretty much runs the office. I guess you'd call her an administrative assistant. I help Sam with his cases. But I'm not a licensed investigator, just a recent criminal justice grad trying to get some experience to help me get the job I really want—as a criminal investigator with the prosecutor's office. But those jobs are few and far between, so I'm working two jobs to make ends meet and trying to get a step up on the competition when the job I want opens up."

She waved her hand again. "Anyway, my point is that I'm his gofer, his researcher. Sometimes I interview clients and things like that. Sam does all the heavy lifting, and I take care of the grunt work."

He studied her intently, as if weighing her every word. "So far I'm not hearing any bad decisions or things for you to be worried about."

She tightened her hands into fists by her sides. "There's more. I screwed up. I mean, really, really screwed up." She let out a shaky breath and met his gaze again. "Sam disappeared a week ago. And before you ask, no, it's not unusual. He's had a tough time since his wife died of ovarian cancer about a year ago. He hits the bottle too hard.

He usually shows up a few days later and will be fine for a while." She clenched her fists so hard the nails dug into her palms. "We always cover for him when he's on a binge. Do you understand what I'm telling you? He could lose his license if clients complain that he's a drunk and messes up cases. And besides that, if he messes up the cases, the income stops rolling in. And, well, Tracy and I both rely on that income. We live paycheck to paycheck. No paycheck means no food, no rent."

He stared at her intently. "You did more than run errands, didn't you?"

She nodded. "We may have…pretended to be Sam to some of the clients, through correspondence in the mail… to close out cases, resolve issues."

"You operated as PIs without a license. You're worried that you may have committed fraud. Even worse, mail fraud. That's a felony."

She winced and looked away.

The silence stretched out between them.

"Jody. There's more, isn't there?"

She nodded slowly.

His sigh could have knocked over a tree. "Go on. Might as well tell me the rest."

She swallowed, then forced herself to meet his gaze. Surprisingly, it wasn't the cold, judgmental look she'd expected. Instead, he looked at her with something far worse.

Pity.

She stiffened her spine and confessed the rest of her sins.

"Sam is dead. Tracy and I killed him."

Chapter Six

Adam dropped his chin to his chest and shook his head. If for even one second he thought Jody was telling the truth, he'd have pulled out his second set of handcuffs and Mirandized her. But in spite of her low opinion of herself, she struck him as painfully honest. In the span of a few hours, she'd confessed more to him than most people confessed to their priests. This young woman didn't know how to lie convincingly, as proven by the fiasco up on the trail. And she'd apologized at least a dozen times in the past few minutes, and meant it. She was riddled with guilt over things she shouldn't even feel guilty about. No way had she murdered someone.

"Okay," he said. "Tell me how you two did the dirty deed. Poison? Butcher knife? Machete?"

"Are you seriously making fun of me?"

He raised his head and gave her a baleful glance. "Are you seriously going to try to convince me you murdered someone?"

"Well, not directly, we didn't. But we might as well have. When Sam disappeared, we should have gone to the police, filled out a missing-persons report and—"

"Which the police would have set aside. They would have told you to give it a few more days because there was no evidence of foul play and your boss has a history of going off on drinking binges."

She crossed her arms, her mouth drawn into a tight line. "Am I wrong? You said he disappeared all the time."

"That's not fair to Sam. He's a great man, more of a father to me than my adoptive father ever was. He doesn't disappear *all* the time. Just sometimes. And it's not like I think we should have reported it the first morning he didn't show up. There was no reason to think anything was wrong. But he's never been gone a whole week before. We should have done something on day five instead of…of… committing fraud. And then maybe Sam would be okay."

Everything about her posture and her tone told him she truly felt responsible. And he hadn't missed the hurt look in her eyes the last time she'd met his gaze. Which was several minutes ago. Now she was staring off into the woods, her pretty face mottled, her jaw tight. She was obviously upset, both because she took the weight of the world on her shoulders and because he'd made light of her claims. She'd really be angry if she knew how hard he was struggling not to laugh, or at least not to smile.

He cocked his head, studying her profile. She'd been through a traumatic experience. Her boss was missing— even though Adam was inclined to think the man would show up alive and well with a wicked hangover. Adam had met Sam Campbell a few times over the years and was well-acquainted with his reputation around town for going on occasional drinking binges—even before his wife's death. Not that Jody apparently knew that. His employees were trying to hide a secret that wasn't even a secret.

But Jody's best friend was *really* missing. And Tracy Larson was *not* likely to show up alive and well. Jody had been chased, threatened, shot at, pulled off a cliff—all in all the kind of morning that would crush most civilians.

But here she stood, her back ramrod straight, her mouth compressed into a mutinous line as she glared her hurt feelings at the mountains around them.

And his teasing, his refusal to take her seriously had only added to her burden.

His shoulders slumped. He'd handled this all wrong. He started to apologize but stopped. What was he supposed to say? *Sorry I didn't believe that you could kill someone in cold blood?* She seemed so young in so many ways. At twenty-four, she was only six years younger than him. His last girlfriend had been younger, twenty-three. But Brandy had been just as bruised by the world and jaded as he was. The years between them hadn't mattered. This girl didn't seem world-weary or jaded and he didn't get the impression that she realized just how horrible or cruel people could sometimes be.

She crossed her arms, the movement pushing up her small breasts in the delicate, lacy bra that her torn blouse did little to conceal. His body's reaction to that innocent display surprised him. He could feel himself tightening, heat pulsing through his veins. And he had to admit, now that he *really* looked at her for the first time since this had all started, there was nothing girlish about her figure.

She was all woman, from her luscious red hair that bounced around her shoulders to the full, pink lips that gave her mouth a pouty, sultry look to her narrow waist that begged for a man's hands to span its narrow curves. Her legs weren't long and lean like Brandy's had been. But on Jody, her short, toned, silky-looking legs were the perfect complement to the rest of her. Even those green glasses on her perky nose were cute. All in all, she was one sexy package. And now that he'd finally noticed, he was cursing himself for the lust that shot through him. Jody needed a protector, not some guy drooling after her.

He forced his gaze back to her face and cleared his throat.

She arched a brow and looked at him in question, the hurt and anger still broadcast in her expression like a neon sign flashing at him. If she ever played poker, she'd lose every round. The art of bluffing was beyond her. Which was, all in all, refreshing. Most people he knew were great liars and couldn't be trusted. He had a feeling he could trust Jody in any situation, and she wouldn't let him down.

Maybe it was time he told her that. And confessed his own half-truths he'd tossed out earlier.

"You didn't sign your boss's name on anything you mailed, did you?"

She frowned. "No, why?"

"Then it's unlikely you committed fraud. All you did was manage the office, continue to send your boss's mail for him, tie up loose ends—stuff administrative assistants do for their bosses every day of the week all over the world. Unless you actually went up to someone and claimed to be a private investigator, you can let that guilt go. You didn't do anything wrong."

"But—"

"But nothing." He squeezed her hand. "I'm sorry I didn't treat your concerns more seriously earlier. You've been through a lot, and you're worried about your boss and your friend. I should have been a better listener and commiserated more."

She cleared her throat. "Well, maybe. But I was being a bit over-the-top when I said we'd killed Sam. It's just that I'm really worried about him. I wish I'd done something more when he didn't show up. Now, with Tracy missing, and that creepy man with the gun thinking Sam had more pictures of him somewhere, I can't help worrying everything's connected and both Tracy and Sam are either in real trouble or—"

"Leave the 'or' to me, okay? That's my job, to worry about stuff like that." He tugged her forward and they started through the woods again. "Let's focus on getting you to safety and then I'll work with the local police to start an investigation and search for your friend. If I were a betting man, I'd bet you that Sam is alive and well, passed out on his couch at home. And your friend is alive, too."

Her hand tightened in his. "You really think so?"

"I do," he lied, seeing no point in making her even more miserable. "And as long as Tattoo Guy thinks you have something he needs, he won't hurt Tracy. He needs her as leverage. His threats up on the trail were a complete bluff."

She stopped, and he did, too, facing her.

"Why do you think it was a bluff?"

"Because he didn't shoot you. In the parking lot, you said he chased you up the trail, then confronted you. If he'd wanted to kill you, he could have. Instead, he threatened you, threatened your friend's life, to get you to talk. To tell him where the pictures are that he thinks are floating around somewhere. That's your bargaining chip. As long as he thinks you have something he needs, he'll keep Tracy safe as leverage."

"Then...those were just warning shots? He wouldn't really shoot us?"

Adam laughed harshly. "Oh no. He'll kill me the first chance he gets. No doubt. And his type, he'll hurt you in a heartbeat. Might even try to shoot you in the leg or bust your kneecap to get you to talk. Or worse." He forced a smile he was far from feeling when he saw the worry in her eyes. "Which is why we don't want to risk him catching up to us if he wasn't smart enough to head back to his car and hightail it out of here."

A deep rumble sounded in the distance.

They both looked up at the sky. Instead of the brilliant

blue it had been earlier, it was rapidly turning dark and ominous with heavy rainclouds blowing in to cover the sun.

"A storm's rolling in. And we aren't anywhere near the next cell tower yet to radio for someone to get us out of here before the lightning show starts."

"That's crazy. There was no hint of an oncoming storm a few minutes ago."

"Oh, I'm sure there were hints. We were just more focused on watching out for thugs than keeping an eye on the weather." He studied the terrain around them, then pointed off to the right. "There, see how the mountain forms a natural depression over there? Away from trees or rocks that will conduct electricity? That's the safest place around here to hunker down when the lightning starts. Won't keep us dry in the rain, but it's safer than being under trees or becoming human lightning rods out here in the open like we are now. Let's go."

He motioned for her to join him and led her down a steeper descent than they'd been taking before. He hadn't wanted to risk her twisting an ankle or getting scraped up on the rocks if she lost her footing, so he'd been leading her around the mountain, taking a more gradual slope down toward the valley below. But storms up here could be deadly. There was no time to waste.

Sure enough, her sneakers weren't up to the task of navigating the rocky path. She wobbled and skittered across some loose stones, her arms flailing as she tried to maintain her balance. He grabbed her waist, steadying her.

"Next time you hike in the mountains, wear some decent shoes," he teased.

She smiled up at him. And it did crazy things to his breathing.

He swallowed and urged her forward again. The breeze that had kicked up helped cool his body and bring clarity to his thoughts. They really did need to find shelter, fast, or they could get struck by lightning, or even drown in a flash flood if they were crossing one of the dry creek beds when the rains started.

Boom!

Jody looked up at the sky. Adam tackled her, wrapping his arms protectively around her as they both fell to the ground. He heard her gasp of pain when they landed, the breath leaving her in a whoosh as her chin smacked his chest. The back of his head snapped against a rock, practically making his teeth rattle.

She shoved against him. "What was that for? The thunder—"

"It wasn't thunder. Move, move, move!" He rolled and grabbed her around the waist, yanking her up with him in a crouch.

Boom! Boom!

A chunk of rock exploded inches from Adam's head.

Jody let out a startled yelp and looked over her shoulder. "Was that—"

"Gunfire!" He shoved her in front of him, shielding her body with his. "Run, Jody. Run!"

Chapter Seven

Chh-chh.

The ominous sound didn't have to be explained. Jody had heard it dozens of times in action movies. It was the sound of a shotgun being pumped.

Adam was already pulling her to the ground before she could react.

Boom! Chh-chh. Boom!

Leaves and sawdust rained down on them from the tree above. Jody let out a squeak of fear before she could stop herself. She started to push off the ground to run again, but Adam pressed her back down.

He held his fingers to his mouth, signaling her to be quiet, then pointed to his right and motioned for her to precede him.

She nodded to let him know she understood, even though she wanted to yell at him for always making himself a human target to protect her. It wasn't right, regardless of what his job title might be. But arguing would only make him more of a target as the men pursuing them homed in on the sounds.

Her bare knees screamed in protest as she half crawled, half duckwalked through the woods, behind clumps of bushes and trees, toward another group of boulders. She tried to avoid dried leaves, twigs, anything that could crunch or snap and give away their location. But everything in this half-burned section of the mountains seemed to make noise when she touched it. All she could do was hope the sound didn't carry to the men chasing them. Their only chance was to give them the slip, find a hiding place and hunker down.

A hand tapped her shoulder. She looked back at Adam. He held up one finger, pointed off to their left and then held his hands out together as if he were holding a shotgun. Her stomach sank, but she nodded in understanding. He held up a finger again and pointed a little farther to the left, almost behind them. This time he held his other hand out, pointer finger extended, thumb raised, in an imitation of a handgun. He must have seen Owen and Tattoo Guy, both closing in on them. One of them had a pistol. How had the other one gotten a shotgun? Had they hidden one in the woods, just in case the threat about Tracy failed? In case Jody managed to escape and they had to give chase?

She nodded, again letting him know she understood. Then she held her hands out in a gesture of helplessness and mouthed, "What do we do now?"

He pointed to the right and once again held both his hands out as if he were holding a shotgun, or maybe a rifle. She bit her lip to keep from crying out in frustration. At least now she knew where Tattoo Guy and Owen had gotten a shotgun. A third man was after them. He must have been a reinforcement, and he'd brought more weapons.

Please don't let there be a fourth thug out here with yet another gun.

He pointed to her, then himself, then motioned behind him. She frowned. That couldn't be right. He wanted them to go back the way they'd already come? She shook her head and pointed straight in front of them, a direct line that would keep the two guys to their left and the other to the right.

His brows drew down, and he shook his head. "Trust me," he mouthed silently. "Come on."

She didn't protest when he grasped her shoulders and turned her around. All she could do was put her faith in him and, as he'd told her, trust him. He was the professional, and she presumed he knew his way around this mountain. She sure didn't.

Her instincts screamed at her to jump up and run. It would be much faster. The ground was almost level in this section of the mountain. They'd descended to a valley or a plateau, perfect for stretching out her legs and putting on a burst of speed and stamina that would take her far away from this place in no time. Years of running, both in school and out, would finally come in handy—if Adam would give her the chance. As long as she didn't have to run an obstacle course—leaping over rocks and trees that had slowed her down on the trail above them—she was confident she could outrun these thugs.

But she couldn't outrun a bullet.

Feeling all kinds of wrong about it, she did as Adam directed. Half crawling, half walking in a deep crouch, turning left or right each time he thumped her on one of her shoulders from behind to let her know which direction to go.

It seemed like an eternity had passed by the time he tugged her hair in what she assumed was his way of telling her to stop. The man was treating her like a horse with his tapping and hair pulling. She wanted to scream in frustration. Instead, she looked over her shoulder and arched a brow to ask him what to do next. But he wasn't looking at her. He was staring off into the woods, eyes narrowed, every muscle tense and alert. He reminded her of a panther: stealthy, alert, searching for prey. Except that in this case, she and Adam were the prey. They were the ones being hunted.

His eyes widened, and he suddenly grabbed her waist, hauling her backward with him. She scrabbled with her feet, pushing back to help him. Once they were behind a downed tree, he shoved her onto the ground and covered her with his body.

Good grief, he was heavy. About six feet, three inches of pure muscle squashed her into the dirt, the musty smell of pine needles and wet moss seeping into her lungs. Drawing a deep breath was impossible, so she breathed shallowly, one after the other, struggling to get enough oxygen.

The sharp crack of a snapping twig sounded close by. She froze. Adam pressed her even harder into the ground, and it dawned on her that he had dark clothes on and she had a white blouse. In the gloom of this part of the forest, her white shirt would stand out like a beacon. He was doing everything he could to keep her hidden and make sure her shirt didn't alert their pursuers.

Another crack sounded, but it was farther away. The men searching for them must not have seen them and were moving off in another direction.

Her lungs screamed for air. Dark spots began to fill her vision. She could feel her energy seeping away. Her limbs went limp like noodles. A strange buzzing sounded in her ears. The weight lifted and everything turned on its axis.

"Jody."

She gasped, drawing a deep lungful of air, then another and another. The dark veil fell away. She blinked and looked up into Adam's beautiful eyes just inches from hers. His brow was lined with worry, his mouth tight as he gently shook her.

"Jody," he whispered harshly. "Are you okay?" He shook her again, his gaze searching hers.

She shoved his hands away. "I'm fine," she whispered. "Couldn't breathe."

He winced. "Sorry," he mouthed silently and held his fingers to his lips, letting her know they weren't alone, that the gunmen were still hunting them.

She pushed against his chest so she could get to her knees and follow wherever he led. Instead, he scooped her up into his arms and ran. He was bent over at the waist, keeping as low as possible so the bushes and trees could conceal them.

She clutched his shirt, holding on for dear life, the trees and bushes rushing past, making her dizzy. She squeezed her eyes shut and focused on making herself as small as possible, pulling in her arms and legs. It was a wild ride, with her bobbing up and down in his arms, feeling like she was going to fall any second. But he didn't let her fall. He protected her, as he'd done since the first moment he'd met her.

Where were the men who were after them? For him to be running like this, they must be close. But no one was shooting at them, so they must not have seen them. Not yet, anyway. She felt his chest rise and fall against hers. Carrying her and running in such an unnatural, bent-over position was taking its toll. His strides were slowing, his breaths coming faster and faster as he struggled to keep up his blistering pace.

"Put. Me. Down." Each word bounced out of her in unison with his strides.

Instead of stopping, he pulled her tighter against him, his mouth pressed next to her ear. "Too close," he rasped.

"I can run faster than you think. Put me down. *Please.*"

He stumbled and cursed, then stumbled again. He

dropped to the ground, spilling her out of his arms onto a carpet of thick leaves and wild grasses. She scrambled to her knees and turned to check on him and ask which way they should run.

Then she froze.

She clasped her hand over her mouth to keep from crying out in dismay, mindful of the footfalls in the distance, pounding against the forest floor. Coming closer.

She scrambled to Adam, careful to stay low behind the grasses and bushes. Tears stung the backs of her eyes as she met his pain-racked gaze. From midchest down, his body was wedged in some kind of hole, a sinkhole or maybe a wild animal's den. He'd braced his arms beside him and was struggling to pull himself free. But every time he moved, his face went pale. He was obviously in terrible pain.

Footfalls sounded harder against the ground, louder, coming closer.

Someone shouted. Another man answered, though Jody couldn't quite make out the words.

"Hide," Adam ordered, his voice low, gritty. Talking was obviously a struggle.

"I'm not leaving you in this hole," she whispered.

"Go." He pushed her hands away when she reached out to help him. He motioned toward the nearest stand of trees. "Hurry, before they see you."

Another shout sounded.

She reached for him again, but he shoved her hand away.

"Jody, get out of here. Head into those trees. There's nothing you can do to help me." He pressed his hands against the ground and strained, his arms shaking from the effort. His body barely moved. He was good and stuck.

She turned in a circle, desperate to find something that might help. There, a thick, broken piece of a branch a few feet away. She lunged for it, grabbed it and yanked it over to Adam. What now? There wasn't any room around his chest to shove the stick into the hole and try to pry him out.

"Over there," a shout sounded. "I think I saw something."

Adam grabbed her arm and yanked her close. "Leave me. Run into the woods. Save yourself, Jody. Hurry!"

"They'll kill you. I can't just hide while they find you and shoot you."

"There's no other choice. I'm stuck. Better that you survive than both of us die. *Go.*"

She whirled around again on her knees, looking for something else, anything, to give him a chance. There were boulders close by, but they wouldn't hide him for long. He was a sitting duck out here. Wait. Boulders. The branch she'd dragged over was too short, but if she got a longer one…

"Hold on," she whispered.

"Jody—"

She scrambled away from him, her heart pounding in rhythm with the footfalls she could hear. Taking a risk, she lifted up just enough to see over the closest bush, then ducked back down. All three men were in sight, about twenty feet apart from each other, maybe fifty yards away. They were searching behind every bush, every tree. They'd be here in a couple of minutes, maybe less. She turned around and around, then she saw it. Another branch, this one thicker, longer, like a bat or a thick cane. It would work. It had to.

She scrambled to it, then dragged it back to Adam and shoved both ends of the branch between some boulders. The main part of the branch was about a foot above him. He gave her a furious look, then grabbed the branch. It held.

He strained against it, twisting and pulling. The ground around his chest moved. It was working.

"Did you hear something, Owen? Where did that come from?"

Adam froze and looked at Jody. "Go," he ordered again. She hesitated.

He strained, pushing and pulling on the branch, twisting his body. He rose an inch, two, then fell back, his face a mirror of pain. The men were almost upon them. They would shoot him, kill him. Maybe they'd shoot her, too, wing her as he'd warned, take her prisoner so they could interrogate her for whatever they thought she had.

She glanced toward the trees where Adam had told her to run, to hide. The boulders and bushes might block her from sight long enough for her to reach cover. But that wouldn't save the honorable man caught in the hole, a man who'd risked his life repeatedly for her.

He was waving at her, his face a mask of fury as he tried to get her to run into the woods. She ignored him. She looked past the woods to the left. The trees were sparser there. But the ground was nearly level. A fast track, as her old high school coach would have said. And it wasn't close to Adam like the trees where he wanted her to hide.

She looked back at Adam, who looked like he wanted to murder her himself.

Please, please let this work. Let him live.

She bent over and ran in a crouch about thirty feet away from him. Then she stood.

"Over there!" Tattoo Guy yelled. "She's over there!"

Jody took off, arms and legs pumping as she sprinted across the open field.

Chapter Eight

Jody whirled around, swinging the knobby length of branch like a baseball bat when one of the men got too close.

The other two laughed as they continued to toy with her, slowly tightening their circle around her in the small clearing.

"What do you want from me?" she demanded.

The pockmarked one named Owen grinned and lunged toward her.

She swung the branch in a wide arc.

He jumped back, laughing and grinning the whole time. "She's feistier than her friend."

Her stomach dropped. "Where is she? Where's Tracy?" She tightened her grip on the branch, twisting and turning, trying to keep tabs on all three of them.

"She's alive," Tattoo Guy told her. "But she won't be for long if you don't tell me where your boss keeps all his pictures and videos."

She gritted her teeth. "Why don't you ask Sam?"

His mouth quirked in a cruel smile. "Already did. He wasn't any more forthcoming than your little friend. I was hoping you'd be more cooperative."

"I told you. I don't know where any more pictures or videos are. Sam locks them all up in the office every day. Are you a client of his? Maybe you got things mixed up. Maybe you thought Sam had more information but he didn't—"

"Where's the cop, Jody girl?"

She clutched the branch harder. "He…he didn't make it. When we went over the cliff. I…had to leave his body there."

"Now, now, Jody." He stopped in front of her, just out of reach of her tree branch while the others kept circling. "And here I thought we were beginning to understand each other. But then you lie to me." He shook his head. "I don't like liars." He made a quick motion with his left hand.

Jody spun around in that direction, swinging her branch as hard and fast as she could. *Crack!* It slammed into the side of Owen's head. His eyes rolled up and he dropped to the ground, blood dribbling from the corner of his mouth.

She stared down at him in horror. Had she killed him? No, his chest moved. It moved again. He was breathing.

"Go on, Thad. Teach her a lesson."

She jerked her head up. Tattoo Guy was standing off to the side, still out of reach. The other man, Thad, was circling her again. But he wasn't smiling. And he was holding a knife.

She tightened her grip on the branch. Her heart was beating so hard her pulse thudded in her ears. Had she really endured this whole horrible day only to die here, two hundred yards from where she'd left Adam? She hadn't managed to give him much distance to get away. Would he be able to escape before they backtracked and found him?

Thad darted toward her, knife extended.

She swung the branch.

He leaped back just in time, laughing again. He was enjoying this.

He feinted left, then jabbed toward her right.

She jumped to the side, bringing the branch around just

in time to slap the knife back. That was close, too close. Her breaths came in short, choppy pants. They circled each other like two boxers. She tried to watch out for Tattoo Guy, keeping him in her peripheral vision. But Thad kept circling and she had to keep turning or risk him stabbing her from behind.

"We're wasting time, Thad. Just stick her already."

Jody's stomach clenched.

Thad's face scrunched up with concentration as he moved in for the kill. He raised the knife over his head, moved closer, closer.

She clutched the branch, knowing she might only get one chance.

Thad let out a guttural yell, a battle cry that made Jody's blood run cold. He lunged forward, knife raised. She screamed her fear, frustration and rage as she swung the branch with every ounce of strength she had.

"No!" Thad yelled, a split second before a dark shape barreled into him, slamming him to the ground.

Jody's swing met empty air. Her momentum sent her crashing to the ground, and the branch flew from her hand.

Vicious curses sounded from a few feet off to her left. Behind her came more swearing and thumps. She shoved herself up to her knees and looked around. Tattoo Guy was the one to her left, his face contorted in rage as he drew his gun. She jerked around to look behind her. Thad was on the ground, wrestling with the man who'd tackled him— Adam! And just a few feet away, the knife blade winked in the light, the prize Thad was struggling to grab.

Bam!

She ducked down and whirled around to see Tattoo Guy, gun out, pointing it at the two men locked in combat. He must have tried to shoot Adam. His jaw was clenched and the pistol kept moving in his two-handed grip as he waited for an opening between the fighting men on the ground.

Jody spun around and dived for the knife. Out of the corner of her eye, she saw Tattoo Guy turning toward her. She grabbed the hilt and threw the knife in one quick motion, twisting around and falling back onto the dirt.

A shout full of rage and pain filled the clearing. Tattoo Guy's pistol dropped to the ground. The knife's blade was buried in his left shoulder, blood quickly seeping around it and darkening his shirt. His eyes shined with malevolence and a promise of retribution as he stared at Jody. A shudder racked his body, and he dropped to his knees. His left arm hung useless at his side, but his right hand was already reaching for the pistol.

Scrambling away, Jody looked around for the only weapon she had, the branch.

Strong arms grabbed her from behind and yanked her backward. She struggled against them as she was picked up.

Tattoo Guy brought up his gun, shouting curses as he raised it.

She fell, something dark filling her vision as she slammed into the ground again.

Bam! Bam! Bam!

She recoiled against the sound of gunshots, but all she could see was the solid bulk of a downed tree directly in front of her face. She started to turn, but strong arms shoved her down—just like they'd done so many times before. Adam!

"Stay down," he whispered harshly.

More gunshots sounded. Wood splintered above her and rained down on her head.

Adam rose to his knees, beside her now, lifting a gun he must have taken from Thad and pointing it at the clearing. His return fire was deafening. Jody covered her ears, squeezing herself into a tight ball as more shots rang out.

A scuffling noise and more cursing sounded from a new direction. She could feel Adam's body against hers, pivoting to the right. He fired once, twice.

Bam! Another shot rang out from the left again.

Adam whirled around, cursing as he ducked behind the tree.

Footsteps pounded against the ground, the sound of men running away. The sounds faded, leaving only Adam's harsh breathing and her own shallow gasps to break the silence.

He looked down at her, gun still clenched in his hand. "They're gone. For now. Are you okay?"

She blinked up at him, noting the fresh blood on the side of his face, his hands, the white line of his lips, clenched in obvious pain. She uncurled and sat up, her gaze sweeping over him. His clothes were filthy and torn, matted with dirt and sweat. Then she saw it, finally, the reason he was in such terrible pain.

"Oh no." Her words clogged her suddenly tight throat as she stared in horror at the thick length of splintered wood that pierced his left calf, protruding through bloody holes torn in the front and back of his pant leg.

"Are you okay?" he repeated, his voice a gritty mixture of concern and raw pain.

"What? Yes, yes, I'm fine. But you, Adam, I can't even imagine how much that hurts." She reached for his left leg, but he jerked back.

"Leave it. We have to get moving. They'll lick their wounds, but they'll be back. It's not about whatever information you have anymore. It's about revenge. They'll kill both of us when they get the chance. We have to get out of here."

"But your leg. You can't possibly walk on that. You have to let me help you. I'll fashion a splint—"

"I made it this far. I can make it a little farther. We have to get to a defensible position. Hurry." He shoved the pistol into his front pocket then braced himself against the downed tree, pushing himself up.

Jody scrambled to her feet and stood beside him, reaching out to help him. Then she saw the body lying in the middle of the clearing. It wasn't Tattoo Guy or Owen. It was Thad. Sightless eyes stared up at the dark sky with its threatening storm that was still holding off, a single small dot of red in the center of his forehead. The ground beneath his head was saturated in blood.

She pressed a hand to her throat.

Adam's jaw worked, his hands clenched into fists at his sides. "That's the handiwork of our nemesis, Tattoo Guy. My guess is he didn't want to leave anyone behind who might give us information about him."

Her gaze flew to his. "He killed his own man?"

He nodded. "Which means he won't hesitate to kill us, especially since you managed to hit him with that knife. He doesn't strike me as the forgive-and-forget type. As soon as he binds his wound and is able to come after us again, he will. And it wouldn't surprise me if he brings reinforcements. We have to get out of here, fall back to somewhere more secure, keep moving until we get in range of a cell tower and can radio for help."

He wobbled on his feet, then braced himself against the tree.

She bit her lip to keep from crying out in sympathy. He was being unbelievably strong, had managed to somehow crawl out of that hole where she'd left him. And even with his leg so horribly damaged, he'd come to her rescue. Somehow she had to find the inner strength to match his, so she could get him somewhere safe and finally look in his backpack for a first-aid kit. Her mouth twisted bitterly. He needed far more than a kit. He needed an emergency room with a trauma unit.

"Let's go. That way." He pointed off toward the left.

"Deeper into the mountains? Are you sure? Shouldn't we head back toward town—"

He shook his head. "Our only real chance is to get in range of a cell tower so I can radio for a rescue team. Back the way we came is by the broken tower, the one destroyed in the wildfires. If we head west, we should be in range of a working tower within a few minutes."

"A few minutes?"

"Give or take."

Relief made her legs go weak. Soon they would have other rangers with guns to protect them, and medical help for Adam. And then they could bring in the FBI or whoever they needed in order to find her friend Tracy. And Sam, if he was still alive. Then they could put Tattoo Guy and Owen in prison where they belonged.

Maybe, just maybe, they'd make it out of here after all.

Adam turned and limped forward.

"Wait." She motioned for him to stay where he was and hurried around the downed tree.

"Jody, what are you—"

"This." She held up the thick piece of branch she'd used like a bat to defend herself after the thugs had caught up to her and surrounded her. "It's thick and heavy and just about long enough to work as a cane." She rushed over to him and held it out.

The lines of pain bracketing his mouth eased, and he offered her a small smile. "That should do the job. Thanks. The one I used to pull myself out of the hole broke in half or it would have been a perfect walking stick." He tested it out, pressing the length of branch against the ground as he took a step forward. He grimaced but quickly smoothed his features. "Works great. Let's go."

Together they hobbled and walked west, keeping near the tree line to give them cover in case the bad guys came looking for them. By staying out of the woods, the going was easier, with fewer obstacles for Adam to navigate around.

"Shouldn't we stop and pull that wood out of your leg?"

He shook his head. "It's controlling the bleeding. It's better to leave it in, even though it hurts like the devil."

She nodded, unconvinced. But since her most recent medical training was CPR in the fifth grade, it wasn't like she had any true wisdom to offer.

"At least the storm is holding off. That's good," she said.

He looked up and nodded. "Looks like it's moving east. We should be okay."

At first, he managed a steady clip. But as they began a gradual climb into the foothills of the next mountain, his pace began to lag. He was leaning heavier and heavier on the makeshift cane. If the broken piece of wood piercing his leg was truly stanching the bleeding, she couldn't imagine how bad it would be if the wood was out. A dark, wet spot was slowly spreading down his pant leg.

She glanced at the ground behind him. Bright spots of blood marked their trail. She worried her bottom lip, not sure whether it mattered at this point. They weren't going fast enough to outrun anyone. Once the bad guys decided to come back to look for them, they'd find them pretty quickly, with or without a blood trail to follow.

"What is it?" Adam asked, his voice husky from the pain.

"Nothing."

He stopped, using the cane for support as he drew a ragged breath. "It's not nothing. What's wrong?"

"It's just that, well, we're leaving a pretty obvious trail. I doubt it matters, but—"

He glanced back, then swore. "My backpack. There should be an extra shirt inside. We can wrap it—"

"I'm on it." She moved behind him and quickly located the shirt, then zipped the pack. A moment later, she stepped back to take a look. The shirt had been wrapped tight around his leg, just under where the stick protruded. It was soaking up the blood and had the added advantage of stabilizing the stick. There'd been some white-lipped moments as he'd endured her ministrations. "That should do the trick," she said. "Hopefully it will help ease the pain a bit when you walk, too."

He took a step forward then another. No blood was left on the ground behind him. But his white-knuckled grip on the makeshift cane told her the pain, if anything, was worse.

They had to get him help. Soon.

"Do you think we're in range of a tower yet?" She moved to his side, wedging her shoulder beneath his to help him hobble forward. It was a testament to his agony that he didn't refuse her help like he'd done earlier.

"Let's give it a few more minutes before we try," he said. "I can picture the park map in my head. I think once we get right about to that tree over there—" he waved toward a group of trees about a football field's length away "—that should do it."

As they hobbled toward their goal, she said, "I never thanked you for saving me in the clearing. I don't know how you managed it. But I was a goner until you got there. Thank you."

"Don't thank me. I'm just doing—"

"Your job, yes, I know. But I guarantee most people wouldn't go to the lengths you've gone to in order to help a stranger. So maybe instead of arguing with me when I thank you, you can just say 'you're welcome.'"

His mouth twitched but didn't quite manage to form a smile. "You're welcome."

She squeezed his side in response, and they continued forward.

An eternity seemed to pass before they reached the trees he'd pointed to. She helped him turn around and sit on some rocks.

He let out a shaky breath and gave her a reassuring smile. "It's going to be okay, Jody. We're going to make it."

"No offense," she said, "but once your fellow rangers finally get here and get us off these mountains, I'm never planning on coming back again. I've had my fill of the Great Smoky Mountains National Park."

He chuckled and unsnapped his radio from his utility belt. Then he lifted it and froze.

Jody swung around, looking behind them. But she didn't see anyone. Or hear anyone. As far as she could tell, they were alone. "What's wrong?" She turned back around to see him staring off into space, a defeated expression on his face. "Adam?"

Without a word, he held up the radio. A bullet hole had been blasted right through the screen.

Chapter Nine

Jody stared at the bullet hole. "Maybe…maybe the radio will work anyway."

He turned some dials. "It's busted. Useless."

"But—"

"Forget it." He snapped the radio back onto his belt and looked past her, his gaze scanning the horizon. "I figure Tattoo Guy will get that shoulder stitched up and some painkillers on board before he and reinforcements come after us. As fast as he got that third guy out here—"

"Thad."

He nodded. "Thad. As fast he got him out here, he's probably got more resources close by. It won't take long." He pulled Thad's pistol out of his holster and popped out the magazine. Then he popped it back in and shoved the gun into the holster. "Six shots left in the magazine and one in the chamber. It's a .40 caliber, like my Glock was. So the extra magazines in my backpack will work. We won't be completely defenseless. We'll need to find a defensible position and settle in, make a plan."

"A plan sounds good. What's our first move?"

He shrugged the backpack off his shoulders and let it drop to the ground. "That first aid kit you've been nagging me about?"

"I don't nag."

He winked, which was amazing considering that he had a piece of wood sticking through his leg.

"The kit is in the bottom of the pack. Can you get it for me?"

"Of course." She dropped to her knees, grimacing when the cuts and scrapes on her skin started stinging all over again. She rummaged through the pack, noting he had some water and energy bars, which would come in handy when they weren't busy running for their lives. She grabbed one of the bottles and handed it to him. "Drink that."

"Not yet." He set the unopened bottle on top of the rock.

She pulled the medical kit out and handed it to him. "You need to hydrate to help your body fight its injuries and replenish the blood you've lost. Why won't you drink now?"

"Because there's something else we need to do first."

He clicked the top of the plastic box open, rummaged inside, then pulled out a spool of black thread and a long, wicked-looking needle.

"If we're going to face off with our enemies," he said, "I can't afford to lose any more blood. And I need to be mobile. I'm going to pull the stick out of my leg. And you're going to stitch me up."

ADAM WOULD HAVE sworn Jody's face turned green when he asked her to sew him up. Now it was completely washed out, almost translucent. Her right hand went to her stomach.

"St…stitch you up?"

"It's a lot to expect," he said. "And I hate asking it of you. But once I pull out the wood, I'll be bleeding from the front and back of my leg. It's going to take both of us to stanch the bleeding and sew the wounds closed."

She shook her head, stepping back from him. "I threw up earlier just because I was upset. Sticking a needle in someone's flesh is a whole other level. I can't do it."

"You can. You're much stronger than you think you are. How many people do you know who could have taken off like you did, leading the bad guys away from me? You saved my life, Jody. You know it. And then you faced down three men with guns and knives and lived to tell the tale. You're a hero and a fighter. You *can* do this."

Her shoulders straightened as his words sank in. Some of the color came back to her cheeks. Then she glanced down at the needle and thread and went pale again. "Please tell me you have anesthesia to numb the pain."

He slowly shook his head. "No. I don't."

"Alcohol?"

"The drinking kind or the rubbing kind?" he teased.

"Either! You have to have something for the pain, and germs."

"Afraid I'm all out of whiskey. But I do have an antiseptic spray. And rolls of gauze."

She raised a shaky hand to her throat. "It will hurt like crazy."

"It already hurts like crazy. Nothing you do could make it worse." He leaned forward and took her hand in his. "I need your help. We're sitting ducks out here. Not enough cover. I'd keep going, look for somewhere better to do this if I could. But in case you hadn't noticed, that shirt you wrapped around my leg is soaked through already. We're leaving a blood trail again. And I'm getting woozy. We have to stop the bleeding, now, or I won't be any use to you at all. I won't be able to defend you. I'll be passed out."

"I'm so sorry," she whispered.

He frowned, thinking she was still refusing to work on his leg. But then she took the thread and needle from him and dropped to her knees. She was probably apologizing because she didn't want to hurt him. He didn't think he'd ever met anyone more sensitive and kindhearted than her.

She set the first-aid kit beside her and located the anti-septic spray. He stretched his leg out in front of him to give her better access. She used his knife to slit his pants and roll the ends up to his knee, out of the way.

Once Jody Ingram set her mind on something, she fully committed to it. She was like a drill sergeant, giving him orders, setting out what she needed.

Getting his boot off to give her more room to stitch the wound was agony. But it was over quickly.

Another of his shirts, the only other one he had in the pack, was sacrificed for the cause. She wrapped it around his calf just below the entry and exit points of the piece of wood, ready to apply pressure as soon as the wood came out.

The confidence she'd displayed as she prepared his leg seemed to evaporate when she looked up at him with shiny eyes. "I'm going to do this," she assured him. "But I'm probably going to cry the whole time and I might even throw up. You'll just have to deal with it, all right?"

He was surprised that she could make him laugh when he was in so much pain. "All right."

She nodded. "Go ahead, then. I'm ready. Pull it out." She squeezed her eyes shut and braced his calf.

In spite of the pain—and the even more pain that was yet to come—he couldn't help but smile at her and admire her. He'd meant what he said. She really was courageous, heroic and strong. She was also sensitive and kind, a rare combination these days.

He crossed his ankles, using his good leg as a brace to keep his other leg still. Then he grasped the two-inch-thick length of tree branch that had impaled him when he'd slid into the pit. His calf already throbbed just from grasping the wood. This was going to hurt like the dickens. And he had to be quiet, no matter how much it hurt, so he wouldn't upset Jody any more than she already was. And so he didn't broadcast their location to the thugs in case they were already back in the mountains looking for them.

He mentally counted. One. Two. Three. He locked his good leg down hard on the bad one, and pulled. The pain was instantaneous, blinding in its intensity, molten lava searing every nerve ending. There was a sickening sucking sound as he tugged and pulled the stick forward and up. It slid through his leg, scraping against bone, rough bumps on the wood tearing his flesh anew much like an arrow might have done. It finally came free with a popping sound.

Jody gasped and clamped her hands down hard against his leg to stop the fresh rush of blood.

Agony ripped through him. He had to clench his jaw not to yell. His lungs heaved. Sweat poured off him. He gasped for air, quick pants as he tried to breathe through the pain.

"It's bleeding too much. I can't stop it."

Her words came to him through a long black tunnel. He struggled against it, desperately tried to clear his vision.

"Adam? Adam!"

He surrendered to the darkness.

JODY'S HAND SHOOK so hard that she almost couldn't sew the last stitch. Only the fact that it was the very last one kept her going. Because she knew it would soon be over. Her stomach clenched as she pierced Adam's skin and pulled the last of his ragged flesh together. She shuddered as she used the knife to cut the thread.

He was still unconscious. But his chest rose and fell in steady, deep breaths. And she'd checked his pulse about ten times out of fear. It too was strong and steady. Maybe the universe was being kind to him by knocking him out so he wouldn't experience the pain of being stitched up. She'd barely managed to keep him from knocking his head when he'd fallen back. But she hadn't been able to keep him from sliding off the boulder.

Now he was lying on his side on the ground, which had ended up being easier for her to stitch the wounds. But without him awake to help her put pressure on them while she stitched them up, he'd lost far more blood than he could probably afford. And she'd had to work fast to try to limit the bleeding. There'd been absolutely no finesse in her needlework. He was going to have horrible scars.

She bent over his leg, inspecting her work, and winced. Hopefully men didn't care about such things. Or maybe a plastic surgeon could fix it later. She glanced around. If there *was* a later. He was right about them being out in the open here. It was called a bald, if she remembered right from the brochures she'd seen. A part of the mountains where there was a huge gap in the trees, where nothing but grass grew. It could have been caused by disease, but judging by the charring on the few trees that were close by, more likely it was a part of the woods that had burned all the way to the ground, leaving nothing in its wake.

And nothing but a few rocks and trees to hide behind.

She grabbed a bottle of water and a bandana from the backpack and gently wiped away the blood on his leg. Thankfully, the stitches had done their job. The bleeding had stopped. Her next worry was infection. She'd sprayed the disinfectant on it throughout the process. And she sprayed it liberally one more time before carefully rolling gauze around his calf.

Once that was done, she pulled a clean sock up over the wound to help protect it. After another quick check to make sure he was still breathing, she worked his boot back on. She almost gave up, but knowing it would probably hurt like crazy if he was awake for the procedure, she persevered until the boot was in place.

She put everything into one of the baggies in his backpack, remembering the "take nothing, leave nothing" mantra the commercials were always touting to tourists. Then she sat beside him and wondered what to do next. Shouldn't he have woken up by now? She pressed the back of her hand to his forehead. It seemed normal, as far as she could tell. No sign of fever. Not yet, anyway. So why wasn't he waking up?

She shook his shoulders. "Adam, it's Jody. Adam, can you hear me?" She shook him again, then sat back and looked around. There were a few trees close by, and the group of boulders he was lying beside. But it wasn't enough to make her feel safe by any means. And she hated for him to be so vulnerable. Maybe she could pull him behind the boulders at least? It would block anyone's view from the woods back where they'd emerged when running from Tattoo Guy. It was worth a try.

A few minutes later, she gave up. A five-foot featherweight like her just wasn't going to be able to drag tall, dark and gorgeous anywhere. It was hopeless. She thought about trying to roll him, but she was worried she'd hurt his leg. There was only one other thing she could think to do—guard him. She pulled the pistol out of his pocket. It was a Ruger, not a brand she'd ever owned or shot before. But it was similar to the Glock she had in the safe at her apartment. It was small enough to fit comfortably in her hand.

After unloading it, she dry fired it a few times. Not the best thing for the gun. But she wanted to be familiar with the trigger pull, see how hard she had to squeeze to make it shoot. It was a little trickier than her own gun, but not overly difficult.

She loaded it again and dug the two extra magazines of ammo from the bottom of the backpack and put them in her pocket. Then she scooted her back against the boulder beside Adam's unconscious form.

Clutching the pistol with both hands, she rested it in her lap, sitting cross-legged on the ground. Then she stared toward the woods, and waited.

Chapter Ten

Blinding, sharp pain shot through Adam's body. He jerked upright, clawing for the pistol holstered on his belt. It wasn't there. He shoved his hands in his pockets, desperately searching for his weapon.

"Whoa, whoa, Adam, stop. You're okay. Everything's okay."

His hands clutched nothing but emptiness in his pockets. He blinked in confusion at the beautiful woman kneeling in front of him. Thick red hair formed a messy, wavy halo around her heart-shaped face, falling to just below her shoulders. Her blouse was partly undone, revealing a lacy bra and the delicious upper curves of her breasts. His mouth watered as his gaze traveled to her full, pink lips, which were curved in a smile as she leaned close.

"Sorry for thumping your leg. You'd slept so long. I was getting worried and thought that might be the only way to wake you up. Looks like it worked." She smiled sheepishly, then her smile faded. "Adam? It's me. Jody. Don't you recognize me?"

He watched her lips move like a blind man seeking the light.

She put her hand on his shoulder and leaned in closer. "Adam?"

It was all the invitation he needed. He wrapped one arm

around her waist, sank the other deep into her fall of gorgeous red hair and pulled her mouth to his. Her lips parted on a gasp, and he groaned, tasting their honeyed sweetness and delving deeper inside.

She was so hot and sweet and soft. He tasted and treasured her mouth, ran his hand down her back, down the sexy curve of her bottom, wanting her with a desperation that didn't make sense. Nothing made sense. He didn't know how he'd gotten here or why this woman—Jody—was in his bed. But he wasn't going to complain or waste the opportunity.

She moaned deep in her throat and clutched his shoulders. Then, finally, she was kissing him back. For such a tiny thing, she was full of passion and exploded like a firecracker in his arms. Her breasts crushed against his chest, and she threaded her hands through his hair, her tongue dueling with his.

He shuddered and caressed her through her shorts. She jerked against him. For a moment he thought she might push him away. But then she was kissing him again. His body hardened painfully. He couldn't take this much longer. He had to have her. Now. He slid his hands back to her blouse and fumbled with the buttons. She was too close. His big hands couldn't maneuver between them and he was afraid he'd rip the fabric.

He broke the kiss and drew a ragged breath as he gently pushed her back so he could finish taking off her shirt. Deep green eyes stared back at him in wonder over green-framed glasses perched crookedly on her nose. A delightful smattering of freckles marched across her flushed cheeks as her gaze dropped to his lips. He undid one button, then another, then he stopped.

A pistol lay discarded on the ground between them, cradled between her thighs. He frowned. That wasn't his pistol. He looked at his utility belt and saw the radio, its cracked screen glinting in the fading light. Fading light? He leaned back and looked around. Little puffs of white mist dotted the mountains all around them, looking like signals from some Indian campfire of old. The Smoky Mountains. They were outside, in the middle of the Smokies. And the sun was going down?

He made a more careful inspection of their surroundings, noting they were out in the open, in a bald near the foothills. His legs were stretched out in front of him. His lap was full of gorgeous redhead. And his left leg was shooting hot jolts of lava up his calf. He winced and bent to the side to see why it hurt. White gauze was wrapped around it just above where his boot ended. The whole lower part of his pants was gone, the hem ragged and ripped, like someone had torn it, or sawed it with a serrated knife.

"Adam?" Her husky voice made his body jerk in response, blood heating his veins, scorching him from the inside out. Good grief, this woman was sexy. He drew a deep breath and turned back toward her.

And blinked.

Recognition slammed into him. Everything clicked together. The hazy fog of lust cleared instantly, and his mouth dropped open in shock. "Jody?"

Her perfectly shaped brows arched in confusion. "Adam? Why are you…" Her eyes widened, a look of horror crossing her face. "You didn't know it was me?"

He stared at her, his face flushing with guilty heat. "I… I knew there was a beautiful woman—"

She scrambled off his lap, smooth toned arms and glorious legs flailing awkwardly in her rush to get away from him. One of her legs slammed into his left calf. Fire ripped through his body. He sucked in a breath and jerked back, clenching his jaw to keep from shouting.

"Oh no, your leg. I'm so sorry. So, so sorry."

She reached for him, but he shook his head and held a hand up to stop her. "Don't." His voice was a harsh croak, the pain so intense he couldn't say anything else. He drew several deep breaths, holding as still as possible, waiting, hoping the pain would ease its grip.

"I'm sorry," she whispered miserably, her eyes looking suspiciously bright, like she was holding back tears.

On a scale of one to ten, his pain was about fifty-two. He rode it out, his fingers clawing at the dirt, panting like a wounded animal. Darkness wavered at the edges of his vision. But he couldn't give in. He realized he must have passed out before, when he'd pulled out the piece of wood embedded in his leg. Thankfully, their pursuers hadn't come back yet or they'd be dead. Or maybe not. As the pain began to ease to about a thirty, he noted Jody had grabbed the gun, expertly holding it with her finger on the frame, not the trigger, pointing it away from him.

"You've…" He cleared his gritty throat and tried again. "You've fired guns before. You know how…how to handle them."

He tried to focus on her rather than the pain. Had he noticed how beautiful her hair was before? It was fire red and hung in thick waves past her shoulders.

She looked down at the pistol in her hand and frowned. "Well, yes. Of course I know how to handle guns. Once I left home and went to college, I was determined to never be a victim again, so I…" Her eyes widened, as if she'd just realized what she'd let slip. "I mean, that I would never *become* a victim, so I learned about guns and—"

"Jody? Who hurt you?"

She looked away. "I never said anyone hurt me."

"You mentioned your family before, that you weren't close. Did one of them—"

"I'm really sorry about your leg," she blurted out, obviously desperate to change the subject. "Is it feeling any better? I didn't mean to bump it. I'm so sorry."

"Stop." The fire in his left leg was bearable now, a paltry eleven or twelve. He let out a shuddering breath. "Stop apologizing all the time. All the bad in the world isn't your fault or your responsibility. Okay?"

She nodded but didn't look like she believed him. "I didn't mean to hit your leg just then. Earlier I did—just a tiny nudge, though. I was worried about you and wanted to wake you…" Her voice trailed off, and her gaze fell to his lips. Her pink tongue darted out to moisten her mouth.

His entire body clenched. He forced himself to look away from the tempting little siren. And just how had that happened anyway? How had she gone from being the young, barely-out-of-college girl to a sexy, mature woman who could tempt a saint? He must have a fever. That was it. It was the only explanation. Jody was far too pure and innocent and sweet for a jaded man like him.

"Make me laugh."

She blinked. "What?"

"Make me laugh. Say something funny." When she continued to look blankly at him, he said, "The pain, to take my mind off the pain. Tell me something funny." What he really needed to do was take his mind off how sexy she was. He clenched his hands into fists to keep from reaching for her.

Her brow furrowed in concentration, as if he'd asked her to calculate some complex scientific equation instead of trying to come up with a lame joke. Didn't she ever laugh? Or really smile and have fun? He found himself craving her smile and laughter even more than he craved her body.

And that was saying something.

"Peter, Patricia, Patience, Patrick and Paul," she blurted out.

He waited for the punch line. "Picked a peck of pickled peppers?"

She frowned. "No. The names. Peter, Patricia, Patience, Patrick and Paul. Those are the names of my adoptive father and my adoptive sisters and brothers."

"Wait, seriously?"

She nodded, looking even more serious than she had a few moments earlier.

"What's your adoptive mother's name? Penelope?"

She shook her head. "Her name is Amelia."

Adam threw his head back and laughed. He laughed so hard he got a stitch in his side. Then Jody had to ruin it by smiling, a genuine, real smile that reached her gorgeous green eyes and made her so beautiful he ached. Again. Oh, how he wanted her, needed her. He sobered and stared at her, his breath hitching when he noticed the tantalizing display she obviously wasn't aware that she was offering. "Jody. Your blouse is, ah, gaping a bit."

She didn't even look down at her shirt. "So?"

His mouth was watering, just from that one glimpse of heaven he'd had, before he'd forced himself to look up, at her face. She obviously hadn't understood what he was trying to tell her. "I can see...ah...your...your bra is...showing."

"In case you didn't notice, I was letting you unbutton my blouse earlier. I'm well aware of the state of my clothes. You may have temporarily lost your mind, forgetting who I was. But I didn't. And I'm not ashamed of that. You're a gorgeous guy. And I like you, a lot. Okay, a whole lot. I wouldn't mind picking up where we left off."

His mouth fell open. He snapped it closed.

"What?" She sounded angry this time, on top of being frustrated. "Does that shock you?"

He cleared his throat. "Well, yes, actually, it does. A little. You're so, so…"

Her eyes narrowed. "I'm so what?"

"Young," he blurted out.

Her expression changed to one of confusion. "I'm twenty-four. Yes, I'm young. But I'm not *that* young. I'm a full-grown woman, Adam. Not some child. Where on earth did you get this hang-up about women who are younger than you?"

He scrubbed the stubble on his face, wondering just how this conversation had turned so bizarre. "You're right." He dropped his hands to his sides. "When we met, I got it in my head that you were much younger than you are, and I didn't for a second imagine ever, well, being attracted to you."

She stiffened.

"Oh, come on," he said. "Don't get insulted now. There can't be any doubt about the state of my attraction for you at this point." He waved at his overly tight pants and his still-painful erection. "I think we crossed that barrier about the time you stuck your tongue down my throat."

She made a choking sound, her eyes wide. She coughed, then covered her mouth with her hands. He had the crazy suspicion that she was laughing at him and didn't want him to know. Likely she was trying to spare his feelings. Because that would be typical for someone who felt guilty over everything from global warming to La Niña and everything else she had no control over.

"I want you, okay?" he gritted out. "And the age thing isn't the problem anymore. The problem, if there is one, is that you're too nice."

Her hand fell to her lap. "I'm too nice? What's that supposed to mean?"

"It means you're too pure, too sweet, too…nice. You

deserve someone way better than me. I'd destroy everything good about you. I'd destroy you. You don't want me."

"I don't?" She sounded suspiciously like she wanted to laugh again. "Because you'll ruin me? That's a bit old-fashioned of you. Besides, I'm not a virgin, Adam."

Something dark passed in her eyes, but it was gone too quickly for him to be sure what he'd seen. Pain? Anger? Resentment? At who? Him, or someone in her past?

"Jody, I'm sorry if I offended you, or hurt you. I didn't—"

"Stop apologizing." She parroted his earlier words back at him. "It's not like I was asking for a long-term commitment." She pulled the edges of her blouse together. "We were just two adults who were about to have fun." She looked wistfully at his lap. "A *lot* of fun. But the moment has passed. And I think that ship has definitely sailed."

His hands curled against his thighs. It was either that or grab her and prove that the ship had definitely *not* sailed. This ridiculous conversation had only done one thing to his appetite for her—whet it.

She pushed herself up and wiped dirt off her legs before straightening. "I need a moment of privacy. When I come back, we'll work on a plan to get out of here and back to civilization."

What should have been a dramatic exit when she whirled around to leave was ruined when she tripped on a tree root. Her arms cartwheeled and she managed to regain her balance without falling. Her spine snapped ramrod straight and her face was flaming red when she once again turned her back on him and marched off to the nearest stand of trees.

Adam groaned and dropped his head to his chest. Everything about this day, from the moment he'd stepped on the Sugarland Mountain Trail, was a disaster. And every attempt he made to fix it only seemed to make things worse.

He shook his head. He wouldn't let anything happen to

the complicated, intriguing, sexy redhead who'd just declared that she was no longer interested in him. It was just as well. Because he needed to focus, to figure out a plan. They needed to alert someone about Tracy, get them searching for her. Which meant he needed to be fully mobile and find that defensible position he'd mentioned earlier.

Even if they didn't find a way out of the mountains to get help, he knew his team would come looking for him soon, if they weren't already. The sun had slipped low on the horizon, and night was falling. His shift had ended hours ago and he'd never called in to report status updates.

His truck was still parked in the employee lot behind the visitor's center. It wasn't like he worked in an office building. He worked in the wilderness. No one would just assume that if he didn't show up he'd gone bar-hopping with a friend to drink away his Saturday night. They had each other's backs and took it seriously when a member of the team didn't report in. But there were thousands of acres of mountain range out here. Without a last known location, they could have several teams of search and rescue out here and never find him.

It had happened before.

Two different people on separate occasions had disappeared in the Smoky Mountains National Park over the past couple of years. They were never found. Not alive, anyway. What Adam had to do was figure out a way to improve their odds, to help the searchers find them. Or reach the searchers themselves.

Which meant he had to stand up.

He also needed a few moments of privacy, like Jody. His bladder was near to bursting. Which meant he *really* needed to stand up. And walk. Neither option appealed to him with his leg throbbing painfully in rhythm with his heartbeat. He had no desire to experience the agony he'd felt when he'd pulled the stick free from his leg, or when Jody had accidentally kicked his leg while scrambling off his lap. But there was no getting around it. He was destined for a bit of torture no matter what. Might as well get it over with. Of course, deciding that he needed to get up and figuring out how to do it were two entirely different problems.

His burning, aching leg wouldn't support him enough to rise to standing. Even rolling over on all fours failed. The leg was pretty much useless. He was beginning to wonder about the wisdom of having pulled out the stick. It had seemed like the only way to stop the bleeding. But his muscles were like jelly now, unable to bear up under any kind of strain.

After yet another try, he got halfway up before his leg collapsed beneath him and he fell face-first into the dirt. He cursed viciously and rolled to his side, panting like a dog as he fought through yet another episode of stabbing pain that set his insides on fire.

When the pain finally subsided to a dull roar rather than a blistering inferno, he stared toward the trees they'd come from several hours ago. The sun had set. The moon was bright, the sky clear, or he wouldn't have been able to see anything this far away from any man-made light sources. Still, the woods were little more than a dark void.

Had Tattoo Guy given up on coming after them? Figuring they'd die of exposure out here? Or was he biding his time, waiting to see where Jody was before shooting at Adam?

Jody. He looked to his right where she'd disappeared earlier. How long had she been gone? More than five minutes, which was all it should have taken her if she had to empty her bladder. Had it been ten minutes? Fifteen?

He hated himself for having spent so much energy and time on his repeated attempts to stand. He had no true concept of the passage of time. And no clue whether she was in trouble, or admiring the stars, or walking off her anger at him and how badly he'd bungled things between them. Regardless, she should have been back by now. He *had* to get up and go check on her. There was no other option.

He looked around, searching for something to use as leverage. The makeshift walking stick might have helped. But the tall grasses and rocks dotting the landscape were hiding it well and good. Wait, rocks. They'd stopped by some boulders to work on his leg. He'd been sitting on one before he'd passed out. He jerked around and let out a string of curses when he realized the boulder had been behind him this whole time. Bracing his arms on either side of him, he scooted back until he was against the rock. Then he rolled over, breathing through the worst of the pain before bracing his hands on the boulder.

With his good leg beneath him and his hands pushing against the rock, he finally made it to his feet. Correction, foot. His bad leg crumpled as soon as he put weight on it. He had to balance on one foot to keep from falling. Leaning against the boulder to remain upright, he looked toward the small group of trees again for Jody. No sign of her. Where was she? At least she had his gun for protection.

Or did she?

He looked around, then groaned. The gun was lying on the ground by the boulder. She hadn't taken it. He swiped it and checked the loading, then slid it into his pocket. Where was his walking stick? He didn't see it anywhere. He snagged his backpack, too, and clipped the strap across his chest to keep it in place so it wouldn't fall with him hopping around like a kangaroo.

On a hunch, he continued his kangaroo impression around the boulder to the back side. *Yes.* The walking stick was lying there, probably having fallen when he'd sat down. He grabbed it and tested it out.

At first his leg wobbled so much he could barely take a step. But he did take a step, so he was encouraged by that. He took another then another. After about ten feet, the leg began to go numb. Probably not a good sign. But it made walking more bearable. And faster. He hurried as quickly as he could across the open space from the boulder to the trees. Then he stopped. Beyond the trees was more empty space.

And no sign of Jody.

"Jody," he called out, his voice just above a whisper. A cool mountain breeze ruffled his hair, bringing with it the scent of rain. The storm that had threatened earlier seemed to be brewing again instead of moving off to the east as he'd expected. "Jody," he called out, louder this time. The only answer he heard was the distant rumble of thunder. A flash of lightning followed, off to the left.

He took another step past the trees and looked around in a full circle for something, anything, that might tell him where she'd wandered off to. Thunder rumbled again, followed by another flash of light. But this time the light didn't turn off. It kept coming. Toward him, low to the ground. That wasn't lightning. And the sound he'd heard wasn't thunder.

It was an ATV, its engine making a dull roar now, the headlights bouncing crazily as it rushed toward him.

He dived for the cover of trees, pulling himself behind them just as the headlights swept past where he'd been standing moments ago.

The ATV wasn't an ATV after all. It was a dune buggy. Tattoo Guy was driving. Owen and another man were in the back seat, Owen with a rifle in his hand, pointed up at the sky. And in the front, her eyes wide with terror, her hands tied to the roll bar above her, was Jody.

Chapter Eleven

Jody bit her lip to keep from shouting a warning to Adam as the buggy bounced across the bald and headed toward the group of rocks and boulders where she'd seen him last. She could only hope that he'd heard the engine, seen the headlights and been able to hobble to another hiding place in time. If he was just crouching down behind the boulder, the men would see him in about, three, two, one…he wasn't there. Her breath stuttered out in relief.

The backpack was gone, too. And the gun.

The buggy continued on its way, circling the area as the men looked for Adam. He was injured. He was also experienced and trained. He would know what to do, wouldn't he? He'd mentioned earlier getting to a more defensible position. Had he done that now? She hoped so. Because there was no doubt what the men with her would do if they found him.

They'd kill him.

"He ain't here, Damien," Owen called out.

Tattoo Guy—now she knew his name was Damien—aimed a sour look at Owen in the rearview mirror. "Unless he sprouted wings, he's here. You saw that stick through his leg in the clearing. He won't be running any marathons any time soon. He's hiding. We just have to find him."

He slammed his foot on the brake, wincing when the action obviously jostled his hurt shoulder. His left arm was in a sling. Adam had been right. He'd had resources close by and got medical treatment, then returned with reinforcements—including the man whom Owen had called Ned, sitting quietly in the back seat studying the terrain, and four more men in a second buggy that was searching the other side of the bald.

The buggy slid to a stop, its headlights illuminating the boulder where she and Adam had been earlier—before she'd gone into the woods to relieve her bladder. It was a mixed blessing that she'd chosen not to stop at the first stand of trees. Because when Tattoo Guy, Damien, had found her, she'd been far away from Adam. And that was the only reason he was still alive.

She'd wanted more privacy, which seemed silly given how intimate they'd already been. Still, it had been good luck that she'd continued on. And that after she'd answered nature's call, she'd seen a beautiful stream sparkling in the moonlight in the distance. She'd been unable to quell the artistic excitement inside her that wanted to see nature's beauty. As soon as she'd stepped up to the stream, Damien had grabbed her.

The radio sitting on the console crackled to life. He picked it up and spoke to his other team, comparing notes about where they'd searched.

Jody rubbed her tongue against the inside of her sore cheek, trying to ease the ache where he'd punched her when she'd refused to tell him where "the cop" was. She imagined the only reason he hadn't beaten her more was that he figured Adam was close by and they'd find him quickly. Since that hadn't happened, would he hit her again?

He slammed the radio back into the console. "Where's the cop?" He called her a foul name and raised his fist in warning. "Where is he?"

She backed against the door. "I don't know. I told you, we split up after the clearing. We were trying to find a cabin, or a road, and I got lost. I couldn't figure out how to get back to where we'd agreed to rendezvous."

"She's probably telling the truth," Owen offered from the back seat. "You know how redheads are."

Damien frowned and glanced back at him. "Don't you mean blondes?"

"Oh, yeah. Those, too. See?"

Damien closed his eyes and shook his head, then looked at Jody again. "Where was the rendezvous point?"

Keep it simple, stupid. The KISS principle one of her criminal justice professors had badgered them with every time they came up with some convoluted answer to a question came to her rescue now. There was evidence by that boulder—blood on the ground, footprints—that would corroborate her story without giving up Adam's current location, wherever that happened to be.

"There!" She poured excitement into her voice. "That boulder, see? I remember it now. I'm sure there have to be some footprints or something showing you we were there." She bit her lip. "At least, I think that's the right boulder."

He stared at her a long moment, apparently not nearly as willing as his pal Owen to believe she was a "dumb redhead."

"Check it out," Damien ordered, waving toward the boulder.

Owen popped his door open.

"Not you," Damien said. "Ned. See what you can find."

With a barely perceptible nod, the second man hopped over the door frame and landed nimbly on the ground. He produced a pen-size flashlight from one of his pockets and shined it around the base of the boulder. As Jody watched, he crouched down and feathered his fingers over some depressions in the grass.

He shined the light all around, his intense gaze seeming to take everything in, as if he could picture what had happened there. Then he aimed his flashlight farther out, toward the trees where she'd run earlier. He stood and motioned toward the trees.

"She's telling the truth. There were two people here, one slight, one heavier, larger. The bigger one—"

"The cop," Damien spit, as if it was an obscenity.

"He lost a lot of blood." He trained the light on the grass again, back to the boulder. "He must have climbed up here, used some kind of stick to push himself to his feet." The light bounced and moved across the rocks, the grass, then toward the stand of trees where she'd gone. "She went that way. He followed."

She sucked in a breath. He'd found Adam's trail? Adam had followed her?

"Back in the buggy," Damien ordered.

Ned hopped over the side and the buggy took off, straight for the trees where she'd run. And, apparently, unbeknownst to her until now, where Adam had gone, too. That must be where he was hiding. And she'd led them straight to him.

She pressed a hand to her throat. What had she done?

Chapter Twelve

Like a rubbernecker on the highway, unable to look away from the scene of an accident in spite of being horrified, Jody stared at the beam of Ned's flashlight as it got smaller and smaller in the distance. Her relief that Adam had not been hiding behind any of the trees in this part of the bald had been short-lived. Like a bloodhound, Ned had easily picked up his trail again, leading straight toward the water.

While she sat in the front passenger seat of the buggy, her hands going numb tied to the roll bar above her, Owen continued to whine in the back seat.

"Why can't I help search for him? I'm just as good a tracker as he is."

"Oh, really?" Damien clutched the steering wheel with his good hand and stared at Owen in the mirror. "When's the last time you tracked anything, or anyone?"

"I tracked that Tracy girl down just fine. It may have been in town instead of mountains. But I tracked her good."

Jody stiffened and looked at Damien. He was staring at her now, probably waiting for her reaction. A slow, cruel smile curved his lips.

"That you did, little brother. Guess I forgot about that. Still, it wasn't like she got very far before we'd realized she took off. And it wasn't at night, so it was a lot easier to recapture her."

Recapture? Had Tracy escaped, only to be caught again? "Where is she?" Jody demanded. "What have you done to her?"

"You really want to know?"

She nodded.

"Then tell me where your boss keeps the rest of his surveillance equipment. Where are the other pictures and videos? Audio recordings?"

"I told you, I don't know of anywhere else he would keep anything. As far as I know, he always keeps it at the office. I don't even think he took his work home with him. It…it was a habit from when his wife was still alive. She made him promise to leave work at the office, literally and figuratively. So both of them could relax and not think about their cases when the workday was over."

"Ah, now. Isn't that sweet?" He leaned toward her, forcing her to press herself against the door to the limits of her bound hands above her. "Tell you a secret, honey. He didn't keep his promise to that dear old lady of his. We found plenty of work files and pictures at his house." His smile faded. "Just not the right ones."

"You…you went to his house?"

He grinned again and relaxed against the seat. "Don't worry. It's not like Sammy boy cares anymore." His laughter made her stomach clench with dread.

Please be bluffing. Please don't have hurt Sam.

Owen chuckled in the back seat, as if the two of them shared a private joke.

"Where's Sam?" she asked, her throat tight. "Please tell me you didn't hurt him."

"Well, now. I would, but then, I wouldn't want to lie."

Bile rose in her throat as Owen and Damien both laughed. Damien hadn't mentioned using Sam as leverage, only Tracy. And from what he'd just said, he wasn't even trying to pretend that Sam was okay. Or was he just saying that, making her think Sam was…that he *wasn't* okay, to make her scared of what he might do to her if she didn't talk? She had to cling to the hope that the dear old man who'd been like a father to her was still alive. She wouldn't be able to function otherwise.

She swallowed and drew a steadying breath. Tracy was still alive. Wasn't she? He was still using her friend as a bargaining chip. She *had* to be alive.

She stared through the windshield toward the water, moonlight sparkling off the little eddies and ripples caused by boulders just beneath the surface as the current rushed over them. Adam was out there somewhere, hopefully okay and hiding. Had he seen Ned? Did he know about both dune buggies loaded with thugs with guns? There was no way he could fight off all of Damien's men with only one pistol.

Don't worry about me, Adam. There's nothing you can do to save me. Don't be a hero. Don't get yourself killed.

The portable two-way radio sitting in the console crackled, startling her.

"It's Ned. Pick up."

Damien grabbed the radio and clicked the button on the side. "Damien here. Go ahead."

"His trail leads directly to the water and stops. Either he fell in or he went in on purpose." Ned's voice, deadly calm and matter-of-fact, sounded through the speaker.

Damien swore. "I want that cop. If he drowned, I want his body as proof. He's seen my face, my jailhouse ink. He knows I'm an ex-con. If he makes it back to civilization, he'll eventually figure out who I am. Once he does, if he pulls the wrong thread, connects the right dots, you can kiss your cut bye-bye. You got me?"

"Understood."

They were talking about killing Adam as if they were making a grocery list. Who *were* these people?

"What's your theory?" Damien asked through the radio.

"If he didn't fall in, he could be walking in the shallow part to keep from leaving a blood trail. With a wound like his, and judging by the blood he lost back at that boulder, I don't see him doing much more than that. The stream is too wide, the current too fast, for an injured man to cross to the other side. But I don't know this guy, how strong or motivated he might be. We'll need to check the far side, just to be sure."

"Owen can do that."

"Bro, I don't want to swim across a freezing-cold stream. Make someone else—"

"Shut up, Owen. Get out of the buggy."

Owen cursed a blue streak, but he popped the door open and got out. His boots crunched on some rocks just outside the car as he started down the rise toward the water.

"What else do you need?" Damien asked through the mic.

"If I'm going hunting, I'll need my pack, plenty of ammo for my nine millimeter and the rifle."

"Owen." Damien motioned to the other man, who stopped to look at him. "Get back here."

When Owen trudged to the driver's side, Damien gestured with his thumb to the back seat. "Get Ned's backpack for him. And your rifle and ammo. Get some nine-millimeter magazines, too."

"My rifle? He's got a pistol. Why's he want my rifle?"

Damien narrowed his eyes. "Who bought that rifle for you? Like I buy everything else?"

Owen threw his hands up in the air. "Fine. Whatever. I'll get it."

When Owen was jogging down the hillside again, this

time with a backpack and rifle, Damien turned in his seat to face Jody. "Don't worry. They'll find him."

He chuckled, as if amused by her distress. But any sign of humor quickly faded as he stared at her. "You've wasted my time all day and caused me way more trouble than you're worth." He motioned toward the sling that immobilized his left arm. "I haven't forgotten that I owe you for this. But I'm willing to forgive this one time, if you give me what I want. Normally I'm a patient guy." He chuckled again, which clearly meant he *wasn't*. "But that little PI firm of yours has been a thorn in my side for three days. And I didn't have time to spare to begin with. Where are the rest of the pictures? You want that friend of yours to live, then tell me what I need to know."

She raised her chin, trying to act brave even though inside she wanted to curl up into a fetal position. "Which friend? Sam, Tracy or Adam?" She swallowed, every muscle tensed as she waited for his answer.

His brows arched up. "Well, now. That's a question, isn't it? I think we both know that Sam's a lost cause at this point." He winked and grinned when she pressed her lips together to keep from crying out.

Sam. Oh no, Sam.

"I admit, I might have been a little hasty with your boss." He let out a laborious sigh. "Regrets can be a terrible thing. Interrogating him first would have saved me a lot of trouble, for sure. As for that cop of yours, well, once again, lost cause. He's not getting out of here alive. That's not negotiable. I've got big plans, and him mouthing off to other law enforcement pigs could ruin everything. I'm not letting that happen. Guess that leaves you with just one friend to be worried about. Your fellow office worker, that Amazon warrior woman with legs that go all the way up. Tall women aren't normally my taste. But she's got some curves, nice melons. I could enjoy some of that. What's her name? Tracy? Yeah, that's it. Tracy Larson. You worried about her?" He leaned forward, his eyes blazing with menace. "Because you should be."

Her stomach clenched, and she pressed back against the door. "Where is she?"

"In safekeeping, for now. But only if you start talking. My infamous patience is about gone. Where are the recordings?"

She flexed her bound hands, which were tingling in the night chill with them tied above her head. "They have to be in Sam's office. That's where he keeps everything."

"Yeah, well, not this time. I've tossed that place high and low, went through every SD card and flash drive I could find. You and that Tracy girl are the only two other people who worked there. So it's up to you to spill the beans."

"What…what makes you so sure there are more recordings?"

He rolled his eyes. "You think I'm dumb? Your boss had date and time stamps on all of his pictures. And there's a gap in them, on a very specific day. He was watching us for a whole week based on the other time stamps. And there's one day smack-dab in the middle that's missing. Tell me where the rest of the stuff is and I'm gone, like I was never here. You'll never see me again. Promise."

She could feel the blood draining from her face. He might have thought his little speech would convince her that Tracy was still alive, that if she gave him what he wanted, she could still save her friend. But after hearing his callous talk about Sam and Adam, and fitting the pieces together, she realized she'd been kidding herself all this time.

Damien's tactics were to kill first, ask questions later. After killing Sam, he'd realized he'd made a mistake. So he'd taken Tracy. He'd no doubt *interrogated* her, and when

Tracy had nothing to share, he'd likely killed her. That was the only reason Jody could come up with for why *she* was still sitting here, alive, relatively unhurt. She was Damien's last chance to get the information he needed. He had to make sure it was secured, maybe destroyed, so no one else would find it. And once he did that, he'd kill her to keep her from talking.

"Good," he said. "You're obviously thinking hard about what I've said. Just hurry it up. Your friend's life, and yours, depends on it. If you take too long, I'll order her killed and cut the truth out of your flesh. You feel me, girl?" He didn't wait for her reply. He turned away and stared toward the water.

Tears burned the backs of Jody's eyes as she followed his gaze. She hated that she cried so easily. But in this case, maybe it had helped her. Damien had to have seen the tears she was trying so hard to hold back and figured she was on the verge of breaking and telling him what he needed to know.

He was right, of course.

She wasn't a strong person, never had been. If she had any clue where other recordings or pictures were, she'd probably have spewed that information back on the Sugarland Mountain Trail. And he would have killed her right then.

She blinked hard, forcing the tears back. If she'd died up on that trail, Adam would have found a dead body instead of ever seeing Damien. He'd be sitting in an office somewhere investigating her death, or maybe others would take on that chore while he went off to do whatever it was law enforcement rangers did. The important thing was that he'd be safe, having never become a target of Damien's wrath.

She clenched her fingers together, trying to keep the blood flowing as she looked through the windshield in the same direction where Damien was looking—down at the water. The second dune buggy was parked by the river now. Flashlight beams pointed down at the ground as the four men from that buggy, plus Ned and Owen, searched for Adam. Six men searching for one, all so they could ensure his silence, that he'd never tell anyone about Damien. Any doubts she'd had about Tracy maybe still being alive died a quick death.

The man beside her didn't value life. And he didn't like being inconvenienced. He'd shot and killed one of his own men to keep him from talking, or maybe to save himself the trouble of dragging him to safety. He was being greatly inconvenienced by Jody right now. No way would he do that if he had another option.

Her best friend in the whole world was dead. And Adam McKenzie—an honorable, kind man willing to risk everything to save a stranger—was going to be dead, too, if she didn't do something to help him. Assuming he wasn't dead already, lying on the bald somewhere, his wound torn open and bleeding out. But what could she do? How could she help him?

She wasn't lying about the pictures. She really didn't know where Sam might have hidden them if he'd stumbled onto something bad and wanted to hide it from her and Tracy for some reason. So where did that leave her?

For the moment, it left her with leverage. As long as this bloodthirsty idiot beside her thought she could give him what he wanted, he'd keep her alive. She could make something up, bluff, buy some time. He'd kill her anyway. Not much she could do about that. But if she could buy Adam some time, maybe, just maybe, with his law enforcement experience and knowledge of these mountains, maybe that would be enough to let him get away and get some help… and survive.

If the legacy of her twenty-four short years on this planet was that she managed to save Adam McKenzie's life, well, that wouldn't be too bad. She could take comfort in that— if she could make it happen.

She watched the lights in the distance. They were still searching, which meant they hadn't caught Adam yet. If he'd passed out from blood loss, they would have found his body by now, wouldn't they? So he was still alive. There was still time to save him.

While she watched the flashlights bobbing through the trees that lined the stream, she came up with a plan. Not a very good one, but better than nothing.

"Damien?"

He frowned and looked at her, obviously not pleased with her using his name. "What?"

"I'll… I'm willing to show you where the other pictures are. But I have conditions."

He grabbed her chin and squeezed it in a painful grip. "How about this condition? You tell me what I need to know. Period. And then maybe I don't kill you."

She jerked her head, but he only tightened his fingers, the nails biting into her skin.

"Kill me and those pictures will be found and made public. I guarantee it. I'm the one in charge of storing all our case files. And part of that responsibility is making sure the files are sent back to Sam if something happens to me. It's…it's in my will, the location of those files. It'll all come out. Whoever handles Sam's estate will get the files. Then they'll be made public."

"You're lying. You're a kid, probably fresh out of college. You don't even have a will."

"Oh, really? I'm a criminal justice major and I work for a private investigator. You think my professors, and Sam, didn't drill into me the importance of ensuring that I have a will, and that any important documents are preserved and turned over to the executor of that will upon my death?"

She wasn't lying about that. Her professors and Sam *had* drilled that information into her. But the glaring flaw in her story was that the papers, and pictures, that she'd mentioned in her will were of course her own, not Sam's. Her storage unit was full of her cameras and SD cards and file cabinets loaded with pictures that she'd taken as part of her other job, as a professional photographer. She had mentioned the unit in her will and left a copy of her key with the lawyer who'd drawn it up. That was part of securing *her* assets. Not Sam's.

But Damien didn't know that.

If she could get him to believe her now, and take her to her storage unit, he could spend days going through all her SD cards looking for the specific pictures he believed to be there. That would buy her a little time, hopefully enough to escape. If not, maybe she'd at least be able to get a note under a door to another storage unit, or somehow leave it for someone else to find, a note that would let them know about Adam so they could send him help.

"Load up your guys into the buggies and take me back to town. If you do that, if you leave Adam alone, I'll take you to where the pictures are stored. And you'll let Tracy go. She's safe and sound, like you said, right?"

She bit her bottom lip, trying to look hopeful, even though she was convinced that her friend was already dead.

He straightened in his seat. "Sure, sure. She's safe and sound. I'll take you back to town, get the pictures and both of you will go free."

"And Ranger McKenzie? What about him?"

His jaw tightened. "He's a threat to me, him being a cop and all." His gaze darted back and forth as he appeared to consider her deal. "Okay, my plans will be taken care of in the next few days. I can pull my guys back, have them watch the trails to make sure your cop doesn't find his way back, for two days. After that, it won't matter. We'll be gone. Of course, I'll have to accommodate you as a guest for those two days as well. You understand. But after that, I'll let you go—if you take me to the pictures."

"And Tracy? You'll let her go, too?"

"Oh, right, right. Her too. Do we have a deal?"

Her heart shattered at how casual he was about Tracy. He'd already forgotten about her. It was so hard to keep up her pretense without giving in to grief, to pretend she was buying the snake oil this viper was selling. "Cut my hands free and we'll shake on it."

He snickered. "No can do. You'll try to get away."

"It's not like we can drive back into Gatlinburg with my hands tied to the roll bar. I'm not going to try to escape. I'm not betting Adam's or Tracy's lives on that."

"I'll cross that bridge when we get there. Your hands stay tied."

She shrugged, as if it didn't matter. Her hands really were going numb. But mainly she'd wanted them free to give her more options. Like maybe she could grab his gun. But he was too careful for that.

"We have a deal?" she asked.

"We do."

She nodded toward the stream. "Your men?"

"Oh, of course." He was all smiles and acting like her friend now that he thought he was going to get what he wanted.

He radioed the change in plans. "Got that, boys?"

"Got it, boss," Owen answered.

Damien frowned. "Why do you have the radio instead of Ned?"

A pause, then, "Ned was worried the chatter would warn

the cop. He didn't want the radio. He gave it to me so he could track him."

As Damien took the opportunity to tell Owen what an idiot he thought he was, Jody tried to focus on the coming challenge, how to draw the time out once they got to the storage unit. Was there something she could use inside to try to get word to someone to come help Adam? Not that she believed that Damien would truly follow through, that he'd pull all of his men off the search permanently. He'd said "your cut" earlier, which implied there was money riding on whatever Sam had seen. He wasn't going to risk Adam making it out of here and ruining that. But at least getting them all out of these mountains for the time being, until Damien could get more men out here searching, would give Adam a head start.

The lawn mower–type roar of the second buggy started up in the distance. All she could see were the beams from flashlights bouncing around as, she assumed, the men got into the buggy. Then the flashlights flicked off. She could tell there were men in the buggy. But she had no way of counting them from this far away.

"Looks like they're ready," Damien announced. "They'll follow us out of the mountains, like I promised." He started up the engine. It sputtered then caught, adding its dull, throaty roar to the sound of the other buggy that was idling down by the water and hadn't yet moved.

"I need to see them," she insisted. "I need to see six men in that buggy. Then *they* can take the lead. We'll follow them out. I have to make sure they're all there, that none of them are looking for Adam."

His eyes narrowed. "You thinking I ain't holding up my end of our deal? You calling me a liar?"

"Trust but verify."

He surprised her by laughing. "You're a lot more like

me than you probably think you are. Wheeling and dealing, probably lying but playing the innocent." He laughed again. "You think I don't see that hamster wheel spinning around in your head a hundred miles an hour? You think you're clever, getting me to call off the search and let you and your friend go. If I thought there was a good chance of your boyfriend making it out of here in the next twenty-four hours, I wouldn't go along with whatever game you're playing. Just make sure you haven't outsmarted yourself. 'Cause if you don't take me to those pictures, I'm not drawing this out any longer. I'll slit your throat and take my chances. And I'll come back here personally and kill that cop."

He floored the gas and the buggy took off, bumping over the rocky field.

Jody squinted toward the other buggy, trying to make out the different silhouettes. The one in the driver's seat was most likely Owen, because he was leaning back against the headrest as if bored, probably whining to everyone else about being cold or something. The others seemed to have their backs to them, looking out at the water.

She tensed. Had they seen something? If Adam was hiding and had made some kind of noise, would they draw their weapons and shoot him, in spite of the fragile deal she had with Damien?

The buggy pulled to a stop perpendicular to the other one, headlights illuminating the group of men.

Jody sucked in a shocked breath.

"What the—" Damien stood up in his seat to get a better view.

There weren't six men in the buggy. There were only five. Ned was missing. But the rest of them were bound and gagged, including Owen. Their own clothes had been used to tie them up. All of them were shirtless. Shoestrings tied their hands together.

Damien let out a guttural roar of rage and slammed the gas, whipping the steering wheel hard left. The buggy spun in the dirt, then took off in the direction of the Sugarland Trail, leaving a wide-eyed and gagged Owen behind along with the other men. A tree loomed up ahead. Damien turned the wheel to avoid it. The headlights suddenly revealed a man standing in their path, about fifty yards ahead, aiming a rifle directly at them.

It was Adam. He was alive!

Damien floored the gas, heading right for him.

Chapter Thirteen

The dune buggy barreled down on Adam. He didn't move out of the way. He carefully aimed his rifle at the driver's side of the windshield, painfully aware that Jody was just a few feet away from the driver. He squeezed the trigger.

Bam!

He heard the crack of the windshield and guttural cursing from behind the blinding headlights. Had he hit Damien? Had he hit Jody? That possibility had his stomach clenching with dread. But he'd had to take the shot. If he let Damien take her out of these mountains, she was as good as dead. He'd had to risk it.

The buggy was still barreling down on him. He aimed for the driver's side headlight, then lowered the rifle bore to just beneath it, going for the tire.

Bam! Whoosh!

The left front tire blew. The buggy hop-skipped sideways. The headlights arced away from him, and he got his first clear look at Jody. Her eyes were wide with fright, but she seemed okay. Relief flooded through him, but not for long. The buggy bounced like crazy, sliding toward him. Damien was wrestling for control with his one good arm, even as he shrugged off the sling on his bad arm. Moonlight glinted off the pistol clutched awkwardly in his left hand, pointing at Adam.

Adam leveled the rifle again.

"No!" Jody yelled. She yanked herself up in the air toward the roll bar and slammed her legs into Damien's shoulders. The pistol went flying.

Adam jerked his rifle up so he wouldn't hit her.

The buggy made a sickening lurch, then careened toward him.

Adam dived out of the way, rolling across the ground, the buggy coming to a bouncing stop about ten yards away, miraculously still upright.

His left leg was on fire, but he fought through the pain, limping as fast as he could to reach the buggy. He rounded the driver's seat, aiming his rifle inside. The seat was empty. Damien was gone.

"Where is he, Jody?"

She motioned with her chin. "He jumped out, ran toward the water."

Adam yanked his knife out of his boot and leaned across the opening. He sliced the rope on the roll bar, freeing her. "Can you drive?"

"The tire—"

"Don't make any sudden turns or stops and we should be able to ride on the rim for a bit on this soft ground. We have to get out of here, now, before Damien finds the cache of guns I took away from his men, or the one who took off looking for me returns. He would have heard the gunshots and could be back any second."

She was shaking her hands, working her fingers. "I'll try. My hands feel like a thousand needles are stabbing them." She stepped over the middle console and plopped down behind the wheel. "What about you? How will you get into the—"

He rolled over the side of the buggy and fell into the back seat. "Go! Head that way." He motioned toward where they'd come from earlier in the day, back toward the Sugarland Trail.

"Your leg. Are you okay? How did you—"

Boom!

The crack of another rifle sounded from the direction of the water.

"Go, go, go!" Adam yelled even as he returned fire.

The buggy took off, tilting dangerously to the right.

"Back off the gas, ease into it!" Adam fired several more rounds, laying cover fire as Jody brought the buggy under control, then took off more slowly.

The buggy straightened out, the ride so bumpy and lopsided that Adam fell back. He scrambled across the seat on his knees, cursing when his makeshift splint caught on a seat belt and pulled his hurt leg. Fire shot up to his thigh, but he couldn't give in to the pain now. He gritted his teeth and brought up his rifle, exchanging shot after shot with the thugs by the other buggy until it fell out of sight behind a rise.

He collapsed, clutching his useless leg.

Jody looked at him in the mirror. "Should I pull over?"

"No! Keep going. I slashed all four tires in the other vehicle and tossed the keys in the water. That should give us a good chance. But it's still a dune buggy. They can ride it with flat tires on this ground just like we're doing. All it takes is one guy who knows how to hot-wire it and they'll be after us in no time."

"Then…what can we do? This buggy can't get back up the mountain where we came down. I don't remember a road."

"There's a road—several. Access roads we rangers use, more like wide footpaths than roads, but they'll do the job. I assume Damien and his men came down one of them to get to us as fast they did. We'll have to keep ahead of them. That's our best chance right now."

A dull roar sounded in the distance. The other buggy, back over the rise they'd just come down.

Jody's tortured gaze met his again in the mirror. "Is there a plan B?"

This was his plan B. Plan A had pretty much ended when he'd had to shoot out the buggy tire to get Damien to stop. He'd hoped to use that buggy for his and Jody's escape. Without a flat tire, they could be going twice as fast as they were now, and escape would have been easy.

He forced a smile even though his leg was throbbing so hard he could barely think straight. And it was bleeding again. And he was pretty sure he was close to passing out. Again. "I'll think of something."

A bright spotlight popped on ahead of them.

Jody slammed the brakes.

Adam grabbed the roll bar and swung himself into the seat beside her, dropping onto his knees and aiming his rifle straight ahead over the top of the windshield.

They came to a shuddering stop, turned sideways, with Adam's side the one facing the lights.

"Drop your weapon!" a voice called out over a loud-speaker.

Adam hesitated.

The spotlight swept off to the side, still lighting up the buggy but not in his eyes anymore. He got his first clear glimpse at what they were facing. A group of at least fifteen men and women formed a semicircle about a hundred feet away. They were all aiming rifles at them.

"Drop it!" the voice ordered again.

Adam pitched his rifle out and held his hands up in the air.

Jody stared at him in shock. "What are you doing?"

He was about to tell her when the loudspeaker buzzed again. "Step out of the vehicle, hands up."

"Go ahead," he told her. "These are—"

Chh-chh. Four men materialized from out of the darkness on either side of them. One had just pumped his shotgun.

"Put the guns away," Adam told them, sounding furious as he leaned over Jody as if to shield her. "I'm Ranger Adam McKenzie."

"Lower your weapons!" Another man jogged into view, shaking his head as he reached the buggy. "What have you gotten yourself into this time, Adam?"

Jody's eyes were wide, her face pale as she looked back and forth between them, her hands in the air.

Adam rolled his eyes at him, but he couldn't help but grin as he gently pressed Jody's arms down. "Jody Ingram, meet National Park Service Investigative Officer, Special Agent Duncan McKenzie. My brother."

Chapter Fourteen

Adam looked over his brother's head, past the foot of the hospital bed to where Jody was curled into a completely uncomfortable-looking chair by the window, passed out from exhaustion.

"Earth to Adam," Duncan said. "She's fine. The doctor checked her out last night, and other than some bumps and bruises, she's okay. You can quit checking on her every thirty seconds."

Adam shoved his brother's arm off the bed railing. "And you can stop exaggerating. I've only checked on her a few times since you came in."

"Yeah. Whatever." He didn't look convinced as he waved a hand toward Adam's left leg, heavily bandaged and propped up on some pillows. "I'm surprised they didn't cut that thing off while I was dealing with your mountain buddies all morning." He winced with sympathy. "It looked awful yesterday. Had to hurt like a son of a gun. What's the prognosis?"

He started to glance at Jody again but caught himself.

Duncan grinned, as if he could read his mind. Maybe he could. The two of them were the closest in age of all of his brothers. They were only ten months apart—Irish twins, as the saying went. Most strangers had difficulty telling them apart. Every time he had to tell someone in front of his mom that, no, they weren't twins, they were ten months apart, she'd blush bright red. His dad would grin with pride, as if his virility had been confirmed. He didn't mind at all being the stereotype behind the slang Irish twins saying that some found offensive. He just pointed to his other two sons and smiled. Or, most of the time to his other *one* son, since the fourth son was rarely ever home, doing everything he could to keep his title as the reigning black sheep of the family.

"The doctor threw all kinds of medical jargon at me. The best I can tell, I pretty much ripped the main muscles apart when I pulled that piece of wood out. Creating a makeshift splint out of tree branches and my shirt and chasing down the bad guys destroyed the rest. If I'm lucky and the antibiotics work like they're supposed to, I might get full use of the leg with a year or so of physical therapy."

Duncan winced again. "And if you're not lucky?"

Adam's hands tightened on the blanket covering him. "They lop it off." He shrugged. "Jody's alive. I'm alive. That's a miracle considering what we were up against. If I end up losing a leg out of it, I consider myself lucky."

"You have a warped view of good luck," Jody's soft, feminine voice called out from her window seat. "And there was no luck involved. You almost killed yourself saving both of us. If the National Park Service hands out medals, you deserve a drawer full of them."

She uncurled her legs and headed toward the bed. She held her hand across Adam to the other side, offering it to his brother. "Thank you for rescuing us, Duncan. But knowing your brother, he'd have found a way to finish the job and bring us both home, even without your help. He's pretty amazing."

Duncan shook her hand. "I'm sure you're right, Miss Ingram. Adam would have found a way. He's a pretty resourceful guy and I'm proud to have him as a fellow officer, and a brother."

Adam rolled his eyes.

Duncan dropped down into his chair as Jody took the one on the other side of the bed. He picked up an electronic tablet from the bedside table and tapped the screen, bringing it to life. "I'm actually on duty, in spite of the obscenely late hour of seven on a Sunday evening—well past my normal dinnertime. I need to take Adam's statement now that he's finally out of surgery and no longer under the influence of anesthesia. My team's heading up the investigation in conjunction with the local police."

"So sorry to have inconvenienced you by having a long surgery," Adam said, rolling his eyes.

Duncan grinned.

"Have they found Tracy? Or Sam?" Jody asked.

"Not yet, ma'am. But I promise you we have every available resource searching for them. We've also got a team looking for that Damien fellow and his right-hand guy, Ned. The rest of them we captured and put into lockup, waiting to be processed. We know their names because of their fingerprints. They're all in the system. We just have to figure out last names for Damien and Ned and make the connections, figure out how and why they ended up together. We're on this. Don't you worry."

She nodded her thanks and rubbed her hands up and down her arms, as if chilled.

Adam started to pull his blanket off to give to her.

She put her hand on his, stopping him. "Don't you dare. I'll go ask the nurse for an extra one. Be right back."

As soon as the door to the hospital room closed, Adam rolled his head on his pillow to look at his brother. "Waiting to be processed? No one has interrogated the thugs you captured?"

"Every single one lawyered up. We didn't get squat from any of them."

"Any idea what their connection is to each other?"

"Career criminals, and not the garden-variety street thugs, either. They all have long records with everything from grand theft auto to breaking and entering. One of them was charged with murder but beat the rap. No question he did it—the prosecutor made some stupid mistakes and he got off on a technicality. But finding links between them has proven difficult. If anything, the lack of links is what's so glaring and concerning. They've all done some time, either in jail or prison, but never at the same places, not at the same time, at least. Two of them aren't even from Tennessee. And the states they're from aren't the same, either. So, again, no links, other than them being lowlifes who will do anything for a buck."

Adam drew the obvious conclusions. "Damien's the leader, so he probably hired all the guys working for him. Instead of bringing on guys he did time with or knew in some way, he purposely went out of his way to hire strangers. He didn't want to risk anything coming back to point to him."

Duncan nodded. "That's my take, too. Which makes me think that either Damien has some kind of connection to whatever is behind the abductions, or someone who hired him does. And that someone is going to great lengths to distance themselves from whatever happens. Even if everything hits the fan, they want to come out lily-white."

"You think someone hired Damien? That he's not the one behind this?" Adam asked.

"Did he strike you as smart enough to mastermind all of this?"

"Hard to say. Didn't you find his fingerprints on the

buggy he drove? He has to be in the system. Those were prison tattoos on his arms."

Duncan's mouth flattened. "Unfortunately, the steering wheel and the rest of the interior of the buggies isn't conducive to giving us viable sets of prints. They're textured, don't provide anything useful in the fingerprint department."

"What about the outside of the buggies, the painted surfaces? Can't you get prints off those?"

"Oh, we've got plenty of prints from the outside. So far, every one matches up to the guys we've already got locked up. Not one of them leads to this Damien guy. Also, the buggies were stolen. So tracing registration is a dead end."

"Figures." Adam blew out a breath in frustration. "The lack of prints doesn't make sense. He wasn't wearing gloves. And I didn't see him wipe down anything. He sure didn't have time to later, when he took off running."

"If he took precautions to only touch the textured plastic door handle on the outside, he wouldn't have left prints. A guy who went to the care he did in order to hire guys who weren't connected to him in any way could have been careful enough to think about fingerprints before touching anything."

Adam stretched his leg, wincing when a sharp pain radiated up his calf. "You have to have a theory about all of this. A group of thugs kidnaps all three employees of a PI firm and threatens one of them if she doesn't show them where some supposed pictures are. Makes sense it's all related to one of Campbell's cases, don't you think?"

Duncan nodded. "The possibility has crossed my mind. This Damien fellow was worried about surveillance photos. The client who hired Sam would have wanted the photos taken. And there wouldn't be any reason for Sam to hide the photos from the guy paying his bills."

"So whoever was in the photos found out that the client hired a private investigator and wants any pictures he took. The question is how did the person in the photos find out. You think Sam got sloppy? That someone saw him taking pictures?"

"Seems like the simplest scenario, and it matches what Miss Ingram said on the chopper on the way to the hospital. Whoever is being followed by Sam sees him and hires Damien to kill Sam and hire a group of guys to toss Campbell's home and office. Only they're still searching the office when Tracy Larson goes to work, and she catches them in the act."

Adam nodded, following the scenario. "There's a struggle, maybe they kill her—either accidentally or on purpose—and then they realize the pictures they're looking for are nowhere to be found. Now they're getting desperate. Was there anything in Campbell's office to let them know that Jody worked there, too? And that she was the only remaining employee?"

"Absolutely. Campbell was meticulous. His payroll records were right in his filing cabinet. Damien knew there were three of them. Without Sam or Tracy around to interrogate, Miss Ingram was the last link to making sure those pictures never find their way into anyone's hands. That's why they went after her." He shrugged. "Makes sense as a hypothetical. But I have to keep an open mind and follow the evidence. We may be on a completely wrong track. If Miss Ingram can remember more details about what Damien and the others may have said in front of her when you weren't with her, that could give us the clues we need to make all the puzzle pieces fit," Duncan said.

"I assume you're talking to all of Campbell's clients?"

"Of course. We sent the files from the office to our team of investigators. They're following up with everyone who hired him in the past month. If we don't get any leads out of that, we'll go back further. Don't worry. We'll figure it out."

"What about finding Sam Campbell and Tracy Larson?" When his brother hesitated, Adam narrowed his eyes. "You found them, didn't you? That's what you really came in here to tell me. But since Jody was here you couldn't."

"I came in here to check on my brother and take a more detailed statement now that you're coherent and off drugs. But, yes, you're right. We found something. Or, rather, some*one*. A body. The autopsy isn't finished yet. They'll need DNA results or dental records to confirm the identity."

"Male or female?"

"Male."

"Sam Campbell."

Duncan nodded. "Most likely but it hasn't been confirmed. Physical description and approximate age matches the body, and there aren't any other open missing-persons cases that could fit. He was dumped in a ditch not far from his office, beside a rural road. Critters and decomp took their toll. Thus the need to wait for dental records or DNA results before making it official."

"Understood. What about her friend Tracy Larson?"

"Based on the quick statement you gave me while the search-and-rescue team hauled you two out in the chopper, I can't imagine that she's still alive. But without a body, we're still treating it as a search and rescue, not a recovery. Not yet."

"No leads?"

"None. Her car was parked at the office, so it seems likely that's where she was taken. No witnesses so far, though. We've canvassed her apartment complex, too, in case this was planned in advance and someone suspicious was hanging out watching her place in the week before she disappeared. Gatlinburg PD is doing a knock and talk, going door to door to follow up with anyone who wasn't home when they did their initial canvass. But the last reported sighting of Miss Larson so far is Friday afternoon, when Miss Ingram left the office."

"I prefer Jody to Miss Ingram."

They both looked toward the door. Jody was just inside, her face pale, her freckles standing out in stark relief.

"How long have you been listening?" Adam asked.

Two bright spots of color darkened her cheeks as she clutched a beige blanket in her arms. "I wasn't purposely trying to eavesdrop. I was about to step inside when I heard you mention Tracy. I didn't want to interrupt, or make you stop, because everyone has been so tight-lipped. It's frustrating. No one seems to want to tell me anything."

She stepped to the plastic chair on Adam's right and sat down, bringing the blanket up to her chin.

Adam exchanged a relieved looked with his brother. If Jody had only started listening at the mention of Tracy, then she hadn't heard that a body had been found and might be Sam. He wanted to keep it that way until the coroner confirmed the identity. "Duncan, can you—"

"Yeah, yeah." He set the tablet on the table and stood. "I'll give you both a few minutes. But then I really need that statement."

"Make it ten."

Duncan nodded. "Ten it is. I'll bring back some coffee. Miss Ingram—"

"Jody."

He smiled broadly, pouring on the charm. "Jody. Lovely name for a fine, Irish-looking lass. Your red hair and green eyes are a perfect foil to black Irish here, with those blue eyes and black hair."

"You have the same blue eyes and black hair," Adam

growled. "And stop with the fake accent. You've never even been to Ireland."

Duncan's grin widened as he continued to stare at Jody. "How do you take your coffee, sweet colleen?"

Adam wanted to strangle him.

Jody smiled. "Cream and sugar, please."

"My pleasure." He headed out of the room.

"Is he always that cheeky?" she asked.

Adam blinked. "Cheeky? Are you going to start talking in a British accent now?"

"I bloody well might," she teased, her inflections a perfect imitation of an English lady's, even if the language she used wasn't.

"Don't fall for his *cheekiness*," he said. "He's married to his job."

"And you aren't?"

He shook his head. "Haven't been on the job long enough to be married to it yet. I transferred from Memphis a few months ago." He held his right hand out, unable to resist the need to touch her, to remind himself there was still some good left in this world. There were many dark times, like now, when he wasn't so sure.

There was no hesitation on her part. She slid her hand through the large opening in the railing. She entwined her fingers with his and rested their joined hands on the mattress.

He squeezed reassuringly and searched her face. She was dressed in clothes a policewoman had brought from her apartment, another white blouse—that unfortunately had all its buttons—and a pair of faded jeans that hugged the curves of her hips and offered a tempting view of her backside whenever she walked across the room. He had availed himself of that view far too often since waking up from recovery to find her in his room this afternoon.

He cleared his throat, forcing himself to focus on the case, not his ridiculous fascination with the beautiful woman just a few feet away. "I'm sorry you heard that, about Tracy. No one has given up hope. They're still searching for her."

She nodded, looking sad but resigned. "You don't think she's alive any more than I do. Even from the beginning, as soon as you heard about her and knew that Damien had confronted me on the trail. You put the pieces together pretty fast, figured out that Damien would have killed me to eliminate witnesses if Tracy was still alive and could tell him what he needed."

He wanted to lie. But she deserved better than that, and she was too smart to fall for it anyway. "You're right. I figured he was eliminating witnesses to whatever he was trying to hide right from the get-go. He didn't strike me as the ruminating type. Act first, regret later. That seems to be his motto." He squeezed her fingers again. "But miracles do happen. Maybe instead of…well, maybe Tracy escaped after all. Damien may have gone after you because you were his last lead and he was desperate to make sure the pictures don't fall into someone else's hands. Your friend may be hiding somewhere this very minute, not sure where to go or what to do. I guarantee she's got the very best possible men and women out trying to find her, both in the mountains and in town. No one's giving up."

She nodded her thanks and pulled her hand free to tug the blanket up higher around her where it had started to fall. The loss of her touch sent a sharp pang of longing through him. He had to force himself not to reach for her again. She was too good for him. There was no chance of a future between them, in spite of the attraction that seemed to simmer every time she was in the same room—a mutual attraction, judging by the hungry looks she'd been casting his way all afternoon as he'd endured exams and bandage changes and listened to long lectures from his doctor on what to do and what not to do.

He frowned and waved at her clothing. "Your hospital gown is gone. I'm assuming they discharged you after keeping you for observation last night. Where do you plan on going when you leave?"

"One of the police officers brought me a key to my apartment that she got from the manager. I guess I'll go there—home. And before you say it, I'm sure I'll be okay. My Glock is locked up there. If Damien or Ned or any other thugs he wants to send after me show up, they won't find a defenseless woman waiting for them. And I've got a phone again if I needed to call for help. A victim's advocate that one of your people called gave me some cash and a pay-as-you-go cell phone from the hospital gift shop to replace mine."

"None of that sounds especially comforting. What about transportation?"

"I can call a cab. You don't have to worry about me. I'll be okay."

"You need protection. Have you asked the police—"

She laughed, without humor. "They're great and all. But they have a limited budget and can't afford to assign officers to watch over witnesses who may or may not be in danger. Especially when half the Park Service is out searching for the guys I'm allegedly in danger from. Apparently, the odds of them being able to get to me are extremely low."

"Is that a direct quote from some jerk police officer?"

"Pretty much. But to be fair, Gatlinburg PD and the Park Service have been great. It was only one jerk. And it's not anyone's fault that they have a limited budget. If I need protection, I've been told to hire my own."

He stared at his bum leg, hating himself for that one

unguarded moment when he hadn't been careful enough and had stepped into a hole. "Will you? Hire someone?"

"I have a limited budget, too."

"When Duncan gets back, I'll tell him to withdraw some money from my account. I can hire someone to guard you for a few days."

She was already shaking her head before he finished. "No. Thank you very much, Adam. But you don't owe me anything. There's no reason for you to spend your money on me."

"I could make it a loan. With a really long payback time frame. Like forever."

She smiled. "You're amazing, you know that? But, like I said. I'll be fine. Now that I know to be careful, I'll be on my guard. And I'll keep my gun beside me tonight, ready to grab. Plus my phone. My apartment's just five minutes from the police station. Seriously, there's nothing to worry about. But thanks, just the same, for being concerned."

"I know you aren't close with your adoptive family. But surely they'd let you stay with them for a while. Wouldn't they?"

She stiffened, but before she could answer, the door clicked open and Duncan stepped inside. As soon as Adam saw the look on his brother's face, he reached for Jody's hand. She clutched it like a lifeline, her face pale as she waited for Duncan to speak.

"I'm so sorry, Jody. They found your friend Tracy Larson. She's dead."

Chapter Fifteen

Jody dried her face with a washcloth and stared at her reflection above the sink in Adam's hospital bathroom.

They found your friend Tracy Larson. She's dead.

Even though she'd been expecting those words, her heart didn't want to accept the truth.

She could see Tracy in her mind's eye, hear her voice, feel her arms around her whenever she'd needed a hug. Which was a whole lot more often than her strong, beautiful friend had ever needed. Tracy was a rock, always had been. Jody had been her weak, needy friend. During the most difficult years of Jody's life, Tracy and her family had been her comfort, her solace, her refuge from the storm. Jody would never have survived if it weren't for their love and support.

She swiped at her tears and straightened her shoulders. Hiding in this bathroom wasn't helping anyone. It was time to pull herself together and tell Adam and his brother everything she could remember about Damien and his thugs. Hopefully some of the details that were coming back to her now that she had finally gotten some sleep would provide the clues necessary to bring justice to her friend, and to Sam, if he too was dead, as Damien had taunted.

She opened the door and stepped out. Two very similar pairs of deep blue eyes looked at her with concern. She forced a smile and stepped around Duncan to take her seat beside Adam's bed.

"I want to help you catch Damien," she told Duncan. "I know that my earlier statement wasn't all that useful. I was exhausted and wasn't thinking straight. But I'm remembering more details now. Like that Damien and Owen are brothers."

Adam and Duncan exchanged a surprised look. "Brothers?" they echoed each other.

"I think so. In the buggy, Damien called Owen his little brother. He only said it once. It could have been a nickname. But if it wasn't, that could help you figure out more about Damien. Right?"

"Absolutely." Duncan pulled out his cell phone and started texting someone. A few moments later, he gave Jody a big smile. "Bingo. My guy brought up Owen Flint's bio. We knew he had a brother, Raymond D. Flint. But hadn't made the connection yet. The D stands for Damien." He held up his phone and turned it around. "Mugshot look familiar?"

"That's him," they both said.

"That's Damien," Jody confirmed. "He's the one who sent those men to kill Adam."

"And *you*," Adam said, frowning.

"Do you remember any other details you didn't mention before?" Duncan asked.

"Three days," she said. "It was part of that same conversation in the buggy. Damien said Sam's PI business had been causing him problems for three days. He had plans, big plans, and Owen wouldn't get his cut if Adam made it out of the mountains and connected the dots."

Adam and Duncan exchanged another look.

"Big plans?" Duncan asked.

"Connected the dots?" Adam asked.

She nodded. "They didn't talk about his plans or what he meant, other than that Adam was a cop and knew he was an ex-con—"

"Because of the tattoos," Adam said.

"I think so, yes. He was worried you'd figure out who he was before he could do whatever it is that he's planning."

"Are you looking at all of Sam Campbell's active cases?" Adam asked his brother.

"His office was crammed with hundreds of case files. We're using his planner to reconstruct a timeline for last week to start, so we can determine which cases he was actively working. So far we're up to twenty."

"He was meticulous with that planner," Jody said. "If he worked a case last week, it's definitely written down."

"Good to know. On the chopper when we were flying you and Adam to the hospital, you said that Damien insisted there were some pictures missing from Sam's office. Any idea why he thought any were missing? And where Sam might have put them?"

"I don't know where Sam would have put them other than the office. But as for thinking some were missing, I imagine Damien was referring to time stamps. I'm not sure if he meant actual dates and times printed on the photos, like I put on most of the pictures that I take for brochures before processing them through an editing program. He might have been referring to the metadata on SD cards that tell you when each picture was taken."

"Photography?" Adam asked. "Is that the second job you mentioned in the mountains? You work for a studio?"

"I work for myself, as far as the pictures are concerned. Sam couldn't afford to hire me full-time. So I run my own photography business on the side. Actually, calling it a business is probably stretching it. I get my clients through word of mouth. I don't have an office or anything like that."

"What do you do, exactly?" Adam asked.

"Work with hotels and cabin rental companies mainly, taking pictures and creating ads and brochures they can use to target tourists." She glanced back and forth between them. "If you're thinking some of Sam's photos could be mixed with mine, I assure you, the chances of that happening are zero."

"How can you be that positive?" Duncan asked.

"Because my photography work is run out of my apartment and a storage unit outside town. And Sam would never allow someone to bring work home. He likes to keep everything under lock and key at the office."

"Assuming you're right—"

"I am." She arched a brow at Duncan.

He smiled. "Okay. Then does Sam have a habit of losing pictures at the office? Maybe putting them in the wrong files?"

She shook her head. "Not in the six months that I've been working there. He's extremely detail oriented, and careful. He'd keep all of the pictures for one case together. It doesn't make sense that any could have been misplaced."

Adam rubbed his left leg as if to try to ease the ache. "It makes sense if Sam purposely put the pictures somewhere else for safekeeping. Maybe he realized he had something important and was checking on some details before going to the police."

Duncan picked his computer tablet up from the table beside the bed. "Looks like it's going to be a long night for us investigators. We should have a preliminary timeline put together by morning. If you don't mind reviewing it, to make sure it looks right, I can bring it to you tomorrow. Does that work for you, Jody?"

"Of course. They've already discharged me from the

hospital. I'll take a cab to my apartment in a little while. The address is—"

"No way are you going home," Adam interrupted. "It's not safe."

"I agree," Duncan said. "Damien and his men are likely looking for you. It's too dangerous. You should go to a hotel until we have him locked up."

She laughed. "Seriously? Did you miss the part where I work two jobs to make ends meet? I live paycheck to paycheck. If I have to pay for a hotel, I don't eat for a week."

"Not a problem," Adam said. "The doctor is discharging me later today. You can stay at my place."

Chapter Sixteen

Adam had expected Jody's apartment to be small. He hadn't expected it to be the size of one of those tiny houses that were all the rage on TV these days. Jody's apartment wasn't even a one-bedroom. It was an efficiency. She didn't have a bed. She had a day bed. If she'd had a couch, there wouldn't have been room for it. She had a lawn chair pulled up to a cardboard box, which apparently acted as her desk.

"Well," he said. "This is…cozy."

"I think you mean minuscule. Now you can see why I keep my cameras and equipment in a storage unit. My goal is to eventually get a full-time job as an investigator with the prosecutor's office. But until that miraculous day happens, I'm stuck in an efficiency."

She opened a door on the far wall, revealing a tiny closet. "I'll pack a bag and grab my Glock from the gun safe. Then we can take that fancy limo you rented and go to your place. Where do you live?"

He was about to answer when he realized she was pulling articles of clothing out of open boxes neatly lined up beneath her hanging clothes and shoving them into what amounted to a large book bag. She didn't even have a chest of drawers or a suitcase.

Thinking about his own home, he suddenly felt self-conscious. He worked hard because he wanted to, not because he had to. He'd never had to struggle financially.

He cleared his throat.

Jody glanced up. "Almost done." She stood and took all of three steps to reach the sink in the bathroom beside the closet. "You never answered me. Where do you live?" She grabbed a few items out of a drawer and snagged her toothbrush from a cup by the sink. "Well?"

"It's, ah, a bit larger than this place."

"I hope your house is huge. We'd be like sardines if we both had to stay here together."

Some of the tension went out of his shoulders. "Then it wouldn't bother you if I had a really big house with a few acres of land?"

"Tell me you have a million dollars in the bank and I'm yours forever."

"I have a million dollars in the bank. I guess we're getting married now."

She laughed and brushed past him to grab her bag. He reached to take it from her, and she rolled her eyes, moving it out of his reach. "You're on crutches. I can carry my own bag. Come on, Mr. Millionaire. I hope you have some New York strip or filet mignon in your freezer and a giant grill to cook them on."

He followed her to the front door, struggling to keep up since he wasn't used to crutches. When she reached to open the door, he said, "Hold it."

She glanced up at him expectantly.

"I do have steaks in the freezer."

She smiled. "Great."

"And a grill."

"Sounds perfect."

"And an outdoor kitchen."

"Okay."

"And a heated pool."

Her smile began to dim. "Any other deep confessions you want to make?"

"I really do have a million dollars in the bank. And then some."

She blinked, all signs of amusement gone. "That wasn't a joke?"

He slowly shook his head. "That wasn't a joke. Do you hate me now?"

She shoved her hair back from her face. "Look, I'm not prejudiced against rich people. Well, not *all* rich people. Just Amelia, Peter, Patricia, Patience, Patrick and Paul. I never mentioned that my estranged adoptive family is wealthy, did I?"

"No. You didn't. Your family has money but they don't share it with you?"

Shadows seemed to darken her eyes, just like they'd done up in the mountains when she'd mentioned her adoptive father.

"Jody?"

"It's...complicated. I don't want to talk about it."

"All right. Then, we're good? You don't mind going to my place?"

"We're good. Just as long as you don't live in Rutherford Estates. It's a ritzy development in the mountains outside of town where my real estate mogul adoptive father lives, along with my adoptive mom." She shivered dramatically. "It's like Mordor and the evil eye looking my way. That's why I'm over here in The Shire, making do with my little hobbit house." She grinned.

"Rutherford Estates?" He forced a laugh. "What would be the odds of your family and me living in the same area?"

"Exactly! Right? I shouldn't have even brought it up. Let's go."

JODY STOMPED PAST Adam into the foyer of his mansion—the one in Rutherford Estates—and didn't even spare him a glance. She was so angry she could spit. Seeing the expensive travertine floors spread out before her for miles made it even more tempting. She'd grown up in a place like this. And she had no desire to go back, or be within a few streets of where her family lived. He knew that and had brought her here anyway.

She clutched her bag and marched to the massive staircase just past the equally massive living area on the left side of the room, keeping her back turned to him. "I assume the bedrooms are upstairs. Which one is mine?"

Click. Click. The crutches sounded behind her as he approached. Part of her wanted to ignore him and run up the stairs, knowing he couldn't follow easily. The other part—the part she really hated right now—wanted to turn around and help him, ease him into one of the surprisingly cozy-looking leather chairs that sprinkled the room and get him a beer. Assuming he even had beer. More likely he drank wine, something French with a hoity-toity label.

The clicks stopped.

"Jody?" As always with her, his deep voice was gentle and kind.

"I'm sorry," he said. "I should have told you where I lived when you asked me instead of tricking you into coming here. But there's an electrified fence around this property, motion sensors, alarms. This is the safest place I could think of to take you."

When she didn't reply, he said, "If you really want to, we can go. I'll call the limo driver back."

She clutched the banister. "Why are you always so nice to me?"

"You want me to be mean?"

She sighed and turned around. "Of course not."

"Okay." He looked thoroughly confused. "I'll book us a room in a nice hotel downtown. I can hire a security guy to watch the door—"

"Stop. Just stop. I'll stay here. And like you said, it's safe. I'll just have to do my best to forget that we're within walking distance of my evil adoptive dad." She forced a laugh and dropped her gaze to his chest.

His fingers gently tilted her chin up. His deep blue eyes searched hers. "I'm a good listener if you want to talk."

"I don't."

"If you change your mind—"

"I won't. Where's my room?"

His mouth tightened with disappointment. "There are four guest rooms upstairs, each with its own bathroom. Pick whichever one you like. My room is down here if you need me."

"Adam, I…"

"Yes?"

She shook her head. "Thank you. I mean it. You've done so much for me. I really appreciate it."

He nodded but didn't say anything.

She started up the stairs, then stopped and looked over her shoulder.

He hadn't moved. He was balancing on his crutches, watching her with an unreadable expression.

"You're not a real estate entrepreneur, are you?" she asked.

His brows raised. "If you're wondering where my money comes from, my great-great-grandfather was a business whiz and started a dozen companies. My parents gave ownership of some of those companies to my siblings and me as we each turned twenty-one."

Her face flushed with embarrassment. "I wasn't trying to find out how you got your money. I just… I'm glad you're not in real estate. That's all."

"Because of your adoptive father being in real estate?"

She swallowed, then nodded.

"But you don't want to talk about him?"

"I really don't. But…if I did…you would be the one I'd want to talk to." She gave him a watery smile, already struggling to hold back the tears that were threatening. "Good night, Adam."

"Good night, Jody."

She hurried up the rest of the stairs and went into the first bedroom she found. After shutting the door, she slid down to the thick, plush carpet and drew her knees up to her chin. She wasn't going to get a wink of sleep knowing that the man she'd hated and feared all her life was just a short walk away. She couldn't tell Adam what Peter Ingram had done to her. She couldn't bear the revulsion that would cross his face. Or worse. She couldn't bear it if he turned out to be just like the rest of her adoptive family. She couldn't bear it if he didn't believe her.

She dropped her chin onto her knees and did what she'd done all her life when times got hard. She wept.

Chapter Seventeen

Jody hesitated at the top of the landing. She hadn't expected any lights to be on downstairs at two in the morning. She didn't want to intrude if Adam was still up, maybe watching a late movie or something.

Everything was quiet. And there were only a *few* lights on. Maybe he'd left them on for her, since she was in an unfamiliar house. He was like that. Nice. Kind. Considerate. Exactly the kind of man she'd always dreamed of, and exactly the kind of man she could never have because she was so dang screwed up.

She sighed and headed downstairs with no particular destination in mind. But she was going stir-crazy in her room, unable to sleep with so much rattling around in her brain. And her heart. Grief was a constant ache in her chest.

Figuring Adam wouldn't mind, she wandered through the sprawling house. It was refreshing to see that not everyone with money decorated their homes like a museum, the way her adoptive father decorated his.

The paintings here weren't modern atrocities of splattered paint with no form or function, calling itself art. Adam's paintings were comfortable, accessible, warm. His love of the outdoors was obvious in his choice of landscapes, most of them featuring mountains, lakes and ethereal forests that seemed so real she could swear she smelled the pine trees.

For such a big house, it didn't feel intimidating. She wasn't afraid that if she touched something it might break. She could easily see children running across the area rugs and bounding up the stairs, giggling and laughing and loving life—as all kids should.

She forced away the dark memories of her own childhood that tried to press in on her and continued her exploration. To the right of the foyer was a short hallway that she assumed led to Adam's bedroom. She paused, longing to go to him. Not because she *wanted* him, although she couldn't imagine ever *not* wanting him. Tonight she *needed* him, needed someone to care about her, to hug her and hold her and tell her that she mattered. That would be selfish, though, waking him up just to give her a hug, no matter how deeply she craved his arms around her. So she forced herself to move past the hallway to the kitchen.

Of all the rooms in the house that she'd seen so far, this one was the most typical of what she'd expect in a place like this. He hadn't stamped his personality in here, his warmth. It was functional and beautiful, with cherry cabinets and black granite countertops. But there was nothing homey. It was too sterile, too impersonal, to be a reflection of him. Which made her doubt he used it much. Maybe he cooked out a lot in the outdoor kitchen that he'd mentioned earlier, or brought a lot of takeout food home.

Thinking of takeout had her tummy rumbling. She hadn't been hungry at the hospital and had only picked at the food on her plate. She had to search for the refrigerator and finally realized it was disguised with cabinet fronts to blend in with everything else.

Mission accomplished. It definitely blended.

Shaking her head, she opened the doors, then laughed.

She pressed her hand to her mouth, belatedly hoping she hadn't been too loud. Then she rummaged through the containers of Chinese takeout, barbecue and leftover pizza. Most of the food still looked edible, and she was about to grab a slice of pepperoni pizza when she saw a plastic-wrapped plate sitting on the next shelf down. There was a note taped to the top.

Jody, just in case you wake up hungry, I cooked you a steak and grilled a potato. Wasn't sure how you like it, so I left the steak medium. —Adam

His thoughtfulness did funny things to her heart and of course had her eyes moist with tears. After all the tears she'd shed tonight, she hadn't expected that. She furiously wiped her eyes and then took out the plate. After warming it in the microwave and preparing the potato, she grabbed a beer—relieved to see he wasn't a wine drinker—and headed toward the dining room. Pausing at the entrance, she eyed the massive, lonely-looking table and changed directions, heading into the living room to the left of the stairs instead.

Now this room was exactly to her taste. Decorated in rich browns and golds, the furniture was plush leather with reclining seats. And a giant TV mounted over the fireplace. She set her beer in the cup holder on the big, cushy recliner that directly faced the TV, then settled down to eat her meal.

The first bite of steak melted in her mouth. She didn't think she'd ever had anything so good. Then again, she hadn't eaten a real meal in a few days, so that could have had something to do with it. She'd eaten half the potato and steak before she finally got full enough to slow down and leisurely enjoy the rest.

As she chewed, she glanced behind her to judge the distance between the living room and Adam's bedroom. She didn't think he'd hear her this far away, so she swiped the remote from the end table and clicked on the television. Just to make sure she didn't disturb him, she kept the volume low. Then she settled back to catch up on what had been happening in the world since she'd received that fateful text from Tracy's phone.

Since it was so late—or early, depending on how she wanted to look at it—local news wasn't an option. So she clicked on one of the twenty-four-hour national news channels. As usual, it was a kaleidoscope of unrest in the world, terrorist plots and political pundits offering so-called expert opinions based on hearsay and no firsthand knowledge. She was about to turn off the TV when one of the news anchors mentioned Gatlinburg.

Curious, she turned up the volume a couple of notches and leaned forward. Their little town was a tourist mecca. But other than the wildfires last season, nothing much happened around here to catch the attention of the national news shows.

Until now.

A picture of one of the local city councilmen, Eddie Hicks, flashed up on the screen. The anchor reminded the audience that Hicks had been killed in a car crash earlier in the week, the same day that Sam had gone missing.

Sam. Tracy. She missed them both so much.

The anchor gave details about the memorial service being held later today. Jody wasn't sure why that made the national news, until another picture flashed up on the screen—Tennessee state senator Ron Sinclair. He was well-known in Gatlinburg and heavily lauded for bringing several economy-boosting projects to town because of his work on an infrastructure subcommittee. Apparently, he was friends with the councilman and would be in town for the memorial. The mayor and other dignitaries would also be in attendance.

The anchor droned on about other events around the world as Jody finished her meal. Then she clicked off the TV and headed into the kitchen to clean up. After loading her plate and utensils in the dishwasher and making sure the kitchen was as pristine as she'd found it, she started toward the stairs again to go up to her room.

Then she noticed the pool through the back wall of French doors.

The water was a gorgeous cornflower blue, lit by lights from underneath. Since the homes around here were separated by several acres, none of them were close enough to have a view of the backyard. It was completely private and looked so peaceful and serene that it drew her forward like a magnet.

She started to open one of the doors, then stopped. There was an electronic keypad on the wall to the right. The security alarm. She hadn't even thought to ask Adam for the code. She pressed her face to the glass in frustration, then froze.

There was a man outside.

She stepped back, ready to run to Adam's room, then hesitated. The man's back was to her and he wasn't skulking around as if he was looking for a way into the house. He was sitting in one of the deck chairs facing the pool. As she watched, he turned his head to look down and picked up a bottle of beer she hadn't noticed before.

Adam.

She let out a shaky breath, relieved that Damien or one of his men hadn't found her. Then she frowned, noticing more details as her eyes adjusted to the dim light through the glass panes in the door. A holstered pistol sat on a small glass table beside his chair next to a legal pad. Dozens of balled-up pieces of paper lay discarded on the ground all around him. His phone was facedown on the concrete as if it had fallen from the table and he hadn't noticed.

What was going on? Why was he out there? Was his leg hurting so much that he couldn't sleep? That thought had her turning the knob and rushing outside.

"Adam, are you okay?" She hurried toward his chair. "Is your leg hurting too much to—" She stopped and blinked down at him. He didn't have a shirt on. He didn't have much of anything on. Actually, all he had on was his underwear—sexy boxer briefs that hugged all his…attributes… like a second skin.

Her mouth went dry as she stared at him, her gaze caressing every inch from his toes to his rippling abs to his lightly furred chest and, finally, up to eyes that reflected a deep blue in the light from the pool. But he wasn't looking at her. He was staring out at the darkness beyond the pool, his jaw clenched with agitation.

"Adam?"

He tipped the bottle of beer up to his lips and took a deep swig, emptying the bottle. Then he tossed it over his head into the pool. It landed with a splash and bobbed up and down before filling with water and slowly sinking beneath the surface.

Jody didn't have to look down into the pool to know the bottle he'd just emptied wasn't his first. And apparently it wasn't going to be his last, judging by the flush on his cheeks and the six-pack carton on the other side of his chair with one more bottle in it.

She put her hands on her hips. "You're drunk."

His eyes slowly rose to hers. "Not drunk enough." He picked up the other bottle and stared at it a moment, then squeezed his eyes shut as if in pain before throwing it unopened into the pool.

Jody lowered herself to her knees beside his chair. "Is it your leg?" She reached for his phone on the ground. "I can call the doctor, get him to phone in a stronger pain prescr—"

"I know about your adoptive father, Peter Ingram."

She went still, the phone clutched in her hand. "Excuse me?" she whispered.

His jaw clenched so tight the skin along his jawbone turned white. "The way you reacted when you mentioned him earlier, calling him your evil adoptive dad, how angry you were that I'd tricked you into coming here…" He scrubbed his face, covering his eyes with his hands before dropping them to his lap. "I know it was your story to tell. But I couldn't let it go. I had to know why you were so afraid of him." His tortured gaze finally rose to hers. "I'm so, so sorry."

"You had no right." Her voice came out a harsh croak. "You had no right."

"I know. Believe me, I know. I'm so sorry—"

"Stop saying that!" She jumped to her feet, finally finding her voice. "What are you sorry for anyway? Abusing your authority and opening a closed file you shouldn't have been able to open? That's what you had to have done. I was a juvenile. They sealed the record. No way could you have gotten that information without breaking a law or some kind of law enforcement code or something. Or are you sorry that you violated my privacy, violated *me* by prying into secrets that were mine to tell or not to tell?"

"Both. I shouldn't have pried, you're right. I abused your trust, my position as a federal officer. I never should have done it."

"No. You shouldn't have. I'm leaving, going back to my apartment. Don't bother driving me. You're too drunk to drive anyway. I'll call a cab." She turned and ran for the house.

"Jody, wait."

His chair creaked. She heard the click of his crutches as she threw open the door.

"Jody!"

She rushed inside.

A loud crack followed by the sound of shattering glass had her whirling around.

Adam lay on his back on the patio, his face twisted in agony as he clutched his hurt leg. His crutches had skittered out from beneath him and lay several feet away, right next to the shattered glass table that had been sitting beside his chair.

She ran back outside.

"No!" His voice was a hoarse whisper. "The glass. You'll get cut."

She stepped around the larger shards as she knelt beside him. "What can I do? How can I help? Are you cut?"

"Stop, Jody. You're barefoot."

"So are you. Can't you just accept help when you need it?" She grabbed his crutches, but when she tried to help him up, there was no way she could lift him. It took all her strength and a lot of cajoling and threatening to get him to even try to help her. Half-drunk Adam was ornery as all get-out and had an incredibly colorful vocabulary.

Finally she got him inside. Once they'd reached the living room, she was so exhausted she didn't even try to steer him down the hallway. Instead she jerked his crutches away and let him fall onto one of the mammoth couches.

He grunted when he landed, bounced a couple of times, then promptly passed out.

Jody's mouth dropped open in shock. Then she snapped

it closed in anger. "Adam?" She grabbed his shoulder and shook him. "Adam?"

He started snoring.

She fisted her hands at her sides and kicked one of his crutches. It skittered across the room before spinning around and sliding halfway under a recliner. How dare he? How dare he invade her privacy, look into the most intimate details of her life without her permission, then not even stay awake long enough for her to yell at him? He should be begging her forgiveness and groveling at her feet.

She closed her eyes. Dang it. He *had* groveled. He *had* begged her forgiveness. And he'd nearly killed himself trying to chase after her because she'd refused to listen to him. She sagged down onto the couch beside him.

"Oh, Adam. What am I going to do with you?"

His soft snore was apparently the only answer she was going to get any time soon.

Obviously leaving him when he was passed out wasn't a good idea. Especially with his injured leg. Plus, she really didn't want to head out the front door with Damien possibly lurking around somewhere. All in all, she was pretty much a prisoner here for the time being. But come morning, when Adam was groaning with a headache over a cup of hot coffee, she'd make him take her back home. She had a gun. If Damien tried to come into her apartment, she'd gladly pull the trigger.

Adam's jaw tightened in his sleep, and his legs shifted restlessly. He reached toward his hurt leg, groaning, obviously in pain.

"You don't deserve my help, you know that, Adam?"

He winced and mumbled something incoherent but didn't wake up.

She shook her head and set about doing everything she could to ease his pain. Which basically amounted to straightening his leg, elevating it on a pillow and applying a cold compress that she'd found in his cavernous refrigerator. But it seemed to help, because he settled down and was no longer twitching in pain.

She sighed and raked a hand through her hair. A slight breeze had her realizing she'd left one of the French doors open. Outside the little pieces of crumpled-up paper still lay by Adam's chair. The broken table glass twinkled in the moonlight like a thousand little diamonds scattered across the concrete.

"A thousand little diamonds I get to sweep up," she grumbled.

Once again she trudged into the kitchen, locating the broom and dustpan in the pantry, exactly where it made sense they would be. Of course they were hanging on hooks, and what little food he had was lined up in neat rows on the shelves.

"I wonder if he folds his underwear, too." Her bin of underwear in her closet was a chaotic jumble. It would probably give him a heart attack. She grabbed a trash bag, conveniently on a shelf next to the broom, and headed outside.

The little table had obviously been made of safety glass, probably the only reason she hadn't cut her feet when she ran outside. But even though the little pieces weren't wicked sharp, there were a lot of them. It took a good ten minutes before she was satisfied that she'd gotten up all the glass. She dumped the last of it into the garbage bag, then set about picking up the pieces of crumpled paper by Adam's chair.

Back inside, she set the legal pad and his phone on the counter and was about to stuff the garbage bag into the can under the sink when she noticed the writing on the pad. She grew still, then very slowly pulled the pad toward her and read the rest of it. By the time she'd read it all, tears were blurring her vision.

She hated that she was such a crier.

She wiped at her eyes, then slid to the floor and pulled the trash bag toward her. She picked out every piece of balled-up paper, unfolded them and smoothed them out so she could read them. Anyone else would probably be horrified at what he'd written. They might even call the police, thinking that he was dangerous. But Jody understood his anger, his fury and his desire for revenge better than anyone. And if she hadn't only known the man for a few days, she'd think she was half in love with him.

Because he was the only person, ever, who'd truly believed her.

The fact that she hadn't personally told him the details about the abuse she'd suffered at the hands of the man who'd adopted her didn't matter. Adam had read the police reports. He'd read the testimony in juvenile court. He'd read what the judge had decided, most likely after being given a substantial bribe by Jody's adoptive father. And still, Adam had believed her. That was what these pieces of paper told her. And to her they were a precious gift, something to treasure.

She carefully set each wrinkled piece of paper on the counter in a neat stack on top of the legal pad and threw the trash away. Then she headed into the family room. She set the pages on the end table, grabbed a blanket off the back of one of the chairs, then sat down beside Adam. She gently lifted his head and slipped closer, cradling his head on her lap. Then she covered both of them with the blanket and closed her eyes.

Chapter Eighteen

The smell of bacon had Adam bolting upright, then falling back with a groan. Pressing a hand to his throbbing head, he blinked up at the familiar coffered ceiling above him. Why was he on the couch? With a pillow beneath his head? And a blanket covering him? The last thing he remembered was sitting by the pool, nursing a beer to dull the pain in his leg, dreaming up all the different ways he could torture and kill Jody's adoptive father for what he'd done to her.

Jody. She'd been there, too. Hadn't she? There was an argument. Blinding pain as he'd fallen against…something. A loud crash. What in the world had happened?

He blinked his bleary eyes and forced himself to sit up. Then he looked over the end of the couch toward the kitchen, where the delicious—and nauseating, given his current state—smells were coming from.

Was she cooking breakfast? He could just catch a glimpse of her as she moved around inside the kitchen. Was she…humming?

She stuck her head around the corner. "About time you woke up. Breakfast will be ready in about ten minutes. Duncan will be here at nine to give us an update on the case. You should hurry up and get ready."

He blinked, certain he'd heard her wrong. "My brother? He called you?"

"Well, actually he called you." She picked up his phone off the island and held it up. "Hope you don't mind that I answered on your behalf." She motioned toward him. "There's a glass of water and some aspirin beside you, and something to settle your stomach if you need it." She looked over her shoulder. "The clock above your oven says you've used up one of your ten minutes. Chop, chop. I don't want your breakfast to get cold while you're dillydallying in the shower."

She disappeared into the kitchen.

Adam had a million questions for her, the most important being why she was so cheerful when he was pretty sure he'd been a moron and a jerk last night. But his roiling stomach, aching head and throbbing leg were taking center stage in his world at the moment. And they wouldn't be ignored.

He gratefully downed several aspirin, chasing them with a huge swig of Pepto and half a bottle of water.

"Six minutes," Jody called out from the kitchen, sounding disgustingly cheerful.

Was this the calm before the storm? Was she planning on poisoning him in return for whatever he'd done last night? He had a feeling he deserved it.

He grabbed the crutches she'd thoughtfully left on the floor beside the couch and hobbled his way into his bedroom. He tried to get ready quickly according to her timetable, but his attempts to shower without getting the bandage around his leg wet were a complete fiasco and he fell twice, finally giving up and just taking a normal shower—to hell with his stitches.

A few minutes later, feeling far more human than he should have thanks to the aspirin and Pepto, he made his way to the kitchen island.

The kitchen was empty.

"You're late."

He turned at the sound of her voice behind him. She was wearing curve-hugging blue jeans and an emerald-green button-up shirt that perfectly matched her eyes and her adorable glasses. Her gorgeous, thick red hair tumbled over her shoulders to hang halfway down her back. Just a touch of makeup made her eyes pop even more than usual. His mouth went dry just looking at her.

"You're beautiful," he breathed.

Her frown evaporated. "You're forgiven. Come on. Your plate's in the dining room."

He stood in confusion, but she seemed determined for him to eat and had gone to a lot of trouble, so he dutifully sat down. She'd made scrambled eggs, biscuits, bacon and hash browns. They were all expertly prepared. She was definitely talented in the kitchen. But in spite of how good everything tasted, he didn't want any of it. He wanted to talk instead, to beg her forgiveness for what little he remembered of his behavior last night, to rebuild the bridges he'd torn down. But she seemed so…happy…content to sit across from him. There were no recriminations on her tongue, no accusations, no tears.

That part bothered him the most.

He was used to her tears. He expected them. This smiling Jody without a seeming care in the world was an enigma. And he didn't know what to make of it.

When he'd finally eaten enough to feel that he wouldn't insult her if he stopped, he set his fork down. "You're a wonderful cook. You shouldn't have gone to all that trouble. But I appreciate it. Thank you."

She beamed at him. "You're very welcome." She took a sip of her orange juice.

"Jody?"

She looked at him over the rim of her glass, brows raised in question.

"Why are you doing this? Why did you cook me breakfast? And why are you being so sweet when I don't deserve any of this?"

She set the glass down and wiped her mouth with the napkin. "Wait here."

He started to ask her what she was talking about. But she hurried out of the room.

He clenched his fists on the table in frustration. He'd wanted to talk it out, see if they could move beyond last night. But she was putting up a front, not letting him in. Where had she gone? Was she upstairs, crying, after trying to be nice in spite of her hurt feelings? All alone? That thought had him pushing back his chair.

"No, please." She'd come back into the room. "Don't leave. We need to talk."

Now this he'd expected. He scooted his chair back under the table. "I know. I was a jerk last night. I abused my authority and—"

"Looked into my sealed juvenile records. Yes, I know." She pulled a stack of wrinkled pages from behind her back and set them on the table.

Adam's stomach clenched. He was glad his appetite hadn't been what it normally was or he'd probably have thrown up right then and there.

"Do you know what these are?" She smoothed her hand over the top page.

He slowly nodded. "The ramblings of an idiot who drank far more than he should have. Jody, I had no right to—"

"No. You didn't. You shouldn't have gone behind my back and used your authority to find out details that were mine to share. Or not to share. I admit, when I realized what you'd done, I was furious, and hurt, and felt betrayed. I was ready to storm out of here."

"Why didn't you? Don't get me wrong. I'm glad you

didn't. I'd have been worried about you and would have had to tear this town apart to find you. But why did you tuck me in on the couch and leave pills for my hangover and go to all that trouble to cook me breakfast? I should have been the one waiting on you, not the other way around. Why did you do all of that for me?"

She tapped the stack of pages on the table. "This. This is why I'm still here, why I'm not mad at you anymore." She held up the first page and squinted at it. "You have really bad penmanship, by the way."

"I was drunk."

"True, which means your inhibitions were lowered and you poured your emotions out onto these pages. Your true emotions, not subterfuge."

"Jody, I didn't mean for you to see—"

"'Castration,'" she read from the first page.

He choked and started coughing.

She looked at him over the top of her glasses and continued reading what he'd scribbled while under the influence of alcohol and an all-consuming rage.

"'Castration would be a good way to kill Jody's father. Bastards like that shouldn't be allowed to procreate.'"

She set the page to the side. "I agree. They shouldn't." She picked up the next page. "'Gunshot wound. Nothing quick or easy. I'd shoot him in the gut and tie him out in the sun to slowly and painfully bleed to death.'"

He cleared his throat again. "I'm actually not as bloodthirsty as I sound. I was just…fantasizing. I wouldn't *actually* do that to someone."

She picked up the next page. "'Caning. Maybe it's time that caning was brought to this country. I'd give cane poles to everyone who'd ever been abused by someone who'd sworn to love them and let them each have a turn at him until the lecherous light faded from his serpent's eyes.'"

"A bit melodramatic," he said, trying to smile as if he thought the whole thing was amusing. But he was pretty sure he failed spectacularly.

"This is a pretty good one." Her voice was tight. She cleared her throat and picked up the next paper, her hands slowly smoothing it out. "'I'd get one of my old buddies from the vice squad to plant seized child pornography pictures on his computer. Once in prison, the other inmates would enact their own form of punishment.'"

"I wouldn't really plant evidence."

"I'm sure you wouldn't," she agreed. She pulled another piece of paper from the very bottom of the stack. "This one is my personal favorite." The paper shook in her hands as she read. "'I'd tie him to a chair and, with his family watching—the vipers who turned their backs on Jody—I'd let her confront him about everything he did to her. I wouldn't let him go until he admitted what he'd done and begged for her forgiveness. And once her family realized they'd been wrong all this time, they'd beg her for forgiveness, too, and she could laugh in their faces. I'd take Jody away from those horrible, awful people and do everything I could to make her forget every bad thing that ever happened to her.'" Her chin wobbled as she read the last part of it. "I would *love* her."

Tears spilled over and ran down her cheeks.

He scooted his chair back, ready to go to her, but he hesitated. Was she angry or hurt or…what? He wasn't sure and didn't know what to do. How was he going to fix this?

"Thank you," she whispered brokenly.

"I'm sorry—what? You're…thanking me? Why?"

"You believed me. When no one else did. You have no idea what that did to me when I read those pages." She waved her hand in the air. "Oh, I know you would never actually do all of those things to Peter. But the fact that you believed in me enough to be that angry on my behalf goes a long way toward healing the holes in my heart." She stood and circled the table to stand in front of him. Then, to his shock, she straddled him in his chair.

He jerked against her, swearing, a bead of sweat popping out on his forehead as he grabbed her arms to lift her off him. "I don't think you're thinking straight. You should—"

She shoved his arms away and cupped his face in her hands. "I'm thinking with more clarity than I have in ages. And you were thinking more clearly when you wrote those pages than you realize. Your heart shined through in the concern you showed for me. And in that last sentence you wrote. I agree with you, Adam. Love really is the cure. Will you love me?"

"Sweetheart." He cleared his throat. "I mean... Jody—"

"I like *sweetheart* better." She pressed a soft kiss against his right cheek.

He shuddered and drew a ragged breath. "*Jody*, we've been through a traumatic few days together. Sometimes that makes people have, ah, feelings that might not prove to be real later on."

She kissed his other cheek, then shifted her bottom in a delightfully sinful way against his lap.

He grabbed the arms of the chair to keep from doing something he knew he would regret, like grabbing her. "Have *you* been drinking this morning?"

"Nope," she breathed against his neck. "I'm stone-cold sober. Love me, Adam."

He grasped her arms and pulled her against him, then swore when he realized what he was doing. He gently pushed her back against the table. "Be careful. My control is hanging by a thread here. I'm trying to do the honorable thing."

She let out a deep sigh and scooted farther back on his

thighs but didn't get up. "I don't know why you think making love to me isn't honorable. It would be two consenting adults who care about each other and want to show their feelings in the most wonderful way possible."

He started to protest her warped view of honorable, but she shook her head and held a finger to his lips.

"Knowing you, I imagine that you're worried I'm vulnerable. But I've never felt so empowered in my life. By believing in me, you've helped me feel less hopeless, more in control, than I have in years. Thank you for that."

He cleared his throat. "Um. You're welcome?"

She smiled, then took his hands in hers. "My parents, my biological parents, were killed in a car wreck when I was a toddler. I barely remember them. Mostly I just know their names—Lance and Vanessa Radcliffe—and that they loved me enough to make sure that I was taken care of when they died. Or at least, that's what they thought—that I'd be well taken care of because of everything they put into place, like designating their best friends, the Ingrams, as my guardians."

"Jody, you don't have to tell me any of this."

"I know. And that's why I want to, because I don't have to. And because…because I've never told anyone the whole story. Not even the judge who oversaw the hearing against Peter Ingram. Not even the prosecutor who pressed the case. Not even Tracy. She knew bits and pieces, but no one knows it all. Except me."

She shoved her hair back from her face and drew a deep breath. "After my parents were killed, the Ingrams took me in, eventually adopted me. Everyone thought they were being good Samaritans, honoring their friends. But they never really wanted me. They wanted the Radcliffe family home here in Rutherford Estates that came with me, and my trust fund. The house has its own trust fund just for its upkeep and taxes, to ensure that I'd never have to worry about having a home."

Adam frowned. "But you live in an apartment. Shouldn't the house be yours now that you're a legal adult?"

She shrugged. "You would think so. The Ingrams showed me the deed and a copy of my parents' will giving them ownership in exchange for taking care of me. I guess my biological parents thought the trust fund they set up for me would be enough once I was out on my own, that I could buy my own house at that point."

"It wasn't enough?"

Her mouth tightened. "It should have been. But the Ingrams made large withdrawals against the fund while I was growing up, supposedly for my care. There was barely enough to get me through college when I came into ownership of the fund and they lost control of it." She held her hand up. "And before you ask, yes, I petitioned the court for an accounting of their stewardship, hoping I could force them to pay back some of the money. But after an accountant reviewed the records, a judge ruled that they hadn't done anything illegal. I could have appealed, but I decided to let it drop at that point."

Adam didn't like what he was hearing. It sounded fishy to him. Maybe he could look into it sometime, if she wanted him to. But it wasn't the financial misdeeds of the Ingrams—if indeed they had done anything illegal—that worried him right now. It was the way Jody had turned pale as she prepared to tell him the details about her childhood.

He didn't want to know any more than what he'd read in the court transcripts.

The house she'd grown up in was just a few blocks away. He knew because he'd looked it up when he'd looked into her background. He already cared deeply about her. How was he supposed to sit here and not run over there and kill the man who'd hurt her? He was afraid of what he might do if she told him in her own words what her adoptive father had done to her.

He was about to remind her again that she didn't need to tell him any of the details. But she was staring at him, her green eyes searching his with a mixture of trust, and hope, and fear. And he knew he couldn't tell her no. She wanted this, needed this, needed to share with him what had happened to her. And he was in awe that it was him she trusted to share it with. So even though it almost killed him, he endeavored to listen and be there for her, and to not go kill Peter Ingram once she was finished.

He drew her against his chest.

She clung to him for several minutes, then relaxed. "The first time he came into my room at night, when everyone else in the house was asleep, I was nine."

Dear God. He closed his eyes and spent the next twenty minutes in agony listening to the harrowing details of her abuse. He remembered, in the mountains, thinking about how young she was, and that she was naive, inexperienced and sheltered in the horrors that existed in the world around her. What a fool he'd been. She was none of those things. She'd suffered horrendous abuse and learned about the ugliness that existed in this world far sooner than she ever should have. He felt like such an idiot for judging her, making assumptions. And now, as he sat here, listening to what had happened to her, all he wanted to do was grab his gun and storm out of the house. He wanted to kill the man who'd hurt her. If Jody wasn't nestled in his arms right now, so trusting and needing him in this moment, he very well might have. He stayed, for her, but it tore him up inside.

The abuse she'd suffered was horrific, far worse than anything listed in the court records. He didn't know how she'd managed to survive and become the well-adjusted, caring, kind person that she was today. She'd been abused by her adoptive father. And then abused again, betrayed, victimized by every member of her supposed family when they took their father's side against her after she finally told a counselor at school what was going on.

And if that wasn't enough, the social worker in the case and the court-appointed psychiatrist took the father's side as well. They claimed that Jody was lying, acting out, wanting attention. And when the proceedings were over, they found the father innocent and forced Jody to attend psychiatric sessions for years—to work on her issues with being needy and attention seeking and being a pathological liar.

And they sent her back to live with her abuser and his family.

As far as Adam was concerned, all of them—her adoptive father, his family, the judge, the psychiatrist, the social worker—should have gone to prison, lost their jobs and anything else that could be legally done to punish them for failing to protect the innocent little girl entrusted to their care.

"After that," she continued, whispering against his chest, "I was treated like a servant, like Cinderella, doing all the chores, eating alone, being pulled out of my school and sent off to the bad kids' school. It was as if I didn't exist to them anymore. I was invisible and I didn't matter. The only good thing was that Peter never touched me again. I think he was worried that his wife was suspicious, that maybe she believed me but wouldn't go against him. The only reason I think that is because the day after the judge made his ruling, a steel bolt showed up on my door. I could bar it from the inside and there wasn't any way to unlock it from the hallway. No one ever said who put it there. No one even mentioned it. But I think it was my adoptive mom. Whoever did it, that bolt was the only thing that kept me sane, gave me hope that one day maybe things would get better."

She sat back and brushed at the tears on her cheeks. "I think I would have died of loneliness and despair if it hadn't been for Tracy and her family. I began spending more and more time with them, until I rarely ever went home. My family didn't care, of course, as long as the trust fund checks kept coming in every month. The moment I turned eighteen, I was out of there. And I've never been back."

She let out a shuddering breath. "Tracy and her family loved me and supported me, but even they were skeptical. It was the one wound in my heart where they were concerned. My family, and the experts, had painted such a terrible picture of me that even Tracy believed I was damaged, maybe traumatized from losing my biological parents at such a young age and that I was an attention seeker."

"How could you have stayed friends with her after that?"

She shrugged. "That's life. It's how it's always been. No one truly believed everything that I said happened. Until you. Why, Adam? Why did you believe me when no one else did?"

"Because I know you, know what's in your heart. We've been through more together in a few days than most people survive in a lifetime. I've seen the good in you, the kindness, the honesty. Why would I doubt you?" He opened his arms, and she fell against him.

It didn't surprise him when she began weeping. If anything, it was reassuring. Crying was her way of coping. She'd just relived her horrible ordeal by saying it out loud to him. The copious tears meant that she'd be okay. Or as okay as she could be with everything she'd been through.

When she started hiccupping, she pulled back. "I'm so sorry. I cry at the drop of a hat. It must be incredibly annoying."

"Not at all. It's part of who you are. It shows you're sensitive and have a wonderful, full heart in spite of everything that's happened to you. It would break my heart if you ever stop having that capacity to care and feel so deeply that you *don't* cry. Don't ever apologize for feeling and being honest about your emotions."

She lay back against him, her arms around his waist. He rested his chin on the top of her head and gently stroked her back. They sat that way for a long time, until the air around them seemed to subtly change. Her fingers curled against his shirt. Her breathing turned ragged. She slowly slid her hands up his chest and entwined her arms around his neck.

"Adam."

Just one whispered word, said with such a mixture of longing and desire, was all it took to send a jolt of raw lust straight through his body.

Then she pressed her open mouth against his neck and lightly touched her tongue to his overheated skin.

He almost came right out of his chair.

His hands tightened around her, trying to stop her wandering mouth. "Jody," he rasped. "Don't."

She kissed him again.

"Jody, no. Stop. You're vulnerable, emotional. You'll regret this later if you—"

She moved to his ear, her tongue doing wicked things that had him hardening in an instant.

He shuddered, his arms tightening around her, drawing her close. *No!* What was he doing? This was wrong. He couldn't act on the chemistry that flared between them every time they were close. Not now, not like this.

"Jody, you're not thinking clearly. You're not—"

She pressed her mouth against his neck and sucked.

He jerked back.

She pulled back and stared up at him and ran her fingers through the hair at the nape of his neck. "I want you Adam. I need you."

"You'll hate me later. When you're thinking more clearly, you'll realize that—"

"Do you want me?"

He swallowed, hard. "You know I do."

"Then love me." She didn't wait for his response. She pulled him down to her and kissed his mouth.

He should have been stronger. Should have set her away from him. But he wanted her so badly he ached. There was something about this beautiful, smart, incredibly sweet woman in his arms that turned his knees to jelly. By the time her tongue darted inside his mouth and stroked his, he was already waving the white flag of surrender. He couldn't have stopped now if a whole army was at his door, trying to break it down. For some reason she needed him. And he needed her just as desperately.

He broke the kiss and gasped for air. Then leaned in and tortured her the same way she'd tortured him earlier. He pressed his mouth against her neck and sucked.

She gasped and almost overturned the chair.

He laughed and pulled back, his mouth hovering inches from hers. "What time did you say Duncan would be here?"

She swallowed, with obvious difficulty. "N…nine o'clock… I think."

He looked past her to the digital readout over the oven. "That's not nearly enough time."

"We'll make it work!" She jumped off his lap, grabbing the table to keep from falling when she tripped over her own feet. She picked up his crutches. "Hurry." She shoved them into his hands and took off down the hall, her bare feet slapping against the tile.

Adam was laughing so hard he could barely keep the crutches under his arms as he followed her to the bedroom at his aggravatingly much slower pace.

Chapter Nineteen

Jody stood naked in the middle of Adam's bedroom, her clothes discarded in a pile at her feet. The *click, click* of his crutches echoed through the house beyond the bedroom door as he slowly made his way toward her. And even though she'd had the occasional tryst in college and had always wanted them this way—fast, furious, two sweaty bodies seeking quick solace before she shoved the man of the hour out the door—suddenly everything about this seemed wrong.

Because this was Adam.

He wasn't like the men who'd drifted in and out of her life. Men who, according to her college counselors when she'd sought therapy on her own, were Jody's way of taking control of her body, in response to the abuse she'd suffered as a child when she'd been completely helpless to stop it. But Adam was different, special. Shouldn't that make… this…different? She looked down at her clothes, her naked body, and suddenly felt shy, nervous.

Click. Click.

She lunged for the chair by the bed and grabbed the blanket off the back.

The door opened behind her.

She spun around, clutching the blanket against her breasts, quickly shaking it out to cover more of her naked skin.

Adam stopped in the doorway, leaning heavily on his crutches, his face pale, eyes wide as they swept her from head to toe. "What's wrong? Second thoughts?"

"What?" She looked down at the blanket, clutched like a lifeline in her hands. "Oh. No, no, of course not. It's just that…" She looked up at him again, took a step toward him. "Are you okay? You look like you're in pain."

"And you look scared. Jody, it's all right. We don't have to do this. I'll just go back—"

"No!" She hurried to him, stopping a few feet away. "It's just…nerves. It's been a while, since college." She took off her glasses and tossed them onto her pile of clothes. "I'm not scared. I could never be afraid of you, Adam. I want you, very much. Don't you want me?" She dropped the blanket.

His gaze dipped. His throat worked. "You have no idea how badly I want you." His voice was thick with desire.

Feeling more confident now, she smiled and slipped into the role she'd always taken with these encounters. She put her hand on his arm and led him toward the bed. Then she shoved the covers back and lay down. She lifted her heavy fall of hair and fanned it out on the pillow, then held her arms up for him to join her.

Some of the heat seemed to leave his eyes as he stared down at her.

She suddenly felt self-conscious again. "Adam? What's wrong? Don't you like the way I look?" Men always did. They loved her thick red hair, her narrow waist, her curvy hips. Her breasts weren't as large as she would have preferred. But they were firm and well shaped. No one had ever had any complaints. "Adam?"

He swallowed again, his knuckles whitening where he was holding on to the crutches. "I think you're the most beautiful creature I've ever seen. And I want you, more than you could possibly imagine. But I want you to want me, too, really want me."

She frowned. "I do. I'm here, aren't I? I'm ready. Let's do it."

He winced. "You make it sound like a chore."

Her face flushed with heat, and she curled her fingers into the sheets. "Well if it is, I'm good at it. No one's ever said otherwise." She grabbed for the covers, pulling them up to her neck. "I don't understand you. We're both adults. We want each other. We should be rolling in the sheets right now, halfway done."

"Halfway *done*? Oh, sweetheart. It would take a lifetime for me to love you the way I want to, the way you deserve to be loved. I assure you we wouldn't be *halfway done* by now."

She frowned in confusion. "Are we going to have sex or not?"

The mattress dipped as he sat beside her. "No. We are not going to *have sex*."

She crossed her arms and stared up at the ceiling.

"We're going to make love. If you want to."

She turned her head on the pillow to look at him. "What's the difference?"

He smiled sadly. "Everything." He reached for her hand.

Aggravated, frustrated, she resisted, keeping her fingers curled into her palm.

He didn't try to uncurl her fingers. Instead, he leaned down and pressed an achingly soft kiss against the back of her wrist. Her skin heated beneath his touch. He moved his mouth along her thumb, kissing, caressing.

Raw pleasure zinged straight to her core.

She drew a ragged breath, fascinated as she watched his long lashes form crescents against his cheeks when he closed his eyes and bent over her arm. The incredibly erotic treatment continued. He worshipped her skin with his mouth, his tongue blazing a trail of lava everywhere he touched. She uncurled her fingers, curious what else he might do. He pulled one of them into his mouth…and sucked.

She jerked against the mattress, her other hand curling into the sheets. Heat unfurled in her belly. Every muscle tightened. Her pulse leaped, her breaths ragged.

And he was only kissing her hand.

He raised his head, breaking contact with her skin. She almost whimpered at the loss of his heat.

"Do you want me to stop?" he whispered.

"Hell no," she gasped.

His mouth curved into a hungry smile that *did* have her whimpering this time. She shifted her legs restlessly against each other and held her arms out to him. But he didn't climb on top of her. Instead, he lowered his mouth to her elbow.

The man seemed to know where every nerve ending in her body was located. He massaged, caressed and kissed her into a frenzy. When he moved to her inner thigh, she came off the mattress, bucking against him.

Still, he refused to hurry, to take what he wanted from her, to slake his body in hers as others had done. The realization shot through her. With others, she'd had sex. This, this was what making love was about. Giving, not taking. Cherishing, gifting her with his body instead of making demands. She'd never experienced anything so incredible, so sweet, so beautiful.

"Jody? Sweetheart? Are you okay?" His breath fanned out across her thigh as he looked up at her.

She realized she was crying. Again. She swiped at the tears. "I'm more than okay. I'm in awe."

"Good tears, then?"

She drew a ragged breath. "Good tears. Um, you're not going to stop yet, are you?"

He grinned and slowly shook his head. "We're a long way from done." Then he lowered his head and flicked her core with his tongue.

"Adam!"

Where before he'd been gentle, slow, tender, now he was a demanding lover, ruthless in wringing every ounce of pleasure from her that he could. She thrashed against the bed, her hands threaded in his hair as her climax exploded through her. Still he kissed her, stroked her, drawing it out until colors burst behind her eyelids and her toes curled against the bed.

She heard the familiar sound of a foil packet being ripped open, felt the bed dip and knew he was protecting her. Then, finally, he moved up her body, fitting himself to her. She was limp, spent, but the feel of him hard and thick against her sent a jolt of heat straight through her. She dragged his lips to hers and lifted her legs, wrapping them around his waist, inviting him in.

This time, he didn't hesitate. He claimed her mouth and her body at the same time, thrusting into her. His hands moved between them, doing wicked things, building the pressure again, spiraling her up to even greater heights. He filled her so completely, so perfectly, his body fitting to hers like they were made for each other. She'd never felt such pleasure, such completeness, such joy before. As if this was meant to be. Destiny. Fate.

She felt him tighten inside her, knew he was close. But her ever-considerate lover placed her needs above his own once again, holding back, caressing, kissing, molding her body with his hands until she was again at those lofty heights, on the brink. Then he thrust into her again, sending them both tumbling over the edge. She cried out in wonder, clasping him to her as they both shattered into pieces and then slowly drifted back down to earth. Together.

Chapter Twenty

Duncan set his coffee down on the dining room table and glanced back and forth between Jody and Adam. "Am I missing something? Both of you are yawning like there's no tomorrow. You're either sleepy or you're worn-out. What have you been doing?"

Jody choked.

Adam coughed, then cleared his throat. Jody was so red with embarrassment that he wanted to grin. But he didn't dare. She'd probably murder him if he did.

"You have new information about the investigation?" he asked his brother.

When Jody wasn't looking, Duncan grinned and winked at Adam, letting him know he knew full well what they'd been doing.

Adam narrowed his eyes in warning. What he'd shared with Jody had been life changing. No way was he going to let his brother's juvenile teasing cheapen it in any way, for either of them.

He gave Jody an apologetic smile. It had been like a bucket of cold water having to hurry and wash and dress before his brother got there. Both of them had wanted to lie in bed all day, exploring the newfound closeness between them. But life wouldn't let them. Cold reality had intruded all too soon. He hadn't even gotten a chance to talk to her about what had happened between them, and whether her heart was as tangled up in the experience as his.

They'd only met a few days ago. But he already couldn't imagine his life without her in it somehow. Did she feel the same way? He desperately wanted to know. Instead, he was stuck here at his dining room table with his brother sitting across from him.

"Why are you frowning at me?" Duncan teased. "Did you wake up on the wrong side of the bed or something?"

"Or something," Adam gritted out, belatedly wishing he'd called his brother and told him not to come over at all. But that would have been selfish. Jody's safety rested on Duncan solving the case. Everything else, no matter how pleasurable, needed to come second.

"Just tell us what updates you have."

Duncan set his briefcase on the dining room table and popped it open. "Saying I have updates is stretching it. For as many threads as we have on this thing, they're unraveling far too slowly and not really leading anywhere."

He took out several folders and plopped them onto the table, then snapped his briefcase closed and set it on the floor. "These are the five cases Sam seemed to be focused on the most in the week before he was killed." He winced. "Sorry, Jody. I should have led with that, with a lot more finesse. The coroner confirmed a body we found was Sam. I'm very sorry for your loss."

She blinked and shook her head as if to clear it. She appeared to be having as much trouble as Adam focusing on the case. "It's okay. I mean, it's not okay. But I'd pretty much accepted that he had to be, that he was gone. To hear you confirm it isn't a shock at this point. It's just sad, and so unfair." She waved toward the folders. "Please, continue."

Adam wanted to pull her onto his lap and hold her, comfort her. But he didn't know how she'd feel about that in front of his brother. Damn it. They needed to talk, privately.

"Like I said, these are the five cases we determined that he was actively working. All of them have stacks of photographs in them."

Adam let out a deep breath and resolved to pay attention, no matter how difficult. He pulled one of the folders toward him and flipped through the small stack of pictures. "I'm not noticing any gaps in time stamps in this one."

Jody pulled another one of the folders toward her and opened it.

"There aren't any gaps in *any* of them," Duncan said.

She frowned. "No gaps?"

"None. We looked in all of the other case folders, too. Like you said, your boss was very detail oriented. Each case has an index listing the pictures that should be there. Everything matches up. We've hit a dead end."

Adam shook his head. "No. You haven't. You've learned something important."

Duncan arched a brow in question, and Jody looked at him, both waiting.

"You've learned that whatever Damien is after isn't related to any cases that Sam was officially working on."

Duncan stared at him intently. Then he sat back in his chair. "You should be an investigator, Adam. That makes complete sense. We've been looking at this all wrong. Sam must have been investigating something else, on his own. Not for a client. That would explain the gap. If he was working something on the side, he'd have no reason to keep the information at his office with his regular cases. He'd put it somewhere else. I would think it would be at his home, so he could keep it separate from regular work. But we searched there, found nothing." He shook his head. "We're still at an impasse. I'm not sure where to go with this. But I'll update the guy working on it. Maybe he can find a thread I haven't thought of."

"Guy? Not guys, plural?" Adam rested his forearms on the table. "What's going on? I thought you had a whole team working on this."

"Yeah, well, I did. We want justice for Mr. Campbell and Miss Larson. And we want to get Damien and Ned and anyone else who may be involved off the streets and locked up where they belong. But, well, resources being what they are, the guys higher up than me make executive decisions based on budget and higher priorities."

Adam swore. "What's a higher priority than making sure Jody isn't murdered? I thought the press had wind of this case and was putting pressure on you to solve it?"

Jody put her hand on his. "Please. Don't fight over me. I'll be okay."

He laced their fingers together. Even with her life on the line, she focused on others, on him. After what she'd suffered in her life, it was a miracle that she wasn't bitter and angry all the time. Instead she was selfless and sweet. He squeezed her hand in his.

"You *will* be okay," he said. "Because I'm not going to let anything happen to you. But you shouldn't have to live in fear wondering when Damien might try to strike. We need to end this. And that means the government needs to put its resources back on the case." He shot his brother an accusing look. "What are you working on if not this?"

"Something that's being kept hush-hush right now. I'm not at liberty to discuss it."

Adam leaned forward. "I'd expect that from Ian, not from you. Spill. Tell me what's going on."

"Who's Ian?" Jody asked.

Duncan gave her an apologetic smile. "Sorry. Ian is our youngest brother. He's always been a bit, well, rebellious.

Doesn't exactly get along with the rest of us on the rare occasions that we even see him."

"Us? Just how big is your family?" she asked.

Duncan turned an accusing look at Adam. "Were you in too much of a hurry to even go through the niceties first?"

Jody's brows drew together in obvious confusion. But Adam wasn't confused in the least. His brother was berating him for making love to Jody without the two of them really getting to know each other first. And he had every right to shame him. Jody deserved better, and he hadn't bothered to share anything substantive about himself with her even though she'd shared the most intimate details of her life with him.

"I'm sorry I didn't tell you more about myself or my family," Adam said. "Really short version for now, I have three brothers—Duncan, Colin and Ian. My dad, William, is a retired federal judge. Margaret, my mom, is a retired prosecutor and—"

"Wait, Judge William McKenzie? I should have made the connection earlier. You're a part of the infamous Mighty McKenzies, aren't you? Your family's a legend at the courthouse. Every member is in law-enforcement in one way or the other, right?"

He winced. "We're not fans of that label. But yes, that's us. Except for Ian. But that's not important right now. The point, that we need to get back to, is that Duncan should be working this case with a full team of investigators. And he's not leaving until he tells us what so-called higher priority trumps protecting you by finding the guys who are trying to hurt you."

This time it was Duncan's turn to look uncomfortable. "I wouldn't put it that way exactly." He held up his hand to stop Adam. "But I'll remind you that I don't set the priorities. I didn't want to tell you what I was working on because I knew it would only upset you even more."

"Duncan—"

"But I'll tell you anyway. Eddie Hicks, a local city councilman, was murdered last week. Turns out he was assisting Senator Sinclair with some local research for an infrastructure bill that was passed by Congress a few days ago after pending in subcommittee for well over a year."

"Infrastructure?" Adam asked. "I vaguely remember seeing something about that on the news. Wasn't the government looking into buying up all the land associated with it?"

Duncan nodded. "A highway and bridge bill. This local councilman has been assisting Sinclair with surveys and research on the tracts of land involved, title searches and things like that. Getting appraisals and, as you said, buying up the land in preparation for the passage of the bill." He idly straightened the folders sitting on the table. "Sinclair and Hicks were apparently good friends."

Adam clenched a fist on the table. "So the senator is using his power to push the National Park Service and everyone else to steer their resources toward finding out who killed his friend instead of protecting Jody. Our taxpayer dollars at work. Nepotism is alive and well."

Duncan shoved back from the table and stood. "Like I said, I knew you'd be upset. I argued against this. In the end there was nothing I could do. I was fortunate just to get them to agree to leave one investigator assigned to the case." He set a business card on the table. "Here's his contact information, Jody, if you think of anything else that might help. I'll check back in with him as often as I can to ensure he keeps at it. And as soon as the councilman's case is resolved, I'll push to get more resources reassigned to your case." He spread his hands out beside him. "I'm really sorry. It's out of my control." He turned and headed toward the front door.

Adam followed, clicking after him on his crutches. In the opening, he let out an exasperated breath. "I'm sorry I'm taking my anger out on you, Duncan. I know none of this is your fault."

His brother gave him a sympathetic look. "You care about her."

"Well, of course I care about her." He kept his voice low, even though he doubted that Jody could hear him back in the dining room. "She's a good person. She doesn't deserve any of what's happening to her. I want Damien and whoever put him up to this found before she gets hurt."

"I know. I'm doing everything I can to help, officially and unofficially. In the meantime, just keep watching over her. And don't hesitate to call me if you need me. No matter what."

"I will. Did you mean to leave those folders?"

"They're copies. I don't think you'll find anything useful in them. But it couldn't hurt to have another pair of eyes on the case. I told the lone remaining investigator to email you if he found anything else significant."

"Thanks. I know that's against the rules. I appreciate it."

Duncan bumped him on the shoulder, his version of a hug, then headed outside.

Adam shut the door and leaned back against it. He was furious with the government for letting politics decide their priorities. But he also knew his brother well, and he knew that Duncan would have already done everything possible to change their minds. Since Duncan hadn't been successful, Adam needed to pick up where the government had left off. He was effectively on leave until his leg healed anyway. Might as well use that time to do what the government should have been doing—solving the case.

He headed to the table, his crutches making a tapping sound on the tile that drove him to distraction. When he stopped beside Jody's chair, she looked up at him in question. He wanted to kiss her so badly right now. But he knew where that would end. And his desire to make her safe outweighed everything else at the moment.

"Pretend you're Sam Campbell."

She blinked. "What? Why?"

"You knew him pretty well, right? Think like him. Tell me about his daily routine."

"I already told Duncan, during the chopper flight to the hospital—"

"I was a bit out of it during that flight. Tell me what you told him."

"Okay. I'll try."

He pulled out the chair beside her and listened to her tell him about her boss. He could see the love and admiration she felt for him. And it broke his heart that she'd suffered two devastating losses of people close to her in a handful of days. But what mattered the most was making sure that she didn't become victim number three.

"Okay," he said, when she finished talking about Sam. "What I'm hearing is he had a regimented schedule and documented everything. Other than when his grief for his wife overcame him, he never veered from that routine. So if he was working a secret case in the week before he died, he would have documented it just like everything else, right?"

"Right. Makes sense."

"But he didn't keep the documents at the office."

"Agreed. But I still don't know where he would have put them."

He tapped the table as he thought some more. "Did he seem afraid before he disappeared?"

"No. Not at all."

"Did he do anything different, out of the ordinary? Anything at all that you noticed?"

She started to shake her head, then stopped. "Well, it seems silly, really. I'm sure it's not related."

"Let me be the judge of that."

"A few days before he disappeared, he was extra nice to me. Not that he wasn't always nice. But he did more things with me than usual. I was his assistant, so usually he worked a case and I was his gofer, running errands for him. But that last week, just a few times, it was like he was *my* assistant instead. I remember it was the anniversary of his wife's death that week, and I attributed it to him being lonely."

"Be specific, Jody. What did he do?"

She thought about it a moment. "He talked to me, in the car, about my family, both my birth parents and my adoptive ones. It was awkward because I never tell anyone about them, or what happened. So it was a short conversation. I certainly didn't tell him about the abuse. He had lunch with me two or three times, asking more questions, like he was just trying to get to know me better. Oh, and one night, after work, he knew I was going to my storage unit and he said he'd like to see what I do when I'm not working for him. He seemed so lonely, so I let him come along."

"Did he give Tracy any extra attention that week?"

She shook her head. "I don't think so. Not that I recall."

"What kinds of questions did he ask you about your family?"

"The usual—whether I had brothers and sisters, where I grew up. I told him I was adopted, that my biological parents were killed in a crash. I remember he asked my birth parents' names, but after that he dropped the questions. I think he could tell I was uncomfortable and he changed the subject."

Adam shoved back from his chair. "Where's that storage unit of yours located?"

"In the middle of nowhere—not far from here, actually. We passed it on the way to your house last night. It's in the last flat section in the valley right before you climb into these foothills. Why?"

He held out his hand toward her. "We're going to take a little trip. If I'm right, we'll find the evidence that Damien was looking for hidden in your storage unit."

She took his hand and slowly stood. "You think Sam was working on a secret investigation and that he put something in my storage unit to hide it? Why would he do that?"

"I don't know. But it's the only place that makes sense, given your accounting of what he did that last week."

"Wait." She tugged her hand from his. "I'm getting my gun. It's in my room."

He tapped the holster on his hip. "I've got mine. It's my job to protect you."

"And it's my job to protect you."

She turned away before he could argue and headed up the stairs.

Chapter Twenty-One

Jody rubbed her hands up and down her arms. On the other side of the small table in the middle of her storage unit, Adam sat flipping through the folder they'd found.

"I can't believe Sam snuck that in here, or that he hid it in a pile of my photographs. Why would he do that?"

Adam didn't answer. She wasn't even sure that he'd heard her. He seemed engrossed in whatever he was reading.

"Adam?"

"Hmm?"

She sighed and glanced over her shoulder at the opening. The rolling door was down. Adam was so worried about keeping her safe that he'd insisted on keeping them locked inside while they searched the place. She never usually shut the door when she was here. It was too much like a cave. Or a prison.

Or her room back home, when she'd watched a similar slit beneath her door and prayed she wouldn't hear footsteps in the hallway.

She swallowed and turned back toward Adam. He was frowning down at a piece of paper.

"More title searches and real estate transactions?" she asked.

"Pretty much. And bills of sale. I'm no expert on that

infrastructure bill Duncan mentioned earlier in relation to that city councilman and Senator Sinclair. But I remember a few local news reports about the government buying up land for right of way." He lifted his gaze to hers. "A lot of these tracts of land mentioned in these bills of sale are ones from the news reports. The buyer is the government. The seller on most of these is a company named Preferred Parcel Purchasing Corporation. That's a lot of P's. Remind you of anyone connected to you?"

Her pulse leaped in her throat. "Peter, Patricia, Patience, Patrick, Paul. You think my adoptive father set up a shell company? And that he's involved in some kind of crooked real estate deals that Sam discovered?"

"We've already established that Peter Ingram is a lowlife. Connecting the dots to shady business deals isn't much of a stretch. Another company listed on some of these transactions is Amelia Enterprises. Isn't your adoptive mother's name Amelia?"

She nodded, her entire body flushing hot and cold. She'd always thought of her adoptive father as evil. But could he be evil enough to have had someone kill Sam and Tracy? Was he trying to have her killed, too? Because of land deals? And money?

"I don't understand," she said. "He's wealthy. There's no reason for him to do anything illegal to get more money."

"Maybe Peter isn't as well-off as you think. Bad investments, a struggling economy, poor decisions—they can quickly ruin someone financially. If he's had heavy losses, he might be desperate enough to make deals with some pretty bad people—like Damien Flint." He held one of the documents up and pointed to a bold signature scrawled across the bottom. "The witness on *all* of these documents is Judge Martin Jackson. Ever heard of him?"

Something about the name sent butterflies loose in her

stomach. "I'm not sure. It sounds familiar. But it's not an uncommon name."

"Maybe." He didn't sound convinced. "I know I've seen it somewhere recently." He flipped the folder closed. "It will come to me. In the meantime, I think we should head back to my house. I'll tell Duncan what we've found and have him send someone for this folder. He'll want to search the rest of the storage unit." His jaw tightened. "When he has resources. Is that okay with you?"

"Of course. If it helps with the case, by all means. Did you find anything in the folder to explain why someone would want to hurt Sam? Or Tracy?"

"Or you?"

She swallowed. "Or me."

"I haven't found a connection yet. But I will. Or Duncan will. Don't worry, Jody. I'll take care of you."

"I'll take care of you, too, Adam."

He smiled, the first smile she'd seen in a long while.

"We'll take care of each other, then," he said.

A few moments later they were heading down the two-lane road back toward town. Barbed-wire fences ran along both sides of the road with cows grazing in the green fields behind them. How ironic that such beauty and serenity could exist just a few feet from their car when her world seemed to be turning upside down.

Adam tensed beside her.

"What is it?" she asked.

"I remember where I saw that signature before, the name Judge Martin Jackson. That's the same judge who ruled on the case involving your adoptive father."

Her hands curled against the seat beside her. "You mean...the abuse case? My abuse case?"

He nodded. "I told you that my dad's a retired federal judge. From what I heard growing up, judges specialize and tend to stay in their specialties. It doesn't make sense to me that a family court judge is signing a bunch of real estate transaction documents. Even if he did switch specialties, the coincidence is sending up all kinds of red flags."

"What coincidence? The real estate transactions have nothing to do with me."

"They have everything to do with you. Your boss was looking into them and hid the evidence in your storage unit. Those have to be the documents Damien was talking about. He said pictures, and maybe there are some pictures, too. But maybe he meant documents, or whoever hired him didn't know if someone had physical printouts or just photographs." He waved his hand. "Doesn't matter. What does matter is that the same judge who signed them played a huge role in your life early on, signing other legal papers associated with you. Sam asked you about your birth parents. And your adoptive parents. Then he hid those papers where you'd eventually find them. Why would he do that if all of this isn't connected?"

He stared through the windshield at the winding road in front of them. His hands tightened on the steering wheel. "Didn't you tell me that Peter was a real estate developer? That he was always amassing property in the mountains?"

A cold chill seemed to run up her spine. "You think… you think he's somehow connected to all of this? Because the papers are about real estate?" She gave a humorless laugh. "That's quite a leap."

They drove in silence for a moment, then Adam slammed a hand against the steering wheel. "The timeline. That's it."

"What?"

"The timeline. Three days. You said Damien told you that Sam's PI firm had been a problem for three days. That was on Saturday. What happened three days before Saturday? What happened on Wednesday of last week?"

The truth slammed into her. She started to shake. "The councilman was murdered."

"Exactly. And he was helping a senator with the infrastructure bill. The government has to buy out everyone who owns land that they need for right of way. Which means researching titles and deeds and finding out who the owners are. That's what the councilman was helping with, because the land involved was here in Gatlinburg."

"Where my adoptive father owns a lot of real estate."

"Do *you*?"

She frowned. "What?"

"You told me your biological parents wanted to make sure you were taken care of. And yet their house passed to your adoptive family instead of to you. That seems unusual, to say the least. Isn't it also surprising that they didn't give you a generous enough trust fund to see you through life, not just college, but they left a huge fund for the Ingrams to take care of a house?"

She rubbed her arms again. "The thought has definitely crossed my mind before, yes."

"A judge ruled against you when you had the trust fund audited. Was that Judge Jackson, too?"

"No. I don't remember the judge's name, but it was a woman. It wasn't Martin Jackson."

"Then the audit may have been legit. Which again brings to question why your parents wouldn't provide better for you. The answer could be that they left you other investments, like real estate. They may have left you a fortune in land thinking it always appreciates in value and you'd be set for life, that you could sell some of it whenever you needed more money."

"But I didn't get *any* assets in the will other than the trust fund."

He tapped the folder on the seat between them. "You

sure about that? Wills can be faked. Sam was tracing the titles on all of the land in this folder, either for a secret client that we haven't found yet or because he heard something himself that made him suspicious and decided to follow up. Either way, it leads back to you. Because he left the information in your storage unit, for you to find. Maybe the land in that folder was actually owned at one time by the Radcliffes—your biological parents. Which means the land should have passed to you but never did. Sam got sloppy, took one picture too many, and Damien or maybe Peter saw him. They went through his things, realized he'd figured out what they were doing—making a killing, probably millions of dollars—selling your land to the government as part of that infrastructure bill. They have to destroy any hint of impropriety about those land deals or they'll lose everything and wind up in prison."

She pressed a hand against her throat. "If you're right, my adoptive father wants me—"

"Dead. So he can enjoy the millions of dollars that were supposed to be yours." He tapped the folder again. "This is what he wants. Once he has it and any pictures that Sam hid, there's no reason to keep you alive any longer. You're a liability, a time bomb waiting to blow up his financial empire if you ever decide to contest the will and dig into your parents' financial history. As soon as we get this information to Duncan, we'll both grab a suitcase and head out of town to lie low somewhere until this is resolved. No arguments. I want you safe and as far away from Peter Ingram as possible."

"No arguments from me."

A black Dodge Charger came into view on the next hill up ahead, coming toward them.

Jody blinked and leaned forward in her seat. "Adam, that

car. It looks just like the one that was parked near the Sugarland Mountain trailhead. The one Damien was driving."

Adam stared hard at the car coming their way. The Charger sped past them with a familiar profile sitting in the driver's seat.

"Adam—"

"I know. It was Damien. Grab my phone. Call Duncan." He kept driving down the road, heading toward his house. When he glanced in the rearview mirror, he swore.

Jody whirled around in her seat. The Charger had hit the brakes. Damien was making a three-point turn in the middle of the road. The car took off, heading straight for them.

"My phone, Jody. Forget Duncan. Call 911."

She grabbed his cell phone out of his pants pocket, her breaths coming in ragged gasps. "What's your pass code?"

He told her, and she punched in the numbers.

Adam grabbed his pistol out of the holster and slammed the accelerator. His car was a sleek sedan with leather seats and all the creature comforts his money could buy. But it didn't have the horsepower the Charger had. Damien was rapidly gaining on them.

"We're four miles from my house. We aren't going to make it." He reached up and slammed back the inside cover of the moon roof.

"What are you doing?" Jody punched Send on the call.

"You're going to hold the wheel while I shoot the bastard. Did you call 911?"

"I did but nothing's happening!" She yanked the phone back to look at the screen. "The call didn't go through!" Her hands shook as she redialed.

Tat-tat-tat-tat-tat-tat-tat!
Bam! Bam!

The car bumped and swerved, skidding toward the drainage ditch on the side of the road.

Adam fought the wheel. "The tires! Hold on!"

"Nine-one-one, what's your emergency?" A tinny voice came through the phone.

She clung to the armrest as the car headed toward the ditch and a group of trees on the edge of the road. "This is Jody Ingram and Special Agent Adam McKenzie," she said so fast the words ran together. "Damien Flint's shooting at us on the road to Rutherford—"

"Brace yourself!" Adam yelled.

She screamed. The car slid off the road, hopped the ditch and slammed into a tree. Everything went black.

Chapter Twenty-Two

"You idiot! Bringing them here was the last thing you should have done. What if someone saw you?"

"No one saw me. I brought you the folder! After all the trouble I've gone through, including getting stabbed, you should be thanking me instead of yelling at me. My guys are hiding the car. No harm done."

A string of violent curses followed.

The words drifted through Jody's mind like a canoe slogging through mud. Someone was shouting at someone else. Both of the voices seemed to be coming through a long tunnel. They were achingly familiar. Not in a good way. She groaned and pressed a hand to her throbbing head.

"Jody?" Another voice, whispering next to her ear. Deep, soothing, full of concern.

"Adam?"

"Thank God." He pulled her close. "Where do you hurt?"

She blinked and opened her eyes. Then promptly closed them, her stomach lurching. "The room is spinning."

"You lost consciousness. You probably have a concussion. What about your arms? Your legs? I didn't see any cuts or obvious breaks. Does anything other than your head hurt?"

"Everything hurts."

"I know, sweetheart. I'm so sorry. Can you try to open your eyes again?"

More shouting. Something about deeds and pictures and…infrastructure? That voice. She knew that voice. It was…oh no!

Her eyes popped open. The room was still moving, but not as badly as before. She was sitting on the floor, her back against a wall. Adam knelt in front of her, the side of his head smeared with blood yet again.

He smiled. "There you are. Better now? The room isn't spinning?"

She reached out a shaky hand. "Your head. You're always getting hurt."

He ducked away. "I'm fine. Now that you're back in the land of the living, let's work on getting out of here. Do you know where we are?"

She looked past him and winced. "My room. My old room. When I was a little girl."

"One of Damien's men carried you up here. After Damien shot out our tires, we crashed. You hit your head on the side window." He framed her face in his hands and pressed a whisper-soft kiss against her lips. "You scared me to death. I thought I might lose you."

She clung to his hands. "What happened? Why are we here? Is that my…is Peter downstairs?"

He nodded again. "Damien had a submachine gun. I lost my pistol in the crash and couldn't do anything to stop him."

She reached down to her side.

"Your gun is gone, too," he told her. "We don't have any weapons. But that doesn't mean we're defenseless. As long as they're arguing, we know where they are. Can you stand?" He didn't wait for her reply. He grabbed her around the waist and lifted her to her feet.

She'd squeezed her eyes shut because the room was spinning again. But when she realized she was clutching his shoulders to steady herself, and that she was bending over at the waist to do it, she forced her eyes open again. Adam was still kneeling on the floor.

"Good job," he said. "I've tied some bedsheets together and anchored them to the four-poster bed. You need to climb out that window and run. Looks like there are some trees ten yards out. That should give you good cover." He tugged her hand to get her moving.

She pulled her hand out of his grasp. "Where are your crutches? Did those monsters take them away from you? I'm not leaving you here."

He frowned. "Jody, we don't have time to argue. We don't know whether that 911 call did any good. You didn't have time to give them an address. We have to assume that help isn't coming."

"I told them Rutherford Estates. And we crashed. They'll see our car, look for us. They have our names. Why are you shaking your head?"

"You said Rutherford. And you gave them our names. They'll look me up and realize I live in Rutherford Estates, so they'll go to my house. Not here."

"But the car. Surely they'll see the crash, know something is wrong. When they don't find us at your house, won't they search the whole subdivision, go door to door? Canvassing. That's what it's called, right?"

"From what I could tell from the yelling downstairs, it sounds like Damien and his guys cleaned up the accident scene. I don't know that the police will have cause to go door to door searching for us." He frowned and glanced past her toward the door, which she noted no longer had the dead bolt on it that someone had installed for her years ago.

"I don't hear them anymore," he said. "You need to

hurry. I'll do what I can to stall them. But you have to get out of here." He pushed her toward the window again.

She shoved his hand away. "You can't even stand. I'm not leaving you."

He grabbed one of the posts on the bed's footboard and shoved to his feet. "There. I'm standing. I'm not helpless. Now go."

"You're as white as a sheet."

"It hurts, all right? But I'm fine. Please, Jody. Just go."

Fresh blood marked the denim of his jeans. He wasn't even close to fine, and they both knew it. She took a quick look around. Everything in the room was eerily similar to the way it had looked when she was little, probably because the house was so large there was no reason to redecorate this particular room. Dust covers were draped over the bed, the chair in the corner, the desk. If all of her things were still here, there were crutches she'd used when her adoptive father had slammed her into a wall and broken her leg. They'd be too short. But maybe Adam could still use them like canes to help him walk, like he'd done with the tree branch in the mountains. She ran to the closet.

"Jody, what are you doing? Get out of here."

"I'm not leaving you. So quit telling me to go." She flipped the light on and rushed inside. Her stomach dropped when she saw nothing that looked familiar. The large closet was obviously being used for storage now. There were boxes stacked in neat rows all across the back. Labels declared them as "crafts." Probably for Amelia. She'd always loved making things and took up new craft hobbies all the time. Or at least she used to. There might be something in these boxes Jody could use.

She started tearing them open. In the third one, she found nylon rope used for macramé, along with a pair of scissors. In another box she found picture frames and a shadow box. She yanked out the shadow box and broke it apart. The pieces of wood were thick and long, perfect for making a splint. She'd have Adam fixed up in no time. Then both of them could climb out of the window together.

Holding the rope and wood in one hand, scissors in the other, she hurried back into the bedroom. Her mouth dropped open in horror, and she stumbled to a halt. Adam was still standing with one hand holding the bedpost. But he had a wicked-looking long gun pointed at him, and Damien was holding it.

"Well, well, well. The last little PI finally makes an appearance." He nodded toward his left arm, still in a sling. "Maybe I'll get a chance for payback after all. Drop the scissors and that other junk." He jerked his head toward the open bedroom door. "Daddy's waiting."

She cast a miserable glance toward Adam and dropped her splint supplies to the floor. He was right. She should have gone out the window. Now there would be no help for him, or her. "I'm so sorry, Adam."

He gave her an encouraging smile without a hint of anger. "Go on. We'll be okay."

Damien laughed. "Sure, yeah, you'll be okay." He chuckled and jerked his head again. "After you."

Jody straightened her spine and headed into the hallway.

"Now you, *cop.* Go."

A loud thump sounded behind her, followed by a pained grunt.

Damien cursed.

Jody spun around.

Adam was on his hands and knees. He must have fallen. Damien pulled his leg back as if to kick him.

Jody ran forward. "Don't touch him!"

Damien turned the gun on her. "Back. Off." He aimed his gun at her abdomen.

"I'm okay. Jody, get out of here. Go." Adam hauled him-self upright, using the bed for support again. "I'm okay."

She rushed to him in spite of his protests and the gun following her every move. She shoved her shoulder under his left arm, acting as his crutch.

He gave her an admonishing look, once again not happy that she'd put herself in more danger to help him. But he didn't argue as he limped with her out of the room under the watchful gaze of Damien and his gun.

Going downstairs was much easier because he used the banister and hopped down each step. But once they were on the ground floor without a banister to hold, he had to lean on her in order to limp into the family room.

"Stop right there," Damien ordered.

They stopped in the middle of the room. Ned and an-other armed man they'd never seen before lounged against the left side of the massive fireplace. A third gunman stood on the right side of the fireplace. Damien crossed the room and joined him. And directly in the middle, ten feet away from her and Adam, stood the man who'd made her child-hood worse than any nightmare.

His dark brown hair was stylishly short with just a hint of gray at the temples. The charcoal-colored suit he wore was tailored perfectly to compliment his broad shoulders and trim waist. Gold cuff links winked in the light of the chandelier suspended from the twenty-foot ceiling above them. To anyone else, he'd look like a handsome business-man, perfectly groomed and ready for an important meet-ing. To Jody, he looked like a monster.

She started to shake.

Adam's arm tightened around her shoulders.

A loud crash sounded off to their left. Everyone turned toward the sound, except the monster. He let out a deep sigh and simply turned his head to look at the woman who'd just emerged from the kitchen and had dropped a tray of drinks onto the travertine floor, shattering the glasses. She stared at Jody, her eyes big and round, her mouth dropping open.

"Amelia," the monster said. "Our daughter has finally come home to visit."

Her mother didn't move, didn't say anything. She just stared at Jody in obvious horror.

Footsteps sounded.

Jody looked toward her adoptive father. His polished shoes clicked against the floor as he strode toward her.

Adam tensed.

Peter stopped three feet away and sighed heavily again. "Jody, Jody, Jody. Always the troublemaker. Maybe I should take you upstairs and turn you over my knee, eh? Teach you another lesson?"

"You'll never touch a hair on her head again, you lecherous pervert," Adam snapped.

Peter's eyes narrowed.

A muffled sob sounded from Amelia. She whirled around and ran into the kitchen.

Peter rolled his eyes and shook his head. Ignoring Adam, he stared at Jody, a nauseatingly hungry look in his eyes. "If I only had more time." He clucked his tongue. "But I have a funeral to attend. A dear friend died tragically in a car crash last week." He chuckled again. "Seems to happen a lot to my friends. Car crashes." He winked.

Jody's stomach lurched at the implication. Her parents, her real ones, had died in a car crash. Had Peter had something to do with that too?

"Fortunately for me—" his voice was lowered in a conspiratorial tone "—my dear friend had finished the task I gave him before his…demise."

"Forging land leases?" Adam accused. "Helping you arrange accidents for the true owners? Convincing Senator

Sinclair to push an infrastructure bill so you could sell all the land you stole to the government and make a fortune?"

Peter slowly turned his head like a snake and speared Adam with his dark-eyed gaze. "To be fair, I bought some of that land legitimately."

"You didn't buy *Jody's* land legitimately. You stole her inheritance. Including this house."

"Well, well, well. Someone's been busy, haven't they? Faking that damn will cost me a pretty penny. I spent years covering that up. And all it took was one very stupid drunk councilman in a bar to complain to the wrong PI about the problems he was having performing title searches to bring it all crashing down around my ears. I gave him explicit instructions to exclude the Radcliffe properties from those searches. But he wasn't the detail-oriented man he should have been. And Sam Campbell started sticking his nose where it didn't belong. Who knew he'd recognize the Radcliffe name? My bad luck that you were working for him. Doesn't matter now, though."

"I'll bet you killed the councilman. And you killed Sam," Jody accused. "And Tracy. And my real parents. For what? Land? Money?" She waved her hand to encompass the mansion. "By all accounts you were quite wealthy even before my parents' deaths. And now you have this. Don't you have enough already?"

He smiled. "You poor, silly girl. You can never have enough when it comes to money."

She surged forward, wanting to slam her fists into his smiling face. But Adam tightened his arm around her shoulders, anchoring her against him. He turned his body slightly as if to protect her from her adoptive father. It caused her arm around his waist to bump against something beneath his shirt, something in his back pocket.

She glanced up at him. He was staring intently at her.

The scissors.

That's what was in his pocket. He must have fallen on purpose in her bedroom so he could grab them. And he was letting her know he would use them when the time was right. But how could the time ever be right with four gunmen twenty feet away? And who knew if Peter was armed? She cleared her throat and looked back at the monster.

"You have the land and the folder," she said. "I don't have any proof that you stole anything from me. It would just be my word against yours. You can let us go."

He clucked his tongue again. "Right. And your boyfriend here would just ignore everything that's happened? He's a cop. Cops don't ignore and let things go. At least, not the honest ones who refuse to take bribes. And word on the street is that he's one of the good guys. Which means, of course, you both have to die."

"Bribes?" Adam said, obviously stalling for time. "Just like you bribed Judge Jackson when Jody went to court? And bribed him again to file those bogus land claims?"

Peter speared him with a look full of hate. "You know way too much, cop."

"What about the pictures?" Damien stepped forward. "I chased them through those stupid mountains to find out where that PI hid the pictures. There weren't any pictures in the folder."

Peter rolled his eyes, a pained expression on his face. "There were never any pictures, *you moron.* I made that up because you didn't need to know exactly what I was looking for. You were just supposed to find out where Campbell might hide any information he collected." He pointed at a folder lying on a decorative table against the wall. The folder that had been in Jody's storage unit. "Everything I need is in there. Now all you have to do is kill these two and I'll be on my way."

"No." The voice, barely above a whisper, came from the kitchen doorway.

Everyone turned to see Amelia once again standing there. This time she was holding a pistol. And it was pointed at her husband.

"Ho, ho," Damien exclaimed, laughing. "Trouble in paradise, boss?"

"Shut up." Peter stared at his wife. "What do you think you're doing, Amelia?"

"What I should have done when Jody was a little girl. Stopping you." Her lower lip wobbled and the gun shook in her hand. "I'm so sorry, Jody. I swear I never even suspected that he might be hurting you until that counselor from your school talked to me."

"Shut *up*, woman." Peter strode toward Amelia. "She lied. I never did *anything* to her."

Amelia wrapped both hands around the gun and brought it up higher, pointing directly at Peter's head. This time, her hands weren't shaking. "Not one step closer. I'll shoot you. I will."

He stopped, his eyes narrowing. "Now why would you do that?"

"Because you hurt little girls!" she cried out. She looked toward Jody. "I swear, I never knew. I asked Patricia and Patience when your counselor brought those charges against Peter. But they said you were lying, that their daddy would never do that. He would never do those horrible, awful things." Tears spilled over and slid down her cheeks. The gun started shaking again. "They were little girls, too. I believed them. I never knew they were scared of him, that they lied. For him. Until Patricia had her baby last month. And she and her husband wouldn't let Peter near the baby." A sob burst between her clenched teeth. "Oh, God. Your own daughters. How could you, Peter?"

His face turned a bright red. He looked at Damien. "Shoot her."

Damien's men raised their guns.

Adam took a limping step forward, his hand going behind his back. Jody grabbed his arm, but he shook it off.

"Adam," she whispered, "please don't. They'll kill you."

He took another wobbling step and pulled the scissors out of his waistband.

"Hold it," Damien said, raising his hand and motioning toward his men. "Lower your weapons."

Adam stopped, the scissors clutched in his right hand. But no one seemed to notice. They were all looking back and forth between Amelia, Peter and Damien.

Adam took another step, and another, moving closer to Peter, the scissors down by his side, half concealed by his hand.

Jody wanted to grab him, stop him. Instead, she moved with him, trying to keep from having a big gap between them to make it less obvious that he'd moved closer to Peter.

Damien faced his boss. "You some kind of perv, man? You like to hurt little girls?"

Peter looked down his nose at Damien. "You're a murderer and a thug. Don't tell me you're suddenly developing a conscience."

Sirens sounded in the distance.

Damien and his men exchanged worried glances.

"Don't be idiots," Peter said. "They're going somewhere else. Not here."

"Yeah, well. We ain't taking that chance," Damien replied. "Not for some sicko who hurts kids." He motioned to his men and they headed for the door.

Peter stepped toward them. "One million dollars. I'll give one million dollars to the man who shoots my wife."

Jody gasped.

Amelia's eyes widened.

All four men turned around.

"A million?" one of them asked, aiming his gun at Amelia.

"No." This time it was Adam who stepped forward.

The man turned his gun toward Adam.

Jody stepped forward. "No!"

Adam shoved her behind him. "You really want to go to jail for a pedophile?"

The man's gaze darted to Peter, who was now glaring at Adam.

"Even if you don't care what he's done," Adam continued, his voice calm, matter-of-fact, "do you think you can trust him to follow through with the money?"

"Two million!" Peter yelled.

The man swung his pistol back toward Amelia.

She stood frozen, tears tracking down her chin. She didn't seem to know what to do and was obviously too scared to pull the trigger on her gun to defend herself.

"Wait!" Adam yelled.

The man looked at him but kept his gun trained on Amelia.

"He's asking you to kill his wife," Adam said. "You really think he'll honor his word to you, someone he barely knows? Everything he does is about money and protecting himself. And you think he'll give you a million dollars, two million dollars? More likely he'll hire someone else to take you out for a few thousand. He kills everyone who gets in his way or threatens what he wants. Listen to the sirens. The police are almost here."

The sirens were much louder now. But were they coming here? Or to Adam's house a few blocks away?

Adam took another step forward. "When the police get here and find Amelia dead, what do you think Peter will tell them? That you killed her. A home invasion. He'll blame everything that happens here on you. The forensics will back him up. You go to prison. He goes on to enjoy his millions."

The gunmen shared concerned looks. One of them headed out the door. Ned followed, leaving Damien and the other gunman.

"Those cops aren't coming here," Damien said, looking like he was considering cashing in on Peter's offer.

"Of course they aren't," Peter said. "No one has any reason to suspect me of anything. You and your men made sure of it."

"Jody called 911," Adam rushed to say. "Right before the crash. They're definitely coming here. Sounds to me like they're three or four minutes out. You'd better hurry and decide whether you want to go to prison or get out of here."

"Check her phone," Damien ordered the other gunman. "Hurry."

"I don't have it," Jody started to say, thinking she'd lost Adam's phone in the crash. But the gunman pulled the phone out of his own pocket.

"Pass code," Damien said. "What's the code to unlock it?"

She gave him the code that Adam had given her in the car. The gunman keyed it in and swiped the screen a few times. His face went pale. "She ain't lying. She called 911."

"Screw it," Damien said. "Let's get out of here. Wait in the Charger. I'll be right there."

His partner threw the phone down and ran out the door.

"Did he really hurt you as a little girl?" Damien asked, looking straight at Jody.

Her face flushed with heat. "Yes."

"Sick bastard." Damien pointed his gun at Peter.

Peter threw his hands up. "My lawyer is working to

get your brother out of jail. You kill me and what do you think he'll do?"

"Come on, man!" A yell came from outside.

Damien's hand flexed on the gun. "You'd better not renege on our deal or I'll come after you, you sicko." He tossed his gun toward Peter and ran.

Peter caught the gun and swung it toward Amelia.

"No!" Adam threw the scissors like a javelin toward Peter.

Boom! Boom!

Peter fell to the floor, the scissors embedded deep in his neck. He gagged and clasped his hands around the wound, blood pouring through the gaps between his fingers. His knees drew up, blood darkening his pants where Amelia's bullet had found its mark.

He'd never hurt another little girl again.

Jody whirled around toward Amelia. "Oh no! Mom!"

Amelia blinked in confusion and looked down. Red bloomed on her breast above her heart and quickly spread, saturating her shirt. Peter's bullet had found its mark, too.

Jody ran to her, catching her just as Amelia's knees buckled beneath her. She couldn't hold her up and fell with her to the floor.

"Mom, Mom. Oh no, please. Mom." She pressed her hands against the wound, desperately trying to stop the bleeding.

Adam dropped to the floor beside her, his phone in his hand. "We need an ambulance." He rattled off the address that he'd found on the internet just last night while looking into Jody's past. "Send the police, too," he said. "I hear them in the subdivision. They're probably at my home from a previous 911 call, but we're here. We're the ones who called them."

"Jody?" Amelia blinked up at her. "Are you there?"

Tears flooded Jody's eyes. "Yes. I'm here."

Adam yanked off his shirt and pushed Jody's hands away. "I've got it." He pressed his shirt hard against the wound.

Amelia gasped, her lips turning white.

"Sorry, Mrs. Ingram. I have to press hard to stop the bleeding."

Jody grabbed Amelia's hand and held it tightly in her own as she gently wiped the hair out of Amelia's face. "Hold on. Help is on the way."

Amelia blinked, and her vision seemed to clear, her hand tightening on Jody's. "Sweet, sweet girl. I'm so sorry. I swear, I never knew. I didn't."

"It's okay," Jody whispered, her tears dropping onto their joined hands. "It's okay."

"No. It's not." Amelia coughed, and bright red blood bubbled out of her mouth.

"Don't try to talk." Jody gently wiped the blood away. "Save your strength."

"I put the lock on your door." Amelia clung to Jody's hand and searched her gaze. "I didn't think you were tell-ing the truth. But I put the lock on your door to be sure, as a test. He never…he never said anything, never took it off. So I thought… I thought that proved me right. That he wasn't the man you said he was." She coughed again and started choking.

"Jody, back up."

She scooted back and Adam rolled Amelia onto her side. She stopped coughing. He moved forward, his knees prop-ping her up while he applied pressure to her wound again.

Jody bent down, maintaining eye contact. Amelia was frighteningly pale, her eyes turning glassy.

"Jody?"

"I'm here." Her voice broke as she clasped Amelia's hands. "I won't leave you. I'm here."

"I loved you, Jody. I should have been stronger, smarter. I should have fought for you."

"You did. He never hurt me again after you put that lock on my door," Jody said, her heart breaking. "I love you, too. You were the only mother I ever knew. It's okay. Everything is going to be okay."

"Forgive me?" Amelia pleaded. "Please forgive me."

"I forgive you."

A smile curved her mother's red-stained lips. Then her hand went slack in Jody's.

"Mama?" She shook Amelia's hand. "Mama?"

"Miss, let us help her," a voice said behind her.

"Mama?"

Adam was suddenly there, pulling her back. "Let her go, Jody. You have to let her go."

"No! Mama?"

Adam lifted her in his arms, then limped to one of the couches and collapsed onto the cushions, holding her tightly against him.

"Shh," he whispered against the top of her head. "Shh."

He stroked her back and rocked her as the paramedics worked on Amelia. Jody drew a ragged breath and closed her eyes, clinging to him and doing something she hadn't done since she was a little girl and a judge sent her back to live with the monster.

She prayed.

Chapter Twenty-Three

Three months later, Jody stood at the entrance to the Sugarland Mountain Trail, a jacket around her to ward off the chilly autumn temps up high in the mountains. A backpack of supplies was strapped on her shoulders. Sensible boots protected her feet, gave her sure footing.

There was no cattle gate across the entrance this time, no warning signs declaring that the trail was closed, no man with a gun chasing her. She was all alone and ready to begin another journey, another chapter of her life.

She pulled her cell phone out of her pants pocket. No bars, no service. But it showed the time. She'd been checking it every few minutes. When she realized the wait was over, a mixture of dread and excitement sent a shot of adrenaline through her. This was it. No turning back now. She started up the path.

Her steps were measured, careful. She kept glancing at her phone, checking the time, checking her surroundings to get her bearings. She didn't want to be late. Or early. She wanted everything to be perfect.

A few minutes later, she reached the curve in the path, the one where Adam had disappeared all those months ago as he chased Damien. The one where she and Adam had run back the other way with two gunmen after them.

Her pulse sped up, her body shaking. She pushed back

the fear, knowing it was silly now. Damien and his men weren't chasing her this time. The police had rounded up everyone involved in Peter Ingram's schemes, and they were all either already convicted and in prison or in jail waiting for their trials. She was safe. No reason to be afraid.

Well, at least not about bad guys, anyway.

She forced her feet forward and rounded the curve, then hurried to her destination. When she reached the spot where Adam had forced her to take that huge leap of faith, she stopped. And looked out at the mountains and the Chimney Tops beyond. And waited.

"Jody?"

His voice sent a jolt of yearning straight through her. She drew a deep breath and turned.

Adam stood ten feet away, having just come around the corner from the other direction. He was wearing his ranger's uniform again, his gun holstered at his side, his new radio clipped to his belt.

"How's the leg?" She waved toward his left leg, which had a metal brace around it from ankle to knee.

He took a step toward her, then stopped again, his gaze wary. "It's fine. Thanks."

She swallowed, hating that she'd been the reason for that wariness. "This is your first day back on the job, isn't it?"

He frowned. "How did you know?"

She took a step toward him. "I asked your brother. Duncan."

His jaw tightened. "He told you I was walking this trail, didn't he?"

She nodded.

"Why? Why are you here?"

She took another step forward. "You're not going to make this easy, are you?"

He looked away, out toward the Chimney Tops. "I don't know what you want from me, Jody. I tried visiting, calling, texting, emailing, until I felt like a stalker and had to stop." He looked back at her. "It's been three months since your... since Peter Ingram died. You haven't contacted me once."

She moved closer. "I know. I'm sorry. I'm so sorry."

"You say that all the time. It doesn't mean anything anymore."

She sighed and raked her hair back. "You're right. I'm trying to stop apologizing so much. I've been going to therapy again, trying to move on, letting go of all the guilt I've been carrying around." She let out a harsh laugh. "At least I've finally figured out why I've always felt so guilty."

"Your sisters. You blame yourself for leaving when you turned eighteen. You've worried that you didn't fight for them, too. You left them behind, and it's always bothered you."

She blinked. "How do you know that?"

He gave her a sad smile. "Because I know *you*, Jody Vanessa Radcliffe."

She blinked again. "How did you know I changed my last name?"

He tapped the badge clipped to his belt. "Cop." He dropped his hand to his side. "Or I might have heard it from Duncan. He told me he'd offered you an investigator job with the National Park Service. You had to put your legal name on the paperwork."

She smiled. "You've been keeping tabs on me."

"Not since the first month. Like I said, I felt like a stalker, so I quit. Duncan, on the other hand, won't stop talking about you. He's torturing me." He clamped his lips together and looked away.

"Torturing you?" She took another step. "Hearing about me is torture?"

His fingers curled into his palms, but he didn't say anything.

"It's been torture for me, too," she admitted. "Being away from you."

His gaze shot to hers. Still, he said nothing.

"My mom's fine, in case you're wondering. You saved her life that day. You kept your cool, thought to grab the phone and call for help when I was completely losing it. The doctors said if you hadn't gotten the EMTs there so fast, if you hadn't kept pressure on the wound, she'd be dead. Thank you, Adam. Thank you for saving her."

He shook his head. "I did my job. And we were lucky you'd called 911 and the police and EMTs were already at my house."

"Maybe. Maybe not. You have a talent for saving people." She took another step forward. "You saved me. So many times. In so many ways."

He stared at her, some of the hostility and frustration easing from his expression. The wariness was back. But along with it was something else. Hope.

"I needed the time, the distance," she said. "From you, from my overwhelming feelings for you. Because I didn't believe it could be real. We'd known each other for, what, a few days? Less than a week? Under traumatic circumstances. I didn't trust my feelings. I had to process them. And I had to process my 'unhealthy attitude' toward sex." She used air quotes. "Apparently my adoptive father did a number on my psyche and I never understood what a normal physical relationship was supposed to be like. Until you."

"You're giving me too much credit."

She shrugged. "Not in my opinion. But I'm working

through my relationship hang-ups. And my relationships with my adoptive family. I had to deal with my mother in the hospital, her recovery, getting to know my sisters and brothers, unraveling the legal tangle that Peter Ingram left for all of us." She shook her head. "It was a mess. I was a mess. That's why I've been going to a therapist."

He started to step forward, then stopped. "Are you okay?" He cleared his throat. "I mean, your adoptive family, the legal stuff."

"My adoptive…my *family* is…well, awkward might be the best way to put it. My sisters weren't abused in spite of Amelia's fears, by the way. Thank God for that. But they suspected what their father had done to me. That's why Patricia wouldn't let him be alone with her new daughter. She didn't trust him. Still, they grew up with him as their dad, loving him as best they could with all that poison running just beneath the surface. I think they blame me for what's happened to the family now. I can understand that. But I don't apologize to anyone for it. Like I said, I'm moving on. From the guilt, from my past." She stepped closer. "I'm moving toward my future now."

He looked down at her feet and smiled. "You're wearing boots."

"And a shiny new backpack with supplies. I learned my lesson from the best. Always be prepared for the worst." She took another step. "But hope for the best."

He stared at her intently, longingly, and took a step toward her. "I saw that your family house is for sale."

She nodded. "The courts awarded me all of the money, the house, even the land that Peter tried to swindle from me. The infrastructure deal is still going through. I didn't try to stop it. But all the money from the land sales went to me."

"You're rich now."

"In some people's eyes, maybe. I gave a huge chunk of it

to my mother and siblings. Including the house. But no one wants to live there because of everything that happened. It was their decision to sell."

"You gave a multimillion-dollar mansion plus more money on top of that to your family? After they turned their backs on you? And didn't protect you?" His tone wasn't accusing, just curious and concerned. As always, it was her he was worried about. Which reassured her that this little trip into the mountains had been the right thing to do. She hadn't built him up in her mind as larger-than-life after all. He really was the wonderful, caring, protective man that she remembered from that dark time in her life that seemed so long ago now.

"I don't blame my adoptive family," she explained. "Not anymore. In their own way, they were all just as much victims as I was. If I kept all that money, it would make me feel like the villain of their lives. There's been too much hurt, too much hate in my life already. I didn't want that. I did it for me, more than for them. I also gave some to Tracy's family. They were there for me, always. So, for once, I was there for them. I'm here for you, now, Adam. If you still want me, that is."

"If I still want you?" He gave her an incredulous look. "Is that a joke?"

"I hope not."

He quickly closed the remaining distance between them. He pulled her into his arms and looked down at her, a fierce, hungry expression on his face. "I'll never stop wanting you. I want to kiss you. If you don't want that, you'd better tell me right now."

She wrapped her arms around his neck. "It's about time."

He groaned and claimed her mouth with his. It wasn't sweet or gentle like he'd been the first time he'd kissed her, when he'd shown her how a man who really cared about a woman treated her. This kiss was out of control, full of longing, yearning, and wild with desire. He was consuming her, and she was bursting into flames in his arms.

His tongue tangled with hers, and his hands roamed over her body, stroking, teasing, tempting. When he finally broke the kiss, they were both panting.

She stared up into his gorgeous blue eyes, gazing down at her with such yearning it nearly broke her heart. "I'm so sorry that I took so long to—"

"No apologizing." His voice was ragged, strained. He kissed her forehead and dragged her against him, his arms holding her tight. "I thought it was all in my head, that I was the only one who felt this way."

She pulled back so she could look up into his eyes, needing to hear the words. "Felt what way?"

He frowned, looking uncertain again. "I love you, Jody. Don't you know that?"

She burst into tears.

He lifted her in his arms. He carried her to one of the leftover stumps that still needed to be cleared from the trail and sat down with her in his lap. He rocked her and stroked her back. "Good tears?"

She hugged him tight. "Good tears. I'm trying not to cry so much. But it's going to take some work to change."

He set her back from him and cupped her face in his hands. "Don't change for me, Jody. Don't ever change. I love you just the way you are. Tears and all."

She hiccupped, and they both laughed.

"I love you, too, Adam. I think I loved you from the moment you threw me off that stupid cliff and sacrificed your own body to protect mine."

"I didn't throw you. I pulled you with me."

She rolled her eyes. "Just don't ever do it again. You scared me to death."

He kissed her, gently, softly, a fluttering caress like soft butterfly wings brushing against her heart. Then he smiled down at her with such reverence and love in his deep blue eyes that her tears started up again.

"I love you, Jody. I may not know everything about you. But I know what matters—your caring heart, your courageous, selfless soul, your kind and giving spirit. And I want to spend the rest of my life getting to know all of the fascinating details that go along with that. I want to build a future with you. If you'll have me."

She straightened in his arms. "What are you saying, Adam?"

His hands shook as he gently feathered her hair back from her face. "I'm saying that I want to marry you. But I know we've only really known each other a short time. I don't count the three months we've been apart. So I'll start out slow. We can date for a while. I'll introduce you to my family—my other brothers, Ian, too, if I can even locate him and convince him to come home for a visit. My mom, my dad. They have a cabin in the mountains where we grew up, where I got my love for the outdoors. I want to take you to Memphis, too. That's where I started my career, as a beat cop, before the ranger position opened up and I could come back here, to my hometown. I want to share everything with you. And then, when you're ready, once you feel you know me well enough, if you still think you love me, maybe then we can work on forever."

She shook her head in wonder. "You're an amazing man, Adam McKenzie. And far more patient than me." She shoved her hand into her jacket pocket and pulled out a small velvet box and held it out to him. "Open it."

He frowned. "What are you doing?"

"What do you think I'm doing? I'm asking you to marry me. There's a gold band in that box. I know it's not the customary thing for a guy to wear an engagement ring. But you're blazing hot and I want every woman who looks at you to know you're taken."

"No."

She grew still in his arms. "No? You don't want to marry me? But… I thought—"

He pressed a finger to her lips. "Hold that thought." He reached behind him and unsnapped one of the small leather holders clipped to his belt. Then he held his hand out toward her. A large diamond sparkled in the sunlight, surrounded by a smaller cluster of diamonds on a white-gold band.

Tears flowed again, and she didn't even bother to wipe them away. There was no point. She seemed to have an endless supply. Her chin wobbled as she held out her left hand.

He slid the ring onto her finger, then handed her the gold band she'd gotten him. She put it on his finger and stared up at him in wonder.

"When? When did you get that ring?" she asked.

"Right after the whole debacle at your old house. Every time one of those thugs pointed a gun your way, I felt like I was dying inside. I knew I was in love with you and there was no point in fighting it. I've carried that ring with me ever since, all the while hoping and praying you'd come back to me. If, or when, you were ever ready."

He lifted her off his lap and set her on the stump, then got down on his one good knee.

"Jody Vanessa Radcliffe, will you make me the happiest man alive and agree to be my wife?"

"Only if you'll agree to make me the happiest woman in the world by being my husband."

He grinned. "I'll do my best."

"You always do, Adam. You always do."

He took her in his arms, and into his heart, and once again, he saved her.

* * * * *

COMING SOON!

LET'S TALK
Romance

For exclusive extracts, competitions
and special offers, find us online: